THE NEON COURT

As he stormed through a door into what I guessed to be the sitting room I followed. He reached out for a phone, and I tapped him on the shoulder. He spun, hands coming up into fists. As he did, we caught him round the throat with our scarred hand. Sapphire fire flared behind our eyes, we felt the hair stand up on the back of our neck. The light flickered in the hall, electricity snapped in the sockets, blue sparks crawled around the handset of the telephone, the TV flickered on and mad static danced over its screen. He wheezed and pawed at our hands as the electrical fire built inside our soul and, for a moment, he met our eyes, and was afraid.

"Hi," we said. "Let us make our position clear. We are the Midnight Mayor, protector of this city, carrier of its secrets and bearer of its shadows. The shadows watch us as we pass, the pigeons turn away at our passage, the rats scurry beneath our feet and shudder at the sound of our footsteps on the stones. We are the blue electric angels, the telephones sing at the passage of our voice, our blood is blue fire, our soul carries a pair of angel wings. We are the killer of Robert Bakker, sorcerer, master of the Tower; we destroyed the death of cities; we came back from the dead, Swift and the angels, two minds become one, two souls in one flesh, in one form, in one voice. We are me and I am we. And we're frustrated."

By Kate Griffin

A Madness of Angels
The Midnight Mayor

By Catherine Webb

Mirror Dreams
Mirror Wakes

Waywalkers
Timekeepers

The Extraordinary and Unusual Adventures of Horatio Lyle

The Obsidian Dagger:
Being the Further Extraordinary Adventures of Horatio Lyle

The Doomsday Machine:
Another Astounding Adventure of Horatio Lyle

The Dream Thief

THE NEON COURT

KATE GRIFFIN

orbit

www.orbitbooks.net

ORBIT

First published in Great Britain in 2011 by Orbit

A CIP catalogue record for this book
is available from the British Library.

ISBN 978-1-84149-901-7

Typeset in Weiss by M Rules
Printed and bound in Great Britain by
Clays Ltd, St Ives plc

Papers used by Orbit are natural, renewable and recyclable products sourced from well-managed forests and certified in accordance with the rules of the Forest Stewardship Council.

Orbit
An imprint of
An Hachette UK Company
www.hachette.co.uk
www.orbitbooks.net

"Who, me?
Midnight Mayor. Protector of the city.
Go figure."

— *Remark attributed to M. Swift, 127th Midnight Mayor of London; probably apocryphal*

There's something at the end of the alley.
It's waiting for you.

— *Anonymous graffito, Soho*

Prelude: The Summoning of Matthew Swift

In which an enemy asks help of the last person in the world you might have expected, a fire leads to more than just minor burns, and a war breaks out in Sidcup.

I thought I could hear footsteps in the darkness behind me.

But when I looked again, they were gone.

I was in the middle of a sentence. I was saying, ". . . 'dragon' is probably too biologically specific a way to look at the . . ."

Then someone grabbed me by the throat with the fist of God, and held me steady, while the universe turned on its head.

There was a hole in the world and no fingers left to scrabble.

I fell into it.

It was my phone ringing in my pocket that woke me.

I fumbled for it and thumbed it on, held it to my ear without raising my head, just in case stillness was the only thing keeping my head attached to my body. My throat was dry. I guessed it had something to do with all the smoke. I said, "Yeah?"

Penny, my apprentice, was on the other end. She sounded too cool, too calm, and therefore afraid. "You vanished."

"Uh?"

"Like . . . hello poof whoops bye bye."

"Uh-huh?"

"You dead?"

"That supposed to be funny?"

I rolled onto my back, every rib in my chest pressing against skin like they had been vacuum-packed into place. Something wet and sticky moved underneath me, made the sound of velcro tearing. My fingers brushed it. It smelt of salt and iron. It had the thickness of thin honey. She said, "So what the fuck happened?"

I licked my lips. They tasted of charcoal. "Summoned," I wheezed. Why was it so much work breathing in here? "Some bastard summoned. Me. Summoned me."

The smoke was getting thick now, grey-black, tumbling in under the crack beneath the door. Through it I could half see the walls, cracked and grey, the only colour on them from scrawled messages in cheap spray paint,

ANARKST 4EVR

JG WOZ ERE

NO GOD GAMES ALLOWED

help

WE'RE WAITING FOR YOU

I said, "I'll call you back," and hung up before my apprentice could start swearing.

My eyes burnt. The room was too hot, the light behind the smoke too bright. Somewhere outside the broken window it was raining, thick pattering on the still London night. I crawled onto my hands and knees, ears ringing. Something warm dribbled into the hollow of my ear, pooled there, then continued its journey down the side of my neck. I felt my head, found blood drying in my hair, and a lump. I looked down at the floor and at the same sticky stuff on my fingertips. Against my skin it had appeared almost black, but in the dull sodium light that reflected off the belly of the night-time clouds, and the glare of the unknown something on the other side of the smoke-tumbling door, it was undeniably crimson.

Undeniably blood.

But not my blood.

That at least was a pleasant discovery, though it came with the snag that it was not my blood because nothing bled that much and lived. It had saturated the thin carpet, splattered across the gutted tattered remains of a couch, smeared its paw marks over the paint-scrawled wall behind a low gas stove and a graveyard of broken beer bottles. It was fresh, and only felt cool because its surroundings were so rapidly growing hot.

Someone had been finger painting on the floor with this blood. They'd painted a pair of crosses. One was smaller than the other, nestling in the top left-hand quadrant of its big brother's shape. Look at it with a knowing eye, and you might consider it to be a sword, not a cross, although when your tool was blood and your surface was carpet, the distinction was academic. What it was, and what there could be no doubt that it was, was the ancient emblem of the City of London and, by no coincidence at all, the symbol once carved by a mad bastard, with a dying breath, into the palm of my right hand – the mark of the Midnight Mayor.

I made it to the window, pulled myself up by my elbows, broken glass cracking underneath the sleeves of my anorak, looked out, looked down. A half-moon was lost on the edge of rain clouds turned sodium orange by reflected street light from the terraced roads below. A line of hills cut off the horizon, their tops tree-crowned and unevenly sliced by the carving of motorway planners. The falling rain blurred everything: the neat straight lines of buildings that peeked up between Chinese takeaways and bus stations; the pale yellow worm of a mainline train arcing towards a floodlit station; the darker stretch of a public heath on a low hill around which tiny firefly cars bustled; the reflection of TV lights played behind curtained windows; big square council estates with bright blue and red buttresses as if the vibrancy of colour could disguise the ugliness of what they supported. But no distinctive landmarks other than to say that this was anonymous surburbia, not my part of town. But still my city.

I looked down. Down was a long way away. Paving stones shimmered black with rain-pocked water, like a disturbance on the dark side of the moon. A play area of rusting swings and crooked see-saws. A little patch of mud sprouting tufts of grass for dogs to run about on; a bicycle rack that no one had trusted enough to chain their bicycle to. A line of garages, every door slathered with graffiti ranging from would-be art to the usual signatures of kids out for a thrill. A single blue van, pulling away up the narrow street leading from a courtyard below and out of my line of sight. The glow of fire where there should only have been fluorescent white floodlights, and somewhere, not very far at all, the sounds of alarms starting to wail and flames eating at the door.

Smoke tumbled past my head, excited by the prospect of open air beyond the smashed-up window. I pulled my scarf over my mouth and my bag across my back. I fumbled in my pocket for the phone, my bloody fingers slipping over the keys, got as far as dialling the first two nines, and a hand closed around my ankle.

We jumped instinctively, kicking ourself free and snatching power from the mains ready to hurl at our unseen enemy, our hair standing on end, our heart beating like the engine of a car about to blow. I looked down, expecting death, pain, an end, a stop, a terror, something nameless that I had not had the wit to imagine until now, and saw the hand. Skin on top dark, deep-roasted cocoa; pink underneath. Soaked in its own blood, too much, too fresh. Arm, covered in a long black sleeve. Head. Wearing a headscarf of white and green that was half knocked off, revealing the long-ago-burnt scalp. Face. Round, smart, angry, lips curled, eyes tight with pain, a tracery of scars down the left side like a map of shifting desert sands. I knew that face. I'd regretted seeing it many times before, and tonight was heading for the clincher.

I wheezed, eyes running and carbon on my tongue, "Oda?"

Oda – assassin, murderer, fanatic, holy woman or insane psychopath, pick one – looked us in the eye and whispered through her cracking lips, the smoke curling around her breath as she spoke, "Help me."

Penny Ngwenya, sorceress (in training) and one-time traffic warden, announced one mild evening as we walked through Spitalfields together, "You know, you were really cool until I met you."

Under normal circumstances, I might have said something rude.

But Penny, whose anger had nearly destroyed an entire city, was not a woman who had much truck with normality.

"Thing is," she went on airily, "you're an urban sorcerer. You bend sodium light with a thought, can taste the rhythms of the city, feed on dust and carbon monoxide and get major hayfever if you go near anything green. And that'd be like, pretty cool, you get what I'm saying? And it's even cooler than that – you're a *dead* sorcerer. Like there's a grave marked 'Matthew Swift, got killed by a mystical shadow or whatever' and an empty coffin, but you're not dead. You came back, and you came back with like, the blue electric angels attached, or whatever, and that's like, you know, Jesus. And you're the Midnight Mayor, which is this majorly pompous job thing that's been going for like two thousand years and you're supposed to protect and save the city and stuff, which is like King Arthur, so . . . you know . . . you're pretty cool. Until you speak."

I thought about this a while.

I said, "Like Jesus?"

She said, "Yeah. You should probably forget I said that."

Oda aka 'psycho-bitch' lay behind the spring-poked remnant of the sofa, in the thickest, deepest pool of blood in the room. It had sunk so far into the carpet that when she moved, little swells and bubbles burst out beneath her, as pressure dynamics did its thing. There was blood on her hands, on her face, in her hair, it had saturated her jumper, and soaked into the side of her leg. There was no doubt that it was hers. Her face was as grey as a face so richly coloured could be, her eyes were bloodshot, pinky-red, her grip round my ankle had the unnatural strength of the newborn babe or the nearly departed dying. We felt our stomach turn, but squatted down and tried to help her up. She grabbed the back of my coat, bundling it up in her fist like a yachtsman's lifeline in a storm. "Help me," she repeated.

"What the bloody hell is happening?" I wheezed.

"We've got to leave this place," she replied, reaching her other arm round my neck to form a crude sling. "Help me!"

"No shit," I growled, and putting my arms round her waist, tried heaving her to her feet. She cried out in pain, an animal shrill of distress, her eyes closing. As she moved, a knife-slice smile opened and shut in the front of her jumper, right above her heart. We half thought we could see something else grinning beneath, and quickly looked away.

She made it to more or less upright, head bumping against my shoulder, her weight dragging down on my neck. "Out," she hissed. "Have to get out."

I half dragged her to the door, felt the heat blasting through it, said, "Can you run?"

"No," she growled through gritted teeth.

"Can you fight?"

"No."

"You got a fireproof suit beneath that jumper?"

She didn't grace that with a reply. "Deep breath," I wheezed, and, wrapping my shirt around my fingers against the scalding heat, took hold of the door handle, and eased the door back.

Flame, brilliant yellow-orange, leapt inward round the door frame.

I opened the door a little further, felt the draught in my hair as the fire, already clothing the walls and ceiling, sensed oxygen behind me and started to surge. Along both sides of the corridor some apartment doors stood open; some were shut; some had been bashed off their frames, pinched for who knew what purpose, some were already half-eaten black cinders, tumbling out smoke that blasted this way and that across the ceiling in giddy twists. In places the flame had found handy little holes between the ceiling's ruined timbers and cracked plaster, through which it was crawling to the floor above. My feet slipped as the soles of my shoes began to liquefy; I felt the hair of my eyebrows and on the back of my neck curl and singe in the heat, could barely breathe for the knives of pain that came with every gasp of oxygenless vapour. Among the carbon and baking damp fungus I smelt petrol.

I half shook Oda, demanded, "Stairs?"

"That way," she mumbled, jerking her head towards the end of the corridor.

Too bright to look at, too much, too hot, just glancing that way dragged the water from my eyes. I adjusted Oda's weight on my shoulder, hissed, "Take a deep breath."

As she inhaled, so did I. The effect was like swallowing a mosquito swarm, that roiled and writhed inside my lungs. Transmutation had never been one of my strong points; on the other hand impending death had always produced my very best work. So, as the burning air settled in my lungs like charred meat swallowed the wrong way, I half closed my eyes, clawed at what little part of my strength wasn't dedicated to staying upright, and inwardly pushed. Something foul and chemical, toothpaste without the mint, rotting eggs and white dust, settled over my tongue, coated the inside of my throat, grabbed my chest from inside. The urge to retch contorted my back once, twice, but I swallowed it down, face aching with the strain of keeping my mouth locked over the pressure and taste trying to crawl back up. Oda's fingers dug into my shoulder; she half closed her eyes against the heat. I waited until my bones could no longer take the strain, then waited half a second more and exhaled.

A white cloud, fine powder on billowing air, burst from my mouth and nose, hard and fast enough to knock my head back and send a shudder down my back that nearly shoved me and Oda off our feet. I steadied myself, instinctively reaching towards the wall for support and then shying away from the intense heat of the flame licking along the cracked old surface. More graffiti, more paint:

hocus pocus

ONE NATION UNDER CCTV

let me out of here

slowly fracturing and popping till it resembled the multifaceted black surface of a bottle fly's skin as the fire raced along.

I couldn't stop myself now, the breath was coming out of me too much and too fast, more breath than I had in me to give, sucking up acid from my stomach and blood from the inside of my nose, its pressure too high as the white cloud burst out from between my lips and blasted down the corridor. The fire recoiled from it, shied and shimmered away, bent backwards and, in one or two places where its dominion was still thin, winked out as if it had never been, leaving carbon scars. And for a moment, I could see the way out. I half fell forward as the last gasp left my body, then heaved in air, shuddering with the strain of it, mouth full of a chemical taste, blood trickling down from our nose, its salt taste blissful against the foulness inside our throat. Oda was already moving, tugging at my coat like she was pulling on the reins of a horse. Even after being blasted by the mixture of magic and fire extinguisher from my throat, the flames were coming back, slithering probes towards us from the ceiling. The glass in the metal-mesh door at the end of the corridor had cracked, turning yellow-green in the heat. I could see the staircase beyond; its metal railings were glowing cheery orange-rose hot, the smoke billowing upwards as if the stairwell were a giant chimney. I peeked down and immediately looked away, half blinded, the after-image of the fires below playing behind my eyelids. Oda risked a glance too, snapping her head away like a frightened bird as the rising heat and light hit the back of her retinas.

"Other ways down?" I wheezed.

"Back there," she replied, indicating the corridor behind us. "Smell petrol?"

"Yep." I looked up. The smoke had blackened the stairwell above, and no lights shone enough to pierce the darkness, but it was moving,

I could feel it moving, drawn up towards colder, more breathable air. I closed my fingers tight together, dragged in a little strength from inside my aching chest, opened my palm and let the sodium light blossom between my fingers, yellow-orange, the colour of street lamps, the light that all good urban magicians summon when they need a guide. I aimed it towards our feet, its glow barely enough to illuminate the steps in front of us, and, heads bowed towards that one light, we began to climb. Oda reached instinctively for the banister, then flinched away with a smell of scorched skin as her fingers brushed against it. The plastic cover on the iron rails had begun to melt and run like tar on a summer's day. On the first landing I found a window, already cracked and foul from earlier times, and smashed it out with a swing of my bag. Smoke spiralled greedily out of it into the open air. I took a breath of the momentarily cold, ice-cold by comparison, blissful pure air of the outside world, and then kept on climbing. The flames were already claiming the floor above, but they had come by easier ways than the stairwell, crawling through cracks in the ceiling, and sending sparks up the tattered remains of curtains. And everywhere there were the graffiti, old dirty paint, cracked pipes and dangling wires that led from nothing to nowhere, mould and fungus and the grey bane-mark of too much time and not enough love, eating as surely as the fire at the heart of this building. Up another floor, and the smoke grew thinner, the fire not yet penetrating this far, but I could still feel it buffeting from below, drawn towards the roof and the wide open sky. We rounded the corner, and there was a body on the stairs.

We nearly tripped over him, feet splayed, arms stretched up like a pinned butterfly in a specimen box. His soot-stained face had once been pale, until someone with a red-hot needle had driven the tip into every freckle across his nose and cheeks, raising swollen pinpricks of scarred red tissue in a dot-matrix printer pattern. He wore the remnants of a black hoodie, starting to smoulder, a pair of blue jeans slashed at the knees and grey trainers, the heels smoking and warped out of shape. Someone had cut his throat; the black-red blood was still working its sluggish way down from the wound. Oda's fingers tightened in my coat, but she didn't speak. We stepped round him, shuffling over the outflung barrier of his arm and upwards, past a pair of empty grey eyes vanishing into the thickening smoke.

One more floor, and the air was almost breathable, the sodium cast from my little summoned light almost good enough to see well by, if you ignored the residual burning pain in the lungs, the cracked lips, the blistered skin, the brilliant yellow-blue afterburn that was visible on the front of the eyes even when you didn't try to close them. One more flight of stairs, smaller than the rest, led to a metal door, its rusted chain long since wrenched off, the lock twisted and broken, a sign dangling by a single screw saying,

ROOF ACCESS – AUTHORIZED PERSONNEL ONLY

I pushed at the door, and it gave with a banshee screech of rust. We tumbled out onto a flat concrete surface, stained with the white tide-marks of a decades-old battle between pooling stagnant rainwater and pigeon crap. The rain was bliss, cold and wonderful and pure. We turned our face towards it, gasped down air, felt the water run down our face and neck, let it. I could hear sirens somewhere below, a distance away but drawing closer. Oda untangled herself from me and flopped on her hands and knees into a puddle of rainwater, gasping for breath, eyes shut, head bowed. The twisted remnants of satellite dishes and TV aerials made up the forestry of this rooftop, and here and there were the sad remnants of beer cans, billowing plastic bags weighed down by pooling water inside them, and limp fast-food boxes. A vent, taller than me, stood dead and silent, some of its bars broken, leaving just enough space for birds to hop inside and nest. A low metal railing ran round the edge of the roof. I staggered over to it, as much to have something to lean on as to get my bearings, and draped myself over it to catch my breath. From here, I could see in every direction, and could fill in the picture that I hadn't been able to complete in the flat below. Canary Wharf, white speckled monuments rising up in the darkness, a hint of silverish water below; the Millennium Dome, a bulb of white before the thicker darkness where the city started to end and the estuary began; Greenwich Hill, a small patch of rising darkness crowned with a glimmer of light where the observatory sat, blasting out a thin green line into the night to declare that here, right here and no more than a needle thick, was the middle of the world.

I was in South London; at a guess, Sidcup or, optimistically, Blackheath. Distances changed their meanings south of the river; short became long, long became expected. I could taste the buzzing magic of the place, tight, full of corners and bumps where a slither of power could suddenly become an overwhelming roar, and a river of magic could dwindle to nothing just when you thought you'd tangled your fingers in it. South, and not as far south as I would have liked, and the familiar silver taste of the city's magic began to give way to the elusive older magics of the countryside, of forests and rivers and the old ways of doing things. We did not like those magics; we neither fully understood nor mastered them, and that left us vulnerable.

I glanced down and saw that the tarmac below the tower was now glowing with the crazy fire dance of reflected light from where the flames were beginning to crawl out of the windows, smoking and steaming in defiance of the falling rain. Blue lights played off the streets around us as the emergency services arrived, their siren sounds calming, a strange reassurance in the night, even though they were much, much too late. The fire had spread too fast, too far, and not entirely of its own accord. I crawled back to where Oda still knelt, head down, resting on the palms of her hands, back arching with the effort of drawing breath.

"You OK?"

She nodded in reply, eyes still fast shut. "Can you get us out of here?"

"Fire's all over the lower floors."

"You can control fire?"

"I can negotiate with it."

"Thought sorcerers loved fire."

"More in a metaphorical than practical sense. It's too big for me to stop it now. And . . ."

"And?"

"It moves too fast. Takes a lot of power to argue with petrol once it's got a big idea."

Slowly she raised her head, and opened her eyes, and for a moment, I thought I saw blood pooling along the rim of her lower eyelids. Then she blinked and it was gone. "You're the Midnight Mayor. You're the blue electric angels. Work something out."

"Oda . . . what the hell is going on here?" She closed her eyes, lowered her head again, and said nothing. "I get us out, you owe me," I said, voice low to her ear. "You *owe* me for this."

"You want to die here?" she asked.

Our lips curled in frustration. Now that the need to survive the next five seconds had receded, other feelings were returning, as hot and raw as the inferno beneath us. I heard sirens below, wheels splashing through water, the voices of men. I stood up slowly, flexing my fingers at my sides, breathing down our anger, and looked into a pair of lilac eyes.

There was a man on the roof.

He was half a foot taller than me, wore black trousers slashed on the inside in that very neat, very minced way that made it fashion, not poverty, wore a cream-coloured T-shirt, five layers of gold chain that at their lowest dropped to just above his diaphragm and at their shortest hugged his throat like a jealous lover, an open black jacket, fingerless white driving gloves and golden spiked hair like a billionaire hedgehog. His skin was white, snow white, painted white, and someone had gone to the trouble of adding to this two great red spikes of paint that stretched up across each eyelid like a mask. He carried a thing that, while not exactly a sword, was well past the point where it could claim to be a knife. It had a handle in the shape of a bottleneck, but of ornate silver wound round with golden wire, and the blade was made of cobalt-blue glass. It looked like it shouldn't be sharp, but the ease with which it tore through the air, sending spinning eddies of rain flying out of its path as it came down towards my throat, suggested otherwise.

I squeaked like a startled rabbit, tried to leap away, banged into Oda, knocking her to the floor, and then fell backwards over her, landing with a splash in the puddle behind me. Oda lay still where she'd fallen, like one dead already, showing none of the usual violent instincts I had come to rely on. So he came after me, face contorted, as if he was a hiccup away from a seizure. I began, "Wait just a . . ." and the glass blade smacked down on the place where my heart should have been. We rolled. Instinct was better than reason, and we were not willing to die in this place, at the hands of this painted bug. We rolled across Oda and then kept rolling up onto our feet, in a half-crouch ready to strike, spreading our fingers to the sides and letting the power flow to them. We took the rain running across our skin, and then we took the faint bite of acid inside it, the faint chemical sting and we pushed it between our fists, let it build up into a bubble of burning not-quite-water that fizzed and hissed as the rain passed across its translucent surface. Surprise, almost comical in its briefness and intensity, passed across the man's face, then he raised his blade high above his head, face contorted again, and gave a battle cry of spit and fury that briefly drowned out the sirens and the flames below. We said, calm and true, "We will kill you if you try."

If he heard us, he showed no sign.

He charged towards us, a man with no other mission in life than to slice our skull in two.

We opened our palms, and let the stolen poison between our fingers fly. It smacked into his face, two fistfuls of burning liquid, and he screamed, clutched at his eyes, blade falling from his hands, screamed and screamed to the little hiss of flesh burning, blood running down between his fingers where he had clasped them over his eyes, a man drunk on his own pain, blind and howling, and my stomach twisted. I tried to grab his shoulders. "Don't touch," I breathed. You're not helping here."

His fingers curled, and for a moment I thought he was going to try and pull his eyes out of their sockets, but he steadied himself, quivering with the effort of control. Slowly, my hands on his shoulders, he dragged his fingers away from his face. I saw eyes turned the colour of wet beetroot, and skin blistered black and yellow, and could not help but look away.

There was a snicker-snack.

The weight of his shoulders suddenly became too much for me to support.

He dropped, face banging into the end of my shoes, dead even before gravity got a look-in. Oda stood behind him, his glass blade in her hands, his blood being washed away by the rain. Her face was nothing, an empty pit with no bottom. She said, looking through me like I wasn't even there, "We must leave this place."

I found my hands were shaking. "You . . . He was . . ."

She turned the blade easily in her hands, tip pointing towards the stair. "This building will burn soon," she said. "We cannot control the fire. We will burn with it. We must leave this place. You will find a way."

She half-turned her head, like a curious pigeon, to one side, and there it was, there was something wrong with her eyes. I thought I heard footsteps and glanced over my shoulder, but there was nothing there, and when I looked back, her face was a crumpled piece of paper and the blade had slipped from between her fingers, limp and weak. "Sorcerer?" she said and her voice was a thin stretch short of a whimper. "I think there's something wrong with me."

"Yeah," I breathed. "Yeah. I think so too."

"Kill me?"

Her eyes were on the floor, her shoulders hunched, back bent, I half thought I'd imagined the words.

"What?"

"Kill me?"

"I . . . I gotta tell you, there's a bit of a queue. I'm barely in sixth or seventh place." She sagged, and I caught her before she hit the floor, dragging her back up. "Come on," I whispered, "think psycho-bitch, OK?"

She nodded dumbly.

I looked for a way out.

It didn't seem likely that the fire would stop short of the top floor. It'd just take that much longer for us to be burnt alive.

Something small, white and limp stirred in the rain, trying to escape the heat and failing. I prodded it with my toe. The sad torn remnants of a Tesco plastic bag, a rip in one side, a puddle of greenish-grey water pooling in what was left of its guts. In my pocket, my phone buzzed. We answered it without looking.

"Hi Penny," I said.

"Hi," she replied. "Still not dead?"

"Still a bit busy."

"Bad time, huh? Only you left me looking like a prat holding half a packet of fish and chips that's getting cold . . ."

"Kinda in a burning building full of the dead, the dying and the should-be both."

"Oh. OK. Bad time." Then, cautiously, "Anything I can do to help out?"

"I'll get back to you."

I hung up, slipped the phone back in my pocket, bent down and picked up the limp Tesco bag with the tips of my fingers. It twitched in the wind, the hot updraught from the approaching flames, trying to escape. I let it go, watched it billow up and away like a demented nervous dove. Oda wheezed, "Any time, sorcerer."

I picked my way across the detritus of the roof and pulled out from a small mound of dead cans and cardboard boxes another bag. This one was blue, whole, dirty, smelling of indefinable rot. I shook the worst of the stagnant water off it, wiped it down on the side of my coat, took a deep breath, held the open lips of the bag over my mouth, exhaled. The bag swelled up. I pulled it shut before the air had a chance to escape and tied the handles together. It tugged and twisted in the heat, even as its surface bent and snapped under the impact of the falling rain. I held it up over my head and let it go, caught almost immediately in the twisted, bewildered wind and carried away past the dead snares of bent aerials. We watched it go. Beside us Oda said, "This had better be good."

"How long do you think before we burn to death?"

"Maybe fifteen minutes. It'll seem shorter."

"Fifteen minutes! I should have brought a book."

"Are you really going to meet death reading trashy fiction?" Oda was swaying, the smoke forming odd eddies around her as it tumbled over the roof. Her eyes were shut again; had she looked too long at the fire?

"If it's a choice between trashy fiction and abject terror, I know which one I'd go for any day." I reached out for her instinctively as pain flickered over her face, then held back, uncertain, not wanted. The body of the man with lilac eyes and hedgehog hair lay between us.

"Getting hot," she breathed, and there was a glow now in the doorway, and a sound of ticking metal beneath our rapidly warming feet.

"All in hand," I sighed.

"I feel sure you should start incanting about now."

"You hate magic."

"We will live."

"We?"

She hesitated, words catching at the back of her throat. I thought I saw something move above and behind her, and looked up, saw the shimmer of something dark and fast caught silver-black in the rain.

"Sorcerer?" What little of Oda's voice had escaped the trap of her tongue was thin and weak. "Matthew?"

"Still here." The building groaned under us, a giant with indigestion, a volcano about to go, drowning out the sirens on the ground a long, long way below.

"There's something waiting for you at the end of the alley."

"Is that a threat, or a geographically obscure statement of fact?"

"It's . . . I don't know. It's true. It's what it is. It is the end."

Something wide and dark caught the orange flicker of the reflected street lamps, turned overhead, gathered more speed and began to dive. "Oda, you're wet, you're burnt, you're a little oxygen-deprived and, if you don't mind me saying it, you've got what looks like a kinda nasty stab wound through your heart. I don't want to leap to any conclusions, but I'd suggest you're not in your right frame of mind."

She looked up, straight into our eyes, and on her face was misery, true and as deep as the darkest ocean. "Help me?"

"You asked; I did. Fancy that."

"Kill me?"

"It's on the list." I held out my hand to her, right hand, twin cross scars aching beneath its fingerless black glove. "Come on."

She hesitated.

Put her hand in mine.

I couldn't remember ever feeling the touch of psycho-bitch's skin before.

"Where are we going?"

I tilted my head upwards. She followed my gaze. Something passed overhead; momentarily, no rain fell around us, and there was the pattering of water on plastic. I pulled her close to me, felt the rain resume across my upturned face, washing away the skin of carbon. She was breathing fast and shallow, but didn't shy away. I heard

water beating on the skin of a drum

rustle of plastic

air beneath mighty wings

And I saw a thing catch the glow of the fire on its belly as it swung round through the sky towards us, as slow, ponderous and inevitable as an oil tanker down a mountainside, its wings of spun white, orange and blue, rolling tapers of plastic streaming back from its parted beak, and it was bigger than an eagle and smaller than a jet plane and wider than a bus and longer than a car and as it swooped down towards us I saw that its belly was sagging with loose plastic handles and its skin rippled and beat in the passing of the wind and on its flesh were written the words:

. . . for Mums who . . .

. . . every penny . . .

. . . thank you for shopping at . . .

. . . finest quality . . .

. . . recycle your plastic bags . . .

And its wings were the same inflated plastic bags that made up the rest of its flesh, rolled and round at the front like the aerofoil of a plane and free, gaping at the back where the mouths of the bags parted. It came towards us, this more-than-eagle, talons of plastic outstretched and I heard Oda draw in breath, I reached up, felt the dry underbelly of bags brush my fingers and caught a handle, twisted my wrist into it and Oda was doing the same, was yanked off my feet by my wrist so hard and fast I thought it was going to pop from the socket. My knees banged against the rail on the edge of the roof, the force spinning me round, plastic biting into my skin, the shock running up the length of my spine. I closed my eyes instinctively as the world dropped away beneath our feet; we opened them again.

Two pairs of feet flapping over a great dark drop.

Blue lights flashing below, firemen with heads turned all towards the blaze, no one marking us, and the tower block was on fire, it was going to go all the way, windows spurting flames like a Satanist's lips bursting obscenities, and both top and bottom now catching alight, the thing already looked lopsided, the place sagging where the fire began as if too tired to fight, it was going to go, the entire thing was going to go and leave nothing but black bones behind. I saw metal glowing red on the lower windows where safety shutters were starting to tick and expand in the heat, I saw workmen's huts and warning signs scattered around its rim and then we were up, swept over it all by my summoned plastic-bag eagle towards the rain, buoyed up by the heat tearing off the building and we saw the city stretching out beneath us, starlight, galaxy-light, an infinity of tungsten stars spread upside down across the universe, flowing rivers of red brake lights and white headlamps, silver snaps of light from the wheels of a rolling train, a horizon of shadow where night sky met night city, magic, pure and brilliant magic the city at night, so beautiful we could have caught fire with the power of it and we saw . . .

I saw a shape move on the roof below us as the plastic eagle turned slowly on the air like a harpist's fingers over the strings.

There was a man, on the roof, bursting out of the door, and he was on fire. His ragged old woollen hat, his stained coat, dirty trousers and his torn boots, his beard that stretched down over his chin and neck, his hair stuck out around his ears: he was on fire, screaming, clawing at his own skin like he would try to pull it free, douse the flames in blood. And he looked at us, and screamed. It took too long for him to die, and it was not a quick turning out of the lights, and he did not stop fighting until his throat had shrivelled too tight for air to pass. The body, when it fell into the pools of water on the roof of the building, kept burning, and steam rose from the ground all around it like a sauna in a mortuary.

So we too closed our eyes.

Touchdown was too dignified a term for our landing. Our plastic saviour came in low over a terrace of houses with freshly painted black doors and the lights out in the clean windows, and as my toes brushed the first blade of grass on the nearby common, the thing I held was no longer an eagle as wide as a truck, but just a plastic bag. I dropped, caught by surprise, falling flat onto damp mud, the orange-yellow street lights round the edge of the common barely twisting my shadow as I fell. Oda landed next to me, and didn't bother to get up again. My arm was the lead handle that had wound a giant catapult: a dead thing reluctant to obey command. Something cold and soft brushed the back of my neck. I pulled it clear. It was a plastic bag. They fell from the sky around us, pattered upon by the rain, spun in wind-drifted shoals, spilling over the grass where the breeze caught them. I dug myself out of a gathering blanket of plastic, caught Oda by the arm, tried to pull her up. She came slowly, her eyes not looking at anything in particular. "Still not dead?" I asked her.

She looked past me, over my shoulder, and I turned to follow her gaze. On the cut-off horizon made by the rooftops of the houses, the sky had turned to pink-crimson. I could just make out the top of the tower block, little more than a giant funeral pyre. Sirens echoed off the streets around us, but there was nothing now to be done but watch it burn.

"Come on," I breathed, pulling her towards the edge of the green.

She managed what in a baby antelope might have counted as a walk. We reached the nearest bus stop, a stand devoid of even a shelter from the weather, and she leant against it, gasping for breath as the rain shimmered between the scars on her face. Only one night bus ran, once every twenty-five minutes. I pulled off my jacket, put it around her. She pulled it tighter.

"Cold."

"What, you want fire, you want rain, you want the earth, gimme a little to go with," I chided.

"Where's the girl?" she asked.

"Which girl?"

"There was a girl."

"Where?"

"In there."

"The fire?"

"Don't know."

"Helpful."

A truck swished by on the other side of the street, sending a spray of water up from a blocked black drain.

Somewhere in the night, a door banged on its hinges. I could hear a female voice screaming, "So you just take it and stick it up your . . ."

The door slammed shut.

The rainwater running off my face was ash grey.

My phone rang.

I answered. Penny again. "Just checking in," she sighed.

"Hey – got out of the burning tower!"

"Neat. Anything I can . . . you know . . . sorta do?"

"Um. Dunno. Look, about tonight's class . . ."

"Yeah, you know I'm still holding your sodding supper?" she replied. "I mean it's fucking freezing and you just kinda vanished and I figured, you know, I'd be big about it and all, but you're kinda taking the mick now, you know what I'm saying?"

"Penny, I didn't exactly *ask* to be summarily summoned into the middle of a burning building . . ."

"And then all you have to say is, 'dunno' and 'I'll get back to you'! I mean some sort of fucking mentor you are."

A pair of bright lights at the end of the street, the low hum of an engine doing too much work for too little maintenance. I held the phone away from my ear and let Penny rant a little. Oda raised her head from a contemplation of her shoes, shied away from the approaching light. I patted down my pocket, found my Oyster card, put the phone back to my ear.

". . . so that's it, I mean what the fuck, it's like so totally . . ."

"Remember what we said about that temper thing you've got going?"

Sullen silence on the end of the line.

"Now I want you to take a deep breath . . ."

"Up yours!"

"Repeat after me: 'Breathe in with anger . . . and out with love . . .'"

I stuck out an arm, flagged down the bus as Penny started on a list of fluent and medically precise obscenities. It was a little red single-decker, the kind of bus I associated with little old ladies nipping out to do the shopping, or kids who rode the buses for nothing better to do.

"Going now! In with anger . . ."

"I *hate* you!"

I hung up as the bus came to a sloppy halt in the gutter by the bus stop, eased Oda on board, beeped in with my travelcard, paid a two-pound bus fare all in loose change for her, stuck the ticket in my pocket. The driver was a Middle Eastern-looking man with a mole on his top lip, who studied us in the mirror and refused to make anything more in the way of eye contact. There were five other people on the bus. A black man with more hair than head held up in a woolly sack on the top of his head, wearing a high-visibility jacket and a pair of steel-capped boots. An old man who smelt of sweat and beer and against whose foot an empty lager can bumped and rolled on every corner; his head was bowed, his nose pink, his eyes lost to another world. Three kids, dressed in oversized duffel coats and trousers that started somewhere around the knee. They looked like they wanted you to be afraid of them, without really knowing why.

I got Oda into a seat papered over with torn free newspapers and crisp packets. She leant, her forehead resting against the cold, scratched glass of the window, looking paler than ever in the unforgiving white fluorescent light. "Where are we going?" she asked.

"Hadn't really thought that far ahead."

"Sorcerers," she muttered sourly. "You never do."

"Remember that major owing me thing? You need a doctor."

"No doctors."

"You need a hospital."

"No hospitals."

"See, both those things sound irrational to me . . ."

"I need a place to sleep."

"Yes, because that'll make everything better."

"Just get me somewhere warm."

"Oda, I have questions . . ."

"Later."

"They're kinda whoppers . . ."

"Later."

So saying, she turned her face away from me, and closed her eyes.

I got off the bus to the south of Greenwich, in that dead space where the reconstruction around the white swell of the Millennium Dome ran into the old industrial dumping grounds of the past; where the air smelt forever of rotting eggs and the off-licence never closed its doors. A yellow-brick building that had once been a pub stood on a triangular street corner, its sign flashing in blue and pink neon, 'HOTEL VACANCIES', above an open glass door leading onto a thin red carpet. Oda moved like a blind corpse, her head bowed, shuffling as if her feet had become dog-chewed slippers on the end of a pair of matchstick legs. There was an inner glass door, locked. I buzzed the buzzer until a young woman with dyed red hair and a silver pendant around her neck reading 'Cheryl' appeared and let us cautiously over the threshold. Inside, the air smelt of baked beans, and carried the sound of a distant TV.

"Yeah?"

"Room for two?"

She looked us up and down a few times, then said, "I gotta get my mum," and scuttled away.

I propped Oda against the nearest wall, beneath a picture showing some long-passed grandmother missing a front tooth and smiling broadly with a chubby babe in her arms.

The girl came back, bringing with her a hard-chinned woman in a large red dressing gown. Her dark thinning hair was held up in a net, and her jaw bore the traces of some grey-green goo that did we could guess not what for her skin. "You want a room?" she asked, looking me and Oda over.

"Yes. For two, one night."

"We're full."

"Sign at your door says you've got vacancies."

"It's wrong. We're full."

"Lady," I snapped, "my friend here is diabetic. She's just had an incident. The paramedics came and shot her full of stuff, and now she can barely stand, but they say she's fine. I don't want to try and get her back to Walthamstow tonight, I can pay, we're not druggies or pimps or whatever, I just need to get my friend to bed, OK?"

Mum looked at Kid, Kid looked at Mum. Neither looked happy.

"Hundred and fifty quid a night," said Mum.

It was a silly sum. I said, "Sure, no problem."

"Paid now."

"Fine."

I saw Kid's mouth twitch with displeasure that their bluff had been called, but Mum's eyes were that little bit brighter. A piece of paper was shoved my way. I made up an address off the top of my head, and signed myself in as Dudley Sinclair. I fumbled in my satchel until I found my wallet, complete with twenty pounds in cash and a receipt for takeaway pizza. Behind it was a card. On the front was a picture of a woman wearing nothing but superimposed black stars over the strategic areas. On the back was a phone number, and a lot of carefully scribbled enchantment in blue biro. I shielded it as best I could with the palm of my hand, and slipped it into the credit card reader that Mum shoved my way. The price being asked on the reader was £175.

I said, "Hundred and seventy-five quid? You said it was fifty."

"VAT," she intoned.

"Right." I entered a random four-digit PIN, and mentally apologised to whatever god of economics I was slighting by this quick and illicit piece of enchantment. The machine thought about it; the machine accepted.

Mum said, "Top floor," and gave me a key attached to a wooden yoke. "Breakfast is seven till nine."

"Got a lift?" I asked.

"Uh-uh." She held out a small clear plastic bag. I took it. Inside was a pink toothbrush, a stubby, half-used roll of toothpaste, and a beige face flannel. "Compliments of the house," she explained.

We smiled the skull smile of death come upon the earth, and helped Oda up the stairs.

Our room had one double bed, a TV on a small wobbly stand, a bedside table the size of a frying pan, a tattered copy of the Bible, a tattered copy of the Yellow Pages, thick curtains, a window that didn't open, a radiator turned up to blasting temperature, and no room to stand. It was, in short, a wallpapered attic, the roof sloping down to within half a centimetre of the headboard. Oda flopped onto the bed, curling up childlike. By turning sideways in the bathroom it was possible to fit yourself in; so long as you had short arms and no desire to move them, there was indeed space inside for you, the toilet, the sink and the plastic shower cubicle. A mirror, cracked and stained mortar grey round the edges, revealed a washed-out ghost, hair singed and eyes too blue for my soot-smeared, rain-streaked face. I looked away, unwilling to spend too much time in this shadow's company, and filled the single plastic cup on the sink with cold water. I took it to Oda, knelt by the bed, said, "Drink?"

No reply.

She seemed already asleep, eyes closed, fists bunched up to her face like the portrait of a frozen scream. I unwrapped the flannel from its bag, dipped it in the cup of water, mopped at her face. The corner of the flannel turned red-black. I eased her out of my coat, threw it into the bottom of the shower cubicle and set the water to run on cold and wash away the worst of the blood. I rolled her onto her back, and she didn't stir. Feeling every part the leery criminal, I peeled the shirt away from her skin.

The little knife-sized hole in her shirt was stiff with dry blood.

Beneath it, there was another knife-sized hole. It went through her skin and flesh, and passed between two ribs and straight down into her heart. Blood had clotted in it, a thick dark plug, and the flesh all around it was swollen and red. It wasn't a slash or a slice, it was a puncture wound to the chest; it went deep.

I cleaned her up as best I could, and folded her under the blankets. Then I cleaned myself up. My fingers stung, were sore and red. The twin crosses ached where they were scarred into the palm of my hand. I sat on the end of the bed, knees tucked up to my chin, and thought. I could think of nothing good in this situation.

And, though I didn't wish it, and the floor didn't encourage it, eventually I slept.

I woke to the buzzing of my phone.

The only illumination in the room was reflected street light slipping round the curtains, and the occasional passing of white headlights outside. Oda lay where I'd left her, though at some point in the night she had rocked and rolled, and dragged the blanket almost over her head. I answered the phone blearily.

"Yeah?"

The voice on the other end was as sharp and precise as the shaved pencils that lined its owner's desk. "Mr Mayor?"

"Uh," I replied.

"Good morning, Mr Mayor, it's Dees here, at the office."

"What time is it?"

"Five forty-three a.m. – did I disturb you?"

"I don't need to be wound up, Ms Dees, I'm already pretty cranked."

"Mr Mayor, I'm afraid something rather important has come up."

"And here was I thinking you'd rung at silly o'clock for something trivial."

"May I ask where you are?"

"Is this a philosophical question?"

"I need to know how quickly you can get to Sidcup."

I sprung upright like a target at a shooting alley. "Sidcup? Why Sidcup?"

"I believe it's where a war which could destroy this city is about to break out. Really, Mr Mayor, I would be happier explaining the details in person; where can I meet you?"

I looked at Oda, still sleeping in the bed. "I'm a little tied up here . . ."

"Shall I reiterate the part about a war which could destroy the city, or are you genuinely handcuffed to a brick wall and unable to secure your own speedy release by the many tools available to you?"

I pinched the bridge of my nose. The pain helped a little. "Ms Dees," I said, "when I was lumbered with the job of being mystic protector of this city, I could have sworn I was told that the Aldermen were on my side."

"We are, Mr Mayor. I think if you look closely, you will see that we are. Can I interest you in a business breakfast?"

The city slept. The rain had paused, leaving silvered-reflective sheen across the blackness of the pavement, and the *drip drip drip* of water off the trees. I walked to the nearest bus stop and waited.

The bus was a double-decker, almost empty. The windows were scratched with names inscribed in the glass.

B n L

Sal ♥ Pete

☺

I caught glimpses of night workers packing up. Barrels of smoking tar being loaded back onto trucks at the end of freshly relaid roads; buckets of steaming hissing paint being covered over and put away. Trucks pulling their doors shut on a few remaining racks of fresh milk. Lorries swooshing away towards the warehouses beyond the M25, the driver's head bouncing to the unheard sound of a radio.

The suburban streets east of Greenwich began to give way to the tall, proud terraces of Greenwich itself. I could see the darker shadow of the observatory on top of its hill. A green laser thinly clipped the sky from its top, shining out to mark the place where the east of the world met the west. The lights were out in the low white-brick enclosure of Greenwich Market, and the shutters drawn across shopfronts selling brass maritime antiques, knotted ropes, maps and compasses, for the home that needs everything. I got out of the bus by the Underground station and walked down the high street, past darkened restaurants and the half-lights of fashion store windows. I could smell the river, a clear coldness on the air that pushed away the usual dirt of the city, which announced its presence only by its absence, like the engine on a ship when it stops running.

Canary Wharf was a cluster of white-silver towers in the night, cloud bristling off the very top of the tallest buildings.

I turned down an alley between a red-brick church and a row of little shops selling everything from Ye Olde Souvenire to **Traditional Sunday Roast Only £12.99** and walked until I came to a sign above a small blue door which said, *'Kim's Korean Restaurant – A Taste of the Orient'*.

I knocked on the door.

The door opened.

I looked down, and then a little bit further down, onto a head almost entirely bald, except for a few loose wisps of grey hair. The head craned up, and a face that had been sun-dried like a tomato peered up into mine. A pair of toothless lips smacked against sticky gums, and this ancient creature replete with green slippers and a bathrobe with a yellow duck on it said, "Are you death?"

"Um. No."

"Are you sure?"

"Um. Yes?"

"Are you an angel?"

We licked our lips. If we had learnt one lesson in our complicated existence, it was never to underestimate the power of little old ladies. "In a way," we said.

"Are you from the council about the rubbish?"

"No."

"Why not?"

"Couldn't really say, ma'am. Um . . . is Mr Kim about?"

She sighed and smacked her lips against her gums a few times. "Busy busy busy," she complained, and waddled inside. I peered past her, down a white corridor with the soul of a parking fine, and smelt something sharp on the air. "Come on come on come on!" she trilled back at me.

I followed her down the corridor.

A silver-metal door at the end opened onto a kitchen of gleaming saucepans and a less than gleaming floor. Steam rose from a knee-high pot in which strange greenish-grey weeds rose and fell on the bubbling surface. The wall was hung with roots and herbs, barely half of which I could name, and on every other work surface were great pink slabs of meat, ready to be sliced. A man sat by a long workbench, head bowed over a bowl of something that required slurping. The woman waddled up to him, said, "He says he's not death or the council or the angels, and I think he lies!"

The man half turned. A small round Korean face split into a thin polite smile. He wore a white freshly ironed shirt and black freshly pressed trousers. He held a bowl of thick soup in one hand, and a pair of chopsticks in the other. "Mr Swift," he intoned, waving me with the chopsticks towards a stool. "It is an honour. Ms Dees is on her way."

I sat on the stool, looked at the tray in front of him. It contained a mixture of little bowls. I could recognise the rice, and the salad, but a bowl of some sour-smelling stuff crinkled like old wrapping paper and a dish of perfectly rectangular grey slabs that looked like they'd been extruded from the end of some obscene machine were beyond me. He said, "Breakfast?"

"Um . . . thanks, I'm fine."

"Tea?"

"That'd be nice."

"Mother!" hollered the man.

The woman scowled. "Tea," she said. "Tea tea tea! I only bore you, you know, I only gave my life for you, your poor father worked to death, my youth, my strength, but don't you worry, tea!"

So saying, she waddled away.

"Ignore the old woman," said my host. "Her time is almost come."

I smiled the best smile I had to hand. "Sorry," I said weakly. "I was told to come here and meet an Alderman. Are you . . .?"

"Community liaison officer," he replied. "The Aldermen employ me to liaise with some mystical communities which might not be used to the idea that you can't go around cursing the business of your enemies in this city without an appropriate permit."

"You need a permit to curse your enemies?"

"Only if you get caught. Are you sure I can't tempt you to something to eat? Kimchi?" A chopstick waggled towards the dish of sour-smelling stuff.

I set my smile to the locked position and mouthed, "I'm fine."

"Just let me know if you change your mind."

The woman returned carrying a tray on which were set a fine white porcelain teapot and two little handleless cups. She laid these down next to us, glared at me, glared at her son and said, "Sugar? Milk? Cream? Napalm?"

"Mother," chided her son, "that will be all."

"Lights going out and all you want is tea!" she tutted, wobbling away.

The man who I guessed to be Mr Kim treated me to another flash of his neat little white teeth. "She used to be a seer of sorts. But the NHS got hold of her and now, you know, the pills . . ."

I nodded, the dumb expression of someone who knew, yes, and understood, yes, and wasn't it sad?

Conversation lagged.

Kim poured tea.

I drank it one sip at a time, in case of napalm.

It was all right.

"You run this place?" I asked finally.

"Yes. Stipend for being a community liaison officer in this time is pittance. Times being what they are."

"Good business?"

"We do well enough. I also offer a freelance service blessing cars."

"How does that work?"

"Oh, there's various different kinds of blessing I offer. The most common one is the blessing of a thousand emeralds; which translated means that all red lights at the car's approach will turn green regardless of their system programming. Cuts commuting times in half."

"How much do you charge for that?" I asked.

"Eight grand for minis; ten for estates; fifteen for trucks and upwards. I charge more for high-emission vehicles."

"How very environmental of you."

"We all have to do our bit. What about you?"

"Me?"

"How do you make your living?"

I thought about this for a while. Then we said, "We destroy the enemies of the city, drive back unstoppable darknesses and purge the night of the things that would make us fear." I thought a little bit more. "Although it doesn't pay very much."

Now it was Mr Kim's turn to think. "You get pension with that?"

"I don't think it's intended I live long enough to find . . ."

There were footsteps behind us, sharp heels on the tiles. I turned, surprised to find myself as jumpy as I was. Leslie Dees, five foot nothing in a sharp black suit, sharp pointed chin beneath a sharp pencil nose, straight mousy hair cut to a sharp line above her straight shoulders, grey eyes above a face of freckles, briefcase in hand, stood in the doorway. "Hello Mr Mayor; Mr Kim," she said politely, a BBC nothing in her accent, nothing in her voice to betray a thing.

"Hi," I sighed. "Tea?"

She seemed to move without use of her knees, and was in an instant standing by Mr Kim's chair, laying her briefcase down beside his tray. "Thank you; no, I had some coffee before I came here. Thank you very much, Mr Kim, for your cooperation in these events."

Even the implacable smile of Mr Kim wavered beneath Dees' well-bred inscrutability. "Always happy to help," he mumbled.

"And it is appreciated."

She didn't gesture, didn't nod, didn't flutter an eyelash, but it was a dismissal nonetheless, that radiated from every neat line of her body. Mr Kim sensed it and did the wisest thing in acting on it, shuffling away, head bowed, leaving his meal to cool on the worktop. Dees took the seat he had vacated and immediately turned to me, snapping open her briefcase.

"The matter, Mr Mayor, is serious."

"Hi," I replied wearily. "Good morning to you too. How are you, Ms Dees? How's the kid?"

"Mr Mayor, you appear to have burn marks on your trousers," she replied.

I looked down.

Somehow, between the blood and soot, I hadn't really bothered to pay attention to my ankles. "You know what, Ms Dees, I do believe you're right."

"May I ask how you acquired them?"

"When you became an Alderman, Dees, were you hired for your tact and managerial sensitivity, or for your capacity to vaporise your enemies at a thought?"

She smiled, diamond teeth glimpsed between a paper cut. "Hopefully you need never find out, Mr Mayor."

"Please don't call me that."

"What would make you more comfortable?"

"Almost anything. Go on. Hit me. What's so ridiculously serious that we have to gather at silly o'clock in a room smelling of fermented cabbage to have a heart-to-heart about it?"

She sighed and leant forward, elbows resting on her knees, chin on the upturned palms of her hands. "A daimyo of the Neon Court has been murdered."

I raised my eyebrows, waiting for something more.

"The Neon Court accuse the Tribe."

I waited for further enlightenment.

"The Neon Court are threatening to declare war on the Tribe."

"And this bothers me . . . how?"

"Mr Ma . . . Mr Swift, do you really want to have two of the most ruthless magical clans in the city attempting to wipe each other out in the streets of London?"

It was my turn to lean forward. We looked her in the eye, and to her credit, she held our gaze. Very few mortals do. "Ms Dees," I said, "let me get this absolutely clear. The Neon Court – a bunch of narcissistic wankers who haven't yet come to terms with the fact that the age of the Faerie Court is over – have this major-league grief with the Tribe, a bunch of self-mutilating wankers who haven't yet come to terms with the fact that the world isn't out to get them personally – and someone somewhere is dead, which is very sad, and they're threatening to kill each other and I care . . . how?"

"Your job is the protection of the city, as regards the rash exercise of magical forces."

"Doesn't seem that rash to me. Neither Court nor Tribe ever pay council tax as far as I can tell, and I don't have much time for the ethics of either. The Court are smug self-satisfied bastards, the Tribe are angry world-hating bastards. Why should I get involved?"

"You should get involved, Mr Mayor, because Lady Neon is coming to town."

I was quiet a long time.

Dees let me think.

I thought.

I reached the only available conclusion.

"Shit."

*

There is a story of the Neon Court.

Actually, there are several stories, but the one I have always liked, and the one which is most often told, goes like this:

Once upon a time, in that old time when life was still magic and life was lived in the trees and the forests and the rivers and the hills, in the old time of wild, ivy-tangled, rain-dropped magic, before the lights burnt neon and the spells flickered with electric fury, there existed the Faerie Court. And it was beautiful, sensual, powerful, rich, decadent and dangerous. One touch from the lips of a faerie and he or she who was touched was enchanted; one whisper from the faerie queen and the course of nations would be changed for ever.

But alas, the Faerie Court did not move with the times, and did not predict how a steam train could carve through the landscape, or how a factory could discolour the sky and, as the times changed, so did the magic, migrating with the people to the cities and becoming rich with smoke and stone and the sound of metal. And so the Faerie Court declined, and those who sought its blessing dwindled, until there was nothing more than a dusty hollow in the carved-out heart of a wood, crumbling with the fall of autumn leaves.

Then one day, one fairly unremarkable day at the beginning of the twentieth century, an enterprising princess of the court, one of the very last, decided that rather than sit at home and watch her world dwindle and die, she was going to explore this new world. So she set out to travel, visiting all the cities of the globe and, as she travelled, she came to understand that new magic, urban magic, and bend it to her will. When finally she stopped, she summoned all her surviving subjects and friends and declared the founding of a new court: the Neon Court, whose heart was in the heart of the cities, and whose magic would be of the new magics, and whose ways would be of the new ways. Soon, in Tokyo and New York, in London and Macau, in Istanbul and Kuala Lumpur, in any city where the lights blazed long into the night and the sound of music could be heard at the end of the street, the Neon Court set up its palaces, to forever revel and entice the more reckless of mankind into its lairs after the sun had gone down. And so there came the daimyos, who ruled each branch of the Court in each city where it came; and the warriors and the thralls, the humans who sold themselves to the Court, body and soul, for what looked like the party of their lives. And when they grew too old, or too ugly, or too tired of playing the Court's games, the thralls would try to free themselves, and find that they couldn't, trapped now as playthings of this never-sleeping monster.

And in time Lady Neon herself became little more than a myth: a figure only ever seen by the shadow of a street light, moving between city after city, forever chasing the night and avoiding the sun, a reveller whose lips could seduce any creature they touched, and, if you believed the darker stories that came from the back alleys of Soho, of Itaewon, Harlem and Galata, a monster and a murderer who struck down all in her way. For the Neon Court had been slow to move into the cities, and there were already many other clans to contend with. The Whites, whose magic was paint; Bikers, whose power was speed; the warlocks who worshipped the power of the Seven Sisters and the ley lines made by the Underground; the Tribe, who prided strength above all else; the Tower, which hungered for life; the Guild; the seers; the sorcerers; the Aldermen. It was only a matter of time before the Neon Court found itself in conflict with one or more of these, and it proved itself a ruthless player of the game. "Beware her violet kiss" became a very literal warning whispered by those lucky enough to survive.

Eventually truces were made, in most cities across the world, with just a few exceptions. London was not the only city with a Midnight Mayor; every city had its own mechanism for dealing with the turbulence of the Neon Court's arrival. But still the Neon Court continued, a fire below the decks, waiting for a chance to spring into an inferno. And while most of the time the fire was contained, if there was one thing guaranteed to send it into a fury, it was the arrival of that queen of the court, Lady Neon.

All of which brought me back to my original conclusion.

I said, "Shit. Really?"

"Yes. She lands from Mumbai in forty minutes. Her ambassador sent out immediate representation to the Aldermen requesting – no, demanding – our assistance against the aggressive actions of the Tribe."

"She demanded that the Aldermen help her?"

"Yes."

"Isn't that kinda naive?"

Dees let out the bare minimum of a breath, that might have been a sigh. "We have a defensive alliance with the Court."

"We have a what?"

"A defensive alliance. Signed in 1959, a mutual pact of accord. When one party is attacked, the other will come to its aid."

My heart found a new low to sink to. "And by we, you mean . . ."

"The Midnight Mayor and Lady Neon signed the treaty."

"I didn't sign it – I wasn't bloody born!"

"But you are the Midnight Mayor. Prime ministers are bound by the treaties of their predecessors whether they like it or not."

I raised a warning finger, extended towards the sharpened point of her nose. "OK, let me get this clear right here, right now. Some bloke is dead, the Court blames the Tribe, and now Lady Neon is expecting me to fight her battles on the basis of some bit of paper signed fifty-something years ago? Which part of what the hell begins to cover this?"

"I'm afraid there's more."

I slumped back against the work surface, elbow bumping a bowl of chilli powder. "Course there is."

"The . . . incident in which the daimyo in question was killed also took the lives of at least five other people, possibly more. The daimyo of the Neon Court, one of his men, and what we suspect are two members of the Tribe, although we are waiting on proper confirmation."

"What, all of them, all in the same place?"

"These are merely the bodies that we could identify, but yes."

"You said five bodies?"

"A fifth individual was caught in the fire, and died. A homeless man, who used to live in the tower. The body was badly damaged; we don't yet have the material for proper identification."

I took my time with the words, careful in case they got ideas of their own. "What . . . fire?"

"There was a fire in an abandoned tower block in Sidcup. The daimyo in question was killed with his own tanto."

"Tanto?"

"A short stabbing sword, easily concealed, with a refined crystal glass blade."

I stayed very very still. "Really?"

"Yes."

"Daimyo . . . that's a senior dude in the Court, right?"

"Very. They are masters of the local Court in the cities they reside in, only one step below Lady Neon in both authority and power."

"And . . . anything else wrong with him? Besides, I mean, getting a sword in the back?"

"I didn't say back," she replied quietly. "I said stabbed."

I shrugged, too much, too easy. "Figure of speech. Anything else?"

We had to force ourself to keep looking her in the eye. "Acid burns to his face and eyes."

"Who recovered the bodies?"

"The fire brigade. The fire was brought under control an hour and a half ago, although the building is still too dangerous to enter. There is no doubt that it was started deliberately; it raged out of control too fast, and it is no coincidence that a daimyo of the Neon Court and two enforcers of the Tribe were found inside it."

"No doubt," I sighed. "And the Neon Court wants war, huh?"

"Indeed."

"Any word from the Tribe?"

"They maintain . . . very poor connections with the Aldermen, and have frequently refused to acknowledge the authority of the Midnight Mayor."

"Any reason why?"

"Disobedience and recklessness is the nearest thing they have to a philosophy."

"Or maybe the Midnight Mayor's always been a bit of a tit," I hazarded.

"Mr Mayor . . ."

"Just saying, just suggesting, you know, pushing that one out there . . ." We were silent a while. Then I said, "OK. What am I supposed to do now?"

"By the terms of our defensive alliance with the Neon Court, we have twenty-four hours to investigate any breach of terms which might elicit an aggressive response."

"And now in little words?"

"We have a day to find out whether the Tribe really did kill the daimyo, start the fire, start a war."

"At the end of which . . .?"

"I believe, in the words of an illustrious American president, the philosophy is, you're either with us, or you're against us."

"You know, Ms Dees, I think perhaps professional practising magicians should leave the terms of diplomatic accords to professional practising diplomats. I mean, it's kind of like me saying, 'Hey, I once put an Elastoplast on someone's right elbow, let me diagnose your herpes!'"

"As soon as the building is safe we will send in forensic teams."

"Does the Neon Court understand the concept of forensic teams?"

"The Court and the Tribe have always hated each other. Their peace, of sorts, for the last few years has been tenuous at best. Rivalries flare; sometimes there are assaults; sometimes there are curses; sometimes there are worse. But this is the first time Lady Neon has come to London for such an event."

"Yeah. She's arrived pretty smartish, hasn't she? I mean, if you only got word that a daimyo was dead an hour and a half ago, and she arrives in forty minutes' time, that's a fairly speedy flight from Mumbai, isn't it?"

Dees was silent. Then, "Yes. It is somewhat remarkable."

Silence again.

Then, "Dees?"

"Mr Mayor?"

"If it turns out that the Tribe didn't kill this daimyo, that they're not responsible for the fire, what happens to the sap who is?"

"The Neon Court will most likely hunt him down and destroy him."

"And we're going to let that happen?"

"It is murder."

"What if it was self-defence? What if this daimyo character was really, really rude?"

"It is not worth risking a war with the Neon Court over one life," she replied. "These are the political realities we deal with."

I nodded, sighed, rose, stretched. "Yeah. That's what I guessed you'd say."

"What are you going to do?"

"I'm going to take a walk. Have a think."

"Is that . . ." Dees stopped herself mid-sentence. "I'll let you know if there are any developments."

"Cheers."

"We're holding an emergency senior management meeting to discuss the issue at nine."

"Spare me."

"Mr Swift?" I glanced on my way to the door. Her face was calm and earnest, her eyes fixed on the papers she was riffling to no effect in her case. "This is your responsibility now, whether you like it or not. Whatever happens here will affect you, no matter what you decide. So you may as well make a decision."

"We know," we sighed. "And it makes us angry." Then, "What was his name?"

"Whose?"

"The daimyo. The servant of the Neon Court, the dead man with the sword in the . . . the stabbed guy with the acid in the face?"

"Minjae San. He was a master of the Soho Court, one of the triad."

"I'm guessing we're past polite reason?"

"I think you guess astutely, Mr Mayor."

"Good morning, Ms Dees," I sighed, heading for the door, one hand turned in an absent wave of farewell.

"Good evening, Mr Swift," she answered, not raising her eyes from the paper. We hesitated at her reply, then half shook our head, and walked away.

Part 1: Lights Out

In which a war escalates, a transport zone vanishes, and a walking corpse stoutly refuses to concede its own mortality.

I thought I could hear footsteps in the darkness behind me.

I stopped to look down the little alley from which I'd come.

No one.

The streets of Greenwich were filling with buses, commuters pressed into every window, faces of every kind, empty faces turned vacantly onto the world outside, seeing nothing but their own thoughts. The uniforms of the working city – suits and ties for the offices, jeans and a T-shirt for the trendy "creative" jobs and hi-vis jacket for the builders. Schoolkids in a special shade of brown known as "poo-humility" shuffled by with black backpacks on their shoulders, mobile phones pressed to their ears. I caught the smell of garlic from the front door of an Italian kitchen, and of fresh bread being synthetically pumped out of a supermarket.

I had to get to Oda.

I headed for the mainline station. South London works on different geographical rules from North London; everywhere is twice as far apart, and takes twice as long to get to. Some time during the great suburban expansion that created places with such unlikely names as Martin's Heron, Winersh Triangle and Carshalton Beeches, a cruel urban god decided to take the transport infrastructure of North London, and stretch it out over South London like a rubber spider's web, to see how far it could go before the strands between each join became so thin that it snapped.

I walked through an early-morning Greenwich, a mishmash of old and new: neat white terraces that had, a hundred years ago, housed the genteel citizens of London who couldn't stand the odours of the old city and, a hundred years before that, their naval grandfathers. Yellow-brick council estates thrown up behind the river where the bombs had fallen or the need for housing had grown faster than architectural pride; shops selling electronics from Taiwan, clotted cream from

Devon, lampshades from the backyard of a craftswoman in Norfolk and sandwiches produced by their thousands in Sheffield. A red-brick church with patchwork stained glass offered God Mondays, Wednesdays, Fridays and Sundays, with judo on Tuesdays, Women's Institute on Thursdays and youth community drama Saturdays, 1–3 p.m.

I became aware of the limo even before it started following me.

It was, after all, a limo, black, with frosted windows and a bass beat coming from somewhere inside it that drowned out even the belching engines of the garbage trucks. The chance that it wasn't following me declined with every step until finally, in the little side street that ran towards the mainline station, I stopped, turned, put my hands on my hips and said, "Oh, for God's sake."

The limo stopped.

The back door opened: a long way back. It was not a car designed for cornering in a city built to a fifteenth-century street plan. A boot extracted itself from the inside of the car. It was leather, it was buckled, it clung to the curves of a calf all the way up to the knee, considered flexibility around the joint, then carried on a little bit further. The flesh that emerged from that was almost corpse-white, clad in fishnet, and fairly promptly – although not promptly enough for some tastes – vanished into a leather miniskirt that wasn't designed to protect against the cold. Above the miniskirt was a corset. It was black, though with a hint of silver and purple running through it that changed with the angle of the light. The corset was also clearly not designed with the weather in mind. A pair of corpse-white arms emerged from this get-up along with a neck of biologically absurd length, wearing some sort of throttling silver bangle with no evident means of release. The whole thing culminated in a face wearing, for its hair, an electrocuted blowfish. We considered this last for a while. Some part of the fragile ecosystem of the planet had suffered to create the hair crowning this head. It was perfectly white, and stuck out in a halo, a lion's mane made of electrostatic repulsion and hairspray. The owner of the head moved; and the hair didn't even droop in the breeze. We wondered whether it was real. We wondered what you had to go through to make it if it was not.

The woman who'd got out of the limo said, "You must be the Mayor."

Her voice was a conspiracy between cigarettes and jazz; low, warm, fuzzy, smooth and probably quite hard to achieve.

I said, "Sorry, mate, you've got the wrong guy," and tried to walk away.

She reached out to stop me.

Her nails stuck out nearly an inch from her fingertips. They were silver, and not just in colour. I stopped before they could lacerate me on my way, and looked into a pair of cool lilac-blue eyes.

"You're him," she replied. "The other guy died."

"The other guy?"

"The guy who went before you. Nair. He died. They say the death of cities killed him, whatever that means."

"Just this once, it does what it says on the cover."

"And you're the new guy."

I craned to see past her, into the interior of the limo. Cigarette smoke, leather upholstery, pounding bass music, low bluey-red light. I said, "And you must be from the Neon Court. Didn't wait long to have a chat, did you?"

She grinned. It was like watching the sun rise over an iceberg. "We wanted to have a quick conversation . . . privately, before matters escalated further. Don't really admire that, considering the circumstances. Can I give you a lift?"

"My mummy told me not to accept lifts from strangers."

"The Neon Court has no ill will towards you, Mr Mayor. In fact, we're practically allies."

I managed a dumb smile. "I'll walk. Cheers."

She stepped directly into my path. The lipstick on her lips was violet, drawn only in the middle, to give her the appearance of a perpetual pout. "Mr Mayor," she said smoothly, "can you imagine how uncomfortable it is to walk in these boots?"

I considered them. They looked like they'd been based on medieval torture devices. "Fairly?" I guessed. "Look, I get it. You guys are pissed, the Tribe is pissed, you're going to kill each other, whatever, major mess, blood in the streets. Hey – if I ask you not to, would that go down a storm?"

Her pout, if it was possible, deepened a little.

"Tell you what, you scrap this whole vendetta business, and I'll get in the car."

"Lady Neon has personally requested you. *Personally*."

"I don't come when she calls."

"She hasn't called until now; and besides, from what I know of the Midnight Mayor, you do." She stood aside, leaving the door open to the smoke-filled interior.

I said, "At least open a window, will you?" and got into the car.

She treated me to another smile. I felt each tiny tooth rattle against my spine on the way down. "I don't think they do. It's not one of the features," and she got in beside me, pulling the door shut.

It was the first time in our life we had been inside a limo.

It made us feel oddly uncomfortable, as if somehow betraying a sea of trusting strangers. The music went up through the seat. The smoke spun little eddies in the air. There was an ice bucket with champagne in it. There was a minibar, containing more liquors, only some of which we could identify. There were no less than five small TV screens pumping out a mixture of financial news, replete with inexplicable numbers and arrows, and MTV videos. The windows made it hard to see anything outside. The driver was lost behind black glass, silent, unseen. The girl with the silly shoes said, "We are grateful, you know."

"For what?"

"For your taking our side."

"I haven't taken anyone's side."

"But you will. There's a treaty."

"And no proof that it's been broken."

She lapsed into a silence that might well have been a sulk. After a while, she stood up and, hobbling, head bowed, the length of the limo, went to a low ice box, and pulled out something orange and frozen, wrapped in plastic. Vapour tumbled out around her wrists. "Want one?" she asked.

"What is it?"

"Vodka lolly."

"Too early in the morning for me."

"Oh, you're sweet. If you were cute, I might like you. But you're not. You're just sweet."

"I forgot to ask how you found me so fast."

"We followed the Aldermen."

"How'd you know to follow Dees?"

"We didn't. We followed the twelve most senior Aldermen. But I was the only one who found you; so I'm the one who'll be rewarded."

"Rewarded, how?"

"Oh," she said casually, "with whatever I desire."

We drove through South London, across that zone where old red-brick blocks of flats faced off across a busy road with the new, balcony-sporting, underfloor-heated, terracotta-tiled apartments that had filled up the former warehouses towards the river. I couldn't see Jamaica Road, not clearly, but I could feel it beneath the tyres of the car, feel the distant plonking of an out-of-tune church bell, smell cleaning liquid and fresh kebab, hear the hiss of buses pulling up. When we crossed Tower Bridge, my right hand twitched, fire – not entirely unpleasant – running through the scars burnt into my skin. The river's magic penetrated even the black windows of the car, washing away, just for an instant, the smell of cigarette smoke. The Embankment was a series of stop-starts at traffic lights; the beginning of the A4 a slog of narrow old roads too small for the great mass of vehicles poured into them. When the A4 became the M4, a motorway hemmed in by roads with names like Elm Walk and Oak Tree Lane, I put my head back against the seat and watched the regular pulse of the pinkish-white street lights across the ceiling of the car.

The magic changed, the closer we grew to Heathrow. Still urban, still our magic, still the kind of power we could tap, but where the Square Mile was a burning brilliance of electricity and shadows, out here along the motorway the magic was a black snake soaked in moonlight, dancing on a frying pan. Hard to see; hard to catch, and once you'd got your fingers tangled in it, you didn't let go. Heathrow didn't sleep; even when the planes stopped, for the few hours that they did stop, lorries bustled in and out, bringing in food and fuel, goods and duty-free barely fast enough for the rate at which they were consumed. I heard the engines of the planes coming in low overhead, felt them shake even a car as fat and decadent as the limousine, even through the relentless music, felt power move around them, caught it like breeze tangling in my fingertips.

I said, as we slowed, "Hope it's not Terminal 5."

The girl made no answer.

"That Lady Neon – smart to come when a crisis strikes, isn't she?"

No answer.

"Must be . . . what? Ten hours from Mumbai? And to think, her daimyos – this Minjae San? – has only been dead for . . . eight?"

"Did you sit silently in the car all this time and think of aeroplanes?" asked the girl with a laugh as light and fake as a snowglobe.

"Ducky," I sighed, "you're a thrall. The silver bangle you wear round your neck is welded on. You're never going to take it off. You were sent to do a job, and being a thrall, you did it. Did they tell you what you were collecting, when you came to collect us? Did they say why our eyes are so blue, or why our hands are so scarred? Did they tell you what we are? Doubt it. Because you probably wouldn't have come, if they had. So, with all due respect, and if you don't mind, shove it."

The limo pulled to a stop as she opened her mouth to answer. I opened the door, kicked it wide with the heel of my shoe, raised a warning finger towards her. "That was the final word, by the by. Enjoy it! And buy some sensible shoes?"

I slammed the door shut before she could start screaming.

I had expected to be at Arrivals.

I wasn't. I was on the edge of a car park. On one side was a field. A rabbit regarded me from behind the chain-link fence separating field from tarmac. A line of red lights announced that the field was probably busier than the rabbit's calm expression implied. In the distance were the white lights of Heathrow stretching off, the control tower a blinking red spike in their midst. To say planes came and went didn't do it justice; planes landed even as others took off, and no sooner had their wheels touched down than you could see the one behind already descending, no room for error, no time for doubt.

I looked across the gloomy, yellow-lit car park as the engines roared and the wind was cool, and the thought dawned somewhere in the back of my mind that something was wrong with this picture. Then a voice said, "Mr Swift?"

I turned.

The man wore a dinner jacket without the bow tie, white silk gloves and sunglasses despite the night. He had come out of nowhere. He said, "Mr Matthew Swift?"

"And you look like hired muscle," I sighed. "Did you have to bring your own gun, or is it one of the perks?"

"If you could come with me, please, Mr Swift."

I shrugged and followed. A chain-mesh gate was set into the fence. He unlocked it with a fat black key, startling my friend the rabbit, and walked down a neat path of square flagstones towards the red lights of the runway. He stopped a few metres from the tarmac, and checked his watch.

I said, "You know, I've got stuff to do, people to see."

"Her ladyship will be here within a few moments, Mr Swift. Trouble with air traffic control."

We waited. Then, without any apparent sign of having looked, the man said, "Ah, here she comes."

I looked up, half expecting to see the lights of a private jet or, at the very least, a 747 heading in to land. No such thing. The skies were clear. Which was, in and of itself, an oddity. A breeze, warmer, smelling faintly of grease, tickled the top of my head. I craned back, looked straight up. Something darker than the sodium-tinted clouds above flickered for a second with a hint of reflected runway light, and then twisted again out of sight. I heard the faintest creaking of metal, and felt something hot bite between my fingertips. I closed my fists up tight, felt the power tingle up my arms, lots and lots of magic, as thick and cloying as steam in a sauna. It made us think of the sound that metal wheels made when braking too sharply on a railway track, and we had to resist the urge to raise our defences.

Then there was a sound, the swish-swish-swish of a tail, the rolling pressure of air being displaced. I shielded my eyes as the wind grew up around the runway, pushing dust and dirt into the air, and looked through a crack in my fingers as a thing made of ebony darkness and pinpointed white light came twisting out of the sky like a paper wrapper in a storm.

It was . . .

. . . not a bird . . .

. . . nor a plane . . .

but resembled more the ancient Chinese dragons of old, a snake-worm of segmented metal parts that slid over and under each other like polished black armour, some thirty metres long and four metres wide. It had a tail that sharpened to a point which swished and snatched at the air; it had four tiny little metal wings, insufficient and insubstantial to the task of keeping it afloat, and not doing any work in that regard. From the polished black metal of its flesh rose spikes of aerials and transmitters, of radar dishes and electronic masts, stretched back across its skin at jagged giddy angles like they'd been beaten flat in the world's largest car wash. In the middle part of its body, which was barely a quarter of its total length, its belly bulged outwards and a few gashes in its skin revealed clear glass through which shone dim blue-white light. Its outstretched legs, four of them, had pneumatic pumps along the thighs and metal claws that glimmered in the dull red of the runway light as they reached out to land; its eyes were two brilliant white lamps, its nose two spinning jet engines, the exhaust visible just behind two bumps that might have been ears, the air distorting from the heat passing through. Its jaw, when it parted the great metal maw of its mouth, revealed a black conveyor-belt tongue licking at the air. It was aerodynamically impossible, as beautiful as a raging fire and the glow left when the fire goes out.

When it landed, the ground shook, and its whole body seemed to arch in the middle as its claws gouged twelve claw-shaped holes in the earth. It came to rest, steam venting from between the joins of its body; briefly its head half turned and those brilliant white lamps of eyes swept over to me. We felt suddenly sad and small, and took a half-step towards the thing, reaching out towards it, to touch its black skin and make the foolish comforting sounds mortals make in the presence of frightened animals lesser than themselves.

But its head turned away, and the hand of the hired muscle man fell on my shoulder and he said, "If you don't mind, sir," and pulled me back.

There was a hiss from one of the central body plates and, as I watched, a piece of metal skin slid back over its neighbour to create a kind of door leading into the creature's belly. Two people – I couldn't see their faces in the darkness and the pouring steam – rushed forwards to secure a ramp from inside and scurried down to secure it at the bottom. Their work done, they then quickly arranged themselves, one on either side, kneeling on the tarmac, heads bowing against the cold ground, hands held forward in front of them, palms down, prostrate at the bottom of this unlikely exit. A small army of attendants promptly descended the ramp and lined themselves up like dignitaries at a state arrival. Six women wearing white silk kimonos, their faces painted the colour of fresh snow, pink cheeks daubed on, hair drawn up tight with gold and silver bangles to keep it in place; four men dressed in black dinner jackets, the guns none too subtly hidden under their arms; two boys, faces sour and pinched, wearing black leather outfits ten years too old for them; a gaggle of eight men and women dressed in not much of everything, some armed, at least three carrying in their belts what I recognised with a shudder as the short tanto stabbing blades that Dees had spoken of, and whose acquaintance I had already made under unpleasant circumstance. Last came a guard of four, shoulders wide, necks thick, heads shaved, suits bulging and, pressed over their features, masks, of twisted crimson and black, the mouths curved into huge, almost comical grimaces of anger and rage, the eyes tight, the features crinkled. I could see no means by which these face-pieces were attached to the heads of those that wore them. These four arranged themselves like a private guard at the foot of the ramp, and the rest of the entourage variously bowed, knelt and grovelled depending on, I guessed, their social status.

Two more people appeared at the top of the ramp, a man and a woman. The man wore what looked like a crimson dressing gown, loosely tied, and a pair of crimson slippers. He too had a mask on, though this one was white, smooth and empty, with just little slits for the eyes and mouth.

The woman next to him was . . .

smell of magic so much magic careful not to drown

purple-scarlet flickers of thought on the edge of sight

silk on skin

. . . undeniably the Big Event. She stood no more than five foot and a half high, and wore a smoke-coloured veil that dropped down from a large three-pointed headdress. Beneath this, someone had taken half a mile of silver shimmer and draped it over and under and around every part of her body, so that no skin showed except for the very end of each hand, from which drooped a set of fingers longer and thinner than any I had ever seen, each adorned with a silver ring, from which occasionally ran a thin chain into the sleeve of her robe, hinting at more expense beneath just out of sight. For all that every part of her was covered, there was no doubting, no doubting at all, that she was beautiful, with the unspecified, undeniable beauty of a woman who knew herself to be the sexiest thing ever to walk the earth and through believing it had, in her walk, her talk, her existence, come to make it so, regardless of the fashion of the time.

She paused on the top of the ramp, head half turning this way and that as though to assess and approve of the grovelling of those around her, and then, one dainty step at a time, left hand drooping at the wrist to be supported by her colleague in red, she descended, and stepped as carefully onto the tarmac of Heathrow as if she were a crusading knight come to the Holy Land. As one, her entourage rose to their feet, bowed once more, and straightened to their full height.

By now, the unseen eyes beneath the veil had fallen on me.

We felt them.

For a curious moment, we almost had a desire to look away. But we resisted.

Then the man in red spoke; or rather, he intoned. "In the name of our trusted alliance, our sacred friendship and our joyous reunion, her ladyship, mistress of the night and most beauteous upon this earth, greets the protector of this city."

I smiled wanly, and found I had nothing to say.

Her ladyship half leant towards the man in red, and I imagined whispers passing between her lips and his ears.

He gave a little nod, then raising his head again added, "Her ladyship is grateful for the assistance of the protector of this city in the just war against the murderers of loyal servants of the Neon Court and expresses the desire that the protector of this city share drink with her war council."

My smile grew strained.

"As a token of her appreciation, her ladyship will bestow upon the protector of this city honorary access to the palaces of the Neon Court within this city, where he may partake of the many wonders of the Court at his leisure."

There was a polite round of applause at this, and the business duly intoned, the party turned to move away.

I raised my hand. "Excuse me?" The party stopped. Lady Neon's head didn't turn, but the man in crimson spared me a glance. "Sorry," I added. "But I think there's been a basic misunderstanding. Now, it's not that I'm not cheering for the continued friendship and stuff, but I haven't yet seen any proof that the Tribe did what you're accusing them of. I haven't seen any proof that this entire affair isn't just another, with all due respect, factional bust-up going down in my streets on my watch. So, all things considered, you might want to hold off on that honorary membership thing, because I haven't said anything about fighting a war."

Silence.

Then the man in red turned on the spot and intoned, "Her ladyship wishes to remind the protector of the city that by the terms of our defensive alliance . . ."

"I must help you if you're attacked. As I understand it, if you start this war unduly, I don't have to do shit."

"Her ladyship wishes to remind you of the consequences of not honouring our alliance: the very . . . unwelcome consequences of such a breach."

I smiled, looked down at my feet, looked up at the sky. "OK," I said. "Sure. I get that. But then again, have you looked at it the other way? You go to war with the Tribe in my city without my help, sure, it'll be messy, it'll be blood on both sides, blood in the gutter. You go to war with *us* and your blood will become dust before it even has a chance to spoil the carpet. This is *our* city. You can lay on this exciting show of strength for me, sure. You can say, 'come here, jump when we say jump' all you like, but if you step one little toe out of line, we will be there, and you will see a war like nothing you can conceive. We are only human in our flesh; burn that away, and underneath you will find blue electric fire. We do not think Neon Court, nor Tribe, nor the fists of hell have the strength to extinguish that. Do we understand each other?"

Silence. That special silence that can only happen when there are armed men thinking long and hard about the use of weaponry.

Then a whisper between Lady Neon and the man in red.

He bowed.

At us.

"Her ladyship appreciates the difficult position you are in. We appreciate that you desire to avoid undue bloodshed; we acknowledge your compassion. Her ladyship will, in light of this, make you an offer, to minimise the casualties of this . . . regrettable conflict."

"I'm quivering like a feather in a storm."

"Her ladyship expresses the wish that, if you can find the girl and secure her release from the Tribe within twenty-four hours, conflict may be prevented."

"Girl? What girl?"

"The chosen one, of course."

"Come again?"

"The chosen one, the one who will end this war."

"Sorry," I mumbled, "I could have sworn I just heard the words 'chosen one' uttered without laughing."

"Find her, bring her to us, and this war need not escalate further."

"Where should I start?"

"The prophets know of whom we speak."

"Yes, because prophets are so good at giving out mobile phone numbers and a postcode – and if I don't find your 'chosen one'?"

"Then the Court will have no choice but to utterly destroy the Tribe, and anyone who stands in our way."

I sucked in air through my teeth. "*Right*. I get it. Sure. Um . . . I don't suppose you have an address?"

Then Lady Neon stepped forward. I thought I saw a glimpse of a face beneath the veil, a shadow beneath the shadow. She spoke. There was a hint of an American accent, a hint of something else, a voice like moonlight through bare branches. She said, "You have very beautiful eyes." And turned. And walked away.

The delegation from the Neon Court got into no fewer than seven black limos and drove away. They didn't offer me a lift, and I didn't ask.

I headed for the Underground. As I walked off, a team of men and women in orange overalls came out of a lorry and started mopping the snake-dragon down with grease and engine oil. It rumbled its satisfaction.

As I headed towards what I hoped was the underground station, I got out my mobile, and dialled Leslie Dees.

She answered within a ring and a half.

"Mr Mayor."

"Please don't call me that."

"Mr Swift," she replied without dropping a beat. "How is everything?"

"Lady Neon's come to town!" I said cheerfully.

"I did inform you . . ."

"I've just met her."

A note of alarm entered Dees' voice. "You didn't permit her to touch you, did you?"

"No, Dees," I sighed. "I neither touched her, nor kissed her, nor shared drink with her; I am, in fact, fully in charge of my own faculties and not under her spell, in fact, I think she's a rather peculiar little woman who's not afraid of mucking me around during a trying time. Oh – and I have beautiful eyes."

"I can't say I ever really looked."

"Thank you for your lack of interest."

"Mr Swift, if it's any comfort to you, I can promise that were I not a happily married woman with a husband I love well," sighed Dees, "you would definitely be in my top two genders of choice."

"You know how to flatter a guy."

"It seemed important to you to hear it."

"Thanks a bundle," I growled. "Serious business, if you please?"

"I can't tell you how long I've waited for you to speak those words, Mr Swift."

I resisted the temptation to hit the phone, as a substitute for something more sensitive. "I've just heard the words 'chosen one' spoken out loud without giggling."

"I see. And who spoke these mystically vague and somewhat portentous words?"

"Some tit in a mask. But he was holding Lady Neon's hand."

"I *see*." Say what you will for Dees, she knew enough about magic to know when to be upset by its misuse. "A 'chosen one'?"

"Yep. Apparently" – sarcasm dripped off the end of my tongue – "there's a 'chosen one' who is going to end the war between the Court and the Tribe, and I have twenty-four hours to find her – hey, she's a girl, I know that much; in fact, that's all I know – before the Neon Court goes to war with the Tribe and anyone else who stands in their way. Which might include me. It's all up in the air. But you never know."

There was a long, judicious silence from the other end of the line. Finally, rather than let the air waves languish, Dees said, "I *see*. Any more information?"

"Apparently we have to talk to the prophets."

"Which prophets?"

"I don't know. I was under the impression most of them were dead after . . . because of Bakker and . . . well, you know. Incidentally, did you know that the Neon Court kept a 747 dragon?"

"No, I did not," was Dees' irritated reply, and I sensed, for a moment, paperwork yet to come. "Obviously I'll have a look into this prophet business but . . ."

"Have you heard anything from the Tribe?" I asked. "I mean, since some of their guys are dead too. Are they threatening hellfire?"

"If they were, they probably wouldn't tell us."

"Is the Tribe one of the many institutions that would happily kill us and drink our blood?" we asked. "Or do they have a sense of self-preservation and perspective?"

"Mr Mayor, I really cannot recommend direct overtures to the Tribe without taking some serious precautions."

"That's me, Serious Precautions Swift."

"You are aware that the Court may have a case, that this could be just what it seems – an act of aggression by the Tribe against our ally . . .?"

"Dees," I began, and then cut myself short. "Yeah. Maybe. Doubt it. Lady Neon arrived too soon, she had to be in the air by the time all this was happening, and the Court found me too easily, which probably means they were looking."

"You are aware, Mr Mayor, then when casually scrying the streets of London, you stand out like a giraffe on roller skates, yes?"

"And even leaving that aside," I snapped, "what the hell's with this 'chosen one' bollocks? You're a cynical lady, Dees."

"I take that as a compliment," she sighed.

"You believe any of it?"

Silence. Then, "No. But we need proof. The Aldermen cannot risk a war on two fronts; we can't be fighting the Court and the Tribe and guarantee the safety of the city from all the other threats that hammer against our walls. Not even you, Mr Mayor, would survive that."

"See if you can find someone from the Tribe to have a chat with," I said. "See if we can have a conversation that doesn't involve the syllable 'ugh'."

"I make no promises."

"Fair enough. What time is it?"

"Eleven ten."

I looked up at the black, plane-speckled sky. "Already?"

"We've all been busy."

Something wrong.

Badly badly wrong.

I couldn't quite put my finger on it.

"Where's the girl?" said a voice, and for an instant, I didn't realise it was mine.

"What's that, Mr Mayor?"

"Just thinking out loud."

Oda.

Where's the girl?

Oda with a hole in her heart, Oda who should, by all reason, be dead, and who I'd left sleeping, unwatched, unguarded, in a hotel in Greenwich. Oda who'd stuck a sword into the back of a man who might or might not have been (but probably was) Minjae San, daimyo of the Neon Court, on a burning tower in Sidcup, while I'd stood and watched and done nothing to make it stop. And I'd been summoned to that tower; someone had summoned me. It takes clout to summon a taxi, let alone a sorcerer who doesn't want to go. And Oda despised magic.

'Where's the girl?' she'd said.

And now Lady Neon had come to town.

Find the girl.

I became vaguely aware of Dees making sounds at me, and mumbled, "Look, I'm going underground a while. Call me if you get anything."

I hung up, and went in search of the Piccadilly Line.

There was something wrong with the Piccadilly Line.

There was something wrong with the map.

I stood inside Heathrow Terminals 1, 2 and 3 station and stared long and hard at the map, and couldn't quite name what it was about it that made me feel uneasy. Tourists with great bags on wheels that snipped at the ankles of strangers jostled around me to look and find their destination; men in sharp suits put away their mobile phones in expectation of going downstairs. Travellers who'd never seen the city's Underground at work tried to stick their Oyster card into the paper ticket slot, and swipe their paper tickets over the Oyster card readers. The attending staff, having seen too many tens of thousands pass through speaking too many languages to ever be learnt, looked on, and made no effort to help. The barriers were extra wide to accommodate the luggage, the escalator a frustrating disorder of tired, bleary-eyed wanderers who hadn't yet come to realise that London was, more than anything else, about neat queues and always standing on the right. The platforms were wide, the board with the orange indicator sign read:

1 Southgate – 2 mins

2 Southgate – 5 mins

3 Turnpike Lane – 8 mins

Beneath it rolled a continual line of text. I watched it; I was the only one who did. **Please keep your luggage with you at all times. The lights are going out. Any unattended items must be reported to a member of staff immediately. It's waiting for you.**

The train was relatively new, the seats still padded, the windows still mostly unscratched, the white paint on the outside only somewhat grey from the passage through the tunnels. I sat down in a small puddle of half-read used free newspapers, picked one up, flicked through it.

'Fire in Sidcup; arson suspected' had made a footnote on page 7. I read the few words. Fire brigade called; tower block due for demolition; haunt of local kids and homeless; locals reported bodies; opposition councillor calls for inquiry into failures etc.

The train rumbled through west London past stations of half-glimpsed pale faces in the platform light, not bothering to slow down for the corners as it sped towards Hammersmith and the City. I read about footballers and their indiscretions, the plight of pensioners and the failure of local government, about a disgrace in the NHS and Charleen's operation to have her bust size increased to change her life. No one ever said that free newspapers were any good.

At Hammersmith I changed to the District Line, a slow, cumbersome rumble of a train that seemed to sit forever at Sloane Square and was for ever delayed by signal failures. The crowds that boarded at Victoria were a strange mix: men and women in suits, carrying briefcases and smart shoulder bags, girls in sparkly shoes with bunny tails on their backsides, young men in hoodies bopping along to an invisible beat, broad-necked blokes red-faced from the pub, theatregoers in pearls and stiff beige jackets earnestly reading the programme notes written for some profound piece. A woman with the 'mug me' bum bag and camera of a tourist sat down next to me, a frown on her face, clutching a bag from the Science Museum close to her chest. I watched her reflected in the opposite window, and she watched me, eyebrows knitted for a long while. Then she turned, and looked me straight in the eye and said in broken, lisping English, "'Scuse me?"

I smiled the patient smile of all Londoners tolerating tourists.

"'Scuse me," she repeated. "But you know where son's gone?"

My smile wavered.

She half shook her head, and looked away. "Sorry," she added. "Sorry. English not good."

At Westminster, I changed to the Jubilee Line, a swish new extension, the train cut off from the platform by a great glass barrier with doors set into it, against which the driver had to meticulously align. The platform was growing empty; I could taste the hour of the Last Train nearly coming, the perpetual last train that went round and round the Circle Line for ever, never stopping, and almost never seen. The Jubilee Line carried me to London Bridge, a grey low slab of a station set only a few metres back from the river, whose platforms stuck out from its back like a raccoon's tail. The shutters were half up, half down over the platforms, the men in blue waistcoats blowing the final whistles for the final trains.

Something wrong.

I headed for the bus shelter. A night bus pulled away as I approached. On the back window, in tiny letters, someone had scratched with diligence and a sharp object,

help me

I could smell the river, catch a corner of its magic in the palm of my hand with the cool breeze that came off the waters. I caught the first bus headed for Greenwich, sat at the very back, above the hot buzz of the engine, feet stuck up on the lip of the window by the emergency exit, arms wrapped round my chest, right hand aching, eyes tired. Back east again, down the Jamaica Road, Canada Water and its dull yellow shopping mausoleums, sprawling grey car parks, gleaming glass stations, smart, soulless apartment blocks overlooking the water. Greenwich again: I caught a glimpse of the drawings of the Whites on the walls, of

half cat, half squirrel, blue eyes raised towards the sky, ice cream cone in one hand, finger pointing east

and of

child holding a wilting flower, face sad

or of

copper in a copper's hat, face smeared out, fingers twisted into broken twigs

I got out a few streets away from the hotel, half ran the short distance to it, didn't know why, had to resist the urge to drag flame to our fingertips.

The front door was locked.

The sign in the window said

HOTEL VACANCIES

I hammered on the door, buzzed the buzzer, tapped on the windows.

Dark inside. Not a light burning, not even in the hall.

I rummaged in my satchel until I found my set of blank keys, dozens of them, every kind of make, and picking the nearest make that matched, coaxed it into the lock and then into the right shape, soothing the lock to obey my commands until, with a reluctant snap, it came undone.

The door swung open.

Darkness inside.

Not a telly hummed, not a radio blared, not a bulb hissed, not a footstep was trod.

I closed the door behind me and fumbled in the dark for a light switch. My foot bumped against something on the floor. A guest book, fallen from its little table by the door and left there. My fingers found the switch. I turned it on. Nothing. Darkness.

I stumbled a few paces further, found the reception desk, considered ringing the bell, thought better of it. I thought I heard the sound of footsteps behind me and turned, electricity snapping to my fingertips, filling the hall with white-blueness around me. Nothing there. My back felt exposed, I thought of knives and things moving in the dark. I spun the electricity around me, made a mesh of it across my shoulders and down my arms, felt my hair stand on end, saw the little yellow sparks build in the open mains sockets by my right foot as I drew power from the things around me. By my blue electric glow, I found another light switch, flicked it on. Nothing. I stood on the chair behind the reception desk and examined the bulb in the ceiling. It was scarred black on the inside, and the hair of the tungsten filament hung limp and dead inside its glass coffin. I headed into the breakfast room. There were plates on tables, toast half eaten on the plates, baked beans, stone cold, congealed scrambled egg, bacon curled up in its own solidified fats. I found a door marked private, standing half ajar. I pushed it back. A man sat, his back to me, hands on a desk piled with books and ledgers, head bowed. I said, "Sir?"

No answer.

"You OK?"

Nothing.

I pushed the electricity away a little from my fingertips, reached out and touched his shoulder. Cold, dead meat in human form. I turned the chair he sat in. He had no eyes. He had two broken red spheres, whites full of blood, irises cracked and full of blood, face streaked with blood that had flowed from the tear ducts – not eyes. Two boiled cherry tomatoes where eyes should have been. The blood had run down his face, dribbled across his mouth, stained his shirt crimson. There was blood in the hollows of his ears, blood in his nose, blood under his nails. Blood in the scratches around the hollows of his eyes where he'd tried to claw them out.

We turned away, stomach clenching, and made it all the way to the door before the urge to puke, without the blissful release of puking itself, caught our stomach in its dusty hot fist and held us. I pushed us into the hall, leant against the wall, breathed deep of the warm musty air, tried to half close my eyes and found I didn't dare. The stairs to the attic where I'd left Oda had been barely a few dozen when I'd climbed them the first time; now, there were hundreds of them, and each step took a lifetime. I passed a door half open on the first floor, and glancing inside, saw the body of a man, half naked, his head turned towards me, his hands clasping the sheets of the bed like rope from a ship in a storm, blood across his face and on the carpet, turning it black, eyes broken. On the floor above, my fingers brushed something sticky on the banister, and we didn't stop to look at what it might be.

No lights on the top floor either.

No smell of death.

The door to Oda's room was unlocked. I eased it open with my toe, looked down at the bed where I'd left her and saw ruffled sheets, disturbed blanket, pillow curved to the impression of a head and no Oda. I eased it back further, drew a little heat from my fingers and cast it upwards in the shape of a sodium-coloured ball of light to cast illumination over the room. The bulb in the ceiling was burnt black, like all the rest; the light switch didn't work. There was no sign of blood on the floor, and only the faintest tracery of blood on the sheets, but that was as like as not from the mess on Oda's clothes as much as anything: old and copper-coloured. I pushed back the door to the bathroom. The mirror was smashed, but there was again no sign of bleeding. My coat lay, damp but drying, where I'd left it in the shower the night before. I picked it up, slung it over the top of my bag, turned back into the bedroom. I sat down on the edge of the bed, sniffed the pillow, smelt nothing particularly untoward, checked the drawers, and saw on the top of the side table a piece of white paper. There were words written in biro on top of it.

They said:

WE'RE WAITING FOR YOU.

And for all we are gods, we wear mortal flesh.

We ran.

I wanted bright lights, clean air and something solid against my back.

Every place I passed, I could think of reasons why it fulfilled none of these desires.

I walked until I didn't know where I was, and stopped, and stood still, and forced myself to breathe. I was in the middle of a small square, cars ringing its edge, bins overflowing between the pigeon-spattered benches. A fox blinked at me from behind the back of a padlocked-up, plywood-boarded public toilet. I turned until I could see the lights of Canary Wharf glimmering over the rooftops, named that direction north, found my way to the nearest bench and sat. My head found its way to my hands. In the distance I heard a window slide open, the sound of a polite BBC radio voice declaiming on the social decline of our times. The phone rang in my pocket. I answered.

"Hi Penny."

"Not too late for you, then?"

I looked up at the dark sky overhead, stained with sodium and scudding clouds. "Dunno. What time is it?"

"Two in the bloody morning."

"Already?"

Wrong.

Something wrong.

I looked at my watch. The hands were on ten past two.

"Hey, don't think like I care or anything, but you OK?" asked Penny. "You seem kinda . . . you know . . . fucked or something."

"What gave you that impression?" I asked, pinching the bridge of my nose.

"Dunno. Just usually when I talk to you on the phone, I hear . . . stuff."

"Stuff? What kind of stuff?"

"Just . . . on the edge, you know?"

"What?"

"Look, can we talk about how fucked you are or what?"

"Penny," I groaned, "come on, cut a guy having a bad . . . night . . . a break. What do you hear on the telephone?"

A sigh, a huff of breath. Then, "I hear . . . and if you call me a prat I'll do you . . . I hear . . . like . . . singing. Just on the edge. Just right below everything else. When I talk to you on the telephone. Like . . . a humming . . . in the wire." We were silent, too surprised to speak. We must have been silent a while, because she suddenly burst out, "Are you laughing at me?"

"What? No. No, honest, no. Sorry. We are . . . we weren't laughing. Nothing like. Hey – by the by – thank you."

"For what?"

"Keeping an eye on me."

"Hell . . ."

"Seriously."

"Matthew," she chided, "you're talking like a total freaked-out pale freak now, and that freaks me out, so just shove it, OK?" Then, "Things that bad?"

"Oh, yeah," I chuckled with raven humour. "They're really that bad."

"You need help?"

"Put it like this – don't turn your mobile off."

"OK."

"And Penny?"

"Yeah?"

"You see or hear or feel anything that freaks the crap out of you – don't be an arse. Just run. Promise?"

"'Cause you ask so nice."

"Cheers. Speak soon, OK?"

I put the phone back in my pocket.

I needed a plan.

What I had was my damp coat. I unfolded it from across my bag, and held it up. There were still suspicious patches on it where the blood hadn't washed out. I wondered how much of the blood was Oda's. I decided to go and find out.

It is surprisingly hard to find a church in east Greenwich. It wasn't that the area lacked for religious houses, but merely that they had been built when the fashion was for short spires if any spire at all, and adaptable spaces and community halls that could cater to sports events and children's clubs when God wasn't in residence. I stumbled on one, a Baptist hall made of dark red brick, with wire mesh over the three low stained-glass windows in its front, hopped over the locked gate and hammered on the heavy blue door.

No answer.

No lights on inside.

I wandered round the back and found, by a small annexe of fresher red brick, a small concrete car park with a large sign saying "DISABLED ONLY, NO BALL GAMES" above the two parking spaces, a recycling bin, the shattered remnants of a broken drum kit, and a fire escape, built by a local council that didn't trust even in God not to start a fire in his own house. It didn't take much to convince the lock on the inside of the back door to snap apart at my command, and the local priest, for all he had felt the need to protect his windows with wire mesh, hadn't bothered with a burglar alarm. I fumbled through the dark until I found a light switch, and turned it on.

I was in a tiny kitchen, containing a pair of tatty stuffed armchairs, a microwave, a sink, a couple of shelves and a small rack of dubiously stained biohazard coffee mugs. On the wall was pinned up a schedule of events, which ranged from local gospel singing lessons through to Italian classes for the over-sixties. A small glass door opened into the main hall, and a switch nearby turned on long rows of white fluorescent tubing in the ceiling. I looked up at a roof of low black criss-crossed wooden beams, along to stained-glass windows depicting, variously, Jesus playing an acoustic guitar, Mary holding a baby and John the Baptist on a drum kit. On one wall were green noticeboards, onto which the local kids had pinned their various understandings of the story of Jesus in A3 crayon form. A box by the main door said, "Please give generously" and a poster above it told the story of Maureen, seventy-eight, and her continued battle to support the lonely, the aged and the lost in the community where she'd lived for forty-five years. The picture of Maureen showed a woman with long drooping cheeks hanging down below the line of her jaw, curly white hair, owl glasses, and a smile that spoke of patient listening that heard all and judged none. I put 50p in the box, and heard it clatter against bare wood inside.

The aisles of the chapel ran between chairs from a stack. At the end was a low trestle table whose purple covering and silver-plated candlesticks proclaimed it to be an altar. Two loudspeakers were plugged in on either side of it, and in pride of place on its own plinth was a much loved copy of the Holy Bible, heavy enough to stun a shark.

I took my satchel off and sat down in the front row before the altar. Jesus looked down at me with sad understanding from above his guitar. He didn't have the face of a guy who held a grudge, so I pulled off my jumper, picked up my coat and wrapped it carefully round my shoulders, just as it had been wrapped round Oda's. I pulled it until the bloodstain that had seeped from Oda's chest was directly above my heart, and held it tightly around myself, eyes half shut.

I thought of psycho-bitch Oda.

I thought of the sound of her voice, low and cold and usually threatening me with death.

Of the touch of her fingers when she'd taken my hand.

Of her weight across my back as I'd helped her from the fire.

The smell of her blood.

The way she ran, when we'd run together from monsters and demons.

The sound of . . .

. . . water . . .

And the smell of . . .

. . . oil . . .

I could taste metal on my tongue.

I pulled the coat tighter, pressed my fingers into the bloody stain over my chest. Close; the thought of her, the sense of her, still close.

I stood up, and was briefly surprised to find that I was doing this thing, but let it happen, moved with it. My feet carried me to the altar. My knees bent. I knelt. My head hung. I felt . . .

. . . shame . . .

And could hear . . .

. . . still water disturbed . . .

And could taste . . .

. . . metal and salt . . .

And could feel . . .

. . . pain here pain pain tear it out . . .

My fingers tightened against my chest, over my heart, and the ache beneath them suddenly rose to heartburn, and then the heartburn became a lance that ran straight through my chest and out the other side, impaling me through the middle. We gasped and rocked back on our heels as the pain hit, felt it pound in our skull, saw it pulse on the back of our eyelids, tried to pull free of the spell and saw

bleeding eyes

and felt

popping ears

and smelt

salt and heat in the nose

and I whimpered, "Oda!"

And for a moment, just a moment, I was in her head, seeing through her eyes, and all she saw was still water, still black water, knee-deep, she was walking in black water and there was pain in her chest, unbearable pain but she didn't seem to care, wasn't crying out or pulling at it, just staring at the water and there was a reflection in it, a face, and the face had no eyes, or rather eyes full of black pudding, sockets stuffed with dead mashed flesh and they were looking at the water and the face was empty and

and then they were looking at me.

And Oda smiled.

Those no-eyes were looking at me.

They *saw* us.

She whispered, a breath of dust on still silent air, "*Sorcerer.*"

And something not entirely unlike the fist of God swung down with the inexorability of Judgement Day, caught us in the belly, picked us up, and threw us as hard as it could, spine-first across the hall.

Villains faint.

Sidekicks pass out.

Heroes are knocked unconscious.

I know which I'd rather be.

I risked opening my eyes.

Still here.

Still in the chapel hall.

Lying in a pile of collapsed chairs, a good five feet from my last location when I was anything resembling conscious, but still here.

Still not dead.

I tried moving and another chair collapsed beneath me, knocking me, if possible, even further to the floor, in even less of a dignified heap. I decided not to risk moving for a while, and lay on my back, eyes closed against the brilliant brightness of the strip lighting overhead, and did a quick physical inventory.

Nothing felt broken.

Splitting headache.

Nosebleed.

No broken nose; just a nosebleed. I wiped the blood away with the back of my hand, wiped my hand on the soggy coat plastered to my skin.

After a while, my nose stopped bleeding.

I considered moving.

I considered it for a very long time.

It remained an unattractive if inevitable prospect and so, after due contemplation, I risked it.

My brain sloshed from side to side with my first attempt, but eventually settled into a reasonably stable form, and I risked getting onto my knees. My passage back and away from the altar had ploughed a small me-shaped rift through the stackable church chairs. I crawled out into the aisle and tried getting upright. I pulled the bloodstained coat off, bundled it into the nearest bin, and set it on fire with a fistful of gaseous blue-yellow flame. I told myself I'd learnt a valuable if unwelcome lesson. I told myself that all the way to the exit, and didn't bother to turn out the lights on my way out.

In the outside world, I fumbled for my phone, and dialled Dudley Sinclair.

He took his time to answer, and his first few words were a slurred mumble. I had succeeded in catching Dudley asleep. I had never thought the day would come.

"Uh? Yes?"

"Mr Sinclair?" I wheezed, one hand holding the phone to my ear, the other clutched to my belly as if somehow that would stop me being sick in the nearest gutter.

"Who is this? Swift? What time is it?"

"No idea," I replied. "You've still got major connections with the Order psycho-bastards or what?"

"Swift?" He was regaining consciousness, and with it, a degree of indignation. "Matthew, what is this about?"

"Remember Oda psycho-bitch?" I asked. "Member of the Order, religious nutter out to kill all magicians et cetera et cetera, got her in mind?"

"Yes – and, as I remember, your last collaboration didn't end particularly well . . ."

"She's in serious shit and I need to find her."

I heard the sound of bedclothes moving as the not inconsiderable mass of Dudley Sinclair, "concerned citizen" and, generally speaking, a man with a plan, hoisted himself into something resembling an upright position. I thought I heard the muted mumble of someone else in the bed, disturbed in restless sleep, but couldn't bring myself to speculate.

"You *care* for this Oda woman?"

"Not really. But it's something about the way she's walking around with a hole in her heart like it was a paper cut and breaking my scrying spells when I try to find her like they were a fucking cheese twist that kinda gets me uppity."

"She's . . ."

"Got a stab wound to the heart and is fine. Well, I say 'fine', I suppose it all really depends on your sense of . . ."

"Matthew, Matthew, please talk slowly," chided Sinclair, now fully back to his impressive, booming self, even by telephone. "What exactly is going on with this woman?"

"Not a clue. Not a dicky bird. But there's a war about to break out between the Court and the Tribe, Lady Neon's come to town, there's a chosen one, apparently, if you believe that sort of shit, wandering the streets of London, and oh yes, Oda is right in the middle of it. So very much in the middle of it. And now I can't find her. And . . ." I stopped dead. "And . . . something's wrong with eyes."

"With . . . her eyes?"

"I don't know. Maybe. There was this hotel and . . . and there's something wrong generally, Sinclair. I can't put my finger on it. But there's something really really wrong. I can feel it. It's . . . we can feel it. We don't know what it is but it's . . . it's worse than Court or Tribe or anything else. It's just out of our reach and it's going to stab us in the back. It's . . . there's something waiting for us and we don't know what it is."

"Matthew" – a little laugh, entirely forced and not a little frightened, rolled across Sinclair's lips – "you sound almost afraid."

"I think I'm going to puke," I moaned, sitting down quickly in the nearest gutter before this became reality. "Jesus! She broke my fucking scrying spell like I was a ten-year-old kid wizard trying to spy on Merlin's love nest. Broke it and sent it straight back at me like nothing. I didn't even have any defences up, I wasn't prepared, she . . . she *can't* do that, do you see? She isn't a magician, she's certainly not a sorceress, she's about as magical as Marmite and she caught me and . . . I've got to find her. I've gotta. Whatever this shit is, she's the heart of it. I shouldn't have left her in that bloody hotel . . ."

"Matthew, I can try and help of course; but do understand, I have my own objectives. I cannot permit . . . exterior forces . . . to damage the very sensitive relationships I have with the various practitioners of magic in this city, and indeed, with their enemies. You are of course aware of this."

"I just need to find Oda," I groaned.

"Very well. I need a little time to make some . . . appropriately discreet enquiries. Say, three hours?"

"Fine. And Sinclair?"

"Yes?"

"If the Aldermen, or the Court, or the Tribe, hear a word of this . . ."

"I would assume," he replied primly, "that you are asking my assistance on this matter for the very reason that you would not wish them to."

"Exactly."

"May I ask, in the interest of the bigger picture, just how far involved you are with something you can't control?"

I thought about it. "About . . . chin-deep?" I suggested.

"So still waving, not drowning?"

"I hope so. Where shall I meet you?"

A judicious drawing in of breath. Then, "How well do you know St James's?"

Three hours.

Dudley Sinclair, "concerned citizen", a man with his fingers into every pie, including, it turned out, several pies that would quite like to eat the other pie.

I could use three hours.

I limped and wheezed my way to the nearest bus shelter.

On the top of the shelter was a single spiky plastic object that looked like some sort of dog's toy.

No good.

I limped and wheezed my way to the next one.

On top of this, amid the smeared stain and dirty greenish-grey marks of mould from stagnant water that would never wash clear, was a mildewed and extremely crinkled copy of the Yellow Pages.

I climbed up on top of a bin to pull it down, and sat on the narrow red bench under the shelter to flick through its pages.

There are business directories, and then there are the business directories that you get on the top of bus shelters. No one really knows how they get there, and no one really asks, but the services these somewhat smelly and decaying items provide are invaluable to the roaming urban magician.

I flicked through listings for magicians, witches, warlocks, exorcists, petty alchemists and full-blown speakers with the dead. Ads proclaimed here and there:

NO GHOST TOO BIG, NO EXORCISM TOO CHALLENGING!!
(Standard call out fee applies.)

Or:

Can't get it summoned?
Magic no longer at your fingertips?
You need Mrs Jameson's Mystic Lift-Me-Up.
Mrs Jameson: The mother of all good magics.

I flicked through "p" for "prophet". No entries.

I flicked into "s", roamed a little too far and found my own entry. I hadn't put it there, but that hadn't stopped the power of the Yellow Pages. It said:

Swift, M. (Sorcerer): c/o Aldermen, 149 Aldermansbury Square, London EC2 9TU.

I sighed and flicked back a few pages, until I came to 'Seers – see also prophets, mystics, visionaries'.

There was one entry, an ad that took up approximately a quarter of the page. It read:

The Future doesn't have to be Frightening!
Get your future read by 20th of December, and get £10 off for a friend!
A discreet, sensitive service.
No terminal patients, wanted fugitives or walking undead please.

There was an address and a telephone number. I wrote both down on the back of my hand, tossed the Yellow Pages back on top of the bus shelter, and went to find the future.

The address was for a house in Mile End.

I rode the bus back to the river, and got out at what the tourist guide proclaimed to be Historical Maritime Greenwich. There indeed were the shops selling bent brass implements of every sort, flags and knots in their windows; away to the right the grand pillared arcades of the old Greenwich navel college; there the *Cutty Sark*, surprisingly small up close, an elegant reconstructed ship with three tall masts where the children could run up and down playing pirates during the day while their parents followed meekly and tried not to bump their heads.

A small green dome was all that announced the long descent to the Greenwich Foot Tunnel. Lights on the ceiling curved down and out of sight, a long spiral towards an unknown depth. Tiles lined the wall, once white turned pale yellow, dirt embedded in the cracks. A pair of wide lift doors faced the exit. I waited. The lift came, great wheels churning and clunking to haul the thing upwards. The doors opened. Inside, a wood-panelled lift car with little seats around the edges was almost entirely empty. A man in a navy-blue jumper sat on a stool beside a small portable cassette player, his head rolled back and mouth hanging open in sleep. I stepped inside. The cassette cracked its way through a song about trampolines and love to the strain of gentle guitar.

We went down.

When we reached the bottom, the sleeping man half stirred, his jaw working slackly, lips smacking, and he murmured blearily as I passed, "Where's the sun gone?"

I hesitated.

But without opening his eyes, he shifted his position on the stool, and went back to sleep.

The tunnel bent away in front of me, dipping down to a point in the middle and then up towards an unseen distance. Tiled walls, bare concrete floor, regularly spaced dull yellow lamps. The doors of the lift slid shut behind me, cutting out the music. I walked. Our footsteps were loud in the too-quiet of the empty space. I felt bare space on my back and wished there was a wall against it. The only movement beside us was the twisting and turning of our shadow, like a mad sundial's point, as we passed underneath and towards each ceiling lamp.

The lift returned again, letting out a little blast of music, heavier this time, lyrics wondering what the story was and why no one else seemed to have got it, whatever it was.

The doors closed again. The music stopped.

I walked on.

I could hear footsteps behind me, a sharp snap-snap-snap on the concrete, louder than the gentle step of my soft soles. I told myself it was nothing. Feeling like an idiot, I stopped. The footsteps stopped a few moments later. I started. They started. I stopped. They stopped. The lift returned, the doors opened. The singing voice drifting down the corridor was running out of battery, dull and distorted against the hard tiles.

I turned and looked behind me. No one there.

I looked to the left, I looked to the right.

No one there.

I risked walking a few more steps.

No sound of footsteps other than my own.

I said, "This isn't funny, universe."

My voice bounced down the tunnel around me, fading at last to a high whisper on the air.

I started walking faster towards the exit, not quite running, not exactly lounging along either. Silence in the tunnel. Just my breathing and my footsteps, nothing else. I could see the lift at the end of the road, see the stairs spiralling upwards towards the other bank. Nothing behind me. Not a sound, not a breath, not . . .

Not music.

I slowed.

I stopped.

The air around me thickened with cold river magic, as I raised my defences. I turned and looked back the way I'd come.

For a moment, I saw someone, or rather, owing to the trick of perspective played by the dip of the tunnel, I thought I saw someone's feet and knees, standing by the other lift, some few hundred yards behind me. They were caught in the light coming out of the open lift door. Then that light went out. Then the light in front of that. Then the light in front of that, a sharp snap-hiss and a brief ultraviolet flash as they burnt to darkness. Then the light in front of that, a moving darkness coming down the tunnel, heading for me.

I turned and, this time, I ran.

*

I stopped running at the top of the spiral staircase that led out onto the north bank of the Thames. I stopped running because my knees were aching, my heart was pounding, and because out here, the lights still burnt and the air was clear. Here was as good as anywhere to stand and fight.

I stood and waited, facing the exit from the tunnel.

Behind, yellow sodium lamps burnt steadily above the neat park benches and between the growing plane trees. The river sounded like thick yogurt being slurped up through a straw. A few cool drops of drizzle fell, promising more rain. No one came.

I stayed there for a good five minutes, waiting as the rain began to thicken from a tickle to a patter, from a patter to a splatter, from a splatter to a downpour, and still, no one came. So at last, feeling every part a fool, and turning as I walked to keep the tunnel exit in my sight until the last possible moment, I let the magic between my fingers go, and scurried away.

The night bus from the Isle of Dogs to Mile End took twenty minutes to come. I now began to miss my coat, huddling under the bus shelter, arms wrapped around me and chin tucked into my chest as though this could somehow protect me from the gathering downpour. Water churned in the gutter, tumbling down into the grates too fast for the drainage system to cope, and forming great pools of water which flew up in sheets whenever the few scant cars drove by. When my bus came, it was a low single-decker, inhabited by a group of three young women dressed for a party, silent, their eyes low, their faces grey, reflected water distorting the make-up on their pale, pasty faces. We swished north without bothering to slow for the empty bus stops, the corners or the rainwater filling the new tarmac streets before us, past fresh green public parks and dully glowing twenty-four-hour convenience stores, past estate agents with little lights still burning in their windows, nurseries with placards all in cheerful red, yellow and blue, past the closed glass arches of the DLR stops raised on their grassy banks, and sixth-form colleges promising to change your life for ever with a diploma in Business Studies with Marketing.

Canary Wharf grew and grew in front of us until the tops of the towers were no longer visible from inside the bus. I leant back against my seat and remembered to breathe, forced myself to take it one steady gasp at a time as the magic of the place, silver, glass, light, razored edges, a buzz at the back of the eyes, an ice that ran to the end of the fingertips and turned them blue, washed over me. Every part of the city had its own magic, and the magic of Canary Wharf, of endless towers and shops and steel and clear running water, though still young, was bursting to make itself felt. We pressed our fingers into the glass of the bus and felt frost form beneath our fingertips, the power bursting out of us whether we liked it or not. The bus slowed as it crossed the security checkpoint into the area, and what little sky there had been became lost, a tiny pinpoint between the tops of the buildings, and what few people there had been became none, empty streets and huge glass doors within which were sleeping reception desks, foyers of bronze and silver, palm trees grown indoors, and shopping centres whose lights never went out.

When the bus finally spun its way out of the area and back across the water towards Billingsgate, I let the magic out with a shudder of breath that condensed on the window in front of me. It steamed unevenly across the glass, forming shapes and patterns where grease was thicker or thinner. I turned my face away from it and, as I did, caught the glimpse of something in the fading pattern of condensation from my breath. It looked a lot like a cross, with a smaller cross that might even have been a sword wedged in its top left-hand corner. I swore, and found my left hand unconsciously curling around the palm of my right, biting into the twin scars burnt into my skin, and bundled off the bus at the next stop.

I was close to Mile End, and quickly too wet to care about getting any wetter. I slung my bag across my chest and shoulder, wiped the worst of the rainwater from my eyes, and went in search of a prophet.

Mile End was a confused part of the city.

At one time, as its name suggested, it had been the end of London, the absolute full stop; but then, the history of the city was one of endless ends, of Field Lanes and Gate Roads marking the places where the city had stopped until, with a great geographical shrug, it had decided to expand. So, over time, Mile End had become not so much the end of the city as the beginning of the end, the place where inner met outer

London, full of terraced houses and council estates, grand royal parks and scrubby little bits of wasteland, overground railway lines leading to Norfolk, Essex and the eastern seaside and little pootling buses that terminated in Aldgate and Liverpool Street. From Mile End it was more than theoretically possible to walk in a straight line into the heart of the city, past Bethnal Green to Liverpool Street. It was equally possible to pick up the end of the Lee River valley and walk with it past canal barges and scrubland until city ended and fields began. It would be a long walk, but a not unpleasant one.

I scampered beneath railway bridges, past stately halls and tumbling semi-detached houses, through grey council estates and down roads of politely austere Victorian terraced houses. My eye wandered over street signs proclaiming:

Slow Down School

and

Residential Parking Zone M – No Parking Without a Permit

and the somewhat vague

Watch Children

and finally came to a pause on the edge of Roman Road, by an off-licence advertising six pints of Polish beer for £4, and red wine at £3.99 a bottle. I checked the address scrawled on the back of my hand in fading biro, fumbled in my satchel for the A–Z, and double-checked my direction on the map. No one can know all of London, all the time.

The rain showed no sign of easing when I neared my destination, a small house with a red triangular roof and net curtains across its small square windows, nestled in between a cobbler's shop and a Polish deli. A tiny front garden containing three flagstones leading up to the door and a tiny patch of grass with a gnome on it was the only thing to mark the house out. The gnome was making a marginally obscene gesture with his left hand, but his face remained merrily benign. There was one light on, on the upstairs floor, behind a frosted window which suggested a bathroom. I rang the buzzer and waited. The light went out upstairs. I rang again. A light came on behind the two thin frosted panels in the front door, and a figure briefly blanked them out. There was the rattling of a chain and the door opened a few inches.

A single watery grey eye pressed itself to the gap and a low, brisk voice said, "Yes?"

"Um . . . I'm here to see a seer?" I mumbled.

"Appointments only," was the reply, and the door began to close again.

I planted my foot in what was left of the gap and said, "It's very important."

"Who are you?" demanded the voice indignantly.

"Um . . . Midnight Mayor?" I suggested.

"Bollocks to that, never believed in the Midnight Mayor and don't bloody believe you're him even if he wasn't a bloody fairy tale, now get your foot out of my door." He tried to push the door shut, squashing my foot.

I put my shoulder against the door and babbled, "Look, mate, but if the job came with a name badge it'd probably lose some of the mystique."

"Piss off!"

For a brief, undignified moment we fought each other for control of the door, before I managed to push him back, driving the door open until it caught on its chain. While he was off balance I reached round inside, fumbled for the chain and managed to manoeuvre it free with only moderate loss of circulation to my wrist. I burst inside and found myself in a hall smelling heavily of cigarette smoke, painted a vibrant sunflower yellow, and lined with ancient caricatures of Indians in various unlikely and questionable poses. The man I'd pushed away was in his fifties at least, with straight, uneven grey hair going thin round the temples, a poorly shaven lumpy chin, worn hands and wearing a blue towelling dressing gown and corduroy slippers. He flapped at me as I closed the door behind me, shouting, "Get out! Get out! I'll call the police . . ."

As he stormed through a door into what I guessed to be the sitting room I followed. He reached out for a phone, and I tapped him on the shoulder. He spun, hands coming up into fists. As he did, we caught him round the throat with our scarred hand. Sapphire fire flared behind our eyes, we felt the hair stand up on the back of our neck. The light flickered in the hall, electricity snapped in the sockets, blue sparks crawled around the handset of the telephone, the TV flickered on and mad static danced over its screen. He wheezed and pawed at our hands as the electrical fire built inside our soul and, for a moment, he met our eyes, and was afraid.

"Hi," we said. "Let us make our position clear. We are the Midnight Mayor, protector of this city, carrier of its secrets and bearer of its shadows. The shadows watch us as we pass, the pigeons turn away at our passage, the rats scurry beneath our feet and shudder at the sound of our footsteps on the stones. We are the blue electric angels, the telephones sing at the passage of our voice, our blood is blue fire, our soul carries a pair of angel wings. We are the killer of Robert Bakker, sorcerer, master of the Tower; we destroyed the death of cities; we came back from the dead, Swift and the angels, two minds become one, two souls in one flesh, in one form, in one voice. We are me and I am we. And we're frustrated."

It was ten minutes later.

We sat on a stool in the kitchen, watching the man in the dressing gown make tea. The kitchen was avocado green, with a single light burning in the middle of the ceiling and surfaces of dirty daisy-yellow. It, like everything else, smelt of cigarettes.

"Biscuit?" he asked.

"What kind have you got?"

"Custard creams."

"Cheers."

A mug proclaiming *'I'M NO MUG – ASK ME ABOUT E-LEARNING!'* was deposited in front of me, along with a half-eaten packet of economy-brand custard creams. We dunked; we ate.

He said, "I got into the prophecy business about thirty years ago. Started out in Enfield, doing just local stuff, you know: relationships, business investments, the dogs. Then that whole business with the Tower happened and it suddenly wasn't safe to be in this city doing magic. There were stories of a shadow that came out of the paving stones, tore out the heart of anyone who could throw a half-decent spell. The sorcerers died. The most powerful magicians in the city, the ones who heard the magic, felt it in their blood, and they all died. All except Bakker, of course. Khan – you heard of him?"

"Yes, I knew Khan," I sighed, taking a slurp of tea.

"Best seer in town, and he still died. I was just a low bit player, but I knew when the heat was too much, so I cleared out. Moved in with my daughter in Belfast for a few years, waited for the trouble to pass. We were O'Rourke and co., seers, prophets and wedding dress makers."

"Wedding dress . . .?"

"My daughter," he explained quickly. "Makes wedding dresses, as well as . . . other things."

"Right."

He sat down on the stool opposite mine, a cup of fruity tea stewing between his pale, hairy hands. His eyebrows were long and white, rolled up and out like an elephant's eyelashes from his grey face. "Then I got a call from a friend of mine – Robert Bakker was dead, the shadow was gone, the Tower had fallen. And you know, I love my daughter, but she had her own family to look after and I didn't really bring in much money so . . . I moved back here."

"The only surviving prophet in all of London," I said. "Must be good business."

He shrugged. "I get by. There's competition moving in, though. New prophets arise, and the Australians, of course, are always coming over here to get work."

"The Australians?"

"Aussie gits," he added with conviction. "Coming over here and they're all like, 'we can tell you the future and give you a sensual massage at cut-price rates'; amateur bastards."

"Fascinating stuff," I sighed, "but you're the only seer listed in the Yellow Pages."

"Well, I'm the only one who doesn't need a work permit," he said huffily. "It's not like we don't have laws, you know." He stared down into his teacup and then demanded, "How'd you survive?"

"What?"

"You're a sorcerer. How'd you survive Bakker, the Tower?"

I smiled and found another custard cream had made its way inexplicably into my fingers. "I didn't." I saw his raised eyebrows, shrugged. "It's complicated."

"And you're Midnight Mayor too?"

"Yep."

"How'd that happen?"

"Oh, the usual. Someone summons the death of cities, death of cities takes on physical indestructible form, kills the previous incumbent, previous incumbent makes a telephone call with his dying breath, telephone call finds us, we get lumbered with the job, destroy the death of cities et cetera et cetera et cetera. It's your fairly standard story of cock-up and disaster, really. Which is, incidentally, what I'm hoping this latest escapade isn't going to be."

"Ah, yes." He pushed the cup aside and leant forward with his professional face fixed for battle. "And what exactly is the problem?"

"Well," I said, also pushing my mug aside and leaning in close, "some total tit has gone and told the Neon Court that there's a 'chosen one' wandering round the city. Care to comment?"

A look of pain flickered over his face. "Ah," he said. "You're here about *that*."

"Wouldn't have been you, by any chance?"

"Perhaps we should go through to the living room," he replied, and before I could answer was on his feet, tea in hand.

I followed him through to the living room, another painted adventure all in rose pink and winter-sky blue. A small round table was set in the middle, two chairs on either side. In the middle of the table was a cardboard box held together mostly by Sellotape, containing within it a Monopoly set. Mr O'Rourke sat down on one side of the table, and gestured at me to sit opposite. He put the teacup on the floor and pulled the lid off the Monopoly box.

"Yes," he said, as he began to set up the board between us, counting out money and laying out cards, "I told the Neon Court about the chosen one. The daimyo – a man called Minjae San – was a regular customer of mine. He came to me for a reading, and I do not lie about what I see. A girl; a chosen golden child, who has the power to end the war between the Court and the Tribe." He held out the chance cards to me. "Cut?"

I cut, not bothering to look at what I did, and said, "End it how?"

"She will destroy either the Court or the Tribe."

"What . . . just like that?"

"Yes. Whichever side possesses her will be the side that survives. Her destiny is unclear, and her power is obscure, but make no mistake – she is the death of one or other of them. Boot or boat?"

"And . . . she's a 'chosen one'?" I echoed dully.

"You look like a boot," he replied, laying down the little metal boot on the start square of the board. "You get one five hundred, four two hundreds, three one hundreds, two fifties, five twenties . . ."

"Sorry," I interrupted as he laid out the paper game money in front of me. "What the hell does it mean, 'chosen one'? Chosen by whom? Is she . . . sorceress, magician, angel, demon, devil, monster, summoned creation, kid who likes to play with fire, I mean, what the hell are we talking about here?"

"She is . . . simply the chosen one," he replied, putting a pair of bright red dice down on the board between us. "She is the death of either the Court or the Tribe, and nothing anyone does can change that."

"And you told all this to Minjae San?"

"Yes; he is a good client and I saw no reason to run away from the truth. Highest roll begins."

"I can think of a few," I growled, scooping up the dice and chucking them down across the board.

"Five and four!" said Mr O'Rourke judiciously, looking at my throw. "Promising start." He picked up the dice and also rolled. Three and five. "You begin."

I grabbed the dice with a scowl and threw them back across the board, moved my piece. The little metal boot landed on Angel, Islington.

"Are you going to buy it?" asked Mr O'Rourke when I didn't move.

"No," I snapped.

He shrugged. "Very well." He rolled. His piece landed on Euston Road. He riffled through his stock of paper money and bought the card.

"So you told Minjae San, the daimyo, that there was a chosen one, who could destroy the Court or its deadliest enemy, loping about London, and what else?"

"I told him that I saw falling rain, and fire, and footsteps alone in the night."

"That must have helped." I rolled the dice, and my boot landed on the Electric Company.

"You buying that?" he asked.

"No."

He smiled, and nodded. "Very interesting," he said, and rolled. His throw took him to Marylebone Station, which he duly bought.

"So, just so I've got this clear in my head. You told Minjae San that there was a chosen one, he goes looking for the chosen one, he ends up dead, and . . . and that's it?"

He shrugged. "I don't really get involved in the politics."

"No shit." My next roll had carried me onto Bow Street.

He said, "I imagine you're not buying that either."

"Oh, you are good," I snapped. "So, did your lack of interest in political affairs run to telling the Tribe about this 'chosen one'?"

"The Tribe are not clients of mine," he replied primly, as his next throw carried him to Free Parking. "They're not really interested in the long-term view of things."

"You think the Tribe killed the daimyo?"

"I don't know."

"What do you know?" I asked, rolling the dice again. My boot moved and landed on Chance.

He said earnestly, "You have to take a card." I snatched the top card off the pack. It read, 'You have won £10 in a beauty contest.' He drew breath in between his teeth and said, "*Interesting*."

"Mate, I've got a war about to break out between the Neon Court and the Tribe, I've got bodies and burning buildings and I've got a chosen one to deal with and, from what I can tell, *you* kicked all of that off. So help me out here, please?"

"That's not all you have to deal with, is it?" he asked, eyes fixed on the Monopoly board.

"Dazzle me," I growled.

He looked up, and his eyes regarded something a thousand miles away, and his breath was a hoarse rattle from somewhere deep in the back of his throat. "It's waiting for you," he managed. "It's waiting for you . . . it's . . . it's . . . where's the sun gone? Where's the sun gone?" His eyes closed, his fingers were claws clasping the edge of the table. He was still, breathing slowly, frozen in place for a long while. Too long. I leant towards him.

"Uh . . . mate? Mr O'Rourke?"

Nothing.

"Mr O'Rourke?"

Something moved round the edge of his eye. It was thin and red. It dribbled down the side of his nose, lingered at the slope of his lip, then plopped onto the table. I reached out a fingertip and touched him on the shoulder.

His eyes opened, and they were bloody, whites turned blood red, blood running like tears, staring straight at me. I lurched back, nearly fell off my chair, knocking the Monopoly board aside. He wheezed, knuckles white in the arch of his hands, back shaking, voice rasping, "It's come back from the edge of the night. It's been waiting so long, so long, and now it will have retribution."

"What is?" I stammered, staggering to my feet and backing away. "What's been waiting?"

"The thing at the end of the alley. The footsteps heard in the night. The shadow beneath the street lamp. It was me, it was me," he crooned. "I did it, I was in the eyes of the man who tore their petticoats, I was in the breath of him who broke the window, it was me, it was me who tied them down to hear them scream, it was me at the end of the alley, not your lover at all, but me, it was me . . ."

Blood rolled down his chin, dripped into his lap.

"Who?" I demanded, raising my hands into the beginning of a defensive ward. "Who is it? Who's come back?"

"Too late," he sighed, head tilting to one side. "Too late now."

"Who is it?"

"It's here. *Blackout.*"

And with due deference to command, the lights went out.

They went out in the house, they went out in the street.

They went out everywhere.

Run.

We wanted to run.

I didn't. I retreated slowly, until my back was against the wall. Then I raised my fingertips and summoned the barest whisper of light.

Mr O'Rourke was slumped over his table, blood running down his face. Still breathing.

I threw my bubble of light over to the door and dropped into a squat, huddling in the corner. I reached into my pocket and fumbled for my mobile. Outside, I thought I heard whistling, the distant tap of footsteps, the patter of rain. Nothing more – should have been more. I dialled Penny's number. She answered instantly.

"Penny?" I whispered.

"Hey – why you whispering?"

"I may need a hand."

"Oh yeah, now he needs help, after all that – what kind of hand?"

"Something's after me. It was in the foot tunnel, and at the hotel. It's here."

"What . . . something?"

"No idea. No idea what it can do or is. That's why I might need a valiant rescue. How soon can you get to Mile End?"

"Uh . . . dunno . . . forty minutes?"

"Make it faster. Take your aunt's car. Drive like a biker if you have to, I really don't care. I'm going to be on the move, may not be able to talk. You going to be OK with all that?"

"Guess so."

"Cheers. Gotta go now."

I hung up, dropped my phone into my pocket.

The patter of rain.

Swish of a car in a distant street.

Splash of water in a broken gutter.

Footsteps somewhere in the night.

I let my bubble of light spread a little, expand to push back the shadows in the corridor outside the living room. I moved over to Mr O'Rourke, felt for a pulse, found one. In the hall, I picked up my satchel, slung it back across my shoulders, turned to face the front door, let electricity simmer into my fingertips from the mains sockets, felt the water in the pipes beneath my feet, and the gas, ready to blow when I commanded. I said, *"Right,"* and opened the front door.

The street, still and silent.

The street lamps were all out, the glass burnt dull black on the inside. Nothing moved, no one stirred. I walked out into the middle of the road, throwing up my bubble of light higher and brighter above my head. Rainwater fizzled off the sphere of illumination, stuck my hair to my face, dribbled off my nose. Pools of water, ankle-deep, had grown out of the blocked gutters and spilt into the street. I sloshed through them, too wet to care, turned three hundred and sixty degrees, looking for a sign of life.

"All right," I called at last. "You know you're here, I know you're here, enough of this."

My voice fell dull and flat on the buildings around. Cold rainwater ran down the back of my neck, made my clothes stick.

"Come on!" I shouted, voice bouncing off the darkened window panes. "Enough of this silly-bugger bollocks! Here I am and here I remain until the sun . . ." My voice trailed off. I thought about it a little longer. I hissed, "Oh hell."

I heard footsteps behind me, turned, and it seemed like they turned too, moving like a child playing hide-and-seek, footsteps in the dark, just one pair of feet but they were everywhere, wherever I didn't look. I forced myself to stand still, half closed my eyes. "Come on," I hissed. "Come *on*."

The footsteps stopped.

Falling rain.

Nothing else.

Not a dog barked, not a child laughed, not a window rattled, not a door slammed, not a brake screeched, not a wheel turned, not a phone rang, not a train rumbled, not a cat miaowed.

I opened my eyes.

A voice behind me said, "Help me?"

It had made no sound when it approached. We stumbled away from it, turning and raising our hands thick with fire, feet slipping and splashing in the rising water in the street. The world filled with blue-white electricity and we saw, by its light, a face, standing not more than two paces behind us, head bowed, staring at nothing.

Oda.

Psycho-bitch.

She was wearing new clothes, the wrong size, style and shape for her, teenage clothes, a puffy black jacket and too-long jeans. She carried no bag or weapon, and stood with her hands calmly in her pockets. She wore a grey T-shirt carrying on it the image of three very angry-looking men and a slogan 'Rock Isn't Dead – But It Will Soon Wish It Was!!' There was a thin stain of fresh blood above the hole in her chest, no more than if she'd cut herself on a splinter, but there.

Despite the darkness, she also wore sunglasses, reflective black wrap-around things that covered her eyes entirely. The air around her seemed to fizz.

"Oda?" I breathed, struggling to gain some sort of balance and decorum, the rain sparking and snapping off the electricity still wrapped round my fingertips.

She looked up, and there was a flicker on her face almost of pain, of a back bending and shoulders arching forward. She said, a voice high and strained, "Matthew?"

"Oda, you scared ten kinds of living shit out of me and if there was any shit left to scare, you'd be scaring it still. What the hell happened to you? What the hell *is* happening to you?"

"Run," she breathed.

"What?"

"You have to run," she repeated. "If you don't run, we'll kill you here."

"Which 'we'?"

A flicker again, something moving in her face that didn't want to be there. "I told you to kill me," she answered. "Why do you never listen?"

"Because I'm an emotionally crippled male?" I hazarded.

Her face darkened, her lips seemed to curl into something almost animal. "Sorcerer," she hissed, "you have no idea. Run."

I raised one shaking hand towards her, water dripping off my fingertips. "What's up with your eyes, Oda? Only I'm noticing, see, a certain pattern, making certain connections. What's with the shades? It's night. It's been night now for . . . for an unreasonably long time."

She grinned. Not her grin. A skull grin, all lip and teeth and no feeling. "Do you begin to understand?" she asked.

"I'm . . . willing to make a few guesses, sure. I mean, after a while, a guy with my mystical credentials, he starts to notice things. Things like . . . how you're walking and talking and have a hole through your heart. And how you're wearing shades. And how people are dead and how you're saying 'we' when you mean 'I' and how the sun isn't coming up. It's not just me going mad: it really, really isn't coming up. And the curious thing is, no one seems to notice or care. Except, perhaps, you and me. Now, why is that?"

"You don't understand," she sighed. "If you did, you'd have torn them out so as not to see."

She reached up, and pulled off her sunglasses.

Her eyes were suet pudding.

There was nothing human left in them at all. They had been pulverised from the inside out, turned to black/red garbage in their sockets, to fried black pudding held in by nothing more than friction and a prayer. But they *saw*. They looked straight at me. I stared, speechless, no sense other than sight able to report any kind of awareness. Then I felt a dull prickling in the corners of my own eyes, which grew to an itching, which grew to a pain. I flinched back instinctively, ran my fingers across my face, and came away with thin red blood. I was crying blood. I looked back up at Oda and immediately the pain grew, scarlet dribbling across my vision, blurring the edges, and a sudden burst of fire inside my nose, that quickly became the taste of salt. I turned my face away, hissed, "What are you doing?"

"I told you," she said flatly. "I warned you. I gave you a chance to make it stop. But you wouldn't, would you? And now it's too late."

I put my arm up in front of my eyes, shielding her from my view, but the blood still dribbled down my cheeks and chin.

"Oda!"

And then she was there, right in front of me, filling what little was left of my field of view. One arm came up and grabbed my raised arm by the wrist, pulling it back. The other locked around my throat and her fingers were cold and slippery in the rain and her thumb dug into my windpipe and pushed like I was made of hollow plastic. I flapped with my free arm, found her chin, tried to push her head back and away from me, but she seemed neither to notice nor care as she pulled my arm away from my eyes. I caught a glimpse of her face, and immediately the pain was back, straight through to the back of my skull, I closed my eyes and wheezed, "Stop! Please stop!"

"This is our night," I heard her say. "This is what we are!"

"Stop!" The pavement buckled beneath my feet, cracked and split as I let the magic go, poured it into the nearest thing I could find. Tarmac began to bubble and boil, became sticky, black, reflective, rose up, tangling into fists and fingers, curled around her feet and up her legs, flesh and cloth smoking, and for a moment her fingers released their hold. Someone else would have screamed in pain, but not Oda, or whatever this thing was that Oda had become; liquid tar laced with jagged grains of stone and dirt bubbled beneath us and I pulled free, slipped on the uneven rolling surface, half fell, feet splashing in tar, oil and rain, turned and ran.

I could hear footsteps behind me, walking in the darkened night, and this time I didn't look back.

The lights were out in the street, the windows dark, the city sleeping. I dragged my bubble of light above my head and staggered through the rain, eyes burning, nose aching, ears popping, throat a crumpled plastic bag. I could feel the shadows moving around me, the rats turning their heads beneath my feet, the pigeons cowering in the rooftops, the foxes scuttling for their lairs. I shouted, "Wake up! You lazy-arsed lot, wake up!" at the black windows of the houses and nothing moved, nothing stirred. I turned my fists towards the cars parked in the streets around me and set the sirens wailing, yellow lights flashing, filled the street with a cacophony of sound; and no lights came on, no one stirred. The rain was above my ankles now in the middle of the road, tumbling downhill towards the river, not a gutter draining. I dragged in magic to my skin, wrapped it around me, and it came slow and heavy, the magic of things in the darkness, of things half perceived.

I waded through the flooding street, past shutters drawn down over sleeping shops and bus stops whose board indicated

No Service

past Tube stations with the gates locked and under railway bridges carrying rusting metal tracks. And still the footsteps followed me, growing neither louder nor fainter as I passed, a constant *tap tap tap* in the dark, as if these feet were not affected by rain nor flood, and could forever find a dry concrete surface on which to walk. I put my hands over my ears to shut it out, and still it was there *tap tap tap* behind my palms. I had no idea where I was going, and I didn't dare stop. I picked a road that seemed longer, with more shops than the rest, shuffling down the pavement against a bouncing tide of rainwater. In the far distance I could see the towers of central London, the Gherkin and the National Westminster Tower lit up blue-green-purple against the night, and fixed them as my destination, though I could hold them both between my index finger and thumb.

A feeling behind me, a disruption in the pattern of the falling rain was what made me turn. And she was there, just a few yards behind, one hand outstretched, fingers curled like an animal's claw. Pain burst again behind my eyes and I ducked, threw a blast of compressed air, hot and smelling of air-conditioning vents, at her belly, which picked her up off her feet and deposited her with a splat onto the bonnet of a car. Shielding my eyes with one hand so I couldn't see her, I slammed my fist into the roof of the car beside me and its engine leapt to life, a raw thrumming that spread almost immediately from car to car down the street. The exhaust pipes belched, rattling and rumbling, and with a crunch of machinery doing something it hadn't been designed to do, began to billow thick brown-black smoke that spun and twisted like a tortured ghost in the falling rain. I staggered on, letting it curl up around behind me, pressing the soaked end of my sleeve over nose and mouth, blinking blood and dirt out of my eyes. I thought I could see a point of light ahead, a pinprick of green that as I watched turned to yellow, then to red. I accelerated towards it, heard feet moving behind me again, real, this time, moving fast, running, water slapping underneath shoes and there was a junction directly ahead, a crossroads, a set of traffic lights blinking steadily back to green as I approached. Then something caught the back of my head by the hair and nearly picked me up off my feet, and something else drove into my kidneys like they'd said something rude about its grandmother and I flopped like a fish, dropping to the ground. Somewhere between the smoke and the pain and the dark, I saw a pair of feet move round in front of me, saw the pink palm of Oda's hand move down and catch me by the chin, pulling my head up. I closed my eyes and she dragged me as easily as a puppy back to my feet.

"Look at me," she said.

I shook my head numbly.

"Look at me."

"Don't make us kill you," we begged, "Oda, don't make us burn."

"Look at us!"

Her voice, and not her voice. Her lungs filled with someone else's breath.

I reached out in the dark, grasped her arm by the wrist with both hands. "Sorry," I wheezed.

"Too late, too late, too late too late too late too . . . !"

I tightened my grip, dug my fingers into her skin and, without daring to look, without opening my eyes, ran straight towards her. I caught her off balance, she staggered backwards, and kept staggering as I came, feet slopping in the rainwater. I swung her round by her extended arm towards where I guessed the pavement was, half opened my eyes as I let her go, saw her stagger against the kerb, fingers curling over the paving edge, raised my arm and shouted, "Do Not Cross!"

Nothing happened.

I sagged, bending over my own internal pain in the hope that my kidneys might one day forgive me, arm made of lead, throat burning, eyes on fire.

Oda straightened up slowly, turned towards me. I didn't remember to look away fast enough, felt the pain again as her gaze locked on mine, felt my world begin to cave in from the edges, dropped to my knees, head in my hands, trying to claw the fire out of my skull, saw, in what little was left of the tunnel of my scarlet-stained vision, the traffic lights change.

Saw a flicker of light.

Something moved in the darkness behind Oda. It was orange-red, approximately five foot nine in height, and was on fire. Brilliant bright red light tumbled out of every part of its body, spilt over the ground around it, distorted the boundaries between skin and air. Its face, such as it was, had messy, blurred-out features which might, just might, have been fixed in an expression of infinite weary patience, worthy of the Buddha himself. The earth sizzled where it walked, the traffic lights hummed. I pointed at Oda and managed to whimper, "There may be special signals for pedestrians. You should only start to cross the road when the green figure shows."

I turned my face away, crawled on my hands and knees, managed to make it onto my feet, staggered a few paces away. Behind me, I heard a sound that could almost have been a snort of derision, heard Oda step out to follow me. The red man moved. A single burning fist caught her arm as she moved after me, and locked tight in place. She struggled to break free and another red fist fell on her other arm, pinning her wrists tight. She looked it in the eye and it had no eyes with which to see, but just gripped her to the edge of the pavement. She tried to kick it and her foot passed straight through its shin. I looked up at the traffic lights, willed them to stay green, willed my summoned saviour to stay where it was, willed the lights not to turn. They wanted to; so badly the lights wanted to obey their programming and let Oda go, and I forced them to obedience while behind me Oda, or not-Oda, or whatever-Oda shrieked, "Do you think you can hold me here? With *this*? This inanimate thing?!"

"If you have started to cross the road and the green figure goes out," I whimpered, "you should still have time to reach the other side, but do not delay. If no pedestrian signals have been provided, watch carefully and do not cross until the traffic lights are red and the traffic has stopped."

I staggered across the junction, felt my control of the spell slipping, felt the amber light start to flicker into life on the traffic lights, felt the presence of the red man begin to fade. This should have been an easy spell, but our head pounded and our eyes were on fire.

"The lights are turning, sorcerer!" called out Oda cheerfully. "You can't stop them for ever, they'll turn and your knight in crimson armour will disappear!"

I staggered down the middle of the street, leaning on the cars as I passed by, back burning, head burning, my vision two blurred slits in either eye. Behind me, I heard a little click, heard Oda jerk herself free, felt the traffic lights change. The red man, my red man, dissolved as quickly as he had come, shimmering away to nothing, his purpose fulfilled. Oda was barely fifty yards behind me. I raised my throbbing head, tried to will the lights of the city a little bit nearer, heard footsteps in my ears and, somewhere just behind them, the sound of an engine being revved in the wrong gear.

I slipped down against the side of a grocer's truck as Oda approached, raised my hands in front of my face. Blurs. Dark brown smudges somewhere in the dark. The footsteps slowed as she neared. I hung my head and let the rain wash some of the heat and terror away.

"Sorry," I wheezed as she stopped in front of me.

The sound of water being displaced, of something moving in the rain.

"You never say what for," she replied, and her voice was for a moment almost human.

"Specifically?" I asked as two grey smudges that might have been her knees crossed my line of sight. "As in right here, right now?"

An engine being pushed up to full speed.

"I think it'd have to be my apprentice's driving."

I felt rather than saw Oda move, and with all that was left of my strength and might I drew my palms together, pushing the stolen sound of the rain and the car and our words and my racing heart into one thin slice of thunder between my fists, and turned my hands outwards and threw it at her. It lifted her off her feet, threw her the width of the road and slammed her into the side of a parked motorbike, which toppled to the ground wailing like a frightened animal. Two bright white points of light rose up to one side and a sheet of water fountained up and deposited itself squarely on my head. I heard an engine, smelt petrol, saw something darker move against the darkness of my sight, heard a window, heard a voice, familiar and scared, shout, "Come on then, move!"

I fumbled my way forward, felt the shape of a metal door, the heat of an engine, the vibration of a car, felt for the handle, pulled it, felt the door open, crawled inside, bundling my knees to my chest, and an arm reached over and slammed the door shut behind me and Penny's voice said, "You bloody bleed on my bloody aunt's car and I'll make you clean it with a fucking toothbrush!"

"Drive," I whimpered. "Drive!"

So Penny did.

Blind.

Not total blindness, not entirely.

Enough light to be offensive, like the smell of fresh bacon to a starving man, out of reach, out of understanding.

We couldn't . . .

. . . it wasn't acceptable to be . . .

. . . we were not prepared to be both mortal and a cripple.

We could not permit it to happen.

We did not care what price needed to be paid.

I huddled in the front seat of Penny's car with my feet pressed against the glove compartment and my hands locked around the handle above the door, saw splotches in the dark, flashes of stained yellow, streaks of white, dollops of pinkish-orange glow, flickers of grey-blue, daubs of darkness stained red, and had no idea where I was, or where we were going, or how long it took us to get there.

"Is she following?" I asked.

"Don't see anything behind," Penny replied, voice hard and busy, far too busy for anything other than a brisk rendition of facts.

"Are there street lamps?"

"Yeah. They came back on at Bethnal Green. Just a power cut. You were in a power cut."

"I think you and I both know that's not true."

She didn't reply.

After any time between a few minutes and a brisk millennium, we slowed, we stopped, we parked, the handbrake came on with a sharp *snack*.

I said, "Where are we?"

In answer, Penny wound down the window.

I smelt onion drifting on the air, heard voices in the distance, the sound of a motorbike engine misfiring, rain falling busily on shop awnings.

"We're near Brick Lane," she said. "You looked . . . so I stopped. I came as quickly as I could." I could hear the sound of her grin, in her voice, in the parting of her lips. "Lewisham to Mile End in twelve and a half minutes – not too fucking bad, right?"

"Bet you broke a few speed limits."

"I fucking broke a few laws of space and time, man! You should have seen me!" She stopped abruptly, the words choking even before they'd finished. I smiled, put my head against the back of the seat. My head pounded, my feet itched, the sticky hot itch of rainwater boiling in thick socks.

"Matthew?"

"Yeah?" I sighed.

"We safe here?"

"Don't know. If the lights are on and people are moving, then yeah, I guess so, for now, until she comes back. What time is it?"

"Nearly dinner time."

"Dinner . . . what about breakfast?"

"What about it?"

"I . . . it's . . ." I swallowed, half shook my head. "We are ten kinds of fucked, apprentice-mine."

"Yeah. You kinda look it. Matthew?"

"Yeah?"

"Can you see?"

"Not so as you'd care to notice."

"Fuck."

"Yeah."

"Is there . . . is there anything we can . . . I mean can we . . ."

"I need to get to Bart's Hospital," I wheezed. "I don't know how long we have before she comes back, I couldn't . . . You look into Oda's eyes and you go blind. Jesus, she killed them, she killed the people in the hotel. She killed them all. Something's got inside her, something's in her eyes, I shouldn't have left her, I should have stayed at the hotel. Bollocks bollocks bollocks!" I hit the nearest thing my fist could find, which turned out to be the dashboard of the car.

"Hey!" Penny's voice snapped across my anger. "That's my aunt's car you're beating up, dripping on and bleeding in, so you watch yourself or she'll do you!"

"Sorry," I heard myself mumble to the sound of the engine starting up again. "I . . . uh . . . I'm a little fried." I fumbled for the grab-handle above the car window, and clung to it as the fuzzy mishmash of lights just beyond the black smoke of my vision swung into motion. "Hey – full marks on the driving. Ten out of ten. Gold star."

Brick Lane to Bart's Hospital was a journey barely worth the petrol it burnt.

I felt the moment we passed across the old line of the city wall, like an electric shock to the belly. I saw the tunnel beneath the Barbican as a continual flicker of whiteness overhead. I felt the streets into Smithfield as a surge in the number of traffic humps beneath our wheels.

Penny parked with merry illegality outside what sounded like a pub, karaoke in full, unintelligible swing. Someone inside was torturing a hippo to a theme by Abba. I heard a glass smash and a bubble of noise. Somewhere else, a lorry with dodgy suspension rumbled by. I smelt old magic, flecked with washed-down blood and sawdust from the meat market. The door opened beside me, Penny's arm found mine. "Where we going?" she asked.

"The church."

"Hey, I've got time for Jesus and all, but you really think this is the right fucking moment?"

"The A and E at Bart's got shut down years ago," I growled, "but they kept a department open in the church."

"Fine," she sighed. "You're the semi-hysterical half-blind blood-splattered one. It'll just make my night listening to you." She pulled me out of the car, held me by the arm, whispered, "They're all staring at us."

"Who?"

"The guys in suits, the City pricks at the pub. They're staring."

"What the hell is wrong with the time?" I snarled. "What are they doing at the pub?"

"Yeah, you're semi-hysterical, remember? Can it."

We turned a corner, the quality of the sound changing, fading, confined. I felt my way with one hand and my fingers brushed flint, jagged sharp edges and old worn stones. I could smell grass and hear the *whush whush whush* of a fan spinning in a nearby vent. Penny pushed at something in front of me and my shoulder bumped a wooden door. The air grew warmer, smelling of wax, thin smoke and wood polish. I heard a couple of voices, American, echoing incoherently in the darkness, whispers caught and amplified by hard stone.

"OK, church, whatever. Where now?" hissed Penny in my ear.

"Crypt."

"And *now* you're taking the piss."

"Isn't there supposed to be this teacher–student relationship?" I growled. "Isn't it the one where I tell you something and you accept it?"

"Uh-uh. See, my cousin Chenaara, right, she went to fucking uni and it was all 'question the system' and 'you gotta find out for yourself' shit, so no, I don't think I do have to accept a word you say."

"Let me rephrase. Please take me to the bloody crypt, Penny, before I scream loud enough to caramelise your small intestine!"

"It's only because we're in a house of God that I ain't fucking answering that," she replied primly, but our feet shuffled, and we did move.

I felt stairs.

What little light there'd been, faded.

Our footsteps were the only thing in the darkness, apart from the smell of damp and a rapid decline in temperature. We paused. I heard a knocking, and reached out to feel thick cool wood embedded with hard bolts. The knocking came again. There was the cranking of bolts, the groan of hinges that no amount of oiling could revive. A cheerful voice said, "You here to bury the dead or what?"

"Don't tempt me," replied Penny.

I felt a rush of cool air as the door was opened further, and the voice said, "Hey! You *are* here to bury the dead!"

An elbow nudged my ribs. "She's talking about you," Penny whispered. "Bet you wish you respected me now, huh?"

"We're looking for the Saint Bartholomew Hospital A and E," I groaned.

"Shut down years ago," came the merry reply. "UCH's your next-best bet."

"We're looking for the A and E for *other* sorts of troubles."

"Other?"

"Oh, for fuck's sake!" snapped Penny. "For fucking magical fucking medical emergencies!"

"I know that," said the voice, delighted at its own entertainment. "I was just fucking with you for kicks. You'd better come on in."

Penny and the unknown voice laid me down on something cold, flat and hard.

I said, "This had better not be someone's tomb, right?"

There was a silence.

Then, "No," soothed Penny. "No, it just *feels* like someone's tomb because of its . . . uh . . . its . . . you know. Qualities and shit."

My fingers quested to the edge, found their way round and down. "There's a slab. With carvings of people underneath it," I said. "This guy's holding a skull."

"OK, so it *is* someone's tomb, but haven't you heard? The NHS is in crisis!"

I heard footsteps in the darkness, a sudden liquid squelch, smelt the peculiar boiled-onion stench of antiseptic hand gel, heard the cheerful voice proclaim, "So, you're like . . . so totally fucked inside your brain, aren't you?"

I said, "Penny, please assure me that the owner of this voice strikes you as being a qualified professional."

Another long, peculiar silence. Then, "Yeah. Yeah, that's exactly what she looks like. Like totally."

"You know, I think I've treated you before," said the voice. "If your eyes weren't like, sorta totally full of blood and stuff, I'd definitely say that you looked familiar. You're not the guy who keeps on getting beaten up by inexplicable mystic darknesses, are you?"

"Oh! That's him!" exclaimed Penny. "That's totally him!"

"Hey!" A fist punched me affectionately in the shoulder. "How's it all going with you? Remember me? Dr Seah? I've given you like . . . oh . . . shitloads of drugs in my time, remember?"

"Hi. I'd shake your hand but . . ."

"Totally get it – no worries! Everything OK with you?"

"Not really," I growled.

"Some shit, huh? Hey – you see this light?"

"Yes, I see it," I groaned as yellow-whiteness flared across my vision.

"Hear any buzzing in your ears, tinnitus, hum . . . throbbing, pulsing?"

"You want a medical answer to that, or am I allowed to get personal?"

"I'll take that as a 'no'. Experiencing dizziness, nausea, loss of muscle control, loss of bowel control?"

"Don't push me."

"Well" – another merry punch to my shoulder – "you're clearly not too bad otherwise you wouldn't be an *issue patient*." She lowered her voice, and in a conspiratorial tone clearly intended for Penny's delight, added, "We have to say *issues* these days because 'problem patient' is considered too negative and unsympathetic. It's all about empathy, you see?"

A little weak "uh" noise was all that got through Penny's self-restraint. Fingers probed around the hollows of my eyes. I heard the snapping of thin rubber gloves. Something sticky and plastic was torn. Something cool and damp rubbed away at my face. "Now! A few standard questions for the history. Do you have any known allergies to medication?"

"No."

"Any history of kidney problems?"

"No."

"Any history of liver problems?"

"No."

"Have you at any point dabbled with necromantic powers that might affect your cellular structure?"

"Um . . . well, I was dead for two years," I admitted. "But since my body was dissolved into raw energy that roamed the telephone wires for that time, I don't really think it counts as 'necromantic powers'."

"I'll put you down as a 'no', shall I?"

"If you say so."

Papers rustled. Something cold and round pressed against my chest. "Breathe in . . . and out . . . and in . . . hey, still breathing normally, what's the problem, you big baby? Are you, to your knowledge, cursed?"

"Haven't checked for a while."

"You don't look cursed. No flaking skin, no rapid hair loss, no protruding veins, no talking in tongues . . . I figure another 'no'. Have you at any point shared a blood link with any of the following: sacred mystical vessels, the undead, demons incarnate, devils incarnate, ectoplasmic interventions, vampires, werewolves, the polymorphically unstable in general, or . . ."

"None of the above."

". . . or creatures from the nether regions of creation?"

"No." I heard a little cough from Penny. "All right," I snapped. "So I guess you could say that I shared a bit of blood with a creature from the nether regions." Another cough, firmer this time. "All right! So I sort of am a creature from the nether regions."

A gentle sigh from Dr Seah. As breezy as a spring morning. "And . . . which particular creature would this be?"

"We are the blue electric angels," we growled. "We wear this flesh but our fire is forever raging. We were summoned out of the telephone lines and I came when we were called, two in one, we wear my flesh to walk this earth. I'm sorry, is this medically relevant?"

"I *see*." Pen skidded over paper. Paper was turned. Pen continued to skid.

After a while Penny said, "So . . . you can help him, right?"

"What? Oh yes, I think so. Oh look – unhealed fresh burn marks too. You haven't been looking after yourself properly, have you?"

"Should I have mentioned being trapped in a fire in the medical history?" I asked meekly.

"In the context of having your brain, like, explode? Probably not medically relevant. Just one last question – how was this particular injury inflicted?"

"I looked into the eyes of a woman with a hole in her heart and black pudding in the sockets of her face who stood in the middle of a world turned to darkness."

"There you are again with those inexplicable darknesses! Well, I wouldn't want to speculate, but based on . . ." Fingers prodded my face, pulling at the lids of my eyes and turning my head this way and that. ". . . based on what I can see here, you're very lucky that your brain isn't dribbling out of your nose! I mean, obviously, it's unorthodox, and not really my field, but if you'd looked much longer you'd probably be like totally dead. Don't quote me on that, though – we'd need further testing to be sure. I don't suppose this woman wants to come in for a check-up?"

"Dr Seah," snapped Penny. "Like, loving the white coat and shit, all very sexy, but can you help him or not?"

"Oh, yes," she said. "You shouldn't believe everything Sarah Palin says about the NHS."

There were noises.

Something that sounded too much like a food processor for comfort.

A machine that beeped when it was done.

Plastic being torn.

Zips being unzipped.

Then something bit my right knee.

"Ow," I offered. "What's my knee ever done to you?"

"Burns," Dr Seah's voice explained merrily from somewhere in the gloom. "No point patching up your bleeding eyes if you then go and get complications from unsterilised burns, is there? Since you don't look too sure, let me answer that one for you. No, there isn't! We pride ourselves on our thoroughness and comprehensive service, especially after that last lawsuit . . ."

"OK, this place, officially freaking me out," Penny added reasonably.

"You freak freak freak me out!" sang Dr Seah. There was a brief silence. "Sorry," she said finally. "Was I the only one who found that funny?"

"This is what my life has come to," I groaned. "Look, thrilled though I am at the care and attention being slavered on my kneecap, can we do something about my sight before I have to face off against a rampaging unknown evil again?"

"Oh, your sight will return of its own accord. Sorry, didn't I mention?"

"No!" shouted Penny.

"No!" I agreed. "When?"

"In about . . . oh . . . a week and a half."

"Dr Seah, I haven't got a week and a half."

"Busy busy busy," she sighed. "*Fine.*" I heard footsteps shuffling over stones, the sound of something metal with a latch being opened. "Technically, this hasn't been approved yet . . ." Something went *splat* into the bottom of a beaker. Glass tinkled on glass. ". . . but I figure, you know, fuck 'em."

"Penny? What the hell is going on?" I moaned.

"Um . . . well, uh . . . there's this stuff that looks like pigeon shit being mixed with this other stuff that looks like chopped tomato . . ."

"Forget I asked."

I heard the faintest clink of something being set down behind my right ear. "Now," said Dr Seah, her voice directly overhead, "this is going to be a peculiar experience, but I want to make it clear – no silly buggers in my crypt! I won't have you do the whole electric flashy flash zingy business just because you can't hack a little basic healing magic, OK?"

"OK," I heard myself murmur.

"Excellent!"

Then a pair of fingers built like the foundations of the Eiffel Tower locked around the socket of my left eye, pulled the eyelid back, and something burning cold and full of teeth was dolloped onto my eyeball.

It was some time later.

I sat on the edge of a cold stone slab with two cotton-wool pads tied with bandage over my eyes and a cup of tea clasped in my hands like the Holy Grail. I focused on the heat; the heat was a good distraction from the desire to prod my eyeballs. We wondered if this was what it felt like to have a glass eye, albeit one two sizes too big for your head and kept in the refrigerator overnight. I could hear the sound of running water and the snap of rubber gloves. I felt a gentle nudge in the ribs.

"I thought you were very brave," said Penny loyally.

"Cheers."

"Apart from the bit where you shrieked like a girl."

The running water stopped. A tin rattled. "We appreciate donations towards the tea bags," said Dr Seah. "20p is the standard contribution."

I heard the sound of change being rattled, and a coin falling into a surprisingly full-sounding container. "Keep it, have it, it's yours," sighed Penny. "How long's this lemon" – another nudge in my ribs – "gotta keep the bandages on?"

"Oh . . . five to six hours?" suggested Dr Seah. "And after that I'd really, *really* recommend not looking straight into the eye of any wandering mystic darknesses for at least another week. Here's the leaflet."

Something papery was pushed into my hand, then snatched away quickly by Penny. There was the silence of concentrated, determined reading. Finally, "Excess hair growth?"

"It's very unlikely," said Dr Seah, "but we do have to list all possible side effects."

"What?" My voice was a lead coffin banging onto the stones. "Side effects?"

"Very, very rare," added Dr Seah. "But I would appreciate a blood pressure check in the next two months, please, and there's a yellow form you can fill out if you notice anything unusual. All medical information is appreciated in these sorts of trials."

"Can I move him?" asked Penny, folding the paper away.

"Oh yes. And have a proper meal. Something with plenty of iron, yes?"

Penny's arm went round my shoulder, helped me to my feet. With the bandages over my eyes, now I could see nothing at all, not even shadows. Dr Seah took the teacup from my hands.

"Bye now!" she trilled as Penny led me up the stairs. "And remember not to fiddle!"

Penny kicked the door shut behind us, cutting off Dr Seah's cheerful voice.

Smell of wax.

Smell of wood polish.

Sound of bells ringing somewhere in the darkness outside.

"So . . ." said Penny finally, as we stood on the cold stones of St Bartholomew's Church. "That was bloody educational, huh?"

"Never let it be said I don't keep the syllabus varied," I replied, groping out in front of me until my fingers brushed the top of a wooden pew. "Which way's out?"

"It's OK," murmured Penny, taking my arm in hers. "I've gotcha. Lemon."

She led me one step at a time towards the door. "Where now?"

"St James's."

"Posh arsehole land? Why?"

"To meet a posh arsehole. You'll like him. He always provides free food."

Penny's aunt's car, upon further examination, smelt.

It smelt of the same dry, fuzzy smell of all cars everywhere, except those with padded leather seats, but also had about it a lived-in stench of old coffee, cheese sandwich, long since dried-up air freshener of the kind sold as a little cardboard tree, and very, very faintly, the acid bite of vomit. I said carefully, "Penny . . . your aunt . . . she got kids?"

"Yeah, four. I said 'you heard of condoms?' and she was like, 'you don't talk that way in my house young lady' and I was like 'aunt, lemme get you a banana and show you how it's done . . .'"

"How old are the kids?"

"Three, five, seven, eleven."

"Any of them get carsickness?"

"That'd be Bets."

"Bets?"

"The youngest. Her name's Bathsheba but we all call her Bets because that way we don't have to talk like tossers. Except her mum. She calls her Bathsheba. 'Cause that's her name."

"I see."

"My aunt's kinda old-fashioned."

"I wouldn't have guessed."

I felt Penny's scowl through the darkness.

We listened to the radio, flicking through channels for something we could both agree on as we headed west.

Blockage on the M25 junctions 5 to 8 almost no movement at all there . . .

He started screaming, they all started screaming . . .

Imagine trying to get that for a pound!

We'll be back tomorrow when funny boy Ste comes into the studio to talk about . . .

It's a disgrace, I mean, them taking our jobs, I've worked here for twenty years and –

I said, "If I said to you 'where's the sun gone?' what'd you think?"

"I guess I'd figure it as one of the wanky cryptic things you say to piss me off."

"What time is it?"

"Ten something. Bloody starving."

"That's odd, isn't it?"

"What?"

"That you're bloody starving. What did you have for dinner?"

"I didn't have dinner because I was bloody saving your bloody life!"

"All right, what did you have for lunch?"

"I had . . . well I had . . ." Penny's voice trailed off. Then, "I guess I must have had a sandwich or something, I dunno, does it matter?"

"Think. Think hard. What did you have for lunch?"

"Sandwich," she said. "That's what I usually have."

"And usually the sun comes up, right?"

"Hey, Matthew, I dunno what that doctor lady put in those drug things, but you're talking like a dork now and it's kinda shitting me out."

I sank back further into the seat. "Never mind," I sighed. "Where are we?"

"Westminster. Shit! I forgot to pay congestion charge! Hey – you think the Aldermen can get me off a fine?"

"I'm not sure they'd regard that as strictly ethical."

"Screw that! What's the point of having a whole connected secret organisation thing doing your shit for you if they can't get you – or your seriously underestimated totally cool life-saving apprentice – out of a driving ticket?"

"I'll ask next time I see them."

St James's was, without a shadow of a doubt, posh arsehole land.

Shops selling cigars and suits, antiques and pictures of ancient naval battles, cufflinks and stationery all bound in moleskin and silver. Wide quiet streets, tall stone houses, private clubs flying the Union Jack, with, inside the massive doors, pictures of the Duke of so and so beside portraits of the Queen and Margaret Thatcher. Every now and then the inhabitants of St James's would claim that the streets between Piccadilly, Buckingham Palace and St James's Park were not as posh as they seemed. This was always a mistake, for if there was one thing guaranteed to piss off the average Londoner more than Silly Money, it was Silly Money that didn't have the brains to realise its own good luck.

And so St James's endured as a part of the *other* city, the one that the tourists visited in T-shirts proclaiming 'I ♥ London', the one where the cars were driven by men in peaked hats, where the tea was always served in a china pot, where the sandwiches were cut to the shape of a triangle, the jumpers were cashmere, the socks were silk, the windows were clean, the booze was £500 a bottle. It was a glimpse of another world, inhabited by another species, one which surely couldn't have bodily functions and spiritual needs like the rest of us, for it did not pine for the smell of fish and chips at supper or get angry at the failure of the 341 bus to come when you needed it, or fumble in its pockets for change for a pack of fags. Certainly, London, the *real* London, the majority experience of London, envied the grand streets laid out around the palace, and even felt a quaint protective streak towards it, as if to say 'We may think that St James's is full of rich tossers, but they're *our* rich tossers and if we could be rich tossers too, we would be. So just because we're rude about it doesn't mean you can be.'

To us, St James's tasted of fog tainted with greenish-grey smoke, of the magics of stones and statues with empty eyes, of secrets tucked just out of sight behind impregnable walls. It was the place to cast defensive spells, and slow, lingering enchantments.

Penny said, "If I park here, will I get towed?"

"Dunno. You used to be the traffic warden – you tell me."

"Pal, my beat was Willesden, it's not like I got to ticket a fucking royal. Fuck it, I'm going to park here."

She did, and I heard the beginning of violent oaths as she found the parking metre. "Twenty fucking pence for four fucking minutes!" she shrilled as she helped me out of the car. "Do you know how much it is for an hour?"

"Um . . . three quid?" I hazarded.

"Magic it," she snapped. "Come on, I've seen you defraud all sorts of wankers with your magicky ways, come on! Magic the fucking thing!"

I gave in, without much of a fight. "Help me to the parking metre."

She did. My hand was laid on a square metal object with only three buttons and no slot for returned change. I ran my fingers down it, making out each button one at a time, thought about it, and then gave the machine a good, hard kick.

Something whirred inside.

Something clattered and clacked.

A piece of paper emerged from a small slot. I tugged it free and held it out towards where I vaguely thought Penny was. "One parking ticket, on demand, ma'am."

"That," said Penny, snatching it from my unresisting fingers, "was fucking awesome. You didn't even have to chant or anything."

"Penny, it may have looked like all I did was kick the machine," I sighed. "But I assure you a lifetime of experience has gone into learning *where* to kick the machine."

There was a door.

It was an automatic door that sounded like glass when it swished effortlessly open before us. There was a hot blast of air from above, sealing off the pristine inner world from the rain-spattered dirty world outside. I could hear the low buzz of artificial lights and a computer fan whirring. There were slippery tiles beneath my feet and the smell of freshly watered plants.

Then Penny rested my hands on something cool and glassy, the height of a reception desk, and said, "Good evening! We're here to see this dude about the imminent destruction of stuff and shit and this here's the Midnight Mayor, very senior fucker, don't mind him, sound cool?"

I wished my eyes were open, so I could have closed them again in despair.

Then a voice from behind the desk, polite and perfectly rounded by years of listening to the BBC, said, "Of course. I'll let them know you're here."

Her voice became the distant platitude of someone talking on a telephone.

"Yes . . . yes, I have a Midnight Mayor plus one to see . . . yes, that's correct . . . I'll send them straight down." A tap of a key on a keypad, then, "If you'd just follow my associate here . . ."

Tile became wooden floorboard, polished and uneven underfoot. The sound of machinery faded, except for the distant thrum of air through a vent somewhere overhead. My fingers brushed rough worn brick, wood, painted canvas inside ornate wooden frames, and occasionally velvet, hanging down from the ceiling here and there like some sort of medieval tapestry. We went down a set of tight spiral stairs, stone, the middle of each step worn to a groove, a thin metal rail added as an afterthought to either side of the staircase. At the bottom the wood beneath our feet had become brick, and the air was colder, the swish of fans in the ceiling a little more pronounced. We walked thirty-two steps and turned left, paused two steps further on in front of a door, knocked.

A voice from inside, muffled but still clear, boomed, "Enter!"

The door opened with a thunk of a heavy metal knocker bouncing on the wood that held it. We stepped inside. The door closed.

The air smelt of food.

Our mouth started watering immediately.

I forced us to stay still, gather the remaining information. Smell of sausages and French dressing, of wine and the kind of cheese that sucked refrigerator doors closed from the inside. Whiff of magic, thick, treacle-black magic, mingling with the shadows.

Then a chair creaked and a voice exclaimed, "Good God! Matthew, what happened to you?"

The voice was loud, as rich and round as the belly that produced it, and spoke of the waistcoat that contained it and the round face that owned it as surely as if sight had confirmed it. It was, in short, the voice of Dudley Sinclair, concerned citizen, dabbler in things that should not really have concerned him, and which, for that very reason, did.

"Evening," I mumbled. "Or maybe morning. Whatever."

"Sit, dear boy, sit!" I was led to a large padded chair padded further with velvet pillows, and sat. I heard something move behind me, that wasn't Penny, and added, "Evening, Charlie."

"Mr Swift." Charlie, Sinclair's silent assistant, a man who was not always, entirely, just a man. Even if my guess hadn't been good, the smell of his magic on the air was unmistakable. "And this is . . . ?"

"Me?" Penny's voice, surprised. "Well, I'm Penny Ngwenya, Matthew's butt-kicking, life-saving, totally awesome apprentice. Um. Hi."

The slightest of pauses, the briefest of hesitations. There had been a time, not so long back, when Sinclair had been of the opinion that the safest thing to do about Penny was kill her; a revelation we all decided at once and in complete silent accord to skip.

Then Sinclair again: "Matthew, your eyes."

"Oh, yes, my eyes! Yes. Unfortunate encounter with Oda, 'psycho-bitch', resulting in temporary – let me emphasise *temporary* – blindness, splitting headache, bleeding nose, bleeding ears, and um . . . no, I reckon that's about it. All of the above. Sorry, is that food I can smell? I'm bloody starving."

"It is indeed food, Matthew – I thought that considering the hour a little breakfast might be called for."

"Supper," corrected Penny casually.

"Do I mean supper? Yes, I suppose I must mean supper. Good grief how peculiar. Yes, of course I mean supper."

"Um, question?" asked Penny, as cutlery clinked and a napkin was folded carefully out across my lap.

"Yes, my dear?"

"Where are we and who are you?"

"Ah – Matthew hasn't filled you in fully, has he?" sighed Sinclair. "Well, then if I may do the honours. We are in the wine cellar of Loveless and Headley Esquires, wine merchants, established 1887, or, to be more exact, we are in one of their private chambers which they lease out for corporate meetings. The food is complimentary – we have an understanding with Loveless and Headley – and while I would love to introduce us all to a bottle of the 1972 Sanchez and Petty, perhaps, considering the circumstances, that may have to be a pleasure for another time."

"But . . . they were OK with Matthew being like . . . Midnight Mayor and shit. So they're up on the magic and stuff, right?"

"Oh, yes. Loveless and Headley have been providing fine wines to most of the major magicians of the city for the last one hundred or so years; theirs was the liquor that graced the table at the 1959 treaty signing between the Midnight Mayor and the Neon Court; they also provide various elixirs, potions of life, as well as an alchemical archive detailing some of the more interesting work on such projects as the fountain of youth, the font of knowledge, the sacred springs of the dryads, the elixir of the immortals et cetera et cetera. But personally, I find them most enjoyable for their excellent collection of fine ports and sherries." Sinclair let out a little breath, a half-sigh, as of a man contemplating both of the above and finding happiness in the process.

I coughed politely. "Funny you should mention the Neon Court . . ."

"Isn't it just?"

". . . but Lady Neon's in town."

"Now you mention it, I had heard something of the sort." A hand closed around mine and a fork was pushed between my fingers. A plate was rested on my lap. I prodded it with the end of the fork, felt something that could have been salad. We impaled what we hoped was a tomato, and took a careful nibble. Disaster failed to strike.

"I hear rumours," went on Sinclair, "that a man called Minjae San, a daimyo, I believe, of the Neon Court, was murdered by warriors of the Tribe?"

"Yeah. I heard that too."

"I heard that the Neon Court was demanding vengeance."

"Yep."

"I understand that by the terms of the treaty you have with the Neon Court, you are going to be obliged to go to war with the Tribe over this breach of the peace?"

"That's the way it's looking."

"I imagine," went on Sinclair, in the same easy, lawyer-at-work tone, "based on some certain information now available to me – for example the fact that you are demonstrating a hearty interest in the woman Oda and appear to be *temporarily* blind – that there is a great deal more to the matter than I, or anyone, is aware. Except, perhaps, you."

I ate another tomato. Penny said, "You're good!"

I swallowed, wiped my mouth with my sleeve, put the fork down carefully on my plate and directed my gaze at what I hoped was roughly the location where Sinclair was sitting. "OK," I said. "Here's how it is. One: the Tribe didn't kill Minjae San. Oda did. Two: I was with Oda when she dunnit, having been summoned to the burning tower block without warning or explanation where various people then proceeded to attack me, and Oda asked me to, in short order, save and kill her. Three: the Tribe was at the tower too. I saw a body in the stairwell. But they did not kill Minjae. Four: Oda has a stab wound to the heart which I think she sustained in the tower from either Tribe or Court or sources unknown. Five: this stab wound hasn't killed her. Six: her eyes are now black mush and if you look at them, you'll go blind and die. Oh yes, and she's talking about 'we' as well as 'I' and is, all things considered, possessed. Seven: many people are dead. Eight: Lady Neon was on the way to London even before her daimyo was killed. Nine: both the Neon Court and the Tribe are seeking a 'chosen one' as prophesied by a guy with a Monopoly board called O'Rourke who was, when I last saw him, lying incapacitated in his own living room having accurately predicted the arrival of Oda, suffering, pain and a blackout, if nothing else. Ten: where's the sun gone? Questions?"

There was a long, gratifying silence.

Finally, "Well . . . it all makes a little more sense now."

"Glad to hear it. Is this thing on the end of my fork mushroom?"

"Some kind of cheese," replied Penny from behind my head. "Looks kinda rank, you know?"

"It's an excellent cheese," replied Sinclair primly, "and in many ways I feel the flavours will be enhanced by your . . . current incapacity."

"We try anything once," we replied, and ate it. It was like eating a kick to the teeth soaked in chilli pepper. Our nose watered.

"Um . . . I kinda got some questions." Penny was either oblivious or uncaring for our cheese-induced traumas. "Like . . . who summoned you to this burning fucking tower in the first place?"

I wiped my nose and wheezed, "At first, hadn't got a clue. I mean, it takes serious whack to just go 'poof' and summon a guy, particularly a guy who doesn't want to be summoned. But thinking about it, I'd say Oda. She was lying face down in her own blood, and drew the symbol of the Midnight Mayor in it. I mean, she's no sorceress, but whatever's got inside her has some hefty magical punch at its command and so I guess with her being in a confused and dubious mental state combined with having that sorta kick . . . yeah . . . Oda summoned me. She asked me to kill her."

"Which would imply that whatever is possessing her, if that's the right term, isn't yet fully in control? Or that she has some sense of her own precarious situation?" suggested Sinclair. "Well, that is promising, at least."

"Did I mention the stab wound to the heart?" I added helpfully. "I mean, leaving aside how I got into the tower block, you gotta ask yourself, what was Oda, Order psycho-nut with a religious hatred thing going down, doing in the same place, at the same time, as a daimyo of the Neon Court and a bunch of Tribe warriors?"

"Do you have an answer to that question?" asked Sinclair.

"No – although you can probably bet your merry backside that it has something to do with wanky complication the second – this 'chosen one'."

"Ah yes. May I say, Matthew, that I detect a certain . . . shall we say . . . cynical lilt to your voice when you say those words together?"

"That's because it's total bollocks," I explained. "'Chosen one'? Seriously? Chosen by whom? God? Destiny?"

"Uh – Jesus?" suggested Penny.

"Yeah, because Jesus went around all the time kicking up wars between the Neon Court and the Tribe."

"Uh – crusades?"

"All right, so there's Jesus. And Mohammed. And like . . . you know . . . those sorts of dudes. But unless you're going to tell me that (a) God has appointed another of his kiddies to walk upon the earth and (b) this kiddie lives in Sidcup and is at the heart of a petty bastard war between two petty bastard factions, then no. Total bollocks."

I heard the sound of liquid being poured into a glass, and a judicious drawing in of breath from Sinclair. "You do raise an interesting point," he said. "Purely from an academic perspective, one must ask oneself what is meant by 'chosen one'. It is possible, for example, that future historians might argue you, Matthew, as a 'chosen one' – not in any theological sense, but merely in that you seem to have a perpetual habit of stumbling into cataclysmic scenarios and surviving through improbable methods."

"By that definition, we should sanctify anyone who's ever served in the SAS," I growled. "Can we get back to the point? Even if you and I know that this 'chosen one' stuff is, from a mystical perspective, ninety-nine per cent sure to be total bollocks, the Neon Court and the Tribe both seem to have gotten wind of it and O'Rourke seemed fairly sure of his crap. Which suggests . . . ?"

"It suggests," sighed Sinclair, with the infinite patience of a man whose brain was having to rewalk routes it had covered half an hour ago, "that Lady Neon's arrival in London was planned even before Minjae San was murdered; that the presence of both Tribe and Court in the same place at the same time was not an accident; and that Oda knows more than she is currently saying about all of the above."

"Which means that this war between the Court and the Tribe . . . ?" I prompted.

"Isn't about retribution, it's about finding this 'chosen one' before the other side does – oh, how very tedious," groaned Sinclair. "And of course Lady Neon has seen the death of her daimyo as an excellent excuse to invoke the treaty between the Court and the Midnight Mayor, forcing you . . ."

"To either get involved with a war between the Court and the Tribe that I don't want to fight, or to find this 'chosen one' for her. Yep. Seems about right."

"Dear boy," Sinclair complained, "why didn't you come to see me sooner?"

"I was amassing information," I replied primly. "And . . . you know . . . getting the crap beaten out of me. Thing is," I went on, putting my plate gingerly down on the floor, "the really bad thing is, that this war business? It's kinda secondary to our real problem."

"You consider the condition of the woman Oda to be more serious than a war between the Tribe and the Court?"

"Yeah. I really do. And I consider it more serious for two reasons. One: she kicked the merry crap out of me. And, as you pointed out, I've got this thing for surviving improbably shitty situations, and I was in trouble. We were . . . we were hurt. She hurt us. That should alarm you in and of itself. Two: where's the sun gone?"

"You keep saying that," said Penny, "and then kinda look like you want us to say something else."

"Yes, do please explain," added Sinclair.

I folded my hands together across my knees, leant forward on my elbows. "So, I've been up and about now for . . . what? I don't know. Hours. Hours and hours and hours. And I can't help but notice, in all this business and adventure, that the sun isn't coming up."

"Well, that's total bollocks for a start . . ." began Penny.

"Uh-uh. Just listen to me. I asked you, Penny, what you had for lunch; you couldn't remember. You, Mr Sinclair, you described the food as breakfast, when in fact it's suppertime. When you picked me up from Mile End, Penny, it was still dark, the middle of the early morning, pre-dawn stillness and a sleep that could not be broken. By the time we got to Smithfield, the pubs were open and there were people drinking. Did you look at them? You said they were just guys in suits, but I bet, I just bet, there was something wrong about them. I took the Tube from Heathrow to the centre of town, and it was wrong: commuters in business suits next to tired drunks next to little old ladies next to schoolkids next to tourists next to party-goers in daft shoes. You get all these things on the Tube, every day – but the Tube has its rhythms, its ebbs and its flows, and it was like all these people were compressed, time-compressed, like it was school-leaving time and rush hour and party hour and happy hour and lunch hour and all hours all at once, packed in together. I bet you if we went outside right now, all of us, I could find twenty things, even blind, that prove something is wrong. Find the seers, find the Old Bag Lady, find the Beggar King, find the Seven Sisters or Upney, the Lord of Tar; find Fat Rat and the deep downers, invoke any spirit of the lonely night you care to name and ask them, just ask them to stand upon Greenwich Hill and look east and tell you what they see, and I can guarantee you they'll say the same thing that I say to you now. Where's the sun gone? Where has it gone?"

There was silence.

Finally Sinclair began, an edge of warning in his voice, "Matthew . . ."

"I am the Midnight Mayor. I am Robert Bakker's apprentice, I was trained by the most powerful sorcerer to screw the city over in the last hundred years. We are the blue electric angels. We see things that others do not. Believe us or be damned."

Silence again.

Then, "You understand that what you are saying is incredible."

"Considering my record, shouldn't that comfort you?"

"Inconceivable."

"Dodgy word."

"Matthew" – a little, uneasy laugh escaped Sinclair's lips – "we all know that the sun has come up."

"And gone down," I added. "We all know it's gone down because it's been dark for . . . well . . . hours. We all remember doing very interesting and potentially dangerous things in the dark, rescuing mentors, researching psycho-bitches and so on and so forth, we can all place activities in the night that we've done recently. And the day? What have we all done lately in the daylight that was quite as exciting as this little chat?"

"You know, right," hazarded Penny, "that you're kinda asking us to believe you're not talking total crap, right?"

"That sounded to me like a woman with *doubts*," I said. "Are you doubting, perhaps, whether you're *not* caught in a nightmare in which time stretches and the sun fails to rise? And more importantly, do you doubt whether it really *can't* be connected to this whole Oda-chosen-one-war crap? Go on. Surprise me."

"You've been attacked," murmured Sinclair. "You're hurt, you're upset, you're . . ."

"The fucking Midnight Mayor, mystic fucking protector of the city!" I snarled. "Two thousand years' worth of tradition and magic in the palm of my hand! Jesus, did every guy who went before me have to put up with all this crap, or do I get special treatment on the basis that no one quite knows what we're going to do next, no one trusts us not to set the sky on fire and everyone knows we can, is that why we are talked to like a child? I am telling you, as the guy in the know, that this is what is happening; now that the thought is in your head, I dare you to go another twelve hours without seeing that I'm right. Cut the mystic crap, I'm just plain *right*."

There was the little shuffling sound of breaths being exhaled, feet being twitched, bellies warping against waistcoats. Then, "All right. Supposing that, perhaps, you are correct about all of this. What do you propose we do?"

"We need to stop a war, and stop Oda," I replied. "Because I just bet you whatever this is, it's connected to one or both of those."

"You mean you don't know *why* the sun isn't coming up?" demanded Penny. "Oh, fat lot of use."

"It's not like this is something that happens regularly!"

"Sure, because you're just a regular sorta guy, like 'hey, this is normal shit for me, what's that, death of cities walking around, is that a dragon, whoo-hoo, let's get zappy on that shit, dude!'"

"This is bordering on harassment . . ."

"Matthew," interrupted Sinclair, "let us say – perhaps – that you are correct about our current . . . temporal hiccup. Let us say that these things are linked to Oda, who is somehow involved with this chosen one business that has the Court and the Tribe up in arms. What action do you propose taking?"

"Well, first up, we need to convince the Tribe and the Court to hold off on the whole massacre thing a little longer."

"Fair enough. And Oda?"

"Need to find her. Need to stop her."

"Kill her?" interrupted Sinclair.

"Can we do that?" asked Penny, an edge of unease entering her voice. "I mean . . . is that something we do?"

"Ms Ngwenya," replied Sinclair smoothly before I could feel ashamed, "Oda is a disciple of the Order. Killing people such as yourself, and Matthew, is something she does. And now you say one look from her eyes and people die? And she has a wound to her heart?"

"Yes."

"I assume a serious injury?"

"Well . . . it's got the words 'wound' and 'heart' in the same sentence, so yeah, we're talking pretty terminal."

"And, despite all this, is walking and talking and saying 'we' when she should be saying 'I'?"

"Yeah."

"And she nearly killed you."

I hesitated. Then, "Yeah."

"You see, Ms Ngwenya," concluded Sinclair, "motive is mounting. All of which leads to the key question – *can* you kill her? Matthew?"

"I . . . dunno."

A hardness entered his voice. "Did you try?"

"I . . . she attacked me and I ran and . . ."

"Did you try to defend yourself?"

"Of course I defended myself . . ."

"Did you try to kill her?"

"I . . . there wasn't really a thought process at work."

"Forgive me, Matthew, but that sounds a good deal like a 'no'."

"Look," I exclaimed, raising my hands defensively, "so it wasn't like I went into being beaten up with a plan, no, and sure, maybe if I did have a plan, I could have . . . stopped her. Sure, maybe, yeah. But this doesn't get round the fact that if you look her in the eye you go blind, and die, so no, I'm not exactly in a tearing hurry to rush off for round two. Besides . . ." My voice trailed off.

"Besides?"

"Possession," I sighed. "Or . . . possession may not even be the right word. Synthesis. Fusion. Possession, you expect just one dominating consciousness, you expect 'hello, I am Argh the Unstoppable, you cannot stop me' and so on. You don't expect . . . *we* feel and *I* feel in the same breath. That's not possession, that's . . ."

"What you do?" murmured Sinclair. "Yes, I had noticed that. And you aren't possessed, are you, Matthew? For all that some would have us think you are, in our extensive dealings I have been forced to conclude that you are simply . . . human plus some. Is that what you're saying Oda has become?"

"Dunno. Maybe. Good news if yes."

"Why?"

"Because she said 'kill me'. Suggests there's some part of her brain still hanging on in there. Some little corner of her consciousness going 'uh-uh, bad roaming nastiness' and holding back."

"Did she hold back when attempting to harm you?"

"Hard call. Don't really want to think about what she could do if that *was* her holding back."

"Erm?" Penny's voice, strained with the effort of seeming calm. "Like, don't want to rain on your parade or anything, but reality check? You seriously talking about killing and stuff like it's OK?"

"Yes, my dear." Sinclair's voice oozed uncle-reassurance. "Yes, I do believe we are."

"What did you find out about Oda?" I asked quickly. "Anything useful?"

Sinclair sighed. His chair creaked beneath an adjustment of considerable weight. "How much do you know about her?"

"Name; occupation. That's it."

"In that case, perhaps there are some things I should fill you in on."

And so he did.

First Interlude: The Life and Times of Psycho-Bitch

In which an acquaintance finally gets introduced.

"The woman," said Sinclair, "that you know simply as Oda, was born Oda Ajaja-Brown in Reading. Her mother was a teacher, her father was a gambler and an adulterer; the first drove him to crime, the second to drink. I'm sure we need not linger on the inevitable psychological consequences. She had an elder brother and a younger sister – we don't know who the father of the sister was. When she was seven years old, Oda Ajaja-Brown was given the privilege of watching the police come in the middle of the night and take her father away screaming abuse and vengeance. Her mother made the tip off. He served fifteen years for a number of offences. But by then, Oda was gone, as was his name from hers; she was simply Oda Ajaja, and had already found her calling.

"You know of Oda as a servant of the Order. Needless to say, she was not always so. The family believed in God, and went to church every Sunday, and the church was kind to them in times of hardship, both emotionally and, when things were bad, physically too. For the children, the local church became a place of friendship, where they were cared for unconditionally, a place of rest, as well as of prayer. The law required Oda to remain in school until she was sixteen, and she did, earning acceptable grades at GCSE. But her school record was a pattern of confusion. She was praised for her voluntary work, for her commitment to those in need, for her dedication to the elderly and almost obsessive desire to help others. She was also reprimanded severely for a temper that, at its worst, led to a seventeen-year-old boy who had been attempting to bully a thirteen-year-old girl finding himself in hospital, nail marks across his face and bite marks along the length of his arm, delivered at Oda's hands. If she was a knight in armour to the child whom she saved from a bully, let no one for a minute think that this armour was white.

"For all this, the history of Oda Ajaja could have been a happy one, were it not for the actions of her elder brother, Kayle. Too young when his father was taken, and too old to find comfort from anything that restored his sisters, Kayle embarked on a journey whose course could only truly end in tragedy. Fuelled by anger at his father, and hatred of his mother for betraying him, Kayle left home at seventeen years old with the resolution that he would be something better, something bigger than the life he had grown up with. His journey took him variously through business schools, entrepreneurship programmes, apprenticeships, and finally by what route we are not entirely clear, to London, and into the world of magic.

"You are sorcerers, Matthew, Penny; you see the city and you see magic, you feel it beneath your feet, you taste it on the air. When rush hour comes, your heart races faster; when you close your eyes you can feel the beat of pigeon wings across your skin and when you flex your fingers, static fills the speakers of the mobile phones all around, as if the air was disturbed with a thing richer than what we can perceive. That, I believe, is sorcery. Kayle saw something too, when he came to London. He looked onto the towers of the city, saw glass and steel, felt time beneath his shoes and power behind the locked doors, heard the rustle of money behind the wall of every ATM and smelt the sex in the sweat of the dancers in the clubs beneath his feet. He saw sorcery, but where I believe your sorcery is defined by a life unstoppable, of hearts beating behind every pane of frosted glass and breath mingling in every corner of every dusty underground tunnel, his was that of a power untameable, of a city that can only exist by every part moving, functioning, working, turning, earning. His magic was about power, and he quickly found those to teach him. This was in the time before Robert

Bakker and his hungry shadow; before the Tower and the creature that came out of the night and killed sorcerers. There were many with . . . shall we say . . . dubious ethics willing to instil what they knew in hungry young Kayle Ajaja, for a reasonable price, or a reasonable percentage of the take.

"And so it continued, for some years. Oda left school and got work in a kitchen on the edge of her home town; her younger sister, just ten years old, continued studying. Her mother grew older, lonelier, throwing herself into supporting her one remaining at-home child, and to the charitable works of the church. Kayle Ajaja neither wrote nor rang, and truth be told, none of the family sought him out.

"Kayle began to . . . how is the phrase? 'Go off the rails' I believe most aptly covers it . . . shortly after his twenty-fourth birthday. He had that delusion that the young and successful can sometimes have, of conceiving themselves a shark in a fishing pond, instead of a minnow in a rolling sea. He had, perhaps, failed to understand that the magicians he saw and met, and who he judged inferior to himself, were merely those who wished to be seen, or who lacked the capacity to disguise themselves. If he had been raised in the city from the start, trained from a younger age, introduced to some more . . . temperate . . . circles, perhaps he would not have acquired the misconceptions he did. But he wanted to succeed fast and young, and as a result fell in with those whose philosophies were those of speed, action without consequence, and no eye for the day after tomorrow.

"I believe the first act of rashness that attracted the attentions of the more . . . concerned citizens . . . was when he tested his abilities on his own father, cursing him, through the rather crude means of extracting waste from the prison sewage facilities and using that as the focus of his spell. Naturally, dozens of others fell under the spell's effect, so much so that the prison warden wrote a report proclaiming that bubonic plague had broken out within his walls. Medical science was baffled, and it was only through the good fortune of one of the attending doctors having had some trifling dealings with magic that an exorcist was called in before the situation grew out of control. It is not the business of concerned citizens to dabble too far in the actions of intemperate magicians; not unless they are clearly out of control. As the situation was contained, and the source of the outbreak unproven, if suspected, no further action was taken.

"Alas, young Kayle's activities did not stop there. His misdemeanours ranged from the petty – ATM robberies to the amount of over £60,000 – and I know, Matthew, that you yourself have been guilty of occasionally defrauding the odd electronic account, but not, I think, to spend on your eighth car, or at any time less urgent than when being pursued for your life. A man Kayle got into a fight with outside a Camden bar was set alight, in public, in the full sight of the street, and later died of an infection to his burns; there were plenty of other incidents of this sort. By now the police had enough images of his face to have put together a criminal case against him for both the attack on the man in Camden and a number of other offences, including fraud, GBH and robbery. At this point, the Midnight Mayor, the then new incumbent Nair, was called in at the warning of the Aldermen, to bring the situation under control.

"According to the official Alderman report, Nair scryed for Kayle and detected him easily, without his subject even being aware of the magic being performed around him. He approached him and informed him that he had three choices: he could either give up magic with immediate effect, in which case he would be tolerated; he could allow himself to be arrested for his crimes and serve his time, in which case he would be redeemed; or he could leave London immediately and never return, in which case he would be simply ignored. Kayle made the . . . regrettable . . . error of laughing in Nair's face, both ignorant of and unwilling to understand exactly what sort of power and authority the Midnight Mayor possessed. Nair gave him twenty-four hours to change his mind. The story says that Kayle spat acid into Nair's face, which Nair simply wiped away with a silk handkerchief. Personally, I believe that aspect of the tale to be apocryphal.

"Twenty-four hours later, and Kayle was, if anything, flaunting his capabilities still further. Nair approached him again on Hampstead Heath, and told him to leave the city immediately and never set foot in it again. Kayle derided him, mocked him, and finally, in a moment of madness, attacked him.

"Kayle may have been a sorcerer, but he was untrained, and unprepared for the power that the Midnight Mayor commands. Nair shook off his attack without creasing his shirt and launched in reply such a storm that they say you can still feel the place where the earth was burnt by it, if you know where to look. Kayle ran, but the city no longer wanted him, the streets themselves cracked beneath his feet, the lights went out ahead of him, the buses wouldn't brake at the shelters, the trains wouldn't open their doors. He ran; he ran until his shoes were torn and his feet were bleeding, through street and across field, down alley and over garden wall, until finally, breathless and hurt, almost a whole day after the fight on Hampstead Heath he ran across the M25 motorway that rings the city, and fell onto the dirt of the countryside around, free from the grasp of the Midnight Mayor's power.

"A wiser man might perhaps have left it there.

"Kayle Ajaja, as I think we have established, was not a wise man.

"He swore retribution, and wandered the country in search of the means to achieve it. But the Aldermen had contacts; in Newcastle and Manchester, Glasgow and Edinburgh, to every place he went where urban magic thrived, the moment he spoke his name the locals turned away, and said it wasn't worth their time to try and explain it to him. London isn't the only city with its mystical protectors. Finally, after months of travel, the penniless, hungry, bleeding, weak Kayle Ajaja returned to the place he had begun; he returned to his family home in Reading.

"And they welcomed him.

"Good people as they were, the family asked no questions, expected no answers, but gave him a place to sleep and food to eat, and let him recover at his own pace. Oda returned to help care for him, for her mother was now beginning to show the first signs of old age, and the diseases that only old age can bring. The youngest sister of the house, a girl called Jabuile, was fascinated to meet her older brother, who she could barely remember from her youth, and the two seemed to strike up a good friendship.

"Alas, neither Oda nor anyone in her family fully understood the reasoning of her brother's mind, for he had come to conclude that there was only one way to amass the power to destroy the Midnight Mayor and all who had slighted him in the past, and that was through a dalliance with the magics of blood.

"I am sure, Ms Ngwenya, that Matthew has given you his little chat about blood magics. I am sure he has explained to you that, for example, his own blood has, upon stressful moments, been known to ignite to the colour and consistency of burning blue electric fire, and that there have been those who, faced with this medical fact, have sought to obtain this blood for their own purposes, usually related to the cheating of death or gathering of great power. I am sure that Matthew has informed you how these . . . little escapades . . . have ended. Even were blood magic not riddled with unwelcome consequences, unforgivable pain and unfortunate risks, it would still be what it indeed is: the last resort of the desperate mortal unable to bear the consequences of a life lived to the full. It seems to me that Oda right now might be an excellent example of the risks of such dabblings, for undeniably the power that can sustain a woman with a knife wound to the heart is immense, as, undeniably, is its cost. I do not say that her elder brother attempted to become a vampire – that's a very specialist area of physiological adaptation, by now well enough publicised to give even the rash some pause for thought before embarking on its attainment. No: what Kayle Ajaja attempted was more akin to the syphoning off of others' power through the medium of a blood bond, the theft of others' lives, of others' strength, if you will, to boost his own. Nor did he practise necromancy, since that implies his victims were dead. Alas, Kayle had discovered all for himself that the greatest power to be obtained came from things that are still living, not from the dead. Life is magic, I believe is a common sorcerer's phrase. Where there is no life, there is no magic.

"So, Kayle Ajaja began to feed off others. It began with vulnerable individuals who he felt had done him wrong, even if this wrong was something as trifling as jostling him when queuing for a bus. Then it became strangers in the street, beggars and runaways, to satisfy his needs. Soon he became organised, and used his abilities to obtain information on local residents that could be incriminating to them, exchanging his silence for services inexplicable.

"In time, his actions grew so flagrant that they could not be contained. We don't know at exactly what point he demonstrated his abilities, gloating, to his sister Oda, but it seems a reasonable guess that the event coincided with her sudden decision to leave home again.

What we do know is that she sought advice from the local priest, who, having no knowledge of such affairs, initially thought she was mad. Fortunately for Oda, he communicated his fears, not with the local council, but with others in the church, of whom a woman called Hale had links to the Order. Oda immediately became a subject of great interest to Hale, who made it her business to become close to the confused young woman, going so far as to put her up, without rent, for nearly two months during this time of domestic crisis.

"Kayle's actions had also attracted the attention of other magicians in the Reading area. It is a peculiar place, Reading, in terms of the sorts of magician it attracts. Urban magicians can function in the town, for there is life enough in it to breathe strength to the fingers of such a practitioner; however, its proximity to the countryside, relative newness and distance from London all make it suitable for more traditional magicians to take up residence on the outskirts, within easy reach of places of older, rural magic. I believe it was this second category of magician who Kayle managed most seriously to offend, through more of his usual arrogance and pranks, and who contacted their urban counterparts to seek a solution. A few tentative examinations of the Ajaja house quickly persuaded the local inhabitants to get in professional assistance from London, and after some more discreet enquiries word reached the Aldermen of Kayle's latest activities. Though outside his jurisdiction, Nair was fully aware of Kayle's potential and danger, and authorised a team of Aldermen to rendezvous with local inhabitants in Reading and conclude the matter one way or another.

"They met. They went to the Ajaja house. There, without even bothering to speak and in broad daylight, Kayle attacked them, and the Aldermen retaliated. You have, no doubt, seen the Aldermen at work – they are as comfortable with guns as with spells, and Kayle was unprepared to oppose either. He was injured, a bullet to the belly that should have killed him, but rather than drop to the ground, he fled, healing even as he went. The Aldermen attempted to follow him, but rushing inside the house found Kayle's youngest sister, Jabuile, lying on her bed, blood slowly filling her belly. Through his practices, Kayle had succeeded in using his sister's strength to heal his wounds, and the act was killing Jabuile.

"The local magicians took the girl to the nearest hospital while the Aldermen attempted to track Kayle, but he was already fled and their powers of detection grew weaker away from the city. Jabuile died two days later in a hospital bed.

"Oda was there when she died.

"Four days later, Kayle's body turned up on the coast three miles east of Hastings. It was a place where the Ajaja family had once gone for a holiday, back when Oda was barely seven years old, the one holiday they had shared with their father. There was a bullet in his brain and three in his chest. Oda was found some three hundred yards away, gunshot residue on her hands, blood on her clothes.

"The police took her into custody, and two days after that, she vanished.

"So did Hale, the woman from the church in Reading. Indeed, it is only through a great deal of bureaucratic innovation that we know Hale even existed to begin with.

"The Aldermen left it at that, as did the rest of the magical community in both Reading and London. With Kayle dead, no one was interested any more. And so Oda Ajaja vanished.

"Oh – make no mistake. A woman with a striking resemblance to her was seen in many different places, on many different occasions. She appeared in St Petersburg, approximately seven months after vanishing from police custody, walking away from the scene of a murder in the metro; except that the body of the murder victim crumbled to dust and there was never any chance to hold an inquiry. I believe in Brazil there is still an arrest warrant out for a woman called Carla Brown, whose physical description matches Oda's perfectly. In Chicago she is suspected of involvement with a fire that killed three old women with a thing for chalk circles and invocation; in Rome, Paris and Berlin there were high-velocity rounds fired from the same rifle which has never been traced, all the victims magicians or dabblers in the craft, all the witnesses silent on who pulled the trigger, except here or there, one or two who whisper that it was a woman.

"What I know for certain, through my . . . special . . . relationship with some of the higher echelons of the Order . . . is that Oda Ajaja came to London nearly four years ago, after a career the details of which are hidden even from me. She quickly established herself as both an excellent detector and skilled exterminator of unwelcome magical influences across the city, finally earning the dubious honour of joining the coalition eventually formed with myself and a number of other factions, against Robert Bakker and the institution known as the Tower. I believe it was in the context of that coalition, Matthew, that you first met her. I further believe that she was under orders to kill you, as soon as you had served your purpose in destroying Bakker, but the orders were rescinded, owing to some . . . considerate advice . . . that suggested that you were more useful alive than dead. Your appointment as Midnight Mayor raised the debate again – was it more important to remove a threat quite as significant as a sorcerer–electric-angel-Mayor fusion from the streets, or was it worth keeping you alive in the hope of manipulating such a powerful weapon? Alas, events prevented the Order ever reaching a firm decision on the matter, when it became apparent that you, Matthew, were the only individual left within the city who had both the knowledge and the ability to prevent the entity we knew as Mr Pinner, or the death of cities, from fulfilling his job description.

"Your success in doing so doubtless continued to justify your existence in the eyes of the Order as a useful tool against such broader threats. However, your actions in achieving this end left Oda Ajaja's position somewhat compromised. She performed a spell; a harmless enough piece of magic, I believe, a cantrip, nothing more, using a pre-prepared spectral trap that you had created. She didn't think, she didn't plan, she merely acted on the spur of the moment, saving, I have little doubt, both your and her lives in the process. She was then injured, rather seriously, in the conflict that ensued between you and Mr Pinner, and having little time available, you were unable to turn back and assist her.

"The physical injuries, for all that they were extensive, were as nothing to the spiritual damnation that Oda has brought upon her own soul. She is a member of the Order; her life has been dedicated to the eradication of magic, upon the theological grounds that it is a sin straight from Satan himself to cast spells and perform miracles as if you were some sort of demigod. And yet this is exactly what she did, that night when Mr Pinner came for you both. She cast a spell. Her soul is, by this logic, damned. Eternity is a very unforgiving time frame – it just takes one sin to merit it, and there's no parole board ready to consider a review at the thousand-year mark.

"And the Order knows all this.

"Holy confession is, perhaps, somewhat less holy when your confessors are armed with guns too. One of their own, one of their best, a woman they had nurtured from her first act, and now corrupted – by you, in fact, Matthew. Injured, weakened and corrupt. She is fallen. They will never trust her again. The best thing, as far as the Order is concerned, is for her to die. They may even have to kill her themselves, but I believe it is more their intention that she should die as she lives – fighting the things she has sworn to destroy, such as yourself – in the curious hope that in such a death, she will find peace. So long, that is, that she does it soon."

Silence, after Sinclair had stopped speaking.

Then Penny's voice, too loud in the hush. "Well, glad I never met psycho-bitch; *shit*."

"Technically, you did," I pointed out. "She was the girl with the gun who you didn't spot standing on top of the stairs when you had a night job cleaning at St Pancras. Not to throw off the joy or anything . . ."

"Psycho-bitch was going to shoot *me*? Why?"

"My dear," sighed Sinclair, "you had, and I mean this in no way at all to question your current commitment or upright spirit, but you had, at the time, by mistake, summoned the death of cities. I'm sure you can see how certain . . . radical solutions . . . came to be considered."

"You mean you thought about shooting . . ."

"But didn't!" I butted in. "Let's focus on the part of the story where we didn't. Besides, all this stuff about Oda is very well and good, but doesn't help us find her or stop whatever it is that's currently wearing her skin like an old hat."

"Have you considered telling the Neon Court about all this?" suggested Sinclair. "If they were aware that their daimyo wasn't killed by the Tribe, and of the risk Oda poses . . ."

"Lady Neon was halfway to London before Minjae San met his maker," I sighed. "This whole dead daimyo business is nothing more than an excuse to make me do her dirty work: all this chosen one crap. Besides, what would I say exactly? 'Hi, you know how you want me to find the guy who popped your daimyo? Well, I kinda got a confession to make . . .'"

"But you didn't kill him."

"I can't imagine Lady Neon seeing it like that. She's already got me going to Heathrow to be impressed by the size of her dragon with this damn bloody treaty business. I'd rather not give her my internal organs on a platter as well."

"Then this war . . ."

"War over a chosen one; therefore a war that is for nothing; therefore a war that is almost certainly being fought for reasons far more bitter, stupid, pig-headed and deep for anyone to own up to it, let alone stop."

"We should inform the Aldermen of all this."

"The Aldermen hate my guts," I sighed.

"You're the Midnight Mayor."

"Yep. And the majority of the Aldermen can't stand it. I got promoted from the outside, a rush job; I'm unstable, we're too dangerous – thank you, but I came to you, Mr Sinclair, precisely because you aren't the Aldermen."

"What about Leslie Dees? Do you trust her?"

I thought about it long and hard. "Less than a snake and more than an Alderman."

"In your own peculiar way, Matthew, that sounded like a 'yes'. Forgive me saying so" – a note of impatience entered Sinclair's voice – "but you are hardly at your fighting fittest right now. While naturally I strive to assist you in such times, my means are more suited to a backseat role than to active involvement with a fight. Obviously you have an invaluable asset in your good apprentice . . ."

"Thank you!" growled Penny.

". . . and your own means are hardly trivial, but in this case, I do believe you may have to seek allies somewhere. Who are you going to turn to?"

I shook my head, shrugged, looked down to where I guessed my feet were. "What would you do?" I asked.

I could practically hear Sinclair ticking the points off on his chubby red fingertips as he spoke. "I would inform Dees at the very least, if not the Aldermen as a mass, regarding all of what you have just told me. I would seek a means to secure a temporary truce between the Tribe and the Court. I would seek clarification on the status of this 'chosen one' from all parties to see whether an amicable diplomatic solution could not be achieved. While doing the above, I would actively seek this individual in order to perhaps use her as a bartering chip in any subsequent negotiations or, as an alternative, to remove her from the conflict zone and hopefully from the equation. I would seek academic guidance on exactly what manner of creature appears to have possessed Oda. I would seek academic guidance on any magics that could . . . perhaps . . . have created the remarkable solar circumstances you describe. I would talk to the Order."

I opened my mouth to say something rude, and he got there first, slipping in under my words before I had a chance to dish out any suitable obscenities.

"The Order," he added smoothly, "will know more about Oda than you do: her habits, life, motives, her actions and deeds. These will all be useful."

"The Order get a prize for hating me more than anyone else in this city, and there's stiff competition at the high levels," I snapped.

"You came to me for help," he pointed out. "As for the rest of my suggestions . . . I suggest you find Oda. I suggest that, after due consideration, you destroy her. I believe that covers an initial plan of action."

Silence again. I heard the swishing of fans in the ceiling, and smelt cheese. Then Penny said, "I've got a question."

"My dear?"

"What kind of 'academic guidance'?"

"Ah – you do raise a thorny point. Alas, Mr Bakker's elimination of a large part of the magical community of London has led to a bit of a dearth of appropriate information, although, of course, alternative sources still exist."

"You just said you don't know, right?"

"If you analyse my words in detail," chided Sinclair, "I think you'll find that what I said was I do know, but I don't think anyone in this room will enjoy the answer. But I really do feel this is a conversation best shared with Ms Dees. After all, sooner or later, Matthew, you are going to have to trust someone, aren't you?"

Phonecalls were made.

By the sound of it, they were made to a lot of different people, by Charlie, Sinclair, and Penny.

Someone found me a nice padded bench to curl up on.

I lay, hands tucked underneath my head, knees folded up to my chin, and dozed, and half listened.

Sinclair's voice: "I understand your concerns, Ms Dees, but he really is very convincing and . . . yes, I am aware of that particular issue, but in this case there may be . . . yes . . . yes . . ."

Charlie's voice; "When I say 'can' we get some people looking into this, what I really mean is 'now' get some people looking into this, all right?"

Penny, always unmistakable, reliable, freaked-out Penny, always trying so hard to sound calm, as she talked to her aunt: "Yeah . . . no, listen, yeah . . . yeah look, if you like . . . no, I know I took your car but I had to, like . . . yeah . . . I'll pick some up on the way back, look, you gonna listen to me or what? It might be kinda like . . . worth going out of the city for a bit. What do you mean 'where?' I don't fucking know do I, just go visit a mate or someone – what about that woman who always sends you those fuc . . . those Christmas cards with the pictures of her kids and the whole kinda 'little Tiddles is four now and has started learning recorder' kinda shit? No, look, I just kinda figure it'd be cool to get out of town for a bit, you know?"

". . . obviously the issue is a sensitive one . . ."

"What do you mean 'they're weeping blood'? Jesus weeps blood. The Holy Mary weeps blood. Scryers being paid forty quid an hour to do a simple job don't weep blood! Well then get them chow mein and put it in the microwave or something!"

"I did not nearly swear! I did not! Look, I've got a fuc . . . I mean, I'm like totally on it, you know?"

And after a while, because it had been a long endless night, our thoughts began to drift into the random currents and giddy tides of sleep.

We dreamt of the lights going out.
We dreamt of footsteps in the dark.
Of lilac eyes and fingers drooping down from white silk sleeves.
Of fire on our back and blood on our lips.
Of endless falling rain.

And woke to the sound of "Well, Mr Mayor, isn't this a mess?"

There was a crick in my neck, and one of my feet had gone to sleep. A hand touched my shoulder. "It's Dees," she added.

"I guessed," I groaned, rolling one cautious limb at a time upwards. My eyes felt dry and itchy, but no longer two times too large for their sockets. Static flickered across my vision as I rose and my head floated momentarily on a hot custard bath. I wondered if this was a good or a bad thing. "Hi, Dees, and before you say anything, I know that it's all a bit of a cock-up and I'm sorry about that."

A sigh as she sat down next to me. I imagined her folding her legs and adopting the clasped hands of a woman trying to be patient in the face of the irredeemably naive. "Mr Sinclair was kind enough to fill me in on some of the details – Mr Mayor, why didn't you come to me sooner?"

"Didn't have enough information."

"We could have helped . . ."

"We or you?"

"The Aldermen are dedicated to the protection of the city . . ."

"And I quote: 'It is not worth risking a war with the Neon Court over one life; these are the political realities we deal with.'"

"We would never betray one of our own . . ."

"And are we one of your own, Ms Dees? Really? When we were first introduced to the Aldermen, as I remember it, a large percentage were all in favour of killing us. After all, the Midnight Mayor, the power and the name, lives on, even if the last poor bastard lumbered with the title is dead."

"I can understand your concerns," she began carefully, "but in this case could you not have risked a certain . . . ?"

"I had no information! Since I last saw you, I've been dragged to Heathrow and back, met a dragon, had a chat with Lady Neon, been concussed out of my own scrying spell, found two corpses with their eyes burnt out in a hotel, been chased by a moving darkness, chatted to a seer and had the crap kicked out of me by a psycho-nutter whose very gaze turns your brain to chicken food! And only at the end of all of this do I have even the beginnings of an inkling of what might, just might, be going on, and that a vague one."

I heard Dees letting out a long, slow breath. "All right," she murmured. "Very well. The situation is not yet irredeemable. We need to find this 'chosen one', whoever she is, and resolve this conflict before it can escalate . . ."

"Not to mention dealing with bloody Oda and the sun not bloody coming up!" I wailed, throwing my hands up in despair. "Let's not forget that little snag."

"Do you have any idea what manner of creature it is that could have caused this? The sun failing to rise, even if the sun is failing to rise . . ."

"Bollocks!" I shouted.

Dees waited, then went on as calm as ever, ". . . the power required to cause such an event of . . . of such magnitude must be immense. To not only elongate time, if that is indeed what is happening, but to enchant an entire city to be unaware of its own predicament, save for, with all due respect, one somewhat . . . harried . . . man? Have you ever considered, Mr Mayor – and please try very hard not to shout when I suggest this – but have you ever considered the dangers to your own . . . mental well-being . . . that some of the circumstances of your life may have created?"

"You're right," I growled. "I am trying very, very hard not to shout and it's a fine balance right now."

"Your appointment as the Midnight Mayor, your dealings with Robert Bakker, your resurrection with another consciousness sharing your own, your death . . . ?"

"I want you to think very hard about the next sentence, Dees, because if the words 'post-traumatic stress' are involved in it I might just start hyperventilating."

"And that in and of itself doesn't concern you?"

"Catch twenty-two! I've either got post-traumatic stress and admit it, or I haven't and am therefore concealing it because of how traumatised I am!" My voice was rising again. "Dees," I said, as slow and calm as I dared, "if I was anyone else, anyone at all, who had this brand on my hand, the mark of the Midnight Mayor, and I came to you and told you that the lights were going out, the sun wasn't rising and whole swaths of the city were turning to blackout, would you doubt me?"

She was silent so long I half imagined she'd left, and forced myself to sit still and patient at what I hoped was her side while she considered this. Then somewhere in the darkness, she said, "No. No, I wouldn't."

"Well then. Let's reach a compromise, you and I. I'll try very, very hard not to stress out, screw things up or generally be an arse, and you listen to me. Deal?"

"Yes. Deal."

"Fantastic. Now, screwy as this Tribe–Court bollocks is, I'm more worried about the walking blackout that seems to go wherever Oda goes and the whole eternal night stuff. Do you reckon we could maybe get someone onto that?"

"We need more information," replied Dees, her voice the hollow thing of a mind working some distance away from the words it made. "Perhaps something similar has happened before?"

"That'd be worth knowing – especially if it came with a tag line on how to stop it."

"I can make some enquiries . . ."

"Beautiful."

"But we really do need to resolve this Court–Tribe matter before it escalates any further . . ."

"Lady Neon gave me twenty-four hours to sort it out, deal with this chosen one bollocks."

"Twenty-four hours . . . since when?"

"You know, I'm really not sure any more. Sorry! But time's got a bit muddled."

"So . . . they could already be at war?"

"I've been busy!"

Even Dees couldn't quite prevent the hiss of frustration escaping her lips. "I'll have our ambassador at the Neon Court ask for an extension of the peace, but we have no such institution with the Tribe, no means of contact . . ."

"Sure we have means of contact," I sighed. "It's just not a very fun means of contact."

"You are proposing . . . ?"

"We ask Fat Rat."

"You see, Mr Mayor, it's exactly statements like that which cause me concern."

"Oh, come on," I exclaimed with forced merriment. "Fat Rat's not that bad. And he goes everywhere and the Tribe practically worship him."

"And how exactly do you suppose the Tribe will react to an overture from us, I mean from you, as Midnight Mayor?"

"I imagine . . . radically."

"I cannot condone this plan, if we're going to glorify it even as that."

"Come up with something better before I get my sight back, and I'll be all eyes," I replied, fumbling my way along the length of the couch for space to lie back down again. "Until then, good luck with that whole war business."

Dees seethed with frustration, but said nothing more.

I lay on a couch in a wine cellar in St James's, and thought about the Tribe.

Up to now, I hadn't given it much consideration, largely on the basis that it hadn't given me any grief, so why bother? The Tribe, as far as I knew, had no reason to come after me, nor me after it, unless the Neon Court got us involved. Sure, I didn't like the bastards; but that was about the extent of my relationship with them.

The Tribe.

Bunch of self-mutilating wankers, caught up in a war with a bunch of all-purpose wankers.

Once upon a time, there had been hundreds of smaller tribes, made up of the various outcasts of the city. Back in the day when you got burnt for your belief, the tribes had been the dissenters, the witches, the criminals and the heretics. They made their lairs in the leper colonies and filled their ranks with the plague carriers whose skin was still burst black with disease but whose bodies would not die for all of this. When times had changed so they had changed again, and their ranks had been filled with the necromancers and the dabblers in profane arts, the ones who wouldn't hide behind gentility or pretend to the rest of the world that they were anything but what they were, but rather flaunted their disregard for the sanctity of humanity, such as it was, and cast dark magics in the quiet places of the night.

But times had changed again, and by the early 1960s the tribes were fracturing into more definitive shapes, and from them you acquired fully formed clans such as the Whites, the Bikers, the deep downers, the warlocks, mercenary magicians for hire and tattooed men and women who found magic in skin. The entity left over was made up of the men and women that no one else really wanted and so they, the last fragment of the tribes, became just the Tribe, a collective that needed no other name, a place for the ones who wanted nothing of society's norms or demands, a shelter for those determined to be alone.

The cruder among the magicians of the city called them the orcs, semi-savage beasts with no place in civilised society, the ones who would eat the flesh of other men, the ones who found honour in ugliness and pride in pain. The sociologists who were lucky enough to live long enough to study the Tribe concluded that this was a misnomer. The members of the Tribe were human, in as much as their base physiology was concerned, but had acquired through the self-infliction of wounds, pains, scars and disfigurement a quality of violent and potent magic that evaded their more mundane human counterparts. Not for them the mainstream trappings of urban spells and urban sorceries, which drew their magics from the world around; theirs was a power that came from them and them alone, a defiant, potent mixture of pain, blood and fury that had no regard for the laws of other men, or indeed, for other men in any form at all.

How the Tribe had come to be on the brink of perpetual war with the Court was a matter of only limited interest; how they'd managed not to go to war with everyone else was more of a curiosity. They were not without their rules, their honour or their gods. Where the Neon Court viewed Lady Neon with an almost divine adoration, the Tribe paid quiet tribute to the gods of the underworld, to Fat Rat, and the One-Armed Angel who tended the graves of the unknown buried in the public cemeteries.

There was a smell of coffee. I said, "Penny, if it's you, and if it's coffee, I'll kiss you."

"You should be so fucking lucky," she replied. A hand found mine, pushed a hot mug between my fingers. "For all you know I've got a bloke anyway."

"Have you?"

"No – but that's entirely my choice! Way too busy to be pissing around with some toy boy."

I slurped coffee, rich and thick and slightly grainy towards the bottom, and tactfully said nothing.

"So," she said finally, "I guess there's kinda a lot of people round here went through the whole 'let's kill Penny' business."

"Yeah. I guess there sorta are. But they're over it now that they've met you and discovered how charming you are."

"I seriously screwed things up for you, didn't I?"

"Hey – you saved my neck."

"I mean . . . you know . . . back when I wasn't being trained proper and you had this whole 'oh shit, death of cities' bollocks crap to sort. Seriously screwed, right?"

"Well . . . yeah. It wasn't a great start to your sorcerous career, but I'm thrilled to say I think we're past the point where you accidentally summon shit like that, right?"

"Right." Another silence. "So . . . did you think about having me . . . you know . . . popped?"

"Nope," I lied, solid as a brick wall.

"You were always like, 'hey, let's try and break this spell without killing the caster', right?"

"Yep."

"But you're willing to kill this Oda psycho-bitch?"

"I'm hoping it won't come to that."

"Why?"

"I owe her a few. I hate her and she hates me, that's kinda in the job description, but she's done me a few good turns and I've done the same."

"I mean – why didn't you join the 'let's kill Penny' society when the membership was going cheap?"

I thought about it. "I guess I have an affinity for screw-ups," I said at last. "I mean, so many people have gone around deciding without ever bothering to have a chat with me that I'm worth killing on the off chance, I figure, why join the club?"

Silence. Then, "How's your eyes?"

"A bit better. How are you?"

"Fine. You know." A long release of breath at my side. "Just fine."

"Hey – you know it's going to be OK, right? I mean, for every wandering nasty darkness out there there's usually something shiny standing on the other side of the street having a kebab, right?"

"And you're it?"

"What?"

"You're the shiny thing having a kebab?"

"I was thinking more theologically . . . or maybe philosophically . . . anyway, point is, there's enough dudes who are keen on the sun coming up that odds are, it'll happen."

Penny shuffled uneasily beside me. "You believe in God?" she asked.

"Nope. Why? Do you?"

"Sort of. I mean . . . I did the church thing as a kid, but it wasn't really my thing. But you know, with all this magic and crap, I'm kinda like . . . there's stuff there that I can't get a cool answer for, and stuff out there that's like . . . you know . . . kinda not meant to be understood and maybe there's . . . something we gotta accept, just something bigger than we understand and maybe it's . . . in a kinda non-beardy-guy kinda way . . . God. See?"

"I see."

"If you're laughing at me . . ."

"I'm not. Honest. I'm not."

"You never get that 'what's it all about?' thing"

"I'm very good at not thinking about it."

"So no God, huh?" she asked dourly.

"We . . . find it hard to conceive of . . . of a *consciousness* whose power, intellect and capacity can be both infinite, and capable of caring," we replied. "We find it hard to accept that there is an unknown thing set above us, to judge us, that we cannot judge in return. Such a concept is, it would appear to us, injustice incarnate, not redemption at all."

"Guess you've thought about it a bit then," sighed Penny. "Which is cool too, you know?"

I felt the steam from the coffee tickle the inside of my nose. "Penny," I began, "I heard you talking to your aunt. About going away for a bit? It might be . . . there might be something in maybe getting out while there's . . . I mean, I'm grateful for the rescue and everything, and you really can look after yourself, but . . . there's no reason for you to end up in a state like me."

"Hey – I figured you might say something like that, you know?"

"Really?"

"Yep. And I've got my answer all worked out."

"It isn't 'fuck it' by any chance?" I asked weakly.

"Hey – not a total dumbo, are you?"

"Penny . . ." I began.

"Uh-uh! You know you're gonna lose this fight, so the only reason that you're trying to have it with me is so you can feel all good about yourself afterwards. So you know what, just shove it and fuck it and I'm staying, cool?"

I gave in, as was always going to happen. "Cool."

"And you're welcome, by the way, for my totally awesome, utterly kick-ass rescuing of your kicked ass."

"Cheers. Although," I added before she could interrupt, "there is one good reason to consider a trip out of the city."

"Uh-huh?" Her voice dripped cynicism.

"To see how far this endless night has gone. I mean, without wanting to wax metamagical on you, are we dealing with an entire world plunged into darkness, or just the city? Is there some sort of barrier after which time resumes in its own quaint way, in which case where? Or are we shut off from the world, no in, no out, just a perpetual repeated night while the universe turns around us, London as a concept and a place forgotten? It's the kind of question that'd tell us whether we're dealing with merely a minor disaster or a serious Armageddon-gods-upon-the-earth catastrophe."

"You sound like a guy with suspicions," mused Penny. "You got an opinion?"

"It's not my field. I've never seen anything like it. But I'm hoping it's just a localised stitch in the universe, a blister of magic, rather than the world as we know it turned tits-up."

"You realise that means it's your problem, and yours alone, right? I mean, if all of London is trapped in darkness, and you're the protector of London . . ."

"Yeah. Figured that part."

"You OK with that?"

"Kinda lumbered with it, whatever happens."

"You know," she added with a thoughtful lilt in her voice, "for all you're the Midnight Mayor, I haven't really seen you do anything . . . you know . . . totally shit-your-pants awesome."

"You should see my pet dragon," I replied coyly.

"Seriously?"

"Oh yeah."

"So . . . why'd you not summon this pet dragon when Oda was like, using you as a piece of loo paper?"

"It's complicated."

"That's your answer for everything you can't answer properly," she sighed. "Some mystic fucking protector you are. Hey – you don't . . . you know . . . *like* her, do you?"

"No," I sighed. "I don't *like* her. There's not much there to like . . ."

"But?" sprang in Penny like a cat onto a ball of string.

"But . . . she asked for my help. She asked and I said 'sure' and she said 'kill me' and I said no and now there's something in her eyes and a hole in her heart and . . . and it's my fault that she cast that bloody bollocks bloody spell and all she's got is the whole psycho hating-magic bollocks and then she cast a spell and . . . anyway. I did that. I'm not going to cry myself to sleep at night about it, but there it is. It happened. Whoops." I heard footsteps approaching and nudged Penny. "Who is it?"

"Dees," she replied without bothering to lower her voice. Then, not to me, "Hi."

"Mr Mayor," Dees answered without bothering to stop for good manners, "we have to go now."

"Go where?"

"The British Library."

"Why?" I asked as Penny took the coffee cup from my hands and helped me up. "What's there?"

"Academic answers."

"Seriously?" asked Penny. "About magic and shit?"

"The British Library," replied Dees primly, "*is* a repository of learning and culture."

"Yeah . . . but . . ."

"Appointments can sometimes be necessary," Dees conceded. "I have a car waiting."

The car smelt of leather. Penny and I piled into the back seats, Dees into the front. I heard Sinclair's voice, muffled through the window outside, though couldn't make out the words. He didn't bother to say goodbye. Dees spoke to a silent creature in the driving seat: "British Library, goods entrance, please."

Penny leant over and whispered to me, "The driver's wearing a hat."

"Try not to let it freak you out," I replied, fumbling numbly for my seat belt. "How's the day looking?"

"Still night," admitted Penny, a note of worry entering her voice. "But that's cool, you know, I mean . . . it can still be night for a while longer, without you being right, right?"

"Right. Just let me know when it becomes wrong. How long have I been wearing these bloody bandage things?"

"Few hours."

"How long till I can . . . ?"

"Few hours."

"Thanks," I sighed. "Didn't Dr Seah give us a prescription information leaflet or something?"

"Yeah, but I never bother reading that shit. It'll only be full of side effects and stuff."

"I think," I began cautiously, "I *think* that might be the . . ."

A mobile phone rang. I fumbled at my pocket instinctively, but it wasn't mine. I heard the snap of plastic being flicked up and Dees' quiet voice in the front. "Dees," she barked, every bit the busy independent financial adviser in the middle of a meeting. "Yes. When? How many? I see."

She talked for less than a minute, voice darkening with every word. When done, I heard the phone snap shut. Leather creaked as she adjusted her position. "The Neon Court has informed our ambassador that a Tribe warband just attacked one of their clubs in Brixton, injuring seven people including five civilians and causing structural damage."

"They got proof?" I groaned, letting my head roll back over the seat.

"I don't believe they'd risk making such an inflammatory accusation without it, forged or otherwise. They are demanding an immediate response from the Aldermen and Midnight Mayor regarding our position and the treaty."

"Terrific. I'm hoping they don't know I can't see right now?"

"I haven't passed on that information, no."

"Good. That's something. Can we buy any more time?"

"Perhaps a few more hours, but that will be it. If we fail to commit . . ."

"It'll get pissy?" I asked. "Yeah. Fine. Buy us whatever time you can; let's see if we can't get something on this whole Oda crap sorted before, say, going to war with two of the biggest lots of wankers in the city."

I heard the little beep of Dees dialling. Then, "Hi, it's me again. Yes. Yes, that's exactly what I'd like you to do. Then tell them he's busy! Tell them that they're little people in a big city, be as rude as you want to be, they still want us on their side, make it clear we couldn't care either . . . yes, I know we do, but they don't need to be reminded of that . . . well then get it sorted! No, I can't right now. No, I won't. No, don't try. Thank you. Yes – thank you."

She hung up. "A few hours," she said. "That's all I can get you."

"Why did the Tribe do it?" asked Penny suddenly from the darkness. "I mean, if they did it, why'd the Tribe attack like this? They gotta know it'll mean war?"

"Perhaps they don't care," suggested Dees coldly. "The Tribe are hardly renowned for their sturdy intellectual reasoning."

"Yeah, but if the Tribe have been at peace with the Court for years, then why all this crap now?"

"Chosen ones," I groaned. "I didn't get a straight answer from O'Rourke, but he told the Court that there was a chosen one, and I guess it'd be fair to assume that the information has made its way into the hands of the Tribe too. If both sides believed it . . ." My voice trailed off. "Oh crap," I muttered. "If both sides believe it, and both sides think that the other side has got their mitts on this 'chosen one' girl, then there'd be nothing to stop them from going sodding nuclear. I mean, that's basically the point, isn't it? Chosen one who can destroy one or the other side, might as well go out fighting rather than just wait for it to happen, might as well go apeshit all out now, consequences be damned. If I had bloody O'Rourke right here, right now . . ."

"We can collect him," suggested Dees doubtfully. "If Oda is gone."

"Might be worth doing."

"I'll make some calls," she replied, and went back to her mobile phone.

The British Library sat like a swollen red-brick portaloo next to St Pancras station on the Euston Road, defiantly as square, unsympathetic and lumpen a bit of architecture as had ever shortened the horizon. That, at least, was how I remembered it. Some attempt at disguise had been made: the bricks were the same colour, if cleaner and newer, as the Gothic palace that was the station next door and, on the inside at least, the British Library managed to maintain a surprisingly airy, open atmosphere for an institution containing what looked like enough books to have pulped the Amazon forests. Two thousand miles of shelving had been bought during the building's initial construction and then, British building being what it was, two thousand miles of shelving had promptly rusted as the roof wasn't put on in time. But such experiences were, it was hoped, in the past, and now the library ran on a smooth computerised system of vaults and sub-levels and ordering slips and reading rooms and would, so the hope went, last until the end of civilisation, as a repository of learning for all.

It was raining when we pulled up at the back entrance, but the walk from the car to the door was only enough to acknowledge this fact, rather than get seriously wet. Smooth concrete underfoot and the smell of oil quickly became tile and the smell of cold, processed air. A voice said, "May I take your bags, please?" I felt a hand fall on the bag on my shoulder. "There's no food or drink allowed in the reading room, sir," went on the voice, tinted with an Indian accent, "only pencil for notes, although we do have laptop power points, and please, no casting of any magics which might damage the documents."

I heard the low murmur of "Jesus. You guys really do have a bloody magical department?"

"Indeed," came the smooth reply, "but only by appointment, and I'm afraid we keep most of the relevant archives in Basingstoke."

"Why Basingstoke?" Penny asked. "I mean, it's like every fucker goes, 'Hey, what's Basingstoke good for? I know! Long-term fucking storage!'"

We were led down an increasingly sloping ramp and through ever colder air to a door that opened with a long, slow hiss. From that was a flight of wide tiled stairs, and a handrail that gave an electric shock at the first touch. The air grew colder still, goosebumps rising on my arms.

When we finally stopped, our guide said, "Now, the archivist is expecting you, but I would be grateful if you'd observe a few common courtesies. This is somewhat unorthodox even for this department . . ."

"Best behaviour," promised Penny.

"We understand entirely," added Dees, "and may I say, on behalf of the Aldermen, that we will be renewing our annual donations package towards this institution."

A door was opened. We went inside. The door closed.

The room smelt of paper, that thick, dry, warm smell of a million million species of microscopic insect and dust mite breeding busily between crispy layers of ink and leather. I could hear a constant gentle hissing in the background, as of wheels on a railway track heard far off; then I heard the little intake of breath from Penny, too sharp and quick for her to hide, and whispered, "Where are we?"

"Um . . . it's ah . . . it's a . . . um . . ."

A voice, ringing with authority and excellent vowels, burst out of the darkness: "Are you the midnight appointment?"

Penny's fingers tightened around my arm a little too hard. "Matthew," she whispered, "I'm freaked again."

"Yes, that's us," came Dees' calm reply, "thank you so much for agreeing to see us . . ."

"You know this is very unorthodox," snapped the female voice, which I could only guess belonged to the archivist. "I was supposed to be attending a lecture on the naval policy of the Ottoman Sultanate from Lepanto to Tzitva-Torok; this is all highly disruptive and of far too late a notice for me to give away my ticket. They tell me that it's important but . . ."

"It's very, very important," said Dees. "And naturally we had to come to an expert for guidance . . ."

"Well, I suppose if you needed an expert," came the huffy reply. "The phone call said something about darknesses and destruction."

"Yes, exactly, yes . . ."

"Not exactly, no!" exclaimed the archivist. "If you put 'darkness' and 'destruction' into the library search engine, even within just this department, do you know how many hits you get?"

"Um . . .?"

"Twenty-one thousand three hundred and forty-three! Even if you put in 'darkness' and 'destruction' and 'damnation' you're still returning over fifteen thousand hits – you have to be specific, do you see? Knowing exactly what you're looking for even when you don't know what it is is the key to academic success!"

"If I may . . ." Dees came in, ". . . now we're here, perhaps we could refine our enquiry?"

"Well do, do!"

"In that case . . . we're looking for any information that might allow us to relate any of the following: a chosen one, a case of possession whose symptoms manifest in bleeding eyes followed by blindness and brain death; also, the lights going out across the city, and the sun failing to rise."

"I'm not even going to bother with this 'chosen one' business," was the prim reply. "Find me an appropriate footnote to reference and perhaps we can look into it, but otherwise it'll only stall the system. What were the others? Sun failing to rise I can probably get you something on, and as for possession . . . very tricky to narrow down without some more specifics. Would you like to come with me, Ms . . .?"

"Dees. Leslie Dees."

"And your friends . . .?"

"This is Ms Ngwenya, apprentice sorceress, and her teacher, Mr Swift, sorcerer."

"Hi," said Penny weakly.

"Hi," I added feebly.

"Yes yes yes," sighed the archivist. "Ms Dees . . . ?"

I heard footsteps on tile, fading into the distance.

I hissed at Penny, "You're hurting my arm!"

"Sorry." Her fingers relaxed a little.

"Now will you tell me what the hell is going on?" I whispered.

"Um . . . well, we're in this library thing . . ."

"I got that much."

"Yeah, but it's like a fucking *huge* fucking library. There's these walls made of glass, right, and there's books behind them on all the shelves, right, but there's also these lifts right, inside the glass? Like those waiter lifts you see in those old films? Only they're carrying books and there's hundreds of them, I mean like *hundreds* of them, all the time, carrying books and bits of paper and folders and boxes and stuff and they're moving around us, up and down, I can't see where they go or where they come from, but they don't look like they're ever going to stop. And there's this desk in the middle of the room with an old PC on it and this archivist lady who's . . . like . . . totally weird."

"Define 'totally weird'."

"Um . . . well, she's like got straight grey hair in a bob, and these eyes the size of tennis balls . . ."

"You being metaphorical?"

"Nope. These huge grey eyes in this kinda old stretchy grey face, and she's wearing these big round reading glasses that are like something NASA might've made and she's got this cream-coloured shirt with like the frills on the collar and sleeves and little sensible green shoes and ankles like sticks and six fingers on each hand, only her fingers aren't grey, they're black. Like they're stained with ink, you see? And you can like see the veins on her neck because she's old and they stand out, and you can see the blood moving in them, and it's like . . . black too. Like she's got ink for blood or something. I don't think she likes us very much."

"Nonsense!" I said with false cheerfulness. "We've got charm!"

"You haven't," she replied sourly. "You've got bloodstains and dirt."

"Is there anywhere to sit?"

"Um . . . no."

"Anything to drink?"

"No."

"Anything to eat?"

"Still no."

I scowled. "Right. If I just lie down and nap for a minute on this floor, do you suppose it'll undermine my gravitas and dignity?"

"Your what?"

"My gravitas and . . ."

"I heard what you said," she replied.

"Some apprentice," I scowled, and engineered myself down onto the floor. It was cold beneath my fingers, and cold through my clothes, but my bones were weary and enough of me was bruised and burnt that the cold was something of a relief. I stretched out on my back, hands folded across my belly, head turned upwards, and contemplated nothing.

After a while Penny's voice, far overhead, said, "So . . . I'll just stand here, right?"

"You could take this opportunity to ponder the great mystical wealth of knowledge that is all around you."

"Why don't you ponder it for me?"

"Don't need to," I replied. "I'm the qualified sorcerer, you're the apprentice."

"God, I can't wait to graduate," she groaned. "Hey – there a time period on that, by the by?"

"Usually there'll come a point when it's pretty damn obvious that there's nothing left for me to tell you, at which there's a fine and noble tradition of the apprentice buying the teacher a Chinese takeaway and a bottle of champagne."

"You're making that bit up."

"Traditions have to begin somewhere. I mean, don't let your imagination be limited just to a Chinese takeaway . . ."

"I'm not listening to you any more."

"Well, that's all part of the learning experience too, I guess . . ."

There was a movement beside me. It took a while to work out that it was the sound of Penny lying down. Silence. Then, "You should see the ceiling."

"Should I?"

"Oh yeah. They've gone and painted it up, words, thousands and thousands of words all across the ceiling."

"What do they say?"

"Nothing. I mean, everything . . . but nothing that has a meaning if you try to string it together."

"Sounds suspiciously like art to me," I said.

"It's not. It's alive."

"What?"

"The words; they're alive. It's a sky made out of words, big and bright and brilliant and alive."

"We're talking metaphorically?"

"Uh-uh. Magic and shit, innit?"

I let out a breath that, for once, wasn't a sigh. "Yeah," I said. "Magic and shit."

We lay still for a very long time.

I felt the dusty drifting of my eyes, the slow warmth of sleep beginning to creep through me. How long since I'd slept properly? Not since the fire in the tower block; not even properly then, just a disturbed doze on the floor at the foot of Oda's bed. She'd said "kill me" and she'd said "save me" and we'd chosen the wrong option for the right reasons. Catch us doing that again.

I must have been on the edge of sleep, because when Penny hissed "Mind," her finger prodding my side, I jerked awake like I'd been stung by a bee. "They're coming back."

I didn't bother to move, but waited until the two sets of footsteps that I guessed had to be the archivist's and Dees' grew loud and stopped. "Hi," I said in the calm. "Anything shiny?"

There was a long, embarrassed silence. Then Dees said, "The sun not coming up – you're absolutely sure about that part?"

"Yep."

Another long silence. Then, "You're not going to like this."

"Wow, because I was expecting good news," I sighed.

"There's a passage in the prophetic works of Alfred Khan . . ."

"Hit me."

"It goes . . ." I heard the unfolding of paper. Dees cleared her throat self-consciously and began to read in the wrong accent and with the wrong inflection, "'So yeah dude there'll be like this major shit you know what I'm saying man and it'll be like the sun is totally not rising 'cause that'll be what's fucking happening you know and shit that's some strong stuff so yeah the sun not rising because the girl with the bleeding eyes is walking the earth but yo! Man! No sweat right 'cause it has happened before you get where I'm coming from and it'll happen again and you just gotta ask the dust. Dust to dust dude. Breathe deep if you wanna see that heaven burn again. I gotta get me a paracetamol, shit.'" The paper was duly folded up again. Silence.

Then Penny said, "That's a prophecy?"

"Alfred Khan," replied Dees, "was one of the most gifted seers of our age."

"And stoned," I added, raising one limp instructive hand. "Let's not forget that part. Well, I don't know about everyone else, but I feel hugely informed."

"There is more . . ." began Dees uneasily. "A footnote to Khan's prophecy."

"I'm all ears."

"It says 'see Bakker, R., 89183, shelf B18; also Blackout, 21631'."

"Meaning?"

The archivist's voice came in, high and sharp. "It's a reference to two different sources. The first is . . . a special archive . . . the second is a document which I have already ordered and should be on its way as we speak from lower storage."

"What do you mean 'special archive'?" I asked, voice dripping suspicion.

"Mr Mayor, do you really feel that this is a conversation to be carried out while you're lying on the floor?" asked Dees.

"Yep. This is where I'm most comfortable, therefore most easily able to think, therefore where I intend to be," I replied with the relentless merriment of the drunkard at the wake. "What special archive?"

"The British Library recently received sponsorship to open up an archive of . . . of extra-media storage material . . ."

"Meaning?"

"Meaning . . ." There was a knock on the door. Dees couldn't keep the relief out of her voice. "To be continued!"

I sat up grumpily, reached out for Penny's arm, hauled myself up by her support. "Why does no one tell me what's going on?" I barked at the stretching pause. "Come on!"

"A moment, Mr Mayor, a moment please," sang out Dees nervously from the door. I heard the low murmur of archivist and Alderman in conversation, punctuated by the occasional louder hiss of "That's entirely an interpretation . . ."

"You regret not going to university and stuff?" I asked Penny quietly as the two argued in a corner.

She thought about it. Then, "Dunno. Kinda like asking if I'm sorry I wasn't born a bloke. Having never had a willy, I can't exactly say if I miss one. Although, thinking about it, that's probably not kinda the same, since it's obvious that having a . . ."

"And already I'm regretting asking," I sighed. Then raising my voice, "Dees! Quit gabbling in a corner and tell me what the hell is happening!"

A lull. Then footsteps approaching. A polite cough. "Um . . . Mr Mayor. We need a little more time . . ."

"What have you found?"

"There are some items which might suggest . . . might suggest that this business with Oda is indeed more serious than perhaps an initial assessment . . ."

"How serious?"

"Serious enough, Mr Mayor, that we would wish to make no mistakes in handling it."

"In other words you're not going to tell me."

"Not yet, Mr Mayor, not yet . . ."

"Right! Penny?"

"Yes?" come the worried voice by my left shoulder.

"Help me out of this place, will you?"

"Um . . . sure. Where we going?"

"Just a little walk."

"Mr Mayor," began Dees uneasily as Penny guided me towards the door, "I hardly think this is a good time for you to be going off on . . ."

"Just a little walk," I replied. "No more, no less! I'll be back before you can say 'whoops where's the sun gone?' OK? Good! Bye!"

I stormed out as quickly as I dared, Penny guiding me as we went.

Dees made no attempt to follow.

Some few minutes later, we stood in the rain.

It was thickening, a proper London-night downfall, tumbling water trying to see if it could dent the pavement.

Penny said, "You know, I don't like Dees much either, but she may have a point . . ." I fumbled for the bandages around my eyes. "Hey hey hey! Whatcha doing?"

"Seeing if I can see," I replied.

Her hand fell on mine, pulling it back. "Hey," she declared, "Dr Seah said to give it five to six hours."

"Hasn't it been five to six hours?"

"Getting there, but you really want to risk getting it wrong?"

"I need to see!" I shouted at the sky and the darkness. "Enough already of this silly-buggers crap, I need to see!"

"Sure, you'll be able to do the mystic protector crap better if you're permanently squinting!"

"We will not be trapped in a cripple's flesh!" we snarled, snatching our hand free of hers and turning away. Before she could speak, we grabbed the bandages around our eyes and pulled them with more than just human strength, the fabric tearing with a long pained sound. We pulled cotton wool free from our eyes and found, as the pressure relaxed, that we hesitated. I rolled the torn bandage up around the cotton pads, and, taking it a glimpse at a time, opened first one, then the other eye.

The world outside was so bright it hurt: a hot sharpness burnt straight through to the back of the eyeball. At first we couldn't look, had to turn our face away and try looking with just one, then the other eye, as slowly our crude mortal organs adjusted to the light. It was nothing, this light: the bright pinkish glow of a street lamp, and yet it burnt. When at last we could risk opening both our eyes at once, we turned our head up towards the light and its edges were distorted, the features of it oddly blurred. I pressed my palms over my eyes a few times, then took them away.

"You OK?" asked Penny nervously.

I half-turned to look at her. Skin the colour of water-soaked dark wood, eyes slightly too small in proportion to her ears. Today her black frizzy hair was being worn like a lion's mane, a vast halo of crinkly dull darkness sticking up from every possible angle as if, freed from its traditional tightly bound style, it had overreacted to the wonders of the universe. She wore a bright silver plastic-leather jacket, a green T-shirt that hung loosely around her shoulders, a pair of too-tight blue jeans, and tight high-heeled black boots that stopped just below the knee and were the nightmare of every street maintenance officer in every local council in the city. We said, "You are beautiful."

She said, "Well, *duh*." Then, "You seeing OK?"

"My eyes hurt, my head hurts – actually, let's skip the inventory and just say I hurt – and you're kinda fuzzy round the edges, but yeah. I can see OK."

"You look kinda boiled, you know?"

"Cheers."

I peered in closer, studying every part of her face.

"Hey – getting pervy here," she mumbled, drawing back.

I looked at her eyes, brown ovals set either side of an impressive nose. I said, "You crying?"

"Fuck no!"

"But there's . . ." My voice trailed away. "Penny?" I whimpered. "Penny, you sure you're OK?"

"Yeah, I feel fine. What the hell's the matter with you?"

"Your eyes . . . you're um . . . your eyes are bleeding."

"They're what?" she shrieked, rubbing her hands quickly across her eyes. Her hands came away clean, but still as I looked I could see the blood welling up in her tear ducts, running beneath the eyes, pooling, and finally bursting to tumble down her face like water from a cracked gutter.

"It's not, I'm not, look, look at my hands, look!" She held up her hands, that should have been thick with the blood on her face but weren't. I closed my eyes, held my head in my hands.

"Maybe it's one of the side effects," she said. "Maybe you see things, maybe you're stressed, you know, or that thing . . . that post-traumatised thing Dees said . . ."

"We are not insane!" we snarled, briefly opening our eyes again. Her face was clean. No blood on Penny's face, none in her eyes; she was clean. I breathed, "It's gone. The blood is gone."

"Well thank fuck for that."

"This is bad."

"Like I haven't heard that before. Look, why don't we go back inside, have a chat with Dees, get you a holiday or something . . ."

"Uh-uh."

"Hey – every guy deserves a holiday!"

"Court, Tribe, sun," I snapped. "My mess."

"Why yours?"

"Because some tit made it mine and everyone expects me to fix it, and, Penny, saviour of the day as you are, I'm really not happy about the thought of you being the last sorcerer left in London with this shit going down!"

A little silence. She looked almost hurt. Then she grinned, a wide flash of crooked white teeth and the brilliant pink inside her lips. "Hell, that's like the nicest thing you've ever said to me."

"What time is it?"

"Still not sun-up time," she replied. "You've got another few hours before you get to prove to me that you aren't like totally whacked."

"Fair enough. Come on then."

"Where we going?" she asked, as I turned towards the red walls and dirty stones of St Pancras.

"Going to have a chat with the Tribe."

"You sure you're up for that? I mean, if you can't see properly yet, and you're seeing weird shit . . ."

"Nope. But let's not tell anyone, shall we?"

She fell into step beside me. I did my best to walk in a straight line. If she noticed, she didn't say anything. "Where we going?"

"Kebabs," I replied cheerfully. "We are going to need lots and lots of kebabs."

Part 2: The Vanishing of Cockfosters

In which academic advice is sought from an unlikely and unwelcome source, a problem is expounded upon and an encounter ends badly for all concerned.

Time was playing silly buggers.

The doors to St Pancras station stood shut, railings pulled across, though the lights still shone inside. On the odd dusty window, where the builders hadn't finished their work, fingers had traced smiling faces, random doodles, and here and there:

help

or

still waiting for the northern line

The traffic wasn't sure whether to put its foot down for the night run along the clear Euston Road, or to crawl in expectation of congestion at the underpass. Buses were trying to get into the red stop zones on the street, even while bus maintenance crews were attempting to paint new lines onto the same. Taxis crawled round the side of King's Cross. The video arcade was open, and a gaggle of grey-eyed kids were playing shoot-'em-ups in the front window. The newsagent was shut. But the kebab shops of King's Cross never closed.

The shop was too white, and too bright, as if somehow the brightness could disguise the embedded greyness trodden into every tile, or the grease spilling over the stainless-steel surfaces behind the counter. The owner, a man with cashew-nut skin and bloodshot eyes, was asleep behind his till, head rolled back and dribble pooling in the corner of his mouth, a half-open newspaper beside him. The radio was on, blasting out the traffic news.

"Congestion on the Cromwell Road heading west owing to an earlier road accident . . . a power cut in Mile End leading to . . . Cockfosters has vanished . . . an overturned truck on the Blackwall Tunnel Approach . . ."

A stained brown-black lump that bore no resemblance to any animal I'd ever seen alive or on the TV spun slowly on a spit in front of an orange grill. Limp bits of lettuce sat in tubs next to chemical pots of white and red gravy. Penny said, "There's nothing like chips at two in the morning."

"It's not for us," I replied grimly, leaning over the counter towards the sleeping man. A little disappointed sigh drifted from Penny's lips. I said, "Excuse me, mate? Mate?"

Magicians have written whole books on the magical power of the word 'mate'. It wove its spell now. The man's eyes flickered open, he jerked in his chair, nearly fell off it, mumbled something incoherent and finally managed to focus on Penny and me. He rubbed his eyes, as if unable to quite believe what he was seeing, and finally, this ritual done, managed a guttural "Yeah?"

"Hi," I said. "I've got . . ." I fumbled in my pocket. "About twenty-seven quid. Penny, how much are you carrying?"

"You're serious?" she asked.

"Penny!"

She scowled, but patted down her pocket and produced at length a much crumpled tenner. I snatched it from her before she could protest. "OK. I've got thirty-seven quid. Give me everything I can buy."

"You what?" he croaked.

"You what?" echoed Penny.

"See my serious, serious face?" I replied. "Load me up."

Thirty-seven quid bought us five white plastic bags of various hideously tortured, grease-soaked meats in white cardboard buns with limp vegetables. As we trudged back outside and towards the line of bus stops on the north side of the road, Penny said, "This had better be one hell of an awesome thing you're gonna do next, Matthew."

"Nag nag nag."

Buses at King's Cross, even in the middle of the night, were fairly regular, and most had a limited choice of places to go. We caught the 205 to Angel, a seven-minute ride in which the smell of congealed, compressed, liquefied and resolidified meat slowly filled the grey interior of the bus. We got out of the bus beside a low blue-grey iron wall with a blue-grey iron door set in it and a blue-grey iron roof sloping down from behind. There was a padlock on the door, but other than that, no indication as to its purpose. I put my plastic bags of food down and fumbled in my satchel for my wad of keys. I found the one whose make most nearly matched the padlock, slipped it inside, and coerced and cajoled until the metal of the key warped enough to fit the tumblers of the lock; turned it, pulled off the chain, opened the door.

Inside was the low deadened white of fluorescent tubing, on a tiled beige floor. We stepped through, closed the door behind us, locked up. A low brick wall that had once been an exterior to another building, now encased, opened through a wide black maw into a hallway of more fluorescent lighting and dark, intense green tiles on every wall. The odd tracery of its former function was still explicit: the mesh grid of a counter, the bolt holes in the floor where there had been ticket stiles. On the wall was a poster advertising a trip to Ongar – 'You Don't Have to Leave London to Go On Adventures!' A thin coating of grey dust stirred beneath our feet. An opening, lifeless darkness, was the remnants of two lift shafts, the occasional lamps that filled its depths dying from too much time and neglect. I could hear water dripping somewhere near by. Half obscured in the shadows was the remains of a London Underground sign, as proud as a coat of arms, proclaiming across its middle, 'Angel'.

Penny said, "Nice. Sweet. What the fuck are we doing here?"

"So impatient!"

The newest feature of the place was a long line of lockers and, beside them, a metal door leading to another room. I eased it open. A small line of showers stood on fresh white tiles. The pooled water around the plughole was grey-brown from dirt, but the water dripping incontinently from the shower heads was clear. I closed the door again, kicked the various lockers until one of them bounced open. Inside was a picture of a toothless grinning child held in a woman's arms, a copy of the *Daily Mail*, an empty, somewhat greying coffee flask, a pair of knee-high boots, a yellow hard hat with a torch on, and a vivid yellow fluorescent jacket. I pulled out the jacket, threw it to Penny. "Take off anything that you love," I said, "put on this, the hat, the boots."

"We're going down there?" she asked, nodding towards the black hollow of the lift shafts.

"Yep."

"Why?"

"Going to have a chat with the Tribe."

"*Why?*"

"Only thing I can do right now, isn't it? Dees is dealing with Oda, can't do anything about the Court; ergo, talk to the only guys I haven't talked to so far, see if they have anything interesting to say about this chosen one bollocks."

"You could, like, you know, go to bed."

"I think you're missing the point of this whole protector of the city business."

She shrugged. "Seems like a good idea to me is all."

"Besides!" I added, gleefully kicking open another locker and pulling out its yellow jacket, "this is all highly educational."

"Yeah," she sighed, dragging off her boots. "Sure. *That's* what it is."

I left my shoes in the vandalised locker, pulled on the yellow jacket, hard hat and safety boots. There was a spiral staircase, two shoulders wide, dirt and dust on its old stones, the handrail cracked, the lights dull yellow pinpoints in old wire frames. It went down past the point where you imagined down had to end, and then a little bit further. At the bottom it opened onto a wide dark hall, made darker and wider by the odd dusty yellow glow of light from a neglected lamp, from which tunnels with no light at all led away. There were some footprints in the dirt, the rugged large shapes of the same reinforced boots we were wearing. I turned on my headlamp, casting the white light over old bits of graffiti and tattered rotting posters.

FLOP CULTURE MAKES FLOP MIND

WRONG WAY →

NO MOUSE

A bright pinprick of light through a crack in a wall revealed on the other side the grey-white glow of the other Angel station, the real Angel station, the one that every day fed thousands of commuters to and from the Northern Line. I thought I could hear voices, far off, somewhere beyond the thin walls separating it from us. I turned away. We walked down a darkened tunnel with no lights at all in it, the walls lined with bare black metal like a nuclear bunker, until we reached a mesh grid at the far end. It was locked. On the other side I could see the bright silver tops of the rails, brilliant among the dull dirt-crusted blackness of the cables that had once been orange and the walls that had once been clean in the tunnel. Strands of human hair were tangled in the mesh of the gate, and dust billowed thinly in the beam of my headlamp. We sniffed the air, smelt the dry heat of the Underground.

"Live rail's off," murmured Penny in my ear. "I can feel it."

"Handy," I replied, fiddling with the lock on the gate until, with a dry reluctant snap and a puff of red-rust dust, it opened. We stepped out into the tunnel, and turned away from the light of the platform some few hundred yards behind us, towards the dark of the tracks. "Which way we going?" asked Penny, voice hushed in the dead silence of the tunnel.

"South," I replied. "Towards London Bridge."

"Kebabs are cold," she said, hitching up the white plastic bags as we started to walk.

"He'll like them that way."

We walked, footsteps flat in the dark, the only light coming from our head torches, the air warm and dead and still. The skin on the backs of my hands was already turning greyish-black from the dirt on the gate and the dirt in the air; my boots were too big and the hard hat made my scalp prickle with rising sweat. It was some small comfort that the gloom, at least, was easy on my eyes.

The silence grew heavier with every step until at last Penny said lightly, "I heard there was a ghost at Angel station."

"'Ghost' is a magically inexact term," I replied primly. "The question you have to ask yourself is this – is a ghost proof of the existence of the soul after death, and thus, by implication, of heaven, hell, torment, destiny and God? Or is it just an echo, a reflection of a life that went before?"

"Well? Which is it?" she asked.

"Buggered if I know. I choose to think an echo, but there's no proof either way."

"You choose to not believe in the soul's immortality?"

"Oh yeah. Because if the soul is immortal, and there is a destiny, and there is a God, I can't imagine he'll have nice things to say to me."

"You don't do *bad* things," she mumbled. "I mean, you may not believe, but you're not a *bad* kinda bloke. Kinda."

"'Bad' is a bit too . . . inexact . . . for my tastes. God might have a different opinion and then how stuffed am I?"

We walked on again in silence a little while more. Then Penny said, "There are footprints in the dirt."

"Men maintain the tracks down here all the time, when the trains stop. Don't worry; they won't see us."

"Because of our hi-vis jackets?" she asked with only nine-tenths of her usual sarcasm.

"Exactly."

I thought I heard a scuttling in the dark, and chose to ignore it. There were sounds on the air ahead, distant echoes of metal on metal, voices in the dark. Penny said, "I know it's kinda late in the day to ask this, but are there . . . rats . . . down here?"

"Oh yeah."

"And . . . and I'm guessing that we're not carrying all this cold kebab for a slap-up feast with the White Rabbit and the Queen of Hearts, right?"

"Right."

"Shit."

"Penny, if you're going to be an urban sorceress, you're really going to have to learn to deal with rats."

"Sure." Her voice was weak and strained. "Yeah, totally. Me and rats. We're like that."

The sounds ahead were growing louder; a spill of white light came tumbling from round the bend of the track. I stopped on the edge of it, pulled my yellow jacket tighter about me, my helmet down over my eyes. There were black shadows eclipsing the brilliant white light from raised tripod lamps, half seen in the dark, voices stirring the air around the tracks. I said, "OK, the rule is simple. You keep your eyes down and your steps fast. Walk like you know you're supposed to be there. Walk like a sorcerer, the magic will come from the movement, from the hat, the boots, the jacket. This is a simple spell of invisibility. You'll ace it."

"Yeah, jeez, great," sighed Penny. "What if someone spots me anyway?"

"They won't."

"But if they do?"

I hesitated. Then I said, "Stand still." I reached up and touched her face, ran my hand over either cheek, across her forehead and round her chin. Her skin was warm and dry. Where my fingers passed, they left a thick trail of dirt, coal black, almost as thick as paint. "There," I said. "You look quite the tunnel-crawler."

"Yeah," she scowled, "I want a wand and a pointy fucking hat, please."

"Move to Glastonbury. Ready?"

"I guess."

I didn't give her time to change her mind, but picked up my plastic bags, bowed my head, and started to stride. It was the confident, easy stride of the kinda guy that has walked these tunnels a thousand times before, who knows what he's doing and where he's going, who has no fear of anything that might lurk in the dark and, above all, is one of us, one of the boys, face blackened and boots worn. The magic came with the walking, quick, easy magic that rose up from the dust beneath my feet and slipped out of the metal wall with the stomach-humming buzz of a million million trains echoing in the dark, magic pulling at the back of my hair like the blast of wind from an oncoming engine, though no wind stirred now in the dark.

As we approached the pool of white light, the faces of the men working became clearer, pale skin stained coal black so that only the hollows of their ears and the shallow places of their necks revealed the skin colour that had gone before. They were working under the rails, and had pumped up a section of track to get easy access. Grease was spilt across the floor around their feet, thick and brownish-yellow sludge from a small black box set on the heart of the curve. There were wrenches and mallets, pneumatic pumps, and devices whose names I couldn't guess, strewn around the working area. As we passed, one or two glanced up, and seemed to look straight at us, into the bright reflective yellow of our hi-vis jackets. Then they looked away again, not so much not seeing, but not seeing anything that was worth the looking. I kept walking, head down, focused on the next step. My feet splashed into a shallow puddle, sending water rippling out around it. I kept walking, but the puddle grew deeper. I glanced up to see if anyone else had noticed this, but no one had. Behind me I heard Penny's footsteps, dry and sharp, walking a little too fast, pushing the spell to its breaking point in her eagerness to get past these prying, albeit unseeing, eyes. I kept walking and the water was now up to my ankles; with the next step it came up almost to the top of my boot. I couldn't see where it was coming from. Something cold and wet hit the back of my neck; I jerked, and in that moment, stopped. Instinctively

I looked up and water fell onto my cheek, ran down it and off the edge of my jaw. Another drop; then another. I tried to see the source of the water in the ceiling, but couldn't make out either a cracked pipe or broken metal plate; but still the water fell, a drizzle now, now a shower, now rain, thick dark solid rain, sending dancing drops of water flying up around my ankle, and I had stopped, the spell was breaking. Penny brushed by me and whispered, "What are you doing?" and her face was soaking, everything was soaking but she showed no sign of having even noticed the water.

I whispered, "Rain?"

"What? What the hell are you talking about?"

I closed my eyes, grabbed her arm, forced myself to keep walking, head down. I had been out of the spell for too long. A voice said, "Uh . . . um . . . ?"

I half turned, saw a man in a white hard hat, a wrench held over his shoulder like a sword, staring at me with the bleary half-recognition of a man who's sure that something here is a little amiss, even if he can't quite name what it is. The rain was gone. The tunnel was as dry as the Gobi Desert. I opened my mouth to mumble something incoherent when Penny said cheerfully, "Morning, mate!"

The man blinked, bewildered. Then smiled. "Morning," he said, and turned back to his work.

Penny half dragged me the next twenty yards back into the darkness of the track. "What the hell was that?" she hissed.

"Sorry," I mumbled. "Uh . . . sorry. Couldn't . . . went a bit peculiar."

"Some educational fucking experience."

"Hey – worked, didn't it?"

"Christ," she hissed. "Me Penny Ngwenya, saviour of the city, plus one token whacked sorcerer. Are we bloody there yet?"

"We'll know it when we see it."

"Terrific," she growled. "If I get electrocuted or hit by a speeding Tube train, I'll be so coming back to get you."

We staggered on, through the dark.

Shortly before Old Street, we found it.

Or more to the point, we trod in it.

It was a turd.

Penny said, "Oh that is just fucking . . ."

"We're near!" I interrupted.

"Near what?"

I got down on hands and knees and pressed my ear against the rail. I could hear the faintest echo of something scrabbling in the distance, of metal on metal, moving fast. "You ever heard of Fat Rat?" I asked, dragging myself back up with a creak of protesting bones.

"Sure, I've heard of him. But I was kinda naively hoping that this waddle into the Underground with forty quid's worth of kebabs wasn't gonna like go that way, you know what I'm saying? What's the deal with this Fat Rat thing anyhow?"

I opened up one of the plastic bags, pulled out a yellow polystyrene box, laid it on the ground, lid open. "Well, some argue that he's just the inevitable biological consequence of a hundred and fifty years of underground sewers and railways. The nuts are convinced he's the product of a scientific experiment, and the magicians obviously regard him as the inevitable result of the exponential expansion of urban magic within the city. Pick one."

We kept on walking, laying down open kebab boxes every twenty yards. "And what do you think?" asked Penny, eyes on the darkness ahead.

"Me? Dunno. I mean, whatever caused him, I know what he is *now*. Fat Rat, king of the underground, lord of the sewers, you know. Doesn't really come up much to play – thing about building a modern city on a Victorian one on a Tudor one on a medieval one on a Saxon one on a Roman one, is you can guarantee there's always going to be more down there than you bargained for. Tribe worship him, though. He's sorta like a mascot at a baseball game? Their protector, their big slobbery all-purpose god and – oh."

Something small and furry moved by my boot. It was a mouse, fur dull grey-beige. It stopped a few centimetres from my toecap and looked up at me thoughtfully, whiskers twitching. Penny said, "Cute."

"Yeah. Charming. Why's it not eating the food?"

Slowly, we turned to look back the way we'd come. The polystyrene yellow boxes were empty, not a shredded soggy lettuce leaf or lumpy cardboard kebab left. Penny said, "OK, did I mention that I didn't like rats?"

"What've they ever done to you?"

"When I was eight, one of them ate half my aunt's breakfast and she made me go to bed early for refusing to admit that I'd done it."

"So it's personal, then."

I glanced back; was the darkness thicker behind our shoulder than it should be, or was the torch on my helmet just giving up the ghost?

We kept walking, kept laying down the kebabs. I could hear something in front, a sound like leaves stirring in a forest. "How'd you know a rat did it?"

"What?" asked Penny, eyes not moving from the darkness in front. She'd heard it too then, a rising sound of twig on twig on the bare winter trees, of skin on skin, of breath mingling with breath ahead.

"How'd you know a rat ate your aunt's breakfast?"

"Saw it two days later trying to get into the fruit cupboard."

"I guess that's pretty conclusive, then – put your bag down."

"What?"

"Drop the bag of food," I said quickly, and the darkness ahead was moving, it was churning, it was the sea swelling before a storm. I tossed my white plastic bag aside and caught Penny by the shoulders as she did the same, pushing her into the wall of the tunnel, against the black racks of cabling. "You really don't like rats?"

"I really don't," she whispered, and her breath was fast and her eyes scared.

I wrapped my arms around her, she put her head into my shoulder and held tight. "Don't look."

She closed her eyes, and here they came, hundreds of them, thousands of them, black matted fur and grey fluff, pink twitching noses and yellow little eyes, claws like shrivelled babies' bones, some no bigger than the length of my index finger, some the size of small terriers with yellowing teeth visible above their worm-tongues, scuttling and clawing and rolling all over each other, climbing over the bodies of the slower rats like a wave breaking onto a shingle beach, obscuring the silver shine of the rails, running along the walls, some with clawed-off tufts of bloody skin visible, others missing half an ear, some with a ravaged black hole for an eye, some with a stubby tail, some coated in grease, others in slime, some stinking of the sewer they came from, white tallow-fat clinging to the fur beneath their bellies, others the dry colour of the dust they rolled in; their claws on concrete were the hard bone sound of locust wings. I felt Penny's whole body tighten as they rolled over our feet, tumbled round the edges of our boots; one climbed up towards my knee to sniff and examine me, trying to work out whether I was poison or feast, before the mass of its comrades knocked it on, and still they kept coming like water draining from a dam, knee-high warm black bodies spinning off into the darkness of the tunnel and there was something behind them, I could feel its footfalls on the ground, the hum of its approach as a regular drumbeat through the pattering, I could smell it, soapy sewer fat, taste the magic of its approach, a rancid thick brown stain on the air.

Then, as quickly as they had come, the flood became a tide, the tide became a trickle, and the rats were past, just a scrambling in the dark behind us as they spread like mist through the tunnel. Penny's breath was a rush in my ear, her fingers digging into my back. I uncoiled my arms from around her and whispered, "You OK?"

Her eyes were still squeezed shut, her cheeks puffed up with the effort of not looking, her forehead drawn. She nodded, but didn't let go.

I felt something warm brush the hairs on the back of my neck. I turned my head slowly, keeping the rest of me absolutely still, and looked into the headlights of a Tube train.

The headlights blinked.

Then blinked again.

I eased myself from Penny's grip and looked up, and then a little more so, at the creature standing before me. It stood some feet taller than me, and the rusting iron mesh over its nose through which air rushed and puffed was the size of a human face. Each eye was the white bulb of a headlamp, its teeth were coated with the same yellow-brown grease the Underground men had spilt on the line, its tongue was ash black where it flickered at the air, its fur was iron metal filings that rose and fell with each breath it took, its lungs pumped the hot blast of Tube air of an approaching train. Human hair was tangled in its fur, long strands of blond and black, and its claws, each longer than my arm, were electricity-conducting copper. It could have taken my head off like I was a jelly baby. Fat Rat, king of the underground. We reached up towards its metal nose, half-glimpsed fan blades whirring just inside the protective rust mesh, felt the blast of air nearly knock us back. My hand was shaking, throat dry, heart headed for my knees as quickly as it dared. Our fingers brushed the quivering surface of its fur, felt it bend and part beneath our hand, soft, as the thinnest of metal sometimes is. It puffed, knocking the hair back from our face, but didn't move, didn't attack.

"Penny?" I breathed.

She still had her eyes shut. "I can hear breathing," she whimpered, "and it's not yours."

"It's OK. You can look."

"Will I like what I see?"

"You've got to look."

"Why?"

"There's nothing to be afraid of."

Slowly, eyelids shaking as if her mind said open and her body said close and neither could win the argument, she looked. Fat Rat turned a head the size of a sleeping human body to examine her. Her breath caught, her body tensed, I felt her pull away as he leant his head down towards her until his nose nearly bumped the top of her head. The ash-black tongue ran around the edge of his teeth, whiskers of thin aerial blades quivered either side of his cheeks. She bent backwards as he considered her smell, and then, his decision made, he drew back again, unexcited by what he found.

"Matthew?" Her voice was shaking, high, a child about to cry.

"It's OK. He's not going to hurt us."

"Doesn't look like he knows how to do anything that isn't hurting us."

We stroked him, looked into the brilliance of his lamp eyes. "We're no threat."

"Too fucking right!"

"He knows we fed his kin."

"No offence, right, but cold kebab isn't my idea of a great peace offering."

"But it'll do. Now he'll take us to the Tribe." I eased round to the side of Fat Rat, pulling Penny reluctantly along with me.

"He will?" she squeaked.

"Yep. That's why he's waiting. Rats are very, very clever, you know. He understands the bargain."

"A bargain to not eat us?"

"Yep."

I led her round to the creature's flank. Great matted strands of tallow-crusted hair hung down from Fat Rat's belly, but along the top of his back the metal of his fur was softer and smooth. We kept stroking his side, glimpsed a tail of metal serrated joins flicker in the air with what we hoped was pleasure and, still stroking, said, "OK, you're going to have to climb up."

I had never seen Penny's jaw drop, but it made it now. "No fucking way!"

"This is the way to get to the Tribe."

"Couldn't we have Facebooked instead?"

"The Tribe are hidden, cut off from the rest of society. The Aldermen don't have an embassy with them because they don't want an ambassador on their turf."

"And these are the psychos you want to have a chat with?"

"Yes."

"But if they don't like the Aldermen . . ."

"I've got charm."

"You're so whacked, Matthew, you know that?"

"Yeah, I know." I formed a stirrup with my hands, pressing my back into the warm flank of Fat Rat for support. With every breath he took, I could feel pistons moving inside his belly, which expanded and contracted like a swollen bouncy castle beneath me. "Come on," I murmured, "this is why you're a sorceress. Don't tell me you aren't excited; don't tell me that you can't feel the life here, Fat Rat's magic. You want to run faster than an Underground train, you want to go places no one else gets to go, see things no one else gets to see? Come on."

"I hate you so much," she hissed, and put her foot in my hands. I boosted her up, and she scrambled, fingers tangling in Fat Rat's fur, up onto his back. He turned his head, all the way, a hundred and eighty degrees to regard us, two bright eyes peeking over the great rolling mound of his slime-greased body. I grabbed a mass of black, oil-coated metallic fur and heaved upwards, felt flesh warp beneath me, saw steam drift from Fat Rat's mouth as he watched, felt Penny's hand curl round my wrist from above as she hauled me up behind her. Her knuckles were white as she clung to Fat Rat, she was bent double, the length of her stomach laid out down his spine for support. I clung on with my knees and fists, tangling my fingers in thin slices of biting metal fur and said, "There? That wasn't so hard, was it?"

Then Fat Rat began to move.

Then he began to run.

I bent low and clung on for dear life as my helmet bounced up and down on my head and flying dirt and oil stung my eyes. Within the black walls of the tunnel the world felt as if it was moving too fast around us, while we ourselves seemed to take on an almost static quality, as beneath us Fat Rat lurched and lumbered like a speeding caterpillar on a grill. I saw blue sparks rising from around Fat Rat's copper claws, smelt electricity in the air, saw little electric bolts arc from the metal fibres of its raised fur, tasted the moment as the live rail spat into furious glory, felt the shock of ten thousand volts come alive below us, so much power, just waiting for us to pick it up and fly with it, blue electric glory waiting to be had and with just one touch we could grasp it and set the world on fire and

and no

we could take hold of that power and

no

burn so bright

I closed my eyes, pushed my face into the oily darkness of Fat Rat's fur. I could hear a sound like the roaring of the Underground train, the rattle of its claws mimicking the de-dum of wheels on an uneven track, the roar of the wind pulling at my skin, the blast of dust and cold racing air filling my eyes, and Fat Rat ran the unstoppable run of the train with the broken brakes, not going to stop for anything, and we let him, and it was free, and it was wonderful. I could feel the sickly churning of my stomach as geography found itself left all behind; half opening my eyes I saw a solid metal wall ahead seem to cave and curl in on itself like a piece of crumpled paper, revealing a darkness that seemed to stretch out on all sides around. We ran into it and when I glanced back there was just darkness behind too, no hint of wall or tunnel or anything. Pipes ran across an empty black sky, supported by nothing, thin green seaweed like moss clinging to their edges, water drip drip dripping down from thin cracks, a skyful of pipes above and below, water sloshing beneath Fat Rat's feet, and the metal of the tracks beneath the water, and beneath that, a universe of yellow, pink, brilliant white and orange stars, the street lights of the city spread below us without bothering to take the architecture of the city with them. I thought I could see a double-decker bus, an old-fashioned red Routemaster with the open doorway at the back, its lights the only thing shining in the darkness, waiting at a red light in the water, black outlines of still figures captured in its windows. A flock of pigeons flew overhead, their eyes red, shedding albino-white feathers. A startled fox passed through the darkness ahead of us, caught in the brilliant light of Fat Rat's eyes, then scampering away through the water, leaving not a ripple behind. Then a flight of stairs ahead, wide, red-brick, leading up to I couldn't see what, and up them we went, into a great vaulted cavern of red-brick arches stretching away as far as the eye could see. Cracked cardboard boxes were strewn all across its floor, bearing the faded remnants of labels proclaiming

Oranges 5d

or

MACHINE PARTS HANDLE WITH CARE

or

Amusement, Beauty and Entertainment Products, *import of Taiwan*.

Then these too were gone as we passed down a narrow tunnel so low we had to press right down against Fat Rat's back to avoid being knocked flat, black metal walls and a floor crispy with curling old envelopes. Thousands, millions, of old paper envelopes, some with the address still written on, some with curling old Christmas stamps, tumbled across the tunnel like ice from a snowstorm. A few sad packages hung by bits of mouldering brown paper from loose bolts in the wall, magazines were caught in old torn cables, their wiring spilt from their blackened plastic sheaths like copper dusters. There was a light ahead, dull orange-yellow, pinpricked with odd flashes of green and blue. I ducked below a sign declaring:

SCHOOL CHILDREN CROSSING

and raised my head again as we burst out of the end of the tunnel onto thick brown mud beneath a starless orange-stained, drizzling sky. Fat Rat slowed here, turned, looked upwards, looked down, looked back at us. We were on a beach, a gloopy, freshly washed mud beach spotted with the usual plastic bags and abandoned trolleys of the English seaside. The beach was on the estuary. To the left I could see, just where the river began to turn, the silver flat-iron shapes of the Thames Barrier, sticking up from the sea as a great gate against the weather. To the right was the Millennium Dome, a low white swell in the landscape, and, beyond that where the river curved, the towers of Canary Wharf. I slipped down from Fat Rat's back into an ankle's depth of wet thick sludge. Penny followed, her eyes bright, a manic look in her face.

"You OK?" I asked.

"That," she said, "*that* was totally fucking awesome." Around the rim of her hard hat her hair was standing on end; I could sense the static in her skin; smell the magic flashing off her.

Fat Rat was already walking away, back towards a narrow tiled tunnel exit breaking out of the concrete embankment wall. I called after him, "Cheers!"

He didn't bother to look back, but slunk into his tunnels with the aplomb of a king.

We were in the East End.

Very much the East End. So much the East End, that technically speaking, the East had ended long ago and we were at that uncertain point where Greater London gave up the ghost and admitted to being Essex.

We found a flight of stained concrete stairs up from the river bank to a flat concrete nothing sprouting weeds between the cracks. A giant arch, rusting metal and broken gears, stood over the old wooden edge of a wharf where once freighter ships had docked. A sheet-iron warehouse, more of a shed for mammoths, sat along the edge of this concrete emptiness. Rubbish tumbled in the wind, littering the waters of the Thames with empty Coke cans and broken plastic bottles. Rainwater dripped off an old sign illustrating that no safety boots + no hard hat = no job. The newest addition was a great mound of blue plastic barrels tumbled down and left to spill across the ground, and a moped parked casually some distance off, a black helmet slung from the handlebars. I wiped my face with my sleeve and it came away black. I pulled off my hard hat and let the rainwater run into my hair and down my skin, turned my face up to the sky. Penny pulled off her hat, felt around the top of her head and said, "This look is not gonna be good for my street cred." I looked at her, and failed to suppress a grin. A glare fit to melt steel lanced from her eyes.

Dull yellow light seeped from one of the warehouse's cracked windows, and thin black smoke drifted from a tear in a bank of rusted pipes set into the wall. Something moved behind one of the windows. Somewhere, a footstep moved on broken glass. I tossed Penny my helmet, dragged off my hi-vis jacket and rolled it up into a bundle.

"We're being watched, right?" she said.

"Yep."

"We going to kick ass or what?"

"You know, I'm sure that there's supposed to be this diplomatic process thing."

"Yeah, right."

I gave her the yellow jacket and my satchel, slinging the strap across her shoulder. "This bag," I said, "contains my whole life."

"That's like the saddest thing you've ever said ever."

"Do *not* lose it!"

I pushed my wet dirty hair back from my face and started to walk towards the warehouse. "Hey!" she called from behind me. "Is this another 'you just wait here' moment?"

"Yep."

"I can help you!"

"I know," I replied. "There's a phone in the bag. If I'm not back in . . . oh . . . two hours . . . you call the Aldermen and tell them to do whatever the nearest equivalent is to nuking this place, OK?"

"Is that it?"

"Yep."

"I can help you! Why'd you drag me all this way?"

"To make the phone call."

"What if you're dead?"

"Then you'll get a phone call from us," we replied. "Death is only a mortal condition."

She flinched. "Yeah," she mumbled. "Right. Whatever. Hey – what if someone comes looking for me?"

"I reckon you'll be up to defending yourself."

She brightened. "Really? You think so?"

"Yeah. I reckon. Just try not to obliterate Essex, OK?"

It was only a few hundred yards between the riverside and the broken metal warehouse, a thing of fractures and twists. It felt like a year of walking. There were eyes watching from the shadows. I thought I heard footsteps behind me and refused to turn my head, kept my fingers to my side and the magic that wanted to crawl out of my belly and set the air fizzing, deep and tight like a fat meal after starvation. As I neared the warehouse I could see that the dull yellow flicker behind the shattered glass was refracted firelight from inside. The water pooling in the cracked concrete outside was stained silvery-purple from oil spilt across its surface. I found a small door, locked. The windows beyond it revealed a small dark office, desk broken and overturned, the stuffing of the chair long since spilled out.

I kept walking, shivering from the cold and the rain, rounded the corner and stepped straight into them. They must have been waiting for us. There were six of them, forming a circle around me. They were young – the youngest looked not a day over fourteen, and had an ugly swollen red scar running from chin to the corner of his left eye, puckered and fresh. Smaller white scars ran in little rows under his right ear. He wore a grey hoodie and his right hand was still wrapped up in old bandage from I didn't know what injury. His left hand held a knife, small and nasty. The eldest of them looked as if time had meant for him to be in his twenties and life had decided to kick him along a little bit further. His head was shaved, revealing a skull of interlocking thick plates and a fat red neck. He wore an old black puffed-up jacket, loose white T-shirt and a pair of faded blue jeans. Tattoos stretched across the skin of his left hand, red and vivid and chaotic, and peeked up from the line of his T-shirt to coil around the back of his neck. His right hand was barely human any more; flesh had bent arthritically, but instead of seized bones, metal was sprouting where there should have been fingertips, cruel jagged slices of metal, and green glass stuck up from the back of his hand along the lines of his vein like the spikes of a hedgehog, vanishing unevenly up his sleeve. But it was his face that commanded attention. Across the top of his skull were stamped in neat parallel lines two rows of tiny metal bolts, like the spikes on the back of a dinosaur; his left ear had a great hole in the lobe where a circle I could have waggled my thumb through had been inserted into the flesh, his right remained intact but was ridged all the way along its curve with hoops of metal. Bars of metal had been inserted at the base and the top of his nose, while from his top lip descended a single silver spike. He was missing a front tooth, and through the little pink remnants of gum I could see that his tongue was equally impaled. His left eyebrow was lined with more silver hoops, and his right eyebrow was also partially lined, while across his cheeks and down the side of his neck were long scars drawn criss-cross without any apparent order, the oldest faded and white, the newest still red and swollen. He looked at me, and the pupil of one eye was round and black, and the other a perfect tiny square, almost imperceptible, unless you knew to look for it. Whatever their shape, their look was one of contempt.

He didn't speak, didn't move, but two of his accomplices, the boy and a girl of some seventeen years with hair half shaven from her head and a raised burn mark in the shape of a V stamped on the side of her neck, came at me from either side. The boy swung a punch, without sound or acclaim, and his knuckles were bronze, bronze bones shining beneath thin stretched skin. I flinched away instinctively and felt something sharp and metal bite at my throat. The girl had a knife, a flick blade with the image of the Blessed Virgin Mary on its white plastic handle. I felt thin hot blood at its biting edge, and stayed absolutely still. Her other hand caught me by the back of my head, pulled me by the hair, exposing more of my throat. Not a word had been said, so I said something instead.

"Midnight Mayor," I wheezed. "Midnight Mayor."

The eldest, who I took to be their leader, held up his hand, and while the pressure on my throat didn't exactly relax, it didn't do anything worse. I slowly stretched out my right hand, uncoiling it to reveal the twin scars burnt into my skin. "First thing you should know," I gasped, careful not to speak too loud in case the volume should propel my neck onto the blade, "is that if we die, the telephones will scream vengeance at you, your words will be fire, your dreams will be burning blue. Second thing you should know is that if I die, the Aldermen will need no further reason not to ally with the Neon Court, as they already want to do, and will annihilate you and yours. Which, I guess, could be a good thing considering the aforementioned electric retribution which we shall pour down upon you from the wires and the radio waves as long as you live. So . . . you guys heard of diplomatic negotiations or what?"

Silence.

Chatty, they were not.

Then the leader jerked his chin, and the boy with the brass bones, and eyes simmering the colour of old overcooked chips, swung his fist, and the world said night night.

We do not fall easily.

I had been in the fuzzy land of bouncing brain cells for less than a minute, but times had been busy. Someone had pinned my hands behind my back with what felt like gaffer tape. Someone else had flung me over their shoulder and was carrying me like a bin-bag, as casual and easy as dirt. There was the taste of blood in my mouth. My head felt like someone had been injecting it with vodka and iron filings. I could see feet: big feet, small feet, feet in boots, feet in trainers, feet in bandages, feet in nothing at all, feet missing toes, feet bursting with blisters and blood, feet that were, really all things considered, reasonably normal if a little world-beaten. The dull glow of firelight was all around, and I could smell burning tyres, heated metal, woodsmoke and baked beans, hear the sound of voices, gabbling, shouting, cursing, swearing, laughing, all raised out of proportion and attacking their words as if it was the power of the sound, rather than the shape it took, which gave meaning.

I was deposited on a concrete floor at the heart of the hubbub, shoulder first with a bang. I curled up instinctively, waiting for bad things to happen, and when they didn't, uncurled a little at a time, and risked looking round. Somewhere overhead, a long way overhead, a voice said,

"Wat is dis?"

I tried to wipe blood away from the corner of my mouth on my shoulder, and crawled onto my knees.

Another voice said, "Som guy says hes from midnite mayor."

A face drifted down to fill my world like a balloon. Metal stuck out of every spare scrap of skin, and where metal couldn't penetrate, scars, ancient and new, had so churned up the flesh of this creature that his features resembled more a map of some craggy range of rocks than any kind of humanity. A hand with two fingers and two little stubs where there should have been fingers caught me by the chin and pulled me back onto my knees. A pair of eyes, irises the colour of tar, whites the colour of cigarette ash, blinked down at me. The owner of the face said, "U from da midnite mayor?"

It wasn't that he didn't speak intelligibly; he made perfect sense. But there was something in the way he formed his words, something deep and cut off, as if he couldn't be bothered to waste his time with this syllables crap.

"I am the Midnight fucking Mayor, arsehole," I wheezed. "Jesus, you know how to hold a party."

"Da midnite mayor is ded. nair. he woz slo n now hes ded."

"I'm the new guy."

"Wat new guy?"

"Didn't they tell you? The Midnight Mayor isn't just one bloke – it's a whole tradition, a power, a wandering job description passed down for thousands of years, one git to another. It's the guy who stops the nightmares, it's the dude who calls the dragons, it's the magic that turns back the tide, and, oh yes, wouldn't you know, it's me and I'm having such a bad day as you would not bloody believe!"

"Yeh," he said finally, "ok yeh. but if u is so powerful, den y u a stinky lil streak of piss?"

I spat a cocktail of blood and spittle onto the floor, and risked trying to climb to my feet. The world wobbled, and for a moment the universe considered kicking me in the kidneys. Then it decided to cut a decent guy doing a tough job a break, and stabilised. I looked my new host up and down. He wore a leather waistcoat, open at the chest, and leather trousers. The waistcoat was open, I assumed, to reveal the mutilation that was his chest, to allow all to see the metal pressed onto his ribs, the steam rolling out from the tears in his flesh, the burns, the scars, the punctures, the still-fresh swollen wounds, the great rises and falls of fluid lost and found beneath his skin, the deformity of his body, puffed up proudly like a warrior's scars. He was a tall man, but no higher than a bear and no wider than an ape. His face, such of it as was still recognisably human, gleamed with pride and contempt. Around him were his warriors, forming a circle with us in the middle, the older the most scarred, dressed in every kind of scrap clothing that the charity shop could reject. The number of scars and the amount of deformity seemed to indicate rank. I looked beyond the circle. The warehouse was lit by flames burning in the bottom of great metal tubs, fuelled largely by tyres and petrol, and everywhere I looked, stretched out among broken beer bottles and across mouldering blankets, spilling along the walls and jeering, were the Tribe. The lost, the young, the scarred, the angry, the old, the lonely, anyone and everyone who wasn't *one of them*, transformed in this place into *one of us*, the outcasts, united by being outcasts. And there were thousands of them, and not one looked pleased to see me. I licked my lips, tasted salt and iron and sand.

"I came to talk nicely," I said, fixing my gaze on a point just between the laughing, discoloured eyes of the man I hoped was a leader, if the Tribe had such a thing. "You going to talk nicely, or am I going to have to get mythic on you?"

"U? u dont lok lik u can shit a spell."

"Thing about me is that I've got two kinds of magics. I've got the nice, sitting-at-home-not-troubling-anyone kinda magics, which is what I'd usually rely on, but which I'm guessing won't cut the ice here. And we have the magics of fire and death, of destruction with no chance of return, of blood aflame and flesh turned to dust, which I was hoping to get through this little chat without deploying. But, as they say, your fate is in your hands. Which of us do you want to meet?"

The smile flickered, perhaps, a little on his face. "Y u ere?" he asked, voice darkening.

"I was told that the Tribe was preparing to go to war with the Neon Court."

"Wer already @ war. dey saw 2 dat."

"Well, thing is, I'm sorta bound by this treaty thing to join the Neon Court in war against you. And I kinda don't want to, because, you know, I figure, death, destruction, chaos, war – these are the kinda things that a decent Midnight Mayor's supposed to put the boot into, right? Hey – I don't suppose if I ask you nicely, you'll stop?"

I smiled my most diplomatic smile. I even got a mild titter of condescending laughter, which I guessed was better than a punch in the teeth. Then it faded, and so did the smile on the face of the man in front of me. "We dont want u n urs. midnite mayor nothin but shit. wen ours were dyin, wen ours were bleedin, da midnite mayor did nothin. Said dat da streets wer al dat matered, said dat sometimes people must die but city must live, dat all dat der is is der city, n we r just passin thru. n he left us wen we asked for help. so dont fink u can come ere now wiv ur scar on ur hand n fink it givs u som sorta authority. cos it dont. not now, not ever agen."

I let out a long slow breath. "Right," I said. "I see. You're narked because of some ancient dead Midnight Mayor shitting all over your lot. That's fine. That's cool. A Midnight Mayor went and shat all over me too, you know? I didn't want this job. Never did. But some tit decided to lumber me with it. And I figure, you know, I've made my bid now, sorry it didn't work out, which way's the exit?"

I turned on the spot, looking for a break in the circle, and finding none, turned back to the leader. There was an unnervingly thoughtful expression in his eyes. "U really da nu bloke?"

"Yep."

"U com ere alone?"

"No – no, sorry, should have mentioned. My apprentice came with me. Her name's Penny. She summoned the death of cities by accident, because she was pissed off one day. That's how I met her, you see, why I'm training her. You never want to get a pissed-off sorceress wandering around the city without giving her a quick tour of magic health and safety 101. You can try and beat her up and tie her up like you've done to me, but I gotta tell you, I'm the patient one pushing a diplomatic accord, and she's the one who doesn't know when to stop. But then again, our patience is not infinite."

"U talk tough."

"I'm fluffy inside."

He grinned, and that was the only warning he gave. A fist, scaled over with dirty aluminium skin that had grown out of his own, green glass protruding where there should have been bone, pumped and fuelled by more than just muscular strength, came up and out from by his right thigh, caught me square in the stomach, picked me off my feet and only dropped me back down to earth because it would be too easy to go through me and out the other side, and still not worth the effort. I never claimed to be buddies with gravity; I fell. The floor offered limited comfort. I lay, tears filling my eyes and bile burning at the back of my throat, curled up around a great black hole of sickly pain, and wheezed. There was laughter.

We rolled onto our knees, pain bursting behind my eyes and static filling my head. We crawled onto our feet, swaying slightly, and blinked away liquid salt. The great man was laughing, a huge deep sound tinted with a hint of broken gearbox. He turned to the crowd like a wrestler, and then turned back to see us. We put our head on one side, blue fire filling our eyes, rage and pain and blood. We said, "Do it again."

"Lol!" he replied.

"Do it again."

He swung his fist again, but this time he went for our face, as slow and merry as an avalanche. We moved; stepped to one side and under his swipe with slightly more than human speed, and as his hand went by, we bit it. It probably hurt our teeth more than it hurt his hand, but he was caught off guard and surprised, snatching his fingers away, two little neat rows of bite marks deep in the top of his hand between his thumb and middle finger, deep enough to draw blood. His friends laughed at this too, and then his other arm came up, more as an afterthought than with any real intent, and caught us round the side of the head like a crowbar, knocking us back to the ground. We fell awkwardly, one leg stuck out behind us, one knee bent, and this time, made no great effort to rise.

He examined his hand, rubbing away the blood that was welling with a casual swipe of his other arm, then looked down at us with a curious expression.

"U bite lil 1?" he asked, as a master might chide an ignorant puppy.

"We bite and we bleed. You may, if you are not too blind and foolish, have noticed that part. When we bit you, some of our blood got onto your skin. Let's just hope some of it didn't get *under* your skin as well."

His look of bemusement deepened, then lifted into a moment's revelation. Not a total fool, then, this mortal. But still enough of one. We closed our eyes, let the blue fire that danced in front of our eyelids spread, fill our mind, fill our body, burn and buzz through our blood, let the power of it, the power of what we were, blue electric angels, gods from the machine, spread all the way down to the toes so that pain became merely a brighter burning in the inferno, and fatigue just a dream on the other side of a nightmare, and we stood, and let our blood catch fire. Brilliant, blue electric fire, the fire of what we were, of our natures, we let it ignite inside us, and on our face, and on our skin, writhing bursting bright blue maggots of flame that snapped and crackled around us, let it burn in our eyes, let it burn under our flesh, let it burn over our skin, let it burn in our hair, let it rage and spill and tumble, brilliant electric glory.

And that little blood of ours that was on his hand: that caught fire too. We saw his face tighten with pain as it burst into electric fire, sparking and snapping over his flesh, biting with little angry lightning teeth. But if that had been all of his bad luck, he might have rejoiced. It was not. A tiny part of our blood, one part in a million, had got from our bite into his skin and into his blood, and suddenly he threw his head back and screamed, clawed at his own hand like he was trying to pull it off and when he couldn't, clawed at his own head like he was going to yank it clear of his shoulders and closed his eyes just a second too late for all not to see the insides of his eyes turn bright brilliant blue, the same blue of ours, and he screamed and screamed and screamed and we let him scream. We let him writhe at our feet and dribble and claw at us and try to shape the word 'mercy', we let him do all that and smiled and

smiled?

and let it burn still, the brilliant glory of it burning and

I said, "Enough."

And blinked away the fire from my eyes.

Slow retreat of glorious flame . . .

I shook it free from my skin, pushed it back into my bones, wiped it off my arms, let it burrow back into my blood. "Enough!" I repeated, louder, as the screaming of the man at my feet broke down to sobs. "Enough."

The others were silent. The entire circle was silent. I tugged at my arms; the fires across our skin had eaten loose some of the gaffer tape.

I tugged harder, and it snapped. There were little plastic burn marks all around my wrists, but the pain felt, to us, distant, an afterthought that would almost certainly plague us in some few hours to come. I knelt in front of the shaking giant man, touched his shoulder with my fingertips. He looked up with eyes back to unnatural grey, shedding dusty tears down his scarred face. He saw us and for a second was afraid, then a tongue pierced through with metal licked his lips and his hand reached up and caught mine by the wrist. Instinctively I reached down inside for power, felt static rise to my fingertips, but paused when I saw the look in his eyes.

He stared straight up into my eyes, into *our* blue eyes, and whispered, so low as to be almost inaudible, "B my god?"

I pulled my hand free instinctively, stood up and backed away a step.

All was silent.

The entire warehouse.

The babble of noise, the laughter, the shouting, the breaking of glass.

I turned slowly on the spot, meeting every eye that dared to meet our own. I could feel blood filling the twin scars on my right hand, thin red lines thickening in the two crosses carved into my skin. I ignored it. "All right," I said finally, when I'd turned a full circle. "You ready to talk?"

The Tribe formed a council of nine.

They sat on overturned boxes, scrap bits of metal and, in one case, a broken toilet.

The youngest looked seventeen.

The oldest was forty.

He had a birthmark, vivid bright purple, that ran across half his face. A few thin strands of hair dribbled down by one remnant of a torn ear, and at some point he had lost an eye, to who knew what, and nothing but a withered hole remained.

He said, "I am da shaman. my name is Toxik."

I wasn't offered a seat, and was too busy trying not to puke to stand. I sat down on the concrete in front of them, cross-legged, hugging my aching, churning belly. "Awesome," I said, waving meekly. "Hi Toxik, I'm Matthew, hundred and somethingth Midnight Mayor, sorcerer, blue electric angels, whatever and so on. I hear you guys are going to war with the Neon Court. Mind . . . sorta . . . not?"

"Dey kiled our wariors."

"What, generally or . . .?"

"Der woz a fire in Sidcup. a tower block. da court started it, da court traped our wariors insid n kiled dem."

"And when I ask you what your warriors were doing there in the first place . . . ?" Uneasy silence. I twisted my position on the floor, trying to find the least uncomfortable way to sit. "Look, guys," I exclaimed, "I know about this chosen one bollocks, right? So if your guys were in Sidcup looking for this chosen one, and the Court were there for exactly the same reason, then let's not beat about the bush; just tell me."

"Yes," said Toxik finally.

"Grand! Glad we got that bit of duplicity out of the way in under thirty seconds. So – your lot went to Sidcup looking for this chosen one, and just so happened to turn up at the exact same moment that the Court did. Because . . . ?"

"Der woz a phon call. we woz told to go den. it woz a court setup; dey caled us 2 trap us."

"You got any proof of that?"

Sulkily: "No."

"So, really, anyone could have made that call. Man or woman?"

"Man."

Not entirely the answer I'd been expecting. "So your lot turn up at the tower, mosey on inside, there's the Court there too, you have a good old punch-up, someone – and let's face it, at this stage it could be anyone – starts a fire on the lower floors, trapping your lot and some Court guys upstairs . . ."

"U no a lot."

I shrugged. "I can be thorough as well as terrifying. Anyway, long story short, everyone dead, you cry vendetta, the Court cries vendetta and then what? You decide 'hey, let's go set fire to some Court shit for kicks, that'll ease the situation'."

"Dey took da girl! wat wer we meant to do? sit bak n wait 4 them 2 take us? we gotta get her b4 dey use her agenst us!"

I leant forward, clinging onto my knees for comfort and support. "Who took what girl?"

"Da court tok da chosen 1!"

"You know that? For sure? They've got her?"

"We got our guys. No bodies of no women woz found in da fire. da chosen 1 is a women; she woz in dat tower."

"How'd you know that?"

"Da seer. he told us."

"Was it the seer – O'Rourke? – was it O'Rourke who tipped you off about the tower block?"

"No. we dont kno who did dat."

I ran my hands through my hair, felt grease and dirt and underground things that I didn't want to think about. "OK. Only, the thing is, the Court seem to think that you've got her. Or someone has. Because Lady Neon has flown to town . . ."

"Lady neon is ere?"

"Yeah."

"Wen did she com ere?"

"Last . . ." I stopped, bit my lip. "OK, wanting to say last night, but that's an abuse of language, so let's skip over that. A few hours back."

Toxik's eye narrowed, a sudden flicker of intelligence, awareness. Then he suppressed it, and mumbled, eye somewhere else, "Shes ere 4 da war."

"Yeah, that'd be my guess. Only, thing is, she wants me to find this chosen one girl. And you think she's got her?"

Toxik was silent a long time. Then he stood up and held out one punctured hand towards me. "Walk wiv me," he said.

The air outside the warehouse was cold, wet, quiet. It smelt of the river, clean washed mud, tinged with a pinch of salt. A flock of seagulls were hobbling up and down by the waterfront, waiting for the new day that was still refusing to come. Toxik handed me something slippery and blue. A plastic mac.

"Wear it," he said. "U lok shit."

I pulled it on gratefully and zipped it up. Pulling the hood over my head, I wandered along hermitlike at the side of the Tribe's shaman. He didn't seem to mind the rain. He pulled a packet of cigarettes from his trouser pocket, offered me one. I shook my head. He shrugged, stuck it in his mouth, lit it from inside his cupped hands, didn't bother with the lighter.

He drew a long puff, held it, and relaxed.

I let him walk and smoke, waiting.

"U a screwd up mother, u r," he said finally.

"Yeah. That's me."

"If u r da midnite mayor, y u let al dat shit go down?"

"What shit?"

"U kno." He gestured, fists punching an invisible enemy in the air, eye tight.

"Oh. That shit. Thing is . . ." I went to rub at the tenderness in my face and changed it at the last moment to an uneasy scratch of my nose. "When you're a sorcerer, and Midnight Mayor, and burning fire runs through your veins, you've only really got two modes. You've got diplomatically passive, and you've got apocalyptically destructive. Finding that middle ground – you know, breaking someone's kneecaps without actually causing them to spontaneously combust – can be a delicate business."

"No midnite mayor givs a shit bout us."

"Hey, don't get me wrong, I'm not exactly Florence Nightingale about this business."

"Den y u bothrin?"

"It's my job. Trying to stop the blood on the streets. And . . ."

"N?" he echoed flatly, drawing another puff of smoke.

"There was a guy in the tower block. In Sidcup. A beggar man, camping out there. He died in the fire too. Burnt alive. He wasn't Tribe, or Court, or chosen one, or whatever. There'll be more like him, many many more, if this gets any worse than it already is."

"So u gotta mak it stop."

"Yeah."

"Court got u by da ass, tho?" He saw my hesitation, grinned a grin of cracked yellow teeth, flecked with black. "I kno u got a treaty wiv da court. every1 kno. midnite mayor always dos wat is best 4 city, not 4 people init."

"I'm not exactly your traditional Midnight Mayor."

"Sorry u got beat up."

I shrugged, and even that hurt. "I get that reaction."

"Bein tribe – its not jus bout respect, u kno? its not jus bout strength or honor or dat. its bout not bein the other guy."

"The other guy . . .?"

"Its bout the whole world screamin @ u, b dis way, walk dis way, talk dis way. u not talkin this way, u not walkin this way, u not lookin, u not speakin, u not bein wat we want u 2 b? den u rnt 1 of us. u r asbo kid, u r hoodie, u r da problem. kids wiv knives, kids wiv guns, kids wiv drink, kids wiv babies, kids dat make da old ladies run in2 da corner an say he didnt lok nice he didnt speak proper he must b out 2 get me, u kno? bcaus u r different, u dont do wat dey expect. n dey gotta b right. someone gotta b right bout something, otherwise dis world is shit, i mean real shit. ders gotta b absolutes, ders gotta be rules else y shuld der b good n bad n right n wrong n true n lie? dese r jus da thins made up by da time we liv in. 1 day right n wrong n good n bad will change agen, like theyve changed b4, n change agen, n agen until 2moro isnt anythin we can name 2day, n all da futur looks back on da big old ere n now n says 'u lived evil – u all lived so evil'."

"That's a lot of big philosophy for a guy who lives in a shed."

He shrugged. "I red philosophy @ uni."

"You're shitting me. What, the world of high academia didn't appeal?"

He glared at me. "U rnt listnin. dat woz wat I woz ment 2 b. *ment*. lik *ment* is al der is 2 b."

"And what's your solution?" I asked. "Just reject good and bad outright? Stop wearing the clothes, stop walking the walk?"

"Yeah. we r da ones who av seen da lie. we av seen dat 1 day, itll all b different anyway, so wats da point?"

"Helpful attitude you have there."

"It maks us free," he replied, flicking ash across the concrete. "Not good n bad – jus free."

I sighed and shuffled deeper into my anorak. "So what's your beef with the Neon Court? Why d'you hate them so bad?"

He looked up into the rain, as if seeking inspiration. "Dey r da opposit. dey say dat power is da beauty, da faces, da voices. but dey dont jus say dat. dey want us al 2 belive dat. dey want us all 2 look at how beautiful dey are n say 'we want dat' n den they say 'u can av it but da price u pay must b ur soul'. u kno dey keep thralls? human slaves who give up der souls 4 a piece of beauty, 4 a few days of da world sayin 'u r d best, u r all we want to b' until da world changes agen n dey get old n dey av nothin but da memory of 1 moment when da world smiled @ dem. y do u allow it?"

"Me? Haven't been in the job long enough to do anything about it."

"U r part of it."

"I have no love for the Court."

"But u dress like dey want, n talk like dey want, n act like dey want, n when they say 'com runnin' u do, bcaus dey talk pretty n look beautiful n dat is all u can c."

"Remember you're judging the guy who went through shit to come and have a chat with you," I pointed out, as he stamped out the remnants of his first cigarette and headed onto the next. "I think I get brownie points for that."

"Mayb. mayb u r somethin different."

He lapsed into cigarette-sucking silence. I flapped my arms against the cold, hopped up and down. I said, "OK, so I get why you don't dress like other guys, and don't talk like other guys, and don't act – hell – don't act like regular civilised bastards; fine, fair enough, so long as you're doing it on your own terms, fine. But I'm not entirely won over by this whole hacking off your own flesh and carving up your own skin. Why that?"

"2 b mor dan da rest."

"To be more than . . . ?"

"More dan human. man is, c, a cockup arsehole shit species. we hate n hurt n do cruelty n hate n hurt n cruelty is done 2 us by dem dat hate n hurt more n they learnt 2 hate n hurt from dem dat hated n hurted n . . ."

"I think I get the picture."

"We dont av 2 b dat. we dont av 2 b nothin we dont chose. only birth made us human, so we chose 2 b somethin else. n u call it ugly, but we cal it free." He held out the cigarette packet to me. "Sure u dont want 1?"

"Cheers, nah."

"Tel me bout blue electric angels," he said suddenly. "Tel me bout them."

"We are . . . what is there to tell? Here we are. Judge for yourself."

He looked at us long and hard. We stared back. His eye skirted ours, and looked away. He tried to disguise his mortal fear with a flick of cigarette ash into the darkness, a casual half-nod of the head. Then, "I av heard of dem, but u shuld b in da telephon. da angels mad when da voices stop, da thought left behind in da wire, da creature mad of al da human emotion tipped in2 da electric signal. y u ere?"

"It's complicated."

"I intrested."

"I got killed by my old teacher. Robert Bakker? Yeah, you've heard of him. He wanted to summon the blue electric angels from the telephone wire, use our power to extend his own life. He wanted me to help him; I refused. I was killed. His shadow came alive, you see – he was a sorcerer and he was out of control and I guess that's how it manifested. Anyway, it came for me, and I couldn't stop it, and it killed me. Very, very dead. But not very quick. Should probably have been quicker, really, but I . . . uh . . . I had time to get to a telephone box. Thought about dialling 999, but then what was the point? Nothing they could do. So I just listened. Listened to the sound of the telephones, that big, wide-open sound of the dialling tone, a whole world just the other side of the connector. And we were waiting. We took my last breath into the wire, dragged me down soul and, I suppose, what was left of my body. We cannot describe the world we came from. Humanity has not invented the words to encapsulate electric godhood. But after a few years, Bakker tried to summon the electric angels again, tried to suck us out of the wire. But he got it wrong. He tried to summon us and instead he got me. I am us and we are me, for ever one. One blood, one mind, one soul."

"But 2 voices."

I shrugged. "It's not a conscious thing."

"R u possessed?"

"Nah."

"R u human?"

"Sure."

"But ur blood burns blue."

"Only when we're really, really frustrated."

There was a moment's uneasiness in his face. Then he grinned, shook it away with a tug of his head. "U rnt lik da midnite mayors dat went b4, r u?"

"I did try to say."

Silence again. Then he said, "If i tel u something dat is freakin me, dat i cant share wiv any of da others, u will listen?"

"Try me."

"I dont think da sun is risin." I stopped dead, stared at him, mouth gaping. He shifted uneasily. "U think im crazy 2?"

"Oh, Jesus Christ!" I exclaimed, grabbing him by the shoulders. He dropped the cigarette and shied back, unsure. I shook him, nearly shouting, "If you weren't an ugly bloke on the verge of a bloody and stupid pointless war, I'd snog you right here, right now!" His eyes widened. I let go self-consciously, coughed. "As it is," I added, more subdued, "you are, so I won't." He relaxed a little. "Lucky escape all round, really," I concluded. "How'd you notice?"

"I c thins."

"Lord be praised and hallelujah for that!"

"Also . . . it is da *other* prophecy."

"Come again?"

He sighed, and looked almost embarrassed. "Der r 2 prophecies bout da chosen 1, not 1. O'rourke made da first prophecy, da 1 we al wanted 2 hear, da 1 in wich da court is destroyed n we live. But der is another prophecy, mad by 1 of da shamans of da tribe in manchester."

"The Tribe has branches in Manchester?" I echoed flatly. "Hell, of course you do. What's this other prophecy say?"

"Says darkness. says dat der wil b nothin but darkness, endless night, if we seek dis chosen 1."

"Something in that."

"Da others dont wana hear it. we want 2 fight, we want 2 go to war wiv da court, n da others say dat da seer in manchester is old n dont kno her stuff any more. but i've looked, i've seen. da sun isnt risin, is it?"

"Nah. It isn't."

"U've seen 2?"

"Yeah."

"N . . . cockfosters has vanished."

"Yeah it's . . . it's what?" My voice rose to near a shriek. He shied back again, as if alarmed I might grab him. "Cockfosters has what?"

"U avent seen?"

"Haven't seen what?"

"Da tube map! cockfosters, high barnet, amersham – dey'r al gon. al da outer stations on da tube map r just . . . gon. lik they weren't never der. n i say dis n people dont think dey wer ever der."

"They were bloody there, I got pissed dressed as a dwarf on a stag night in Barnet!" I was on the verge of shouting; Toxik waved me urgently to silence.

"Dey think it is madnes."

"Too bloody right it's madness, how long has this bloody been happening and why hasn't someone told me?"

"People dont kno. like dey dont kno the sun isnt risin, like dey cant c. n it all hapened after sidcup. watever happened in dat tower, sinc den nothin but bad has com."

I thought of Oda and her bloody eyes.

"You think it's connected to this chosen one?"

"Has 2 b."

"What do you know about her? Do you have a name? A picture? A postcode?"

"A name. O'rourke gav us a name."

"That's something. What is it?"

"JG."

"JG?" I echoed. "What kind of a rubbish name is that?"

"He said her name woz JG n she woz the chosen one. n den we got da call telin us 2 go 2 da tower in sidcup n . . ."

"'JG woz ere'," I murmured.

His eye flashed, head angling up towards me. "Wat?"

"Um . . . graffiti. Written inside the tower. I saw . . . well, it was there."

He nodded slowly, drew another puff on his cigarette, held it up carelessly in the falling rain. Then, "I thougt da fire destroyed da whole place."

"Thorough, remember?"

He smiled, but said nothing. We turned another corner, began lap two of our tour of the docks. "So," he said finally, "wat u goin 2 do now?"

I shrugged. "Don't really know."

"U cam al dis way n dont kno?"

"My plan was to try and convince you lot to not kill each other for a while, and get more information about this chosen one. Is that really all you've got? A name? JG?"

"We kno she woz in the tower when it burnt, n we kno her body werent found when it stoped. we think dat lady neon has her but if u arent so sure den wat we gonna do?"

I tried to huddle deeper into my coat, and found it had no depths left to plumb. "What if there's something else happening here?" I asked finally. "A third party, some other bugger mixed up in this?"

"Lik who?"

"I don't know. Someone who wants war, someone who's playing silly buggers with the Court and Tribe both." Then, "You heard of the Order?"

"Nah."

"Bunch of religious nutters, fanatics, out to destroy magicians and all their works."

He shrugged. "Bit midle ages innit? y u think dem involved?"

"Maybe?"

"U kno dat thin u said bout duplicity n how we shuld b past it?" he asked with a crooked grin. "I likd dat."

I looked down at my boots, and smiled. "Yeah. Ignoring the casual violence, it's all gone OK. Can I trust you?"

"I trusted u, yeh?"

I sighed, wiped rainwater off the end of my nose, tasted blood on the inside of my mouth. "I know there's more going on here than just the Court and the Tribe. I don't know what – yet. But there's definitely other people mixed up in it, and this whole . . . endless night, Cockfosters vanishing business . . . isn't necessarily about this chosen one at all." A thought hit me, late and hard. "Unless, that is, your chosen one walks around with pudding for eyes?"

"O'rourke . . ."

"Didn't specify?" I asked with a sigh. "You astound me. You know, I met O'Rourke? Seemed kinda like an arse."

"Seers r rare now dat most of dem r dead."

"Just saying, a hole in the market doesn't necessarily attract top-quality service providers, you know? Look – if I can find this chosen one ducky, and if I can square things up with you, her, and the Court, can we put off this whole war business?"

"Da others wanna fight," he replied, sadness tinging his voice. "We r proud 2 b difrent, but we jus end up da same. angry n violent, hatin every1 cos dey hate us til we cant remember who did da hatin 1st."

"You don't strike me as particularly angry and violent."

He shrugged. "Im old enogh now 2 want somethin more dan da thins i believed in wen a kid."

"What kind of things?"

He sucked in air thoughtfully between his crooked yellow teeth. "I think . . . free prescriptions on da nhs, posture-corectin matres 2 sleep on, holidays by da seaside, n central heatin." He saw my face. "Dont tell no 1. i havent got no 1 if i havent got da tribe."

"Your secret is safe with me. So how about not having that raging war?"

"I dont av dat much power dese days. kidz jus wanna fight. kidz jus wanna scream but dont av no way 2 do it cept in da dark."

"You'll try, though?"

He scratched his chin carelessly, white skin dragging and flaking beneath his metallic nails. "Ill try but dont make promises."

"Fair enough." I pulled off my coat, twisted it over my arm, passed it to him. "Thanks for the loan." He took it with a shrug, tossed it carelessly against the wall. I held out my hand. He hesitated, then shook it. His skin was cold and clammy, his grip made of wrenches and steel. I tried not to shake the blood discreetly back into my fingers when he released it; then grinned, and turned to walk away.

He said, "Swift?"

I stopped, looked back. "Yeah?"

"If u find her – da chosen 1 – if u find her n she isnt wiv da court, u better bring her ere."

"I had?"

"Yeh."

"Why?"

He fumbled another cigarette free from his pack, stuck it between his lips. It waggled as he spoke. "Cos if u dont, da tribe wil think u r on da courts side n kill u, n kill da chosen 1, rather den let lady neon av her. jus sayin. jus so u kno."

I grinned, all weakness and teeth. "Thanks for the warning."

He shrugged, and lit the cigarette.

"Hey, Toxik?" I half turned, looking back at him, face lit faint orange in the dark. "This war, this thing you have with the Court? As Midnight Mayor, I've gotta tell you – it's a wanky piece of piss. The city is much, much bigger than what you two have going on tonight. You kill Lady Neon or she kills you, at the end of the day, when all the cards are counted and the chips are laid across the table, no one will really care."

There was a flicker of something in his carved-up features that might have been sadness. "Is al we av," he replied softly. "Is al we r."

I found Penny some four hundred yards away from the metal warehouse of the Tribe, curled up on a pile of tyres, hard hat pulled down over her face, huddled beneath the overhang of an abandoned lorry-loading dock. Her eyes were shut, her lips parted, her breathing long and slow: fast asleep.

I knelt down next to her and unhitched my bag from her shoulder. She stirred, head lolling as if it was trying to rise, before gravity and fatigue pulled it back down. I fumbled open my bag and pulled out my mobile.

There were three missed calls on it, all from Dees.

I dialled.

She answered almost instantly. "Mr Mayor?" Her voice was low and urgent.

"Hi."

"Where are you? Are you all right? You can't just walk off like that . . ."

"I'm in Woolwich, I'm fine, and I can, thanks for asking."

There was a long slow huff as Dees got her anger under control, and when she spoke again, her voice was cool and level. "We need you to come back to the British Library as soon as possible."

"OK – why?"

"This . . . matter of the sun not rising. There may be more to it than I initially thought."

"And?" I prompted.

"And?" she echoed. "And what?"

"And, this is where you say, 'Goodness, Mr Mayor, there may be more . . .'"

"Oh, yes, of course," she said, as realisation dawned. "Yes, sorry, Mr Mayor, you were right, and the collective wisdom of the entire city and all its extensive training and wisdom was, just this once, wrong, and I'm very sorry that reason has failed, and you have prevailed and I will try to doubt you with more politeness and, I trust, a wiser soul from here on in." A pause. "That is what you wanted, isn't it?"

I sighed. "I'm on my way."

Waking Penny was a necessary guilt.

Finding a working Underground station was a struggle.

After two buses, we found our way to Bromley-by-Bow, a District Line station whose main function seemed to be servicing the Blackwall Tunnel flyover and a recycling centre. The gates were open, the blue-uniformed men and women at their posts. Their eyes were bloodshot, their faces addled. The sun was failing to rise, and humanity, with its finely tuned body clock, was beginning to pay the price.

We sat on the train as it ran west, clunking through stations of dirty ceramic tiling and general suburban neglect. Penny said, "Sorry."

"For what?"

"Falling asleep. Should've been . . . you know . . . butt-kicking and shit."

"It's fine. We're all tired."

"You've got this kinda fist-sized red mark . . ."

"To quote classic American foreign policy – stuff happens. It's fine. Go back to sleep."

She sighed, shrinking down further into the criss-cross-patterned seat of browns and blacks. Her eyes began to drift closed again. I pinched myself to stop my own eyes following her course, focused on sitting upright, on staying alert. On the row of seats opposite us sat a mother, her face ash grey, her hair unbrushed, holding a briefcase in one hand and a child in the other. The child looked about five and was wearing a scruffy blue uniform. The child said, "I wanna go home."

The mother said nothing.

"I wanna go home I wanna go home I wanna go home! Mummy!"

She didn't even look down, but stared blankly into nothing. The newspaper on the seat of the train was the same newspaper I had read on the ride back from Heathrow, the same headlines, the same trivia, only more scuffed than before. Penny's head bumped against my shoulder. I thought about chosen ones, about prophecies and all that they entailed. I had never known any good come of either.

On the concrete walls of Mile End, some wit had written:

WAITING FOR YOU

Someone else had replied, equally witty;

at the end of the alley

Next to them was a giant ad demonstrating the extraordinary abs a guy could get from wearing Marks & Spencer underwear. I wanted breakfast, and thought I could smell Fat Rat in the tunnels, hear footsteps in the clunking of the engine.

We tried changing trains at Monument, and were told that, due to vital and ongoing refurbishment, such a thing was impossible. We got out and walked the few hundred yards between Monument and Bank stations overground, while I seethed and wondered how much extra this little wander would make the ticket to Euston cost.

The Northern Line carried us duly north, to the minor maze that was Euston station, a trap of escalators and signs to this line that way, but not that line this. There were rumours of clever sorcerers who'd learnt to bend the rules of space and time in Euston station, make minutes pass in hours, hours pass in days. Sometimes, so the rumours went, you could see a reflection in the curved mirror on the corner of the stairs, that had no body attached to it round the bend. I wasn't sure if I believed it. Bank station seemed a far more likely time-bending location.

The main concourse of Euston, a dull flat white space inside a dull flat black rectangle of a building, was dominated by huge orange boards proclaiming what train was leaving next. I looked up. The train to Birmingham Snow Hill was cancelled; most of the rest were indefinitely delayed. I stopped by a map of the London Underground and examined it as Penny bought us a breakfast of sausage rolls and black coffee. It was a stunted multicoloured map of an arterial system starting to suffer from congestive failure. The usual ends of most lines had vanished, leaving just whiteness. Cockfosters, Amersham, Uxbridge, Upminster, Epping, Morden, even Heathrow had all been sliced off, as if they had never been. Penny stood next to me, handed me a hot plastic cup of coffee and a bag containing nine parts grease to one part pastry and meat. I ate gratefully, and through a splattering of pastry shards said, "Notice anything odd?"

She stared long and hard at the Tube map. "Dunno," she said finally. "Should I?"

"Cockfosters, Amersham, Uxbridge . . . ?"

Blank emptiness on her face.

"Heathrow?"

"I've heard of Heathrow!" she said. "It was that . . . that uh . . . that thing . . . that place where you went to . . . um . . . that other place . . . you know . . . uh . . ." Her voice trailed off. "Nah," she said finally. "Sorry. Drawing a blank."

"Airport?" I suggested.

"That's the shit! Jesus! Mind not with it today."

"You notice something else?" I asked, waving with my coffee towards the departures board.

"Uh . . . ?"

"None of the trains leaving London are actually leaving. Cancelled or indefinitely delayed. Strike you as odd?"

Her face furrowed with concern. "Uh . . . no?" We both lapsed into silence. Then she added, "Shit."

"Hum?" I asked through a mouthful of sausage roll.

"'No's the wrong answer, innit?"

"Yep," I replied brightly.

"I can . . . feel . . . it's . . . I can't feel like . . . when there's a spider's web in front of you and you walked through it by mistake and you're sure you pulled it off yourself but you're not sure whether there isn't a spider in your hair? That's what I feel like. Mean something?"

"Yep."

She poked me firmly in the shoulder. "Means . . . ?"

"Oh – you're under a spell," I replied calmly. "Your mind tricked into not caring that there's nothing beyond London, that the map is shrinking and the sun isn't rising. Don't beat yourself up over it; everyone else is having a similar thing. And look on the bright side! You're one of a select minority who's actually noticed it. Eight out of ten, well done!"

Penny stared at me for a long while. I finished the sausage roll and got down to the serious business of licking pastry crumbs off my fingertips. She said, "You're one weird mother to be fucking saviour of the fucking city, you know?"

"Thanks," I said, finishing the last of the crumbs and scrunching up the bag. "That's a great comfort. Come on, we've . . ."

I turned.

There was a man standing behind me.

His hair was white, his skin had been slow-roasted beneath a brilliant sun. Today he was wearing a suit jacket and neat blue shirt, jeans and a pair of squash shoes. He looked unarmed, but that didn't really mean anything. He was smiling, and that meant even less. His eyes were focused on the departures board above, but his words were all for me. He said, "Is it truly a tragedy that the train to Coventry is cancelled?"

I wiped crumbs off my lips with the back of my hand, found to my surprise that the hairs were standing up with static all up the length of my arm, magic ready to be thrown, that I hadn't even noticed myself preparing. I looked slowly around the concourse, checking the windows of every shop and walkway. A man in a café turned away. A woman buying her ticket bent down closer to the machine. A pair of travellers, their bags carrying goods not intended for casual travel, examined novelty ties in a shop display. I wondered if Euston station was any good for positioning snipers, and if so, whether they'd ever be caught.

I said out of the corner of my mouth, "Penny, give us a moment."

Penny stared with all the rudeness of the defiantly fearful straight at the man and said, "Who the fuck is this?"

I opened my mouth to reply, but he got there first. "My name, young lady," he said, "is Anton Chaigneau. I am the head of an organisation entrusted by God with the destruction of you and all your kind. You used to be a God-fearing, devout young woman, Penny Ngwenya. I have prayed for you, that when you have suffered the fires of eternal hell, you may yet be redeemed."

Penny's eyes widened. "You are shitting me."

"Hey, at least he prayed for you," I sighed. "That puts you one up on me. What do you want, Chaigneau?"

"To talk, Mr Mayor, as if you and I were almost civilised people. I am alone."

"Like you don't dig that martyr complex," I growled.

"It concerns," he added, a flicker of irritation in the corner of his eye, "the woman Oda. Who is, I believe, an acquaintance of yours?"

I deflated. "Step into my office."

There's never anywhere good to get a drink near railway stations, and Euston was no exception. The pub we found ourselves in had the advantage of convenience, emptiness and dark, shuttered corners away from windows and the passing of strangers, and not much else to recommend it. A fruit machine dazzled with a constant flicker and flow of brilliant yellow and orange lights that raced up and down it like frantic ants in a boiling maze; the carpet was thin, with spilt beer trod in deep, the barmaid a bleary-eyed student with an Eastern European accent who handed out drinks in glasses still carrying the lipstick scars of their previous owners. She looked too tired to sourly judge our order of tap water, two packets of cheese and onion crisps and a glass of cranberry juice for Chaigneau, price: extortionate. A TV in one corner was showing repeats of ancient 80s sitcoms, in which all the female voices rose to earth-shattering pitches, and the audience cackled at every waggling eyebrow. The stained beer mats on our glass-topped table promised that no one knew how to party like the Aussies, and invited attendance to the 2001 Rugby World Cup to test this theory.

In our dull, underlit corner I sat next to Chaigneau, Penny on my other side. I wasn't sure whether I was protecting her from him, or the other way round.

He said, "Does your apprentice really have to be here?"

I looked at Penny. "I don't know," I said. "Why don't we ask her?"

Penny beamed and gave a cry, only slightly subdued by fatigue, of "I just dig those religious psycho-bastard fanatics, shit."

"Yes," I translated for Chaigneau. "I think she does. Talk – tell me about Oda."

"I'm here to help you, sorcerer," he said.

"Sure."

"I have information that could be relevant to the safety of the city."

I let the silence hang, hoping that my expression was at least partially receptive, mingled to dilute our natural hate.

"The Order has come across information that the woman Oda has engaged herself to dark powers."

I waited. "Are we talking . . . rings, bells and a honeymoon in Ibiza?" I queried at last. "Or do you mean something specific?"

"This is hardly a time for flippancy."

"I'm sorry; it's my defence mechanism. So Oda has gone and got herself mixed up in dark powers. What dark powers and why?"

He hesitated. Then, eyes fixed on a point somewhere just above my head, "We're not sure."

"Of which bit?"

"Both. But she has . . . killed . . . at least two people that we know of, in a hotel in Greenwich. We think she may have killed more. And her means were not of God's creation. I will not lie to you; our relationship with her has cooled."

"Before or after the dead people in Greenwich?" asked Penny sourly.

His eyes flashed. "Oda lost her path some time ago. She has not been a true scion of the Order for . . . many months."

"You think it's been a long-term engagement with darkness and death?" I asked through a fistful of cheese and onion crisps.

"In a way."

"And what exactly, Anton Chaigneau, psycho-nutter who goes around killing guys and thinking that's a good thing, do you want me to do about it?"

"She could be a threat to us all. If you encounter her . . ."

"You'd have me kill one of your own?" I asked. He didn't answer, and didn't need to. "Blimey, but you're a right bastard."

Muscles worked in his jaw. "My place may not be in heaven, Matthew Swift; I accept that. It is not my fate that motivates me in this, but the fate of many, many others."

"Sounds like sanctimonious shite, if you don't mind me saying so," offered Penny from over the edge of her glass.

Chaigneau turned to her, and I felt a shimmer of something that might have been fear, might have been anger as his eyes met hers. "Have you asked yourself, Miss Ngwenya, what your magic is good for? You are adept at fighting other magicians, you are skilled in destruction, you are gifted in the art of making tragedies or, at the very best, averting tragedies that magic has already made. Do you heal? Do you work, do you toil, do you assist the greater good? What use are you?" She slurped in reply, but there was a light in her eyes that I had seen only very rarely, and which usually portended fire. Chaigneau saw it too, for his eyes flickered back to me. "*If*," he declared, "if you see Oda, know that the Order will not consider it an act of aggression should you take action against her. She is a threat to everyone and everything; she has lost her path, her light and her soul. I tell you this as Midnight Mayor, as a necessary evil, who even I must occasionally cooperate with if many many more are to be protected and saved."

He stood up, pushing the barely touched cranberry juice to the middle of the stained table top. "Do with this what you will, Mr Mayor."

"Thanks a bundle."

He eased himself out of our corner, moved as if to go, then hesitated at the last, turned back, looked us in the eye. "It's your fault," he said, voice low and weather-worn. "No one else, Matthew Swift. What happened to Oda, to her body, to her heart, to her mind, to her soul. It's your fault. Think on that."

He turned away.

I said, "Chaigneau?"

He paused, but didn't look back. I could see his shoulder blades pressing against his shirt.

"There's a chosen one in Sidcup," I said.

He didn't move. Breath pushed fabric out, pulled it back in again.

"And the sun's not coming up," I added.

His head half-turned, he looked at me over his shoulder, as if he couldn't be bothered to grace me with more of his presence than he had to. "That," he replied, "is exactly the kind of problem that inspires us to keep you alive."

Drawing himself up, he stalked away.

Penny watched him go. She reached across the table, and started drinking his cranberry juice. Her nose wrinkled in distaste. "Never as good as I think it'll be," she concluded after a few sips. "Hate wasting stuff."

"That man . . ." I said.

"Yeah?"

"Remember him."

"Sure. Why?"

"Because when I'm dead, he'll come after you."

Penny raised her eyebrows.

We looked squarely at her. She wasn't meeting our eyes. Her fingers were tight around the glass. I held out my hand to her, stood up. She took it tentatively, allowed me to pull her to her feet.

"You know," I murmured as we gathered our few meagre things, "this whole being shit-scared thing . . ."

"Yeah?" Voice a little too loud.

I hesitated, felt words reducing to empty platitudes. "Way smarter than the alternative," I stumbled.

"Sure," she said with a shrug. "Whatever. Where we going now, boss?"

Back to the British Library. The front doors were open, lights shining inside, the main hall a vista of broad stairway. The security guard was asleep, the receptionists looked tired and grey. A woman with curly brown hair was wearing a blue suit jacket over a sequinned dress, and stood in the middle of the hall with a rucksack in one hand, not sure if she was coming or going. I looked around at the high ceilings and down at the slippery tiles on the floor and said, "I have no idea which way to go."

Penny grinned. "See how much you rely on me?"

She led the way downstairs into a series of corridors that looked like they'd escaped from a local swimming pool, past giddy artwork of crazy proportions and strange lines, into a locker room of grey steel, through a door stamped with the words "**Authorised Personnel Only**" in firm black letters, and down. I heard the same vents humming as before, the same lift shafts whirring, smelt books and cleaning fluid. She pushed back a pair of heavy, brass-handled doors that seemed to be the only exit, and stepped into a small carpeted reception area. "See?" she began. "Just like I . . ." A man in a flat black hat looked up from behind the desk, put his fingers to his lips and interrupted her with a pronounced "*shush*". Penny's face fell a little, but she pushed back the next set of doors and led me through to a hall of endless moving books behind glass, vast ceiling, sprawling cold floor and, in the very middle of it, a desk that would have shamed

Ikea with its rickety simplicity. Behind the desk was sat an Alderman in his long black coat, small shield-shaped badge bearing the crosses of the city pinned to its front, fast asleep. A small door stood open in one corner of the room, white fluorescent light spilling out. There was the faint sound of voices from the other side. We walked over to it, peeked round the corner, saw shelf upon shelf upon shelf stretching away to an uneasy heat-haze-lost distance, Aldermen poring over every part. One spotted us, showed a tiny flicker of recognition and scurried away. Penny said thoughtfully, "So this is academic shit, huh?"

"Wouldn't really know," I answered. "Not my thing."

The Alderman came scurrying back, Dees in tow. She put a hand on my arm and pulled me quickly along a row of shelves and down a corridor smelling of old paper and string. "Welcome back, Mr Mayor. I'm glad you're here. I see you can see again then? Good, excellent, there have been developments . . ."

I struggled to keep up. How such little legs on such a little frame could carry Dees with such speed was a mystery. Penny puffed along behind. We spun round a corner and down another corridor that could have been the first. A few titles caught my eye.

Necromancy: Proof of God and Proof of Hell?

Invocation for Idiots (2nd edition)

Everything I Learnt about Magic I Learnt from a Gnome Called Reginald: a fond magician's recollections

Summoning Unleashed – Who's Got Your Back?

Another corner, another blur. A door ahead, low, grey metal. Dees pushed it back, shooed me through in front of her, and then turned, barring Penny's path. "We need to have a private chat, Mr Swift and I."

"Oi! I'm his fucking apprentice, I'm the fucking bitch who's done all the fucking legwork all this fucking . . ."

"The matter is highly personal," Dees replied, "and while we're all very grateful for your efforts, this is something that must be handled quickly, privately, and alone."

Penny fumed. I said cautiously, "Dees? How personal and how private?"

She turned back to me, and there was something in her face that might almost have been regret. "It concerns Robert Bakker."

I raised my eyebrows, struggling not to do anything more extreme. "OK. Yeah. We should probably talk."

Dees nodded smartly, closed the door, cutting us off from the rest of the world, and locked it behind us.

We were in a medical examination room.

The British Library had a medical examination room. There was a high black couch, covered over with white paper, a white curtain, standing open, a low desk with many drawers and a silverish metal canister on top of it, a blood pressure monitor, a set of scales, and, as if the situation needed it, two Aldermen who looked like they took themselves too seriously, and a man in a white coat. Dees said, "Please, sit down," indicating the couch.

I perched on the edge, leaning back on the palms of my hands. "Dees," I said, "you should know that we do not like medicine. What's going on?"

She sighed. Suddenly she looked too small, too frail, tired and alone. Somewhere in South London was a husband and a kid, who might by now be wondering where the missus had got to. She pinched the bridge of her nose and with her eyes still half screwed shut said, "All right. The sun isn't rising."

"Tell me something I don't know."

Her mouth twitched in displeasure. "The edge of the city is shrinking. The boroughs furthest out, Barnet, Amersham, Croydon, they're all . . . gone. We didn't notice, none of us noticed, until I tried to call my family and discovered that I had forgotten my home telephone number. There are others of the Aldermen who also know people in the suburbs. They couldn't make any contact. It's as if the city is closing in on itself." Then, sharper than she'd probably intended, "Did you know that?"

"Yep."

"You're not just . . ."

"An elder of the Tribe told me. Nice guy. Studied philosophy at university."

"You went to . . ." She caught her breath. "Yes, of course you went to have a talk with the Tribe, why wouldn't you? The fact that the Neon Court's ambassador is threatening to declare war on *us* for non-cooperation would in no way hinder you from . . ."

"I'm sorry, the part where I convinced the Tribe not to go to war any time soon and found out more about this 'chosen one', a girl, by the way, going by the catchy name of JG, who the Tribe think is in the hands of the Court and vice versa – that wasn't of any use, was it?"

"You could have been . . ."

"And yet happily I wasn't and we had a lovely little chat and all things considered, I think advanced the situation. I even talked with the head of the Order, psychopathic guy by the name of Chaigneau, who asked me very nicely if I'd kill Oda and was, incidentally, lying about something but I don't know what. Isn't it nice the way I let myself get beat to crappiness despite our potent desire to obliterate all before us, just to ease these little diplomatic transactions?" My smile was fixed like a bayonet. Dees was almost shaking with exhaustion, with tension seeking release through some crack in her faultless exterior. We let the moment stretch, then said, "Anyway, about this whole sun not rising . . . ?"

Her shoulders bent, her head lapsed to one side. She said, in a voice that would never have admitted it was close to breaking, "We found references. This has happened before."

"That's something, I suppose. Did you find O'Rourke?"

"No. His house was empty. There was blood on the carpet."

"Has anyone tried to get out of London?"

"It's not . . ." she began. "It's not as easy as that. There are no trains leaving the city. When we ask, we are informed there's a delay on the line, and any further enquiries go round in circles. When will the trains run? When the delay finishes. Why is there a delay? An incident. What incident? There's a delay. The city isn't aware that it's under this spell. I ordered a car to try and drive out of the city. The M11 slopes back in on itself long before it reaches the M25. You drive round a junction and the next thing you know, you're heading back into town. The same on the M4, the M40, the M2. The Blackwall Tunnel has been closed owing to flooding. The Woolwich Ferry isn't running. Roundabouts spin you round and round and then throw you back the way you came. Streets are become cul de sacs, and on the walls where there was once a road, someone has written, 'end of the line' in ancient fading paint, as if the words were there all along. The map of the city . . . well . . ." She gestured with the end of one pale finger at the nearest Alderman.

He produced an A–Z of the city from a deep dark pocket of his deep dark coat, handed it to me. I flicked through it. There were blank pages, dull creamy-yellow colour, mixed in with all the rest, where there should have been busy streets on the edge of the city. I handed it back to the Alderman, said, "I'm very tired now."

"As are we all."

"What good news do you have?"

She shifted uneasily. "We know what it is."

"And you look like you've just swallowed a baby mouse because . . ."

"You're not going to like any of it. Not one tiny part."

"Astound me."

So she did.

Second Interlude: Aftershocks

In which the story of the creature called Blackout is recounted in the basement of the British Library.

She said, "It's old. Almost as old as the city. When this city was founded by the Romans it – he – was the devil with the club, the mad native spirit that waited behind the temple of Mithras to bite and tear and claw at his enemies in the dark. Then later, when the streets became alleys and the roads became mud, he became the man on the edge of the torchlight, the half-seen shadow that puffed out the torches of the wandering guards and beat their heads out on the sides of the churches. They say he inspired the Mohawks to run mad in the eighteenth century, raping and maiming not because they felt any great need to do so, but because it was sport, and because they were bored, and life didn't matter. When the streets were cobbled over he began to resemble what we know now, the footsteps heard on stone that you cannot see, turn your head and the sound may be there but he is not, blink and you die. When the Victorians began to introduce street lighting, he was the shadow at the end of the alley, half seen and then gone, who always shied away from the light, and when the gas went out, there he was. The more fanciful accounts say he was Jack the Ripper. I regard the evidence for this as faint. The Blitz gave him strength, of course. The lights went out all across the city; the moonlight was cursed for leading bombers to London, the curtains drawn, the streets still and silent. The perfect place for the one wandering air-raid warden to hear footsteps in the night that were not his own, and then look, and then die. That's where he got his name – Blackout – the shadow at the end of the alley, the footsteps half heard in the night.

"You may ask: but what is he?

"The answer is, no one is entirely sure. An idea, perhaps, that roams from body to body, age to age, inhabiting the minds of the cruellest, the most frightened, the most lonely and driving them to perform terrible acts. We call him 'he', which is a misnomer – he has no gender, he has no physical form – but his habit has been, until now, to occupy the minds of men, not women, and drive them to commit deeds that even the most hardened criminal would shy from. He does not simply kill; he murders. He does not simply stalk; he hunts, and wherever the lights go out, there he is, just the other side of a breath drawn in fear.

"But only once before has Blackout been powerful enough to stop the sun. Only once did he inhabit a mind whose rage, whose fury, whose anger and whose passion was great enough to stop the sun from rising, to keep the city from turning over, to kill all chances of escape.

"The best way, therefore, to understand Blackout is, perhaps, to understand this.

"I have said already that Blackout reached the peak of his power during the Blitz: fear, horror, doubt, these are the fuels that sustain him, and make minds most open to his presence.

"What I have not said is that the years immediately following the Blitz were also ripe for his endeavours. Soldiers returning home from five years of fighting found their homes destroyed, their families changed, their children dead or grown, their minds blackened by the things they had seen. England in the 1950s was not a good society in which to expose the scars of the time; the Dunkirk spirit was, regrettably, less than amenable to the shedding of self-indulgent, emotional tears. Minds were open to Blackout. The smog was thick and black, the streets gloomy, full of holes and dirt. He was able to influence the thoughts of men without trying, hunting with impunity. His victims were easily identifiable: their eyes turned to blood, blood in their ears, their noses, brains burst from the inside out. Those, at least, were the simple deaths. The police could make nothing of it, and the Aldermen, I am sorry to say, hushed up the majority of cases to prevent the nature of the crime being too extensively explored. We knew what Blackout was, but a creature that roamed from mind to mind, body to body, was next to impossible to stop, harder still to kill. The Aldermen had killed plenty of his vessels; the morgues were rich with the bodies of men whose eyes were turned to slush and whose nails were black-red with the blood of their victims – but still Blackout, the idea, the thing at the end of the alley, persisted.

"Then, in 1958, Blackout entered the mind of a young man, one of the Tribe – a boy called Woods. The Tribe then was not like the Tribe now – it changes with the times, so that when a thing becomes accepted, it forgoes it, and moves on to embrace some new way of being outcast. This young man had not lived in times that were sympathetic to his condition. An orphan of the war, like many, raised in a care system that had yet to come under any form of appropriate scrutiny, I think it is fair to say that he had been abused, and shown at an early stage that there was nothing for him in this life but the abuse of others. A sensitive boy in a time in which sensitive men were not the fashion. The details of his life are heavily shrouded; neither the state system nor the Tribe kept records of them.

"The Tribe gave Woods some refuge, for a time, and he embarked on the usual processes of transformation that characterise the Tribe's actions: self-harm, cutting, dressing skin with ink and blood, and through these things acquiring new strengths and new magics, becoming, so I believe the philosophy goes, *more* than human through systematic destruction of those characteristics that we use to define humanity. But even with the Tribe he was unhappy, since they, for all their talk of being free, conform to each other, and to an idea of difference that can make them all very much the same. And the elders of the Tribe, looking at Woods, could see in him a darkness, a pit of tar at the bottom of his soul, deeper and more violent than anything they were used to even among the denizens of the Tribe, and it scared them.

"For what action, we do not know, Woods was expelled from the Tribe, and some few weeks later attempted to take his own life. He failed, and for trying to commit suicide he was given a prison sentence. In prison he attempted suicide again, cutting his wrists in his cell. He bled out and should have died, but at the moment of death, something changed in him. His eyes turned, according to one source, totally black; another corrected this, saying that his eyes weren't black, but it was like spilt ink and burst flesh mixed up together to make his eyes seem black, whereas each was more like an ink–meat pudding in his skull. Pale from blood loss, the cuts on his wrists still bleeding, he rose, and calmly walked out of his cell. Stories then become chaotic. Some say the lights went out and all went silent except for the passing of his footsteps. Others say that the guards tried to restrain him, and by simply looking him in the eye, they died. Some hid. Some ran. Some tried to escape when he did. One says a guard fired a shotgun straight into Woods's chest, and that Woods simply staggered, then raised his head and kept on marching out.

"Whatever stories you believe, the Aldermen's records give us twelve dead, four blind, two with significant brain damage from internal bleeding. Matter hushed up as quickly as possible. And then, of course, the sun failed to rise.

"I regret to say that the pattern on this occasion was similar to what we see now. Few individuals in the city noticed the failure of the sun to rise: the Midnight Mayor, the Old Bag Lady, the Beggar King, one or two others, the odd seer and sorcerer. But the Midnight Mayor's word was law, and once others were made aware of the problem, it was easy enough to convince them. I regret that times have changed; we now live in a more dynamic corporate age. A meeting was called of all the most senior figures in the city – Tribe and Court included – and it was resolved that together they would find a solution for the problem of Woods and Blackout, and end the matter once and for all. The Court was still a small operation, and the Tribe reluctant to engage with one of their own. An agreement was made, however, with the Midnight Mayor as its head. His name was Aronson – a peer, as a matter of fact, but then again, these were very different times. Aronson, with a team of Aldermen, assisted by various seers, sorcerers and magicians, tracked Woods down and attempted to capture him. Eleven people died, four survived, Woods was not captured. Aronson was one of the dead, his eyes turned to nothing, a fist-sized hole punched through his heart.

"The next Midnight Mayor was, rather against the fashion of the time, a lady, called Manswala, who wasn't even an Alderman, but rather

Aronson's personal secretary. There was some unease at her succession, but it soon became clear why she had acquired the title: she was more cautious, and less arrogant, than the norm. Rather than engage Blackout directly, she embarked on research. Some have criticised her for the slowness of her response to this matter, for in the days she spent attempting to work out every detail of Blackout's and, indeed, Woods's existence, seven people died slow, cruel deaths at the end of the alley.

"One of those killed was a member of the Neon Court, a thrall, a favourite of Lady Neon for her beauty and charm. An Indian, it was said she had eyes the colour of emeralds and hair as black as night, and that Lady Neon loved her, and worshipped her, and she returned the honour. It was, no doubt, that beauty and charm which led Woods to take extra care with her, keeping her alive, so the pathology report said, for nearly two days while he performed on her . . . deeds that I suspect we can all imagine. Lady Neon was furious and immediately ordered the Court to send out a force against Woods. Manswala argued against rash action, but Lady Neon was mistress of her own people and they could not be stopped. The body of the daimyo that led the attack was found hung upside down by his ankles outside the main palace of the Neon Court a day and a half later, the body mutilated both before and after death.

"To this day, she has always blamed the Tribe, Woods's people, for what happened to her daimyo and her favourite; the mutilation, and their failure to curb Woods when they had a chance, were merely two excuses to fuel the fire of a long-held mistrust, and in the face of such humiliation and disgust, it was hardly surprising that she needed someone to blame.

"Lady Neon spoke to Mayor Manswala again, this time agreeing to follow the Midnight Mayor's policy in all matters relating to Blackout, and to assist in whatever way she could in curbing the threat to the city as a whole. That arrangement formed the foundation of the 1959 treaty between the Court and the Aldermen that is causing us so much concern now; I fear, in the Aldermen's haste to secure aid against Woods, we may have played diplomatically into Lady Neon's hands.

"And still the sun did not rise.

"Five days, if you can call night without ending 'day', Manswala talked and argued and thought about how best to bring down Woods, and all that time he grew more out of control. Soon it became almost impossible to hide Woods's activities from the civil authorities. He flaunted the ineptitude of the people around him, and killed increasingly senior targets – daimyos, Aldermen, Tribal elders – daring one and all to try and bring him down. But this was in many ways the least of the Midnight Mayor's problems. As the sun continued not to rise, and the city remained cut off from the rest of the world, the people as a whole became affected. Under Blackout's spell, they lived in a world of body-clock confusion, not sure whether they were supposed to be at work, or at play, or be asleep, or be on the buses or the trains or open the shop or close the shop or any manner of activity. A form of sleepless, wandering delirium seemed to set in, as if the whole city was suffering from jet lag; shelves were not restocked; some parts of the Tube ran while others were shut; water supplies and power became erratic; parents slept while children ran in the street; violence increased and the police didn't know whether they were on call or not; hospital admissions increased and the doctors on the night shift did not sleep and did not sleep, so that by the fifth day no one dared perform an operation for fear of killing the patient. There were hallucinations and terrors; ordinary people were afraid to leave their homes for fear of the footsteps at the end of the alley, of a thing half seen under the lamp, for Blackout's magic is the magic of shadows and fear, of reason saying one thing and instinct saying the other. And at the end, everyone just started falling asleep. All across the city, people fell down where they walked, just fell asleep where they sat or where they lay, and could not be woken. Even the magicians, even the ones who knew what was happening, could not do anything but sleep.

"In the face of this, Manswala felt that she had to act, and with an alliance of sorcerers, Aldermen and Court soldiers, went after Woods once more, ready this time with a plan to trap him, hold him, study him, and, they hoped, contain Blackout for ever, which should stand a good chance of succeeding.

"They found him.

"The spell was cast; but they hadn't had time, and they were too tired and too afraid, and though they fought and fought, they could not contain him. He killed them. Dozens of the most powerful magicians of the time, he killed them all; some quickly, some slowly, but all dead. Manswala he killed as slowly as he could. They say she stopped screaming long before she died.

"Only a few were left alive, hiding and cowering in the dark away from Woods, eyes closed, frozen with terror.

"Except one.

"The apprentice to a sorceress had followed his teacher into the battle, and watched everything, hidden in a corner. We don't know how or why this young man, still a teenager at the time, had felt the need to risk his neck for this, but he did. He was more powerful, this apprentice, than any of his peers, a great craftsman of magic in the making, who was eventually to be hailed as one of the greatest sorcerers of the time. He watched Blackout kill his friends, his colleagues, his teacher, watched them all scream and die and, while he watched, he prepared his own plan, and made his own spell. He took the power from the survivors, from the few pitiful remnants of that group, took their magic and their strength, summoned light above his head and, alone in all that blood, stepped out, and faced Blackout, and fought back. The rest ran, or crawled, or did whatever they could to get away, leaving this one apprentice standing his ground, and when the battle was over and the lights had finally gone out, they looked east, and saw the sun rise.

"He had banished it.

"Blackout.

"He had banished Blackout, this sorcerer's apprentice. After hours of battle in the dark, he had managed to find that weakness in his enemy's armour and banished Blackout from the city. Woods was dead, his body torn to pieces, just a few bones and scraps of skin left behind, and the sun was rising. But the apprentice gave a warning – Blackout could return, would return. The lights had to be kept burning, the streets had to be kept safe, eyes watching, people waiting, wherever there was a darkness deep enough, there Blackout would be.

"That was another reason why the alliance with the Neon Court was struck. The Midnight Mayor and Lady Neon agreed to maintain a mutual watch on the city streets, and ensure that the lights burnt brightly enough to keep the shadows away.

"And so the city woke and forgot that it had ever been asleep.

"And, I am afraid, others forgot too. Magicians, Aldermen, even sorcerers, who had at the very last fallen asleep after five days of endless night, woke, not entirely sure what had happened or why their clothes smelt so bad, and, as mankind does, shook their heads and went about their daily business, without trying too hard to contemplate things that might unsettle this convenient pattern. Both the Midnight Mayors who had participated in this battle were dead; the new incumbent hadn't even been exposed to the case. Things were written down, by what few survivors there were, but Lady Neon was reluctant to keep a record of such bitter defeats, and shortly left the city for palaces in other lands, rather than be reminded of the blood that had stained her doorstep. Those Aldermen that had lived made records, but these were quickly lost in the mass of case notes that make up the history of our organisation, and with Blackout banished, and no sign of his return, the story became a warning, which became a legend, which became a myth, which became forgotten, all in a matter of a few passing generations. Aldermen do not live very long lives, traditionally. Nor, I suspect, did those who had survived long wish to remember. A combination of carelessness, fear, the after-effects of an enchantment and the strong desire to forget and be troubled no more, all affected the records of these events. We thought he was gone; so why should we remember?

"Besides, only one man really knew what had happened the night Woods died, and he almost never talked of it, except to give his one command that the street lights should be kept burning in the night. It was said he had seen too much blood that night, that some part of his soul had died, or been twisted into a form unmentionable. Furthermore, this sorcerer's apprentice went on to become a sorcerer of incredible power and talent, and his deeds in his middle years were so remarkable that few people bothered to ask or even remembered the way in which his story had begun. However, old age corrupted him, turned his power a darker way, so that by the time he died his name was spoken of with curses by almost all that knew him, and this, alas, only made his previous life's wisdom and achievements harder to accept.

"I suspect, Mr Mayor, that you can guess the name of this sorcerer.

"He was, after all, your teacher.

"And, of course, your killer.

"And it is you who brought this part of my story to an end, the night that you killed him.

"However, as I am sure you can guess, death is never really the end for a man like Robert Bakker."

Dees finished speaking.

I looked down at the floor, then up at the ceiling. I said, "Dees? Did you really drag me all this way to tell me that the only guy who knows how to stop Oda is dead?"

"No."

"No. Didn't think so."

"Robert Bakker is dead," she said. "Be that as it may. He was the only person who managed to stop Blackout, but regrettably he left us with less than coherent details on how he did so."

"Isn't that just bloody typical?" I sighed. "You know, if I had a penny for every time prophets forgot to footnote their mystic utterings . . ."

"And now Blackout is back," she interrupted.

"Yes. He is, isn't he? Get to the point."

She sighed. "Mr Mayor – we have Robert Bakker's last breath."

I forced a smile and said, soft as a swollen sea, "You have what?"

"When the allies you made in the Kingsway Telephone Exchange stormed the Tower on the last night of Robert Bakker's life, we were of course aware. The Aldermen chose not to intervene because Bakker was useful to us in maintaining order in the city. A killer, no doubt, and potentially a liability we ourselves might have had to deal with in the near future. But you solved that problem for us. However, we were uncertain of the outcome of your encounter and deemed it prudent to have observers on the scene."

"You . . . knew what was happening?"

"Yes."

"You . . ."

"We are the Aldermen," she said sharply. "Rest assured, if either you or Mr Bakker had threatened the city itself in any significant way, we would have acted. As it was, you seemed set on destroying each other, rather than us. We saw your allies storm the Tower; we saw signs of battle. We saw, in the middle of the night, a build-up of magical forces at the very, very top of the building, a meeting of magics unlike anything the city had seen for nearly fifty years. Are you aware, Mr Swift, that during your encounter with Mr Bakker, two substations in the central and west London areas shorted out? Are you aware that half a mile of water main had to be replaced under New Oxford Street, and there was a gas leak off Charing Cross Road? No one ever considers the logistics of these things. You two fought; Bakker fell. He was, needless to say, dead at impact, barely worth the coffin he was buried in. But our observers were quick; they saw the value of maintaining some part of this extremely powerful and learned man. So one of our number got a plastic bag, and as Bakker let out his last breath, she tied it around his head, to capture the air from his lungs. We had our people take him to our mortuary, where the breath from his lungs could be contained for posterity. In other words, Mr Mayor, his dying breath; the sum and conclusion of his life captured. I think we all here are aware of the power in such things."

"And if we had fallen, instead of him? Would you have done us the same service?"

"No," she replied. "Our observers had no orders to catch your last breath."

"That's . . ."

"We were, however, prepared to extract, examine and document your blood."

We looked up, eyes flashing, fingers tightening knuckle-white. "You were . . ."

"Mr Mayor, it is nothing personal. You are a mystical oddity, something unique. It is always worth documenting and recording such things. You are one of us now; I'm sure you understand."

We stood up, clenching our fists at our sides to contain the anger prickling within them. "We are not, Alderman, nor never shall be, one of you. We are not . . . some mortician standing by to dissect, we do not . . . stand by in the face of such things as these."

"Matthew," she said, "I am being honest with you."

I felt cold. My eyes burnt. I said, "So what do you propose?"

She indicated the metal canister on the desk. "Do you know the power of dying breaths?"

"Yeah."

"We need information." A pause, then she became the brisk professional again, reciting facts without feeling. "It works best if the individual concerned had a close link to the dead; a sympathy for magical operations is a bonus – a seer would be ideal but, unfortunately, we have neither seers nor time to find one – having shared blood with the deceased helps. Robert Bakker, I believe, did have a fascination with your blood, did he not?"

I didn't answer.

"The process manifests in different ways. Sometimes it's subtle: a simple awareness of that which the deceased may also have known. Sometimes it's more profound; a weak mind can sometimes be overwhelmed by the presence of the deceased, assume traits, personality aspects, of the dead consciousness. Sometimes it manifests in other ways. It is not something recommended to anyone suffering from mental conditions such as hallucinations, delusions, or violent dreams. The condition is temporary. Possible side effects can include a dry mouth, a sense of impending doom, and, if the deceased died violently, an echo of pain. But it is just an echo. A man's dying breath doesn't hold his soul, even if we were to consider that such a thing existed. Just a fragment of what he was."

She looked at me uncertainly. "You don't strike me, Mr Mayor," she added, "as someone for whom a weak will is a problem."

"No," we said. "We're not that."

Her fingers tap-danced over the edge of the canister. The Aldermen round the room were silent, their eyes fixed on us.

"We wouldn't be having this discussion if there was an easier way," she added.

"You do it," I replied sharply. "Go on. You open the canister, you share Mr Bakker's last breath. Enjoy having the knowledge, experience, wisdom, and psychopathic murdering tendencies of a dead sorcerer whose shadow grew claws when the sun went down and who went around gutting his friends, rollicking around your brain. We're not doing this."

"If I could do it, I would – I trust you believe me when I say that."

"Your trust is flattering."

"You shared blood with Bakker. Before he died; you shared blood. That creates a potent link with his last breath almost as good as if you were a seer . . ."

"I have auditory and visual hallucinations," I retorted. "There you go. Screw it."

A reproachful look passed over her face. "Mr Mayor . . ."

"I do! Ever since I stopped being blind, remember then? I see weird shit."

"You are the Midnight Mayor of this city, at a time when it's under attack . . ."

"A few hours ago you were wanting to diagnose me with post-traumatic stress! You really think getting me to share my brain with the dead echo of the guy that killed me is going to chill me out?"

She sighed, pulled her hand away, shrugged slightly too dramatically. "Very well. It's entirely your choice. We wouldn't force you."

"Glad to hear it."

"But . . . do bear in mind this."

"What?"

"That two Midnight Mayors died attempting to fight Woods. Your encounter with Oda left you half-blind and clawing for help. Do you want to be the next name on the list of corpses?"

I stared down at my feet. They were still wearing the big heavy boots I'd stolen from London Underground. I said, "My shoes and coat are in a locker in the disused section of Angel Tube. I want a large cold drink, a hot shower, a clean shirt, an apple and a Kit Kat. One of those big ones – not the two-finger wanky jobs. And not the dark chocolate or orange ones or shit: a proper, authentic, Kit Kat."

"We can do that."

"Right. And if there's any pills you lot have which you use to help you keep awake during major-league crises, I could probably do with that, because I haven't slept in what I guess counts as days, even though the sun hasn't happened."

"Again, we can provide."

"Good. And someone give Penny a proper meal and a warm safe place to lie down and catch a few winks, set someone over her, make sure she's safe, ignore the abuse."

"We can do all these things."

"Right." I swung my legs up onto the black couch, lay back to look at the ceiling. "How many dying breaths have you guys collected down the years?"

"A lot," she replied, picking up the canister and moving it towards me. "The British Library recently started a catalogue. We have no fewer than seven last breaths of Merlin, although of course we have no way to test which one may actually be real other than having someone inhale them, which, while academically fulfilling, does carry its risks."

One of the Aldermen detached himself from a wall, and wheeled over a box on a trolley. There was a clear plastic mask with a rubber band along the back, attached to a clear plastic tube that ran into the device. He parked it next to me.

I said, "You'd better do it quick, Dees, because I reckon you've got all of thirty seconds before I change my mind and run out of that door gibbering."

She slid the canister into a slot that seemed designed for the purpose on the side of the machine. Something inside went *clunk*. "You know," she went on, pulling the breathing mask down over my head and tightening the strap behind, "an unofficial survey six months ago found no fewer than fourteen Merlin's skulls wandering around the underground markets, and seventy-nine finger bones, with or without mystical adornments. There are probably at least twenty dealers offering fraudulent vials of your blood, Mr Mayor. You could start a business."

A flicked switch on the side of the machine produced the sound of a thousand giant ants doing riverdance on the inside of its metal case. One of the Aldermen moved towards the end of the bed; one towards the head. I strained to see them clearly: faces like prison walls. A small light on the side of the device went red; then yellow; then green. Dees laid a hand on my chest, palm pressing down on the middle of my breastbone like she was about to do CPR. "This could be a novel experience," she said, and something at the back of the machine went *click-hiss*.

Nothing happened.

I waited a bit, breathing fast and scared through the mask, and nothing went on not happening.

A breath.

Another breath.

I could feel my heart slowing down.

I said, "You sure this thing is switched on?"

She thought about it, lips pursing tight. "I'm not sure," she replied. "Let me check." Then she leant forward, pulled the mask away from my face, peered into its clear plastic shallows, tossed it aside. She leant down over my face, until her nose was hovering a few inches above mine, and then, very slowly and thoughtfully, pressed both her hands palm first over my nose and mouth. I tried to mumble, then I tried to scream, wrapped my hands around her wrists, tried to pull them free, but the Aldermen were holding down my feet and arms, and her fingers were growing silver claws and her eyes were turning the mad, empty red of the city dragon with its rolling tongue that guarded the old gates of London, and we screamed, our voice lost beneath her fingers. I tried to bite and couldn't even open my lips, felt as if my teeth were about to be bent out of my mouth, my nose broken, I could feel blood in every tiny capillary, hear it in my head in the small veins round behind my ears, feel the inside of my chest seem to burn and shrivel like ancient dry popcorn, we tried to bring fire to our fingers and it wouldn't come, the fire wouldn't come, and Dees just looked at us, with mad empty red eyes and there was nothing human in her face, skin of silver and a rolling thin red tongue that curled and lashed at the air, hair turned to wire, back bending and breaking upwards as the lizard spines burst from the back of her coat. Static burst across my eyes like fireworks breaking and we thought

no no no no no nonononono can't die can't die can't die haven't lived haven't lived haven't lived

and the Pacific Ocean burst behind our ears and there was a pain in my belly like a fist made of barbed wire slicing through flesh and our whole body jerked and twisted and a sound like a dinosaur exhaling its final breath and our whole body snapped, lifted up off the couch, arching onto our shoulders and heels as every bone tried to break free of our chest and still Dees held on and we couldn't breathe we couldn't breathe and . . .

and there was a man standing just behind us.

His head was upside down, but so was the world. His face was old dressed up as merely middle-aged, skin bright, eyes sharp and cheerful, hair receding to reveal a round skull containing a round face that was happy with who and what it was. He was leaning on the palms of his hands, arms stretched out either side of him, like a surgeon examining the patient and wondering whether he should really bother. Then another burst of pain twisted our whole body and we screamed again, his face blurring behind a burst of salt in our eyes that crawled out of our skin as if all water had decided to jump ship while it had the chance. Something was wrong with the lights, somewhere overhead a darkness that wasn't just the cave being built in stone around the edge of my eyes, spreading, and then we jerked again and there he was, shaking his head sadly and leaning over to look us in the eyes. His pupils were grey, ringed with pale brown, and as his gaze met ours the pain in our flesh parted and we lay gasping and still, our body a limp bundle of communications interrupted. He sighed. His voice, when he spoke, was deep, level, calm and familiar. It was the voice that had taught me everything I knew.

He said, "Well, Matthew. This is a mess, isn't it?"

I found I had nothing to say in reply.

His face was the last thing I saw as the world went out.

Part 3: A Fully Rounded Education

Because there's no such thing as "can't get worse".

I opened my eyes.

This was an error.

Bakker was sat at the side of the black couch.

He was wearing a striped suit and a grey tie.

He was smiling.

Dead Mr Bakker.

I closed my eyes. I said, "Dees?"

A voice said, almost kindly, "Matthew?"

"Dees – the guy who killed me and who I killed in return is sat next to me and did you try to throttle me?"

There was a brief pause, that might have been something nearing consternation. Then, "No . . . and no. You started screaming."

I opened my eyes again.

Bakker was still there. He leant forward, putting his chin on the top of his upturned hand. "Interesting," he said.

I half turned my head, and there was Dees, sat near the other side of the couch, face pinched tight with weariness and doubt. I had never seen doubt in her before, but the universe had managed to pull a number even on Leslie Dees, Alderman and financial adviser to the ridiculously wealthy. "Bakker says 'interesting'," I wheezed.

"You are aware," she began, "that he is both dead and not real?"

"The dead aren't real?"

"I meant . . . in a strictly practical sense."

On the other side, Bakker said, "She's absolutely right, you know. What you are experiencing is arguably no more than a metamagical manifestation shaped by a mystic echo highlighted by my own death – which don't think we're not going to discuss, by the by – rather than any sort of profound theological or philosophical experience." I turned back to him. He beamed. "There's no point attempting to construct this event as anything other than what it is. Although make no mistake: the fact that you are seeing me so strongly, so promptly, and your reaction to inhaling, if you don't mind the concept, my dead breath, suggest that the near future will be . . . all things considered . . ." His lips puckered in concentration as he tried to find the words. His skin was too pale, thin and translucent. ". . . I believe the vernacular term which I shall deploy in the interest of being both brisk and to the point – is shit."

I looked back at Dees. "I want that drink now."

Wordlessly she handed me a stainless-steel flask. I sat up slowly, angling myself so my back was to the place where Bakker, or not-Bakker, or the thing that was most definitely and absolutely not Bakker's ghost, was sitting. I unscrewed the lid, saw milk. Dees held up a Kit Kat. "Cup of cold milk," she said, "and chocolate. The milk should be in a glass, really, but wonders do not universally abound."

I took the Kit Kat, ripped open the package with my teeth, broke off a stick of chocolate, ate slowly, drowned it with a gulp of milk. When this was done I said, "You still not seeing any ghosts of sorcerers past?"

She shook her head, smiling apologetically.

"Where's Penny?"

"At a hotel; sleeping."

"How long was I . . . ?"

"Screaming, howling, foaming at the mouth?"

"Yeah, all of that."

"Only a few minutes. Then you . . ." Her lips thinned. "I believe the term is 'passed out'. As would anyone, under the circumstances."

I put the flask of milk to one side, felt my throat, rubbed my knees and elbows, checking for injuries. Every part ached, but nothing more than the usual background throb of sleepless beaten-up fatigue.

I had another stick of chocolate.

Dees watched.

I had another slurp of milk.

I wiped my mouth with my sleeve.

I started on my third line of chocolate.

Dees said, "How exactly does this work?"

"How does what work?" I asked through a mouthful of biscuit.

"How does Bakker's knowledge work relative to your consciousness?"

I hesitated. "Dunno," I said. "Try me."

She shifted her weight on the stool where she sat, leaning forward with elbows on her knees. "All right," she said. "How do we destroy Blackout?"

Bakker was standing just behind her. He hadn't been at the beginning of the sentence, and there had been no word at which he appeared; just a breath and there he was, a faintly appreciative expression on his face. I screwed up my eyes tight and thought. "No idea," I said finally. "Sorry. Not a clue."

"She's very to the point, isn't she?" said Bakker, craning over her shoulder. "A woman who knows what she wants, what she needs, and intends that nothing prevents her from acquiring both these things. She likes you, you know."

I bit my lip, felt heat rise somewhere.

"Not," he added quickly, "in any sexual way. No more than is the usual chemical response of a pair of XX chromosomes to the presence of an XY combination. Not sex. But she likes you." He leant down close, until his lips nearly brushed her face, and she didn't move, didn't twitch as the non-air of his non-breath ran over her skin. "Not that she will ever admit it. Far too dangerous to grow close to someone who spends as much time in danger as you do. Decisions could be flawed. Emotions could be damaged. Careers compromised. You'll never get an invite to watch the kids play hockey from this one, I'm afraid."

"Mr Mayor? You look . . . distracted," said Dees.

"Uh . . . just appreciating a surreal and psychologically traumatic experience here," I whimpered, gesturing vaguely in reply.

"These two though," went on Bakker, straightening up and turning a stern gaze onto the Aldermen, "these two would kill you, if they weren't afraid that they'd miss. They have it in their eyes: that voice saying do it do it do it do it kill him; but there it is . . . just on the edge, in the hollow of the tear duct, that other voice saying he'll kill me he'll kill me he'll kill me if I try. You've done well, Matthew. While resembling a chewed-up rodent you've still managed to make them afraid. Then again, I imagine your blue blood helps."

For a second, there was a flicker of something else in Bakker, something that sank his cheeks into bone, turned teeth yellow and lined like ancient rotting bone, made scraggly his hair, black his fingers, nails turned to claws, just a flash, just a flicker, bursting out of the suit and, for just a moment, Robert Bakker cast no shadow. Then it was gone, and he was ambling round the room, trailing his finger along the black couch, turning his head this way and that to examine every detail of his surroundings.

"Oh, look!" he said idly. "You have an apprentice." My throat tightened, I could feel every lump of phlegm there and every drop of saliva in my mouth. "Fascinating, the inside of your brain, Matthew. An apprentice who you would fight for, die for and, of course, kill for. A sorceress who nearly destroyed the city and you took one look at her and thought 'she's a train wreck on legs, a liability and a danger to all around her, let's take her in because she'll make excellent company'. I always wondered what made you pick the fights you did, Matthew. Maybe the Alderman is right. Maybe you do need therapy. Post-traumatic stress. Your blood tasted good, when you died."

I became aware of something slippery under my fingers. The chocolate of my last stick of Kit Kat was melting beneath my touch. I rubbed my fingers clean on my sleeve, all the while hypnotised by Bakker's slow wander round the room.

"I knew the last Midnight Mayor, of course," he went on. "He was more imaginative than anyone ever suspected. Making you his successor, of all people! I underestimated him. Not that this knowledge does me any good now, since I am, of course, nothing more than a projection of some traumatic echo of consciousness given shape by my dust, your magic and . . . of course . . . your overly stimulated and somewhat disturbed brain."

"How long is this going to last?" I asked Dees, and was surprised at how dry my voice was.

"It varies. There's nothing set. But the longest . . . was no more than a few days."

"Even when the sun isn't rising?" asked Bakker, sitting down next to me so close I could almost feel the not-heat from his not-body. "Difficult, defining 'day' when there is no daylight. The Norwegians probably have a trick to it. Very underestimated people, the Norwegians."

I kept my head locked dead ahead, not looking at him. Dees said, "Mr Mayor? What exactly are you experiencing?"

"All sorts of weird bad shit. If I start talking to myself, you won't call the guys in white coats, will you?"

"I think we're all past that, don't you? Is there . . . do you have any further thoughts on . . . Blackout?" she ventured.

"You could ask," suggested Bakker, examining his nails.

"I'm going to go to the bathroom now," I said, easing myself off the couch. "Where the hell is it?"

Bakker wandered with me down the corridor, examining everything.

The bathroom was made of dull beige tiles and smelt of cheap dull air freshener. There were cubicles down one side, and mirrors down the other.

There was an Alderman there washing his hands.

I said, "You – out!"

He took one look at our face and left.

I waited for the door to close, did a quick scan round the edges of the ceiling for CCTV cameras, and turned on Bakker. He was leaning against the wall by the hot air puffers, casually running his hand underneath them to see if they'd work. They didn't. He looked up as I turned, raising his eyebrows expectantly.

"Right!" I said. "A few ground rules! You're dead, which means the you I'm seeing right now is entirely dependent on my brain as the living bit of the equation. Therefore, no playing silly buggers! I say jump, you jump, savvy?"

He sighed, scratched his chin. "That's all very easy to say," he sighed, "but, alas, current evidence suggests that this relationship may not be so straightforward."

"Uh-uh," I snapped, wagging a finger at him. "No complicated shit we're doing this for a very simple reason. Oda is possessed by Blackout; you killed Blackout; you tell me how to do a repeat number. That simple, end of story, we all get to go home."

"I take it you're choosing to ignore the fact that by now the Neon Court will have concluded you are not going to honour your alliance and will be sending people to kill you, and the Tribe will have by now decided that they just don't trust you and will equally be preparing reprisals? All very tactfully of course – no one will be admitting to it, but so it goes."

"Yep!" My voice was rising towards a shrill. "Yep, totally choosing to ignore that. Totally, utterly, totally, because you know what, civil war has nothing on the sun not coming up or my having to share my brain with your ghost."

"And we're not going to handle this slight conflict of interest?"

"Slight conflict of interest?" I echoed, ready to shout.

"Naturally," he replied, detaching himself from the wall. "I mean, my dying breath was collected, by definition, as I was dying, capturing my very last thoughts, state of mind and being. Needless to say, your having just pushed me off the thirty-sixth floor left me in a rather absolute frame of mind regarding my relationship with you."

"Let's not get schoolkid about this," I replied with a scowl. "You killed me, I killed you, you started it, boo sucks boo, end of rant."

He was walking towards me. I stood my ground, clenching my fingers to stop them shaking, looking at a point just between his eyes and hoping he'd mistake my glare for the real thing. "It's hardly going to be that easy," he said, stopping within throttling distance in front of me. "Issues all round, and we do know how difficult issues are in sorcerers. Your apprentice had issues and the city was nearly destroyed. I had issues and . . . well . . ."

He waggled his eyebrows towards the mirror behind me.

Instinct turned me where sense would have made me stand my ground.

There was a man in the mirror.

His hair was a few stray strands of wilting grey, his skin was stained with liver death, his teeth were yellow, his eyes were watery grey, he wore a coat – a familiar coat – stained with blood – familiar blood. He grinned, revealing a black gullet to a bottomless belly, and as he did so, he leant straight out of the mirror, dragging the glass with him, the glass bending like water trapped behind a rubber bubble, leant right out, his fingers stretching towards me, nails black cracked bone, mouth opening wider and wider and as he came he screamed, "I'm *HUNGRY*!!"

I fell back, lost my footing, landed on my wrist on the floor, covered my head instinctively, electricity rising to our fingertips. The light flickered and hummed, sound of an angry wasp nest poked with a stick, and death, in the form of two sets of claws dragged from a reflection that shouldn't have been there, failed to come.

I risked peeking.

The mirror was empty.

Bakker's foot tapped, bored, on the tiles of the washroom floor. If a ghost taps its foot unseen in the forest, does the foot tap? Discuss.

I uncoiled, picked myself back up, forcing down long slow breaths, feeling the pain in my chest where once those claws had done their work, many, many nights ago, focusing on the ends of my shaking fingers, numbing them one at a time, until I felt strong enough to raise my head, look Bakker in the eye and say, "Very funny."

He shrugged.

"I see death doesn't lead to repentance," I added with a scowl.

"Matthew, we could stand here all day – well, maybe not that – debating the ethics of guilt and innocence."

"Let's not."

"If you insist."

"What we need," I added, forcing the words out one at a time, "is, in fact, to get over the whole cock-up that is my current metamagical, post-psychological, moderately psychical . . ."

"You're misusing the word."

"What?"

"You're misusing 'psychical'."

"Yet you are in my head and you knew exactly what I mean and do you really feel it's necessary to correct my usage, that being the case?"

Bakker sighed. "Do go on."

"What we need – leaving aside the current psychic baggage – is a plan."

"I would say that was a reasonable position."

I waited.

He waited.

I said, "Well go on then, Mr Bakker. You've stopped Blackout before. Gimme a plan."

He examined the ends of his nails. "It's a pity you never shared my taste for the fine things in life, Matthew. A gourmet meal and a glass of Sauvignon does wonders for the intellectual processes."

"How about a kebab and a Ribena?" I snapped. "It's bad enough having to share my brain with you, I'm not about to throw in the digestive system as a job lot."

"Matthew . . ." he began again, in that special voice reserved for the particularly foolish pupil who is quite deliberately refusing to understand the matter at hand.

The toilet door opened.

It was Dees.

I said, "This is the men's and I'm having a moment."

She looked slowly round at the empty bathroom. "You know," she said finally, "this is the first time I've been in a men's toilet and I can honestly say it fails my expectations."

"Dees! There are social norms and I'm still having a moment!"

"It's Lady Neon," she replied. "Without wishing to alarm you, she's *here. Now*."

I pinched the bridge of my nose. The pain had enough rivals for attention across my body that it didn't really make much difference. "Would you describe her current position as volcanic?"

"Krakatoa," she replied.

"I'm guessing that the Neon Court are pretty pissed, huh?"

"The ground beneath their feet clatters with the broken glass of metaphorical vodka bottles."

I waggled a finger at where Bakker was perched casually on top of a curved bin. "To be continued." I caught the flicker in Dees' eyes as I turned back. "Yes, my imaginary friend," I snapped, "keep it to yourself, OK?"

We went upstairs.

The foyer of the British Library was indeed occupied.

Two dozen men and women in various states of leather-clad skimpiness, ozone dying around their sprayed hair and skin gleaming with sweat, sweat substitute, and make-up to make the sweat seem sensuous instead of sticky, were arrayed throughout the broad, complex indoor space, with various weapons pointedly unsheathed. I saw glass blades, nasty stabbing things that reminded me of the smell of smoke and the look of surprise in the burning eyes of Minjae San the night he died. Even when armed for war, the Neon Court managed to make itself look like something out of a fashion shoot, beautiful people preparing for an ugly thing like it was ballet, not death. Their magic was a sticky perfume on the air. We could feel it as a fuzziness behind our eyes, a woolliness in the head. It made us angry. The anger made it easier to fight.

The Aldermen were arrayed at the top of the wide stairs, black silent shapes in long black coats. They weren't beautiful people, and they never intended to be. When you died by their hand, and die you likely would, it would be a cold and quiet death.

No one seemed to have anything to say.

Lady Neon stood in the middle of them all. Even when the sun failed to rise, she found time to change. She wore pristine white, unaffected by dirt, dust or the rain, thick swaths of silk that clung to every surface of her body so that while next to no skin was revealed, they still managed to leave very little to the imagination. Her face was covered by a gauzy veil that obscured the details of her features, and she stood small and still, a spider guessing – no, knowing – that it *is* faster than the snake.

She said nothing, but we could feel her eyes on us. Her gaze made our head hot and fuzzy, set off a tingling in the pit of our stomach, made every cell of our blood feel too thick for our veins to hold it. Her magic – it was overwhelming, all-encompassing, like trying to find a grain of salt in a dish of chillis, and left no room for clear thought. Then a man stepped forward. He wore a floor-length red coat, trousers that could have been engineered to taut perfection by a team from NASA, and was apart from that bare-chested, not a hair on him, just oiled, polished skin. His complexion was pale almond, his eyes narrow, flecked with street-lamp yellow, his skull perfectly shaven. We imagined that he was what the times called beautiful, a work of art, not a human at all, assuming there was anything of the human left in him. He looked young; far too young for the glare of contempt he now gave us.

We stopped, Dees and I, near the bottom of the stairs, and waited.

He said, "Are you ready for war?"

"I'm guessing that was a rhetorical question," I said, as our fingers itched to strike.

"We gave you time. More time than you asked for. You haven't found her. You haven't found the chosen one. You have consorted with the Tribe. If we didn't hold you in such high regard, we would have destroyed you for all this."

I sighed. "Thanks for that. I feel all fluffy inside." We looked straight past him, to Lady Neon. "Sun's not coming up, my lady."

Silence.

"And the city is folding in on itself. You got a way out? You got an escape plan?"

"War!" barked the man in red. "Betrayal, then war!"

"There's a creature called Blackout doing the rounds," I added, ignoring him entirely. "The thing that crawled out of the shadows at the end of the alley, creature of night. Got pissed off when the street lamps were turned on, when the night grew that little bit less scary. Got banished after, may I say, a disastrous attempt by the Neon Court and Midnight Mayor to push it back, that ended in blood all around. That thing. Blackout. Back, right here, right now. It's waiting for you."

"Your lies are . . ."

Lady Neon raised one hand. The man in red fell silent. She took one delicate step forward. She didn't raise her veil or her voice, but her words carried like a breeze from an open summer sky. "Do you think they are not related?" she asked softly. "Do you believe all this can happen by pure change, together, tonight; this endless night?"

Our mouth was dry at the sound of her voice. We struggled in vain to speak.

"The last time Blackout came to this city, the Court allied with the Mayor," she went on. "The Tribe attack us. We cannot help you, unless you help us. If you wish your city to be consumed in darkness, your memory lost to all time, then continue on the path you have chosen. Our price . . . is not as high as that we usually charge for such services."

"This is hardly the time to consider the smaller picture," blurted Dees.

Lady Neon's head turned a fraction, and I felt Dees, Leslie Dees who never shied back from anything, rock on her heels as if blasted from an open furnace door. The look in her eye wasn't fear, but an all-purpose sensory overload.

"You think your city matters? You think the world will care when you are destroyed? I am Lady Neon. I have no need for just one city."

Bakker was at the bottom of the stairs, circling Lady Neon slow and steady, head tilted on one side. "Fascinating specimen," he offered.

"And entirely sincere, I believe, in her intention to exploit this situation for her own gain. She really doesn't care what happens to you and yours. You're just not . . . interesting enough. That must be a rather humiliating consideration for a man of your ego, Matthew."

Dees whispered, "War with the Court . . ."

"It won't come to that," I replied.

"This chosen one is . . ."

"Relevant," snapped Bakker. He had one hand on Lady Neon's shoulder, like a possessive lover. "Perhaps not in the way anyone expects, but you know, and therefore I am entirely free to say it, that Lady Neon is correct in one sense. You do not get coincidences like this in politics or magic. The idea may turn your stomach, but that's the truth of it."

"Fine," I said. And then louder, for her, "Have it your way."

"You will swear," Lady Neon insisted, "to seek the chosen one immediately."

"I swear," I replied.

One hand reached towards mine, slender pale fingers uncurling. "You will swear," she added softly, "to bring her straight to me."

I was aware of every ridge in my mouth, the lingering taste of blood on my tongue. "What will you . . ."

"You will swear!"

"Careful," warned Bakker. "Careful."

"The Tribe have never been our allies, Mr Mayor," whispered Dees. "The Court have."

"Fine," I breathed. "Fine. I'll . . . do as you ask."

"Swear it."

"I swear."

She smiled.

We felt a sickness inside, a fist in our belly, a more-than-words pressure in our throat.

Her hand relaxed and she turned away. Immediately her followers, thralls and servants, began to bustle towards the door, moving as one, ants serving their queen. Umbrellas were raised as she stepped outside, gate opened, stretched cars standing with their doors ready to receive, and as quickly as she had arrived, Lady Neon and all of hers were gone.

Bakker said, his voice low and dark, "Words are power, power is magic."

I bit my lip hard enough to taste the blood.

The man in the red coat was still standing in front of us.

He said, "I'm coming with you."

"You're what?" I blurted.

"Sir," interjected Dees smoothly, "the Midnight Mayor is quite suitably protected by the Aldermen, and while we appreciate your offer of assistance . . ."

"I'm coming with you."

"Mate," I said, "it's pissing it down out there and you aren't even wearing a T-shirt."

"You have not proven reliable, Mr Mayor," he snapped. "I am here to guarantee reliability."

Bakker said, "Take him." My eyes flicked uncontrollably to him. "The man is clearly an assassin, but an assassin for hire. He will attempt to manipulate and use you, but you are aware of this fact and can play the game better. No – not true. *I* can play the game better. Take him with you. If nothing else, he will provide useful distraction should you need someone to put between yourself and Oda."

I looked back at the man in the red coat. "You've got a name, mate?"

"Theydon."

I raised my eyebrows. "As in . . .?"

"Just Theydon."

I shrugged. "Fair enough, sunshine jimbo. I should warn you that in the course of the last however many hours it's been, I've been chased, burnt, blinded, dropped from great heights, threatened with all manner of weapons ranging from the magical to the mundane, tied up, beaten up, chatted with a giant rat and shared my consciousness with the ghost of a sorcerer renowned for the systematic murder of all his kin."

"Systematic is a curious choice of word," offered Bakker. "But I sense now is not the time."

My smile grew a little thinner. "So sure: you want to come along for the ride, come along. It's up to you."

His knuckles looked like they were about to pop out from under his skin. But all he said was "I'll make the arrangements."

*

I took Dees to one side.

"Bakker's not being cooperative."

"That's hardly fair!" exclaimed Bakker, flicking his fingertips idly at the drooping leaf of a potted palm tree and sighing as it failed to stir at his incorporeal touch.

"Having no better plan for the moment," I went on through gritted teeth, "I'm going after this JG person."

"JG?" echoed Dees.

"The chosen one."

"Because of the Court?"

"Because of the Court, the Tribe, O'Rourke, the prophecy, because all this can't be a coincidence, and the fact that Oda said 'Where's the girl?' And because, at the end of the day, Dees, Lady Neon was right – it's all gotta be connected somehow."

"'Where's the girl?'" Dees' voice was the hollow emptiness of someone who has opened the fridge on a hungry night and found nothing left but a lump of rotting cheese and half a lemon: resigned to what must be.

"You want to have the Court and the Tribe and Oda on your back all at the same time?"

"Not especially."

"Well, then."

"Are you sure this is . . ." She gestured uneasily. ". . . the most prudent course?"

"You have a better one?"

She thought about it. "If I suggested a meeting, you would make an inappropriate sound, possibly coupled with derogatory remarks?"

"Yep."

"I thought so. And how exactly do you propose finding this chosen one?"

"Start where it all began: Sidcup."

Silence. Dees studied her shoes. I waited. When I could wait no more I blurted, "All right, come on! What's wrong with this otherwise flawless scheme?"

"Sidcup," she echoed.

"Yes, Sidcup, the place of the fire, the place where Court and Tribe went looking for her, the place where Oda was stabbed and I was summoned: Sidcup, oh, Sidcup, yes?"

Dees coughed politely to cut me off before I could embark on my ode to irritation. "Sidcup," she said gently, "vanished from the pages of the A–Z about forty-five minutes ago."

Silence.

When the silence was reaching critical mass, Bakker added, "Oh dear."

"Define . . . 'vanished'."

"There are empty pages where Sidcup should be. It has become like Cockfosters: a memory of a name without a geographical reference point."

"I imagine that makes it . . . difficult to get to?" I hazarded.

"All roads are cut off, all maps are blank, no train nor bus will go to it," she intoned.

A thought slipped through the dull fog of my brain and waltzed all the way to the tip of my tongue. Before it could be stopped, I'd blurted, "Your family live south of the river."

Dees' eyes flashed, a moment of something bright and fierce and dangerous in her face. Then, very quietly, "Yes. They do. In Croydon, to be exact."

"And Croydon is . . ."

"It was one of the first boroughs to vanish from the map. No trains reach it, no bus, no car. The roundabouts send traffic back the way it came, brick walls block the cycle paths, ancient paint on the stones declaring 'end of the line' or 'wrong way' or 'no way out'. Croydon, to all intents and purposes, no longer exists, if it ever did."

"Your family . . ."

"Both mobile and landline numbers are no longer recognised." She didn't look at me as she spoke, but stared at some distant thing out of reach and out of sight, for her eyes only.

I said, "Sorry."

"We know what this is," she replied. "It has been remedied before. It will be so again." Dees looked smaller, all the same, than I had ever seen her. The bruised weariness of her eyes was too deep and dark for her subtle make-up to disguise.

Theydon called out: "I'm ready."

Dees said, "So, Mr Mayor, can you think of a way to get to a place where no one else can?"

I heard a chuckle next to me. "Oh, yes," said Bakker. "Of course you can."

"Yeah," I sighed. "I can think of a way."

There was something I had to do, before going back to Sidcup.

Penny found me sat by a bank of indoor plants, flicking through my battered and much loved copy of the A–Z London street map. Dozens of pages were empty, nothing but a number in a corner to indicate that anything had been there to begin with.

Penny sat down next to me, said, "Well, *I've* had a lovely snooze and a cup of coffee. How about you?"

I didn't answer.

"Nah," she agreed. "Didn't think your day was getting better. What now, Mr Man?"

I closed the A–Z, dropped the little book back into my bag. "I'm going back to Sidcup in the company of an assassin from the Neon Court to find a chosen one who may or may not be responsible for either a war or the end of daylight."

"Yep," sighed Penny, "as ideas go, it's another fucking winner."

"I don't have a choice any more. This chosen one – JG – is all I've got left to go on."

"I heard on the grapevine that Sidcup has vanished."

"Along with most of suburban London," I added with a scowl. "The city's contracting in on itself, throwing up walls, and on the other side . . ."

Bakker said, "And on the other side, you can be assured, there is nothing good."

Penny spoke over him, unaware there was a third party to our conversation: "What do you want me to do?"

"The way the city is shrinking – edges first – suggests that central London will be the last place to get swallowed up by whatever this is. So find somewhere bang smack in the middle."

"Hide?" she echoed. "Is that it?"

"Not this time, no." I glanced left, I glanced right, saw no one within ready earshot, lowered my voice for luck and leant close to her. "You remember how to do a recorded delivery?"

Her lips tightened, muscles moved in her throat. But she nodded and said, "Sure, yeah, I remember."

"I may need one in the next few hours. Me at the very least, possibly one, maybe two others. I may need a very fast rescue – faster than your car can get from Lewisham to Mile End – and that takes planning. Can you do it?"

A flicker of hesitation, a moment of indrawn breath. Then she nodded, all stubborn chin and unwavering eyes. "Yeah," she said. "Sure. I can do it. Hey – you expecting this assassin fucker to try and pop you?"

"I'm expecting *everyone* to try," I replied, trying to rub some of the weariness out of my eyes.

"And you think you aren't psychologically damaged!" offered Bakker.

"Besides," I added through gritted teeth, "the sun not rising, the city shrinking, Oda going psycho-shit, Sidcup, the burning tower – dig that connection."

Penny raised her eyebrows. "You think Oda's still gunning for you?"

"Of course she is," sighed Bakker.

"Probably," I added.

"All this," Bakker went on, "every single part of it, they're all tied up together, strings in the hand of a puppet master. Your apprentice is terrified, Matthew."

Our eyes went to Penny's face. Her lower lip was curled in, as if she was trying hard not to bite it. She caught our look and flashed an uneasy smile. "Gotcha," she said brightly. "OK. One fucking recorded delivery coming right up. I'll charge my phone and everything."

"Terrified," added Bakker, leaning in until his mouth almost brushed her cheek. Then he drew back again with the slight hiss of a satisfied conclusion. "But not of you. I sometimes saw this look in Dana too, before she died."

My head snapped round, the words were past my lips before I could stop them. "Don't you dare talk about . . ." I bit back on the rest of the sentence, but too late.

Penny said, "Uh – what the fuck?"

I half closed my eyes, tried to shake free of the anger. "Sorry," I mumbled. "Trouble with the staff."

She hesitated, then a strange smile spread over her face. "Hey," she said, "you know, you don't have to do the hero business alone."

"I know."

"Sure you do. Sure. You going to kill this Oda?"

"I –" I began, then faltered. "I don't know."

"Of course you are," said Bakker easily. "I mean, are we even pretending you aren't?"

"She helped me in the past," I said, finding myself unable to meet Penny's eye and unwilling to meet Bakker's. "She wasn't . . . not a friend . . . but when you do all that together, then . . . but she is the cause, the reason why the sun doesn't rise. If I can get this Blackout creature out of her I will."

"You can't," said Bakker.

"And if you can't?" asked Penny.

"We'll see how busy the waters are below that particular bridge when we come to it."

She looked up, met my eye. There was something there that was almost concern. Almost something more. "You be OK, OK?" she said.

"That's my big party trick," I sighed, stretching. "Everyone's gotta have a talent."

It was raining outside.

It seemed to have been raining for a very long time.

"Yes," said Bakker, head tilted upwards to study the orange-black-sodium sky. "That happened last time too."

Nearby stood a hotel of white walls and glass, windows lit up in the reception area. The lift stood still, a little box of light in a tube of darkness. In the restaurant a waiter had fallen asleep over a half-cleared table of picked bones and smeared sauces. A pile of suitcases, off the train from Paris, filled a tall gold trolley, which showed no sign of moving. Outside in the street, the traffic lights were set to red. The buses queued four to a bus stop, no one waiting to board. In the second-hand bookshop opposite someone had stuck up a sheet of paper with words written in felt-tip pen – *NO ONE HOME NOTHING TO SEE* – as a substitute for the "closed" sign. One couple ate pizza in the restaurant next door, four waiters gathered round one table, not sure if they were coming or going.

I mumbled, "What time is it?"

Dees instinctively moved to check her watch, then hesitated. "Does it matter?"

The man called Theydon, his coat forming a peculiar shape about his hips where it just clipped the edge of the two hidden blades strapped to his back, gave a little half-shrug. Muscles bunched and unbunched; here was a man who wanted you to know that he could carry a mammoth on his back, without the crude embarrassment of actually telling you. Our dislike deepened.

"Well?" said Dees, and it took me a moment to realise she was talking to me. "I gather an official car is out of the question, so just how are you planning on us getting to Sidcup?"

"Night bus," I replied.

Silence.

I outwaited Dees by a microsecond.

"Well, we're all quivering, Mr Mayor," she blurted. "Enlighten us. Exactly how does a night bus break down the magical walls currently closing in on this city, where all other means of transport fail?"

"Ah-ha!" I intoned.

Bakker said, "Was I as insufferable as you when imparting the ancient mysteries of our craft?"

"First thing you need to do," I went on, "is get very, very uncomfortable."

It took twenty minutes.

I walked up Grays Inn Road, shoes tied together and slung round my neck, socks saturated black from soaking through in a heartbeat, sleeves rolled up, head bare, flesh goosebumped, eyes stinging from the rain. Behind me came Theydon, coat pulled off, feet bare on the rain-reflective paving stones, looking, to our intense annoyance, as bedraggled as a superstar in the movies. Behind him walked Dees. She had arguably got the worst deal of us all, since we had discovered on leaving the British Library that one of the receptionists had a similar (yet not quite right) shoe size, and was, praise be, wearing particularly silly shoes. They were red, with a high heel that should have been outlawed along with landmines and mustard gas. Dees was limping. Her suit jacket was open, and her shirt was wet enough to sag. Her skin had turned a chicken-flesh colour, with hints of blue about the lips, and in her eye was the look of someone who, having knowingly committed to the most inane plan in the world, would stay committed to the death.

Behind her was Bakker.

Dry as dust and ashes.

His shadow was not his own. His shadow had claws.

Grays Inn Road was not, by any standards, a beautiful road. A one-way system led to the kind of junction where anyone lied who told you it was quicker to stay on the bus till the next stop. Victorian terraced shops still carried half-visible daubs of faded paint advertising penny cures and machine weights, but their windows offered suspicious fruit, lipsticks, tights, milk and half-price telephone calls to Somalia. A shop selling office furniture declared "closing down – everything must go!" and had done so for five years. The lights were down inside sandwich bars and little greasy cafés, bicycle repair shops and chemists offering free Botox consultation. I could feel the city below my feet, tunnels and pipes and gleaming tracks; there was more than just the Underground happening beneath Grays Inn Road.

We halted some hundred yards short of a bus stop. It had no shelter, but was just a stand with a sign. Dees made an instinctive beeline for a doorway, but I caught her and said, "Uh-uh! We gotta get as cold and miserable as possible!"

Dees staggered obediently back into the middle of the pavement. A van swooshed by, sending up a sheet of water that fell across our feet.

"This may just be a failure of imagination on my part." I could hear Dees' teeth knocking as she spoke. "But I can't conceive of getting much more cold or miserable than I currently am!"

Theydon said nothing, but his knuckles were white and his face was drawn.

"Good!" I exclaimed, running my hands through my hair and releasing a small waterfall down the back of my neck. I flinched: a curve of my back had evidently been dry, and was no longer so. "That means it's nearly time!"

An estate car, its back seats ripped out to make way for speakers, thundered by to a *boom boom boom* of bass beat. In the distance I saw it rounding a corner, the lights turning red behind it. The road fell silent:

the thick, silken, sudden silence of engines stopping, of blood pumping in your ears, the sound you were born with and hadn't known you were hearing.

Dees felt it.

Then Theydon too.

I looked back the way we'd come, wiggled my numb toes in my soaking socks, breathed, "It won't stay long; we get one chance." I looked at Dees and added, "You may want to lose those shoes."

She pulled them off gratefully.

Nothing moved.

Not a car, not a bike, not a soul stirred.

Then I heard it: an engine coming up to speed on the straight after rounding the corner; then I saw it, a pair of bright headlights in the distance, obscuring whatever the thing was behind it; but I knew, didn't need to see.

I said, "Run!" and turned and belted for the bus stop as fast as my slipping frozen feet would carry me.

Theydon was by me in a second; then overtook. I risked glancing over my shoulder: Dees was right behind me. And there was something else, flickering in and out of the reflections from the shop windows: a grinning shadow, yellow teeth, grey eyes, loose tangles of hair, keeping pace with us, a thing that should be dead. I strained to look further behind, saw the lights, heard the engine, the swoosh of the windscreen wipers, saw a tall dark shape behind the light, hurtling towards us with the reckless abandon of a boy racer; the night-bus drivers of London had always enjoyed putting their foot down. The bus stop was ahead, Theydon nearly there, then the bus, a double-decker, the redness of its paint so deep and thick it was almost that blood black of a dried scab; brakes screeching, it slid by, steam bursting from the grating at the back of the engine, and stopped, its front door dead level with the bus stop. Its windows were yellow-grey from internal light diffused through thick condensation; impossible to see more than shadows inside. On the back, in tatty yellow-on-black, was the number N1. The rear doors opened with a hiss and a snap. A single woman got off. She was old, face like a roast pumpkin, a mass of hair sticking out from an ancient velvet hat. A huge purple coat, folded down over a stumpy pair of legs, that might at some point hide knees. In one hand she pulled a small shopping bag on wheels. In the other she held a walking stick of black wood. She looked us straight in the eye, and knew us, then turned away with a little humph of contempt and started rattling towards the traffic lights.

The door at the front of the bus opened. Theydon reached it first, got one hand inside the frame, then stopped so suddenly I nearly ran into him. I looked past him to where the driver sat. With skin the colour of dirty bath water, he sat bolt upright in his seat, head turned stiffly forward, more robot than man. He wore a little black cap, and every time he breathed there was the rattle of broken pipes inside his chest. There were chains on his wrists, at his throat, around his middle. Big, black iron chains, bolted into the bus itself. Theydon opened his mouth to say something and I heard the warning beep of the door about to close. I shoved him hard in the middle of the back, pushing him inside, grabbed the panting Dees by the wrist and dragged her up onto the deck as with a hiss of steam and whine of ancient pistons, the door slammed shut with enough force to break bones. The driver's head didn't turn. He didn't move. I reached down and found my fingers shaking from cold and something else besides, and touched my travelcard to the reader. Dees followed suit.

Theydon said, "I don't . . ."

The driver's head snapped round, metal clanking, and a pair of eyes glazed over with silver-purple cataract stared straight at him. Dees fished in her pocket, produced a couple of pound coins, dropped them into the small dish between driver and passenger. Slowly, the driver's head returned to normal position. The ticket machine beeped and rattled. The bus began to accelerate away from the stop. I pulled free the ticket that the machine had produced and looked down at it.

It said:

Single.

Stage 1 to 387

Valid once.

Terms and conditions apply.

Have a pleasant journey.

I looked on the back.

In tiny letters, someone had printed over and over again,

nowhere to run nowhere to run nowhere to run nowhere to run nowhere to run nowhere to run nowhere to run nowhere to run

I handed the ticket to Theydon. "Next time you decide to join the let's-save-the-city club," I growled, "buy a bloody travelcard."

He took the ticket, his face halfway between a sneer of contempt and a shudder of shame.

We staggered, dripping and shivering, inside the bus.

We were not the only ones riding the night bus.

Sprawled across most of the back seats above the engine, the warmest and most shaken part of the bus, was a man with a tatty beard stained with tomato ketchup, a broken red nose and a face that had gone straight through ripe and out the other side. He was snoring loudly. A single empty beer bottle rolled downhill between the seats as we decelerated, and back the other way as we accelerated, bumping and banging with a regular *tonk tonk*.

A child sat next to the door. She looked about five years old. She wore a black and grey school uniform, including a felt bowler hat with a grey ribbon round the base. Her eyes were old. Her teeth were too small and sharp. She looked at me, she looked at Dees, and her lips parted in hate. "Upstairs," she said, voice small and high. "Your kind isn't wanted down here."

I shrugged and headed upstairs, Theydon following. But Dees paused at the foot of the stairs, then turned and looked the child straight in the eye. "You got a licence, little girl?"

The child's scowl deepened. "No rules on the night bus."

"When you get off, if you get off, call us," replied the soaked, bedraggled Alderman, and from somewhere inside her suit produced a creased, damp business card. The child took it reluctantly, cowed by the force of Dees' glare. We went upstairs.

On the top deck there sat just one Chinese woman. She was tiny, from her tiny straight black hair to her tiny shoes, from her hands, almost too tiny to grasp the rail on the seat in front of her, to her tiny brown eyes in a tiny oval face. The only big thing about her was the cream lace collar that stuck out from her tiny grey jacket. She had no baggage, but sat leaning forward in her seat as if any moment she expected the bus to crash and everyone to die except her, who had taken the precaution of clinging on. Her smile was friendly enough.

I sat down. The condensation on the windows was too thick for us to see anything outside other than splodges of street light. Blobs of sodium pink, flares of brilliant white, on-off flashes of red and blue circled round us like flies to blood. The heat was the jungle heat of suspended moisture with a hint of suffocating humanity. On the cold window panes, smiling faces had been traced, doodles, messages in a dozen languages.

Super mouse!!

GET OFF THE BUS

Left at Dulwich

wasnt me lik they said it was

Dees sat down and examined her feet. The shoes I'd forced her to wear up the length of Grays Inn Road had bitten into her heels. Theydon's nose wrinkled in distaste as he examined the tatty blue-and-red coverings on the seats, before perching on the edge of one he judged the least grimy. I rummaged in my satchel and produced a small towel. It was little more than a grey furry tissue, wrapped round the toothbrush and toothpaste that were the sum of my domestic property. I handed it to Dees. She looked at it longer than was necessary, then cold overcame all other senses and she took it from me and started vigorously rubbing at her arms, her feet, her face, her hair, as much trying to warm with friction as dry herself off. Theydon looked at her, looked at me, then turned away from us. He covered his features with his hands and I half wondered if he was about to cry. Then he swept his hands back from his head and I tasted, just for a moment, the sugar-tingle touch of magic on the tip of my tongue. He looked back, and what had been before a man soaked in rain and prickled with cold was now Alpha Male, Natural Man, every bit the hunter-gatherer who could stand before the elements and proclaim 'the tempest holds no fear for me'. His physical appearance hadn't particularly changed, but now it was as if the elements had become just another coat he had decided to wear, and there was defiance in his eye, and pride, the cocksure pride of a man who knows that yes, he does look that good. We scowled.

"Cheap tricks," we said.

"Rich enough for the company I'm in," he replied.

"I'm guessing you won't want the towel, then?"

In answer, he stretched himself out further over the seat, achieving that posture seen on any form of public transport whereby one man and his testicles, by the simple act of sitting back and spreading his knees, can occupy enough space for five.

Dees finished with the towel and passed the soggy rag back to me. There was a sharpness in her eye that, to my surprise, fixed on Theydon.

"You – Neon Court man – let's establish a few essential rules," she barked. "While in the company of the Midnight Mayor you will address him as 'Mr Mayor', and if you are extremely lucky he might deign to reply. When the Mayor tells you to do something, you will do it immediately, and without question. This is not merely because you are a stranger in our affairs; it will be for your own survival. Do you understand?"

Silence.

I waited for the knives to come.

"Do you understand?" Dees's voice was ice, but there was fire in her eyes, a red tint around the iris, a touch of the madness that you could see in the image of the dragon that guarded the gates of London, and her fingernails were tinted silver, and just a little bit too long. I'd seen the Aldermen fight, seen the changes that came over them when they did; but I had never associated Dees with that power, until now.

Theydon considered being an idiot.

Then he changed his mind.

"Yes," he said, voice dead and flat.

"You understand?" snapped Dees.

"Yes," he repeated. "I understand."

She smiled, and I could smell metal magic shimmering off her as she relaxed. "Good," she breathed. "I'm sure we'll all find this relationship mutually beneficial."

She sat down. Bakker was next to her, sat with his chin resting on the palms of his hands, leaning forward like a child towards the front window of the bus. I hadn't seen him get on, but then again, he didn't need to.

"I hope you know where this bus is going, Matthew," he said.

In vain I tried drying myself off with the tatty towel. Outside, flares of colour flashed and danced like oil being burnt in the desert.

Theydon raised a languid finger to the condensation, thought about writing something in it, changed his mind. Dees said, "You could have told us, Mr Mayor, that you were planning on catching *this* night bus."

"Yeah," I said with a shrug. "But then you might have refused."

"What is this thing?" demanded Theydon, looking around. We were surprised he bothered to ask.

"This is the night bus," I replied. "It has all the characteristics of any night bus in London. It drives far too fast down roads where during the day there is usually clogged traffic; it misses half the stops where you'd expect it to pull up; its inhabitants are usually less than salubrious; it only runs after midnight; and it gets you into places where nothing else can go."

"For example . . . ?" said Dees.

"Sidcup. The night bus is one of the big unstoppables of London magic. There's no wall I know of can stop it getting where it's going to go."

"And the driver?" prompted Theydon. "He was . . ."

"Chained, yes," offered Bakker, a finger trying to draw in the condensation and leaving no mark. "Condemned, quite literally, to perpetual night."

"They say there's a curse," I answered. "It binds its victims to service on the bus for twelve years. No rest, no food, no drink, just the night and the driving."

"It's a rumour," added Dees. "The Aldermen have seen no proof of such an accord."

"It's real," said Theydon, utter certainty in his voice. "I have seen things like it before."

I raised my eyebrows. "Really? I had heard that the Neon Court wasn't exactly employer of the month, but . . ."

His eyes flashed. "You know nothing about us."

"I know," I replied, "that when you grow too old or ugly or tired or unwilling, you are thrown out. Not the nice-pension-with-benefits thrown out. The Neon Court is everything to those in it, life and bread and universe. Thrown out is on-the-streets-without-a-toothbrush thrown out. It is old age – very briefly – without friends. And that's just what happens if Lady Neon is bored with you. Christ knows what happens when she's angry."

"And what about the Midnight Mayor?" he replied. "I don't hear about many of your kind living to collect benefits."

"You'll watch your tongue," sighed Dees, as light as a summer spring, "if you hope to keep it attached to your gullet."

Sulky silence resumed.

Bakker said, "He makes a valid point, Matthew. You are already aware that you are going to die in this service. Five years? Ten perhaps, if you are lucky? Of course, your life expectancy would be hugely increased if you were capable of a few essential management skills. If you were able, for example, to put your faith in other people, delegate! But then, how you would moan when others died the death that had been waiting for you. Your level, Matthew, is perpetual NCO."

Theydon said, "Do we have a plan to find the chosen one? Besides, I mean, attempting to cross into a part of the city judged to be either non-existent or utterly inaccessible?"

"Mr Mayor?" prompted Dees.

"Yeah," I lied. "There's a plan."

"Care to share?" suggested Theydon.

"No."

"Of course" – Bakker again – "if there really was a chosen one, then she'd probably stand out like a bonfire in Antarctica. But there isn't, is there? After all, chosen one equals a god doing the choosing equals a higher power equals a plan equals a purpose equals a point to this universe, which of course there isn't. Can't be. For if it were, then you and I would both be utterly damned."

"Why these shoes?" asked Dees suddenly. She was wearing a politely quizzical look and holding up the pair of ridiculous red shoes in which she'd limped down Grays Inn Road.

"Oh, yes, sorry," I said. "The night bus – *this* night bus – obeys the rules of its more mundane counterparts in one other way."

"Being . . . ?"

"It'll only ever come when it's absolutely pissing down, you're freezing cold, soaking wet, and horribly uncomfortable and frankly you've given up on the bus ever coming and just decided to walk home while wearing the world's worst shoes. And even then, it'll only come when you're a good hundred yards off the nearest bus stop and you're going to have to belt it to reach the stop in time."

"The spell to summon the night bus is based on *pain?*" asked Theydon.

"No no no no no!" I replied. "You've missed the point. The night bus is about alleviation of pain, it is the revelation, the relief, that thing that comes when nothing else is running and when you've reached the absolute depths of misery, the thing that saves you! Unfortunately, of course, you have to be at the depths of misery already, in order to be plucked out of them. Sorry about that."

Sulky silence all around.

Then the woman, the little Chinese woman with the friendly smile, leant forward and said, "Excuse me?"

We all turned. She nodded politely to each of us and then, her smile not even wavering, nodded to where Bakker sat and said, "Good evening, I hope you don't mind the intrusion."

"It's the night bus," I replied with a shrug. "It's a great place for social weird."

"I couldn't help overhearing you talk; am I right in thinking, ma'am, that you're an Alderman?"

"Yes," replied Dees carefully. "May I be of assistance?"

"Such an honour to meet you!" exclaimed the lady. "You know, I've admired your work for nearly two hundred years."

"Oh . . . well, I'd love to take credit for all that," mumbled Dees. "But, alas, you know how linear temporal mechanics generally relate to the human lifespan . . ."

"And you!" added the lady, cheerfully turning her attention to Theydon. "May I say that you look fabulous for your age. If Mr Wong and I didn't have such fantastic sex, I would, I must admit, find your glamour irresistible, your charm utterly tempting. What do you put in your eye cream? Newborn babe's blood, or something a bit richer?"

Theydon blurted, "Who the hell are you?"

Her face crinkled, disappointed at his rudeness. "Oh dear," she sighed. "Only a little time now until her ladyship grows bored of you, and then they'll laugh. Drip drip drip goes the cistern and knock knock knock no one to answer the door. So sad. But! Can't be helped, really, can it?"

Finally she turned to me, and her beam was a lighthouse on a foggy night. "And you!" she exclaimed. "All three of you, busy busy busy!"

"Hi," I said. "And . . . hi and hi," I added helpfully.

"Two corpses and an angel, bless, all wearing one face, and it a sad one."

Bakker leant in suddenly, held out his hand to the little woman. "A pleasure to meet you, ma'am; may I say, as one dimensionally challenged soul to another, it is an honour."

She attempted to shake his hand, but her fingers just passed through thin air. "Whoops," she chuckled. "Difficult difficult difficult, isn't it?"

Theydon breathed, "The woman is mad."

Dees' face was tight, every part of her scrunched in concentration. "No," she murmured. "Not mad. Not that."

"You fine people wouldn't be adventuring to battle unspeakable evil, would you?"

"Oh, no evil is unspeakable!" replied Bakker. "How may you fight a thing if you will not name it?"

"True, so true," sighed the woman. "First time on the night bus?"

"Yes," I replied.

"No," added Bakker.

"Well, for those of you who do have corporeal frames which may sustain injury," she said cheerfully, "may I advise holding on tight to something?"

Dees opened her mouth to put a question.

I held on.

Something in the engine beneath us went *clunk*.

Something bright and sodium flared in the condensation on the glass.

Then the fist of a giant curled round the shell of the bus, picked us up in all defiance of gravity's whims, and shook. We were snowflakes in a glassy globe. My feet hit the ceiling and my head found itself staring down at the floor as the bus lurched out from underneath me, knuckles white on the cold metal of the handrail on the back of the bench. My stomach had just about managed to catch up when the entire contraption tilted onto one side and the grip I had with one hand failed, swinging me round like a pendulum. I caught the upright bar of a handhold in passing, hooked my elbow into it; and someone had tied stones to my legs, was trying to drag the entire bus sideways with the inexorable slide of lead weights. The lights inside were flashing with an epilepsy-provoking pulse, and as I tried to crawl my way upwards, one inch at a time, wrapping myself round the bar I'd found, I could see the words dancing in the condensation on the window glass, changing with every lightning strike of fluorescent flashing white

Did not . . .

Have not . . .

Meant to . . .

Been there . . .

Saw that . . .

Theydon was sprawled across the back window, pinned like a butterfly, his spreading coat a pair of glorious red wings. He'd drawn one of his short stabbing glass swords, beer-bottle green, but had nothing to strike at, and each time he tried to raise his head he fell back, crushed beneath an invisible mass. The little Chinese lady sat as calmly as before, her body at ninety degrees to the angle at which I dangled, so it appeared to me for all the world as if she protruded from the wall. She was smiling away with a hint of regret, as if apologising for her lack of team spirit in not getting involved. Of Bakker and Dees I could see no sign.

Then the bus lurched again, flinging us back to something resembling an upright position. My knees slammed against the floor, my head bounced against the back of a bench, my grasp loosened and I dropped down, dazed. The lights inside the bus were out, but cold grey light from outside diffused through the mist on the glass and, by its glow, I could see that the bus was now packed. Dozens, hundreds of people, maybe more, pressed in on top of each other, inside each other, folded out and over and around each other, one seat carrying five people whose shadowy forms had blended into one, and who were only distinguishable by here the move of three arms not two, or there the nod of another head emerging from the first. So many were crushed together that there was no one clear feature or face in the entire pile, but rather formless ridges and dunes of grey skin. I was trapped in a maze of pale legs, bumped and bustled all around; and this in silence. Not a voice, not a breath, not an engine stirred. I eased my way up, found that the figures around me were just a whisper cooler than room temperature, and at my passage they parted easier than air. The little Chinese woman was gone, but there was, perhaps, a shadow that might have been like her, sitting in a medley of shadows on the bench where she had been. I could partly see Theydon, his arm lying limp, the fingers bent and loose. Gravity's resumption of normal service had dumped him at the foot of the stairs. I made my way through the shadows, until I reached the front of the bus. There was no indication of anything else alive. I went to wipe away the mist from the window and look outside, and hesitated.

Below the palm of my hand, dribbling water, someone had, once upon a time, written these words:

We be light, we be life, we be fire!

We sing electric flame, we rumble underground wind, we dance heaven!

Come be me and be free!

We be blue electric angels.

We drew our hand back, watched the drops of water running down from the letters distort the characters below.

A hand fell on our shoulder. It was cold; colder by far than the grey ghosts packed a hundred to a dozen into the seats of the bus. Its nails were cracked and thick, stained sickly yellow. Its fingers were long, ridged skin over thin bone. It gripped hard, tight, deep. I looked up and saw the reflection of its owner's face in the glass. Thin. Grey. Withered. Teeth rotting. Hair falling out. Eyes a familiar watery grey. The face grinned. Those rotting teeth were still sharp, a dark tongue passing behind their battlements.

The voice said, "Hungry!!"

I tried to turn and push him away but he already had his mouth at my throat, his fingers in my spine. I felt hot pain break out in the soft hollow between my shoulder and my neck, tasted phlegm and blood and bile thick enough to suffocate, screamed and scrabbled at his face, tried to bury our fingers in his eyes. We found something that yielded in his features, and the hot pain became cold as, with a shriek of rage, Hunger, Bakker's shadow, the thing that had come alive as he started to die, resisted. Still trying to turn, we found electric flame flickering unbidden to our fingertips, hairs standing up on end, the smell of gas in our nose and taste of dust on our tongue; but his hands curled like a vice around our skull and slammed us temple first into the thick glass of the window. Static burst across my vision and for a moment I saw out of the corner of my eye

STOP! CHILDREN CROSSING!

and heard

engines rumbling louder than cracking earth

and saw

headlights swerving to avoid the outline of a child

too late

and then the floor was there, I was landing on the floor, breath knocked out of me. We tried to force ourself up, but the frame of flesh that we were trapped in, sluggish and mortal and sick and slow, wasn't obeying our commands. Hunger's hands caught us by the throat, pulled us round so he could see into our eyes. His face filled our world, his breath was rotting stomach-sick, and he said, "More fire?"

I closed my eyes.

He shook us, and we could feel blood swerve and dribble down the side of our head.

"More fire?" he breathed.

Hard to think through pain.

We reached inside ourself, caught a fistful of sickness, found the needle-sharp point of pain at the front of our skull, focused on it until it became a throbbing, a burning, a raging pinpoint of flame.

"Beautiful blue angels," whimpered Hunger. "Just want to live, is that so bad? Just want to live . . ."

We opened our eyes.

Sapphire brilliance across our vision, and we could see him clearly now, the thing that was Bakker-Hunger, could see straight through him, dust and shadow, right out the other side and we laughed, and the engine of the bus roared with our laughter, shook and hummed and spat back into life, and the mist of the windows of the bus dribbled and flowed downhill, sweeping the glass clean to reveal a giddy chaos of light outside that bore no relation to geography, space, time, or any of those piddling mortal considerations that humans liked to wrap themselves in.

We found our hands free to move, reached up and grabbed Hunger by the throat, saw his eyes flicker and widen in fear; and our fingers were on fire, blue electric fire that spun and twisted down the length of our arm, made our spine hum like cables in a storm, sent sparks flickering off us with each move we made, filled the air around us with the snapping of electric flame, made the air freeze with each breath we took. Hunger scrabbled at us, trying to pull himself free, but we held on, clung to his ghostly neck as his fingers of nothing scratched and clawed, picked ourself up, pulled him up until his feet no longer touched the ground, and the air around us bent and shimmered with the flame, we could feel it burning across our back, and for a moment, in the reflection from the window

I saw a creature that wasn't human

Beautiful

Burning blue fire

Laughing as it throttled a shadow

Pair of angel wings in blue electric flame

Not human

Not me

And the creature in our grasp had Robert Bakker's face, and Robert Bakker's weak withered old arms were scrabbling at ours, and his old face was turning beetroot purple, then dry-ice blue: his lips, then the hollows of his eyes, then the rest of his skin, and he wheezed, "Matthew! Please!"

We just laughed, and squeezed a little harder, felt his not-flesh collapse beneath our grasp.

Then something moved at the back of the bus.

It picked itself up, stretched.

It had metal skin, silver-steel metal skin, laced with veins of red. Its breath was thick black smoke, its tongue was lizard-licking, its hair metal strands that stood up like poisoned spines, its eyes burning red madness. It said, in a voice that rattled like a misfiring engine in the night, "Mr Mayor?"

We were aware of pain in the palm of our right hand.

Curious, we looked at it.

A pair of twin red crosses, carved into skin.

They ached.

"Mr Mayor?" repeated the creature of metal skin. The light was bending around it, too frightened to come any nearer than it had to, and in the shadows that formed at its feet, things tried to crawl their way out of the darkness.

I opened our fingers.

Bakker/Hunger collapsed backwards, wheezing, clawing at his throat, gasping for air.

I stared at the crosses in the palm of my hand, then at the thing, not exactly human, not exactly dragon, stuck somewhere in between, that stood at the back of the bus. I whispered, "Dees?"

The blue electric fires began to go out.

The lights outside began to fade, until all that remained was the blue electric glow that rose off our skin.

"Dees?" I added, and there was just a shadow at the end of the bus, still and dark, no red fire in it any more. "I hit my head," I complained.

And then, even the blue fires went out, plunging the bus into the dark.

There was a sign outside the window.

It was the first thing I saw.

It said:

Halal

Open 24/7

Next to it, picked out in little blue and green LEDs was the picture of a happy smiling man eating a hot dog over and over and over again.

Then it passed in the night.

The lights, yellow anonymous lights, flickered back on, one at a time, running up the length of the bus. Theydon was crawling to his feet in the stairwell. He looked breathless, ragged. His hair had fallen free from its perfect slicked-back shape and there were long dark streaks of dye running down his face like blood from a scalp wound. As we looked, we saw traces of grey in the edges of his hair, thin traces of pallor in the former perfection of his looks. He met our eyes, and quickly looked away, sweeping his hands back and over his face: and that was it, all streaks of dye and hints of grey immediately gone, banished as he restored his perfect mask of youth. But we had seen, and he knew it.

Dees said, "Well . . . that was informative." She was sat by the stairwell, doing up the buttons on her sleeve, as normal-looking as a woman with no shoes can ever be on a bus in the middle of the night. She said, "Injuries? Anyone?"

Theydon deposited himself on a seat opposite her and said, "No."

She looked at me. I mumbled, "Fine."

"You appear to be bleeding, Mr Mayor," she replied.

I felt my neck. The blood was already sticky, like half-dried glue. I felt a little lower. The skin felt hot, burnt. I wiped my hands clean on my trousers, tried to pull my coat a little tighter around my neck. "I'll live," I said.

"Of course you will, Mr Mayor," replied Dees. "You're very good at that."

I looked round for Bakker.

Not there.

Theydon said, "Is that going to happen again?"

I saw that there was a pair of handprints pressed onto the glass, fingers too long, glass scratched by the too-long nails. I could just hear, over the sound of the engine, the pattering of falling rain, see water being dragged backwards along the glass by the pull of the wind. I took a deep breath, and swept the condensation clear from the glass, obliterating the marks as I went.

Theydon and Dees moved closer, pressing up against the glass to see the world outside.

Rain.

Hard to see for all the rain.

The drains had given up long ago, water pooling in dirty lakes, spilling across the pavements, pushing against doors, ankle-deep. Dead leaves spun and twisted as we swished along roads where the street lamps had forgotten to burn, just a dull wire-thin glow of lingering red within each light. Behind the windows of the houses there was no sign of life. Not a pedestrian walked in the streets. Not a car moved, but sat like crocodiles in deep mud. The only light came from the bus headlamps, slicing out two cones of white in the dark, and from the occasional shop sign. Nothing moved except us, not a man, woman, rat nor fox.

I breathed, "We're here," and rang the bell.

*

There was a bus shelter.

On the roof of the shelter someone had thrown a child's toy, a bright blue rattle, that sat in a black-encrusted dirty pool of water which had overspilt the roof and was now running in waterfalls all around the shelter.

Inside the shelter the light had gone out.

The light had gone out everywhere.

And as the night bus pulled away, its windows the only brightness in this place, even that light faded.

I closed my fingers into a fist, put what little warmth I had into the hollow of my hand, opened it out. Pink-sodium light bloomed, rose up from my fingers, hovered at head height, snapping and fizzing with every drop of water that splattered across its surface. When I moved, it moved, providing a small circle of illumination around me. I could see the timetables and local maps fixed to the inside of the shelter. Their paper was thin and grey, curling up where the rain had got in. Across the timetable, someone had stuck a yellow piece of paper proclaiming:

NO BUSES TODAY.
NO BUSES EVER.

I heard Theydon's sigh.

I glanced at him, and saw that, even though he wasn't inside my bubble of light, he still had about him a glow, no source, no colour, but he was still clearly visible as if what little light there was had decided to be his friend, let the rest of the world suffer. My eyes moved to Dees, and her eyes, when she tilted her head to one side, flashed bright like a cat's in the night, though I had seen no cat's eyes ever flicker that shade of red.

I looked back at one of the maps on the wall.

Sidcup.

In all the excitement, I hadn't really noticed us arrive.

"Where now, Mr Mayor?" asked Dees.

"Back to where it all began," I sighed. "Back to the tower block."

Our footsteps were too loud.

There is no silence as dead as the sound of the engine stopping, no silence so complete as the city when the traffic stops moving. For chirruping country insects the city made human voices constant in the night; for the rustle of leaves and wind there were air vents in the sides of buildings; for the sound of mud underfoot, the clip clip clip of hard soles on tarmac. There should always be something, somewhere, making noise in the city.

Just not tonight.

We didn't talk as we walked.

We were all too busy minding the sound of our feet, contemplating the simple fact that our light was probably the brightest thing in this black landscape, a beacon to all the nasties that weren't making themselves known in the dark.

We walked down the middle of the road, following the broken white line, in a place where traffic should have been. The rain was unstoppable. It gurgled and splattered in the gutters, dug momentary craters in the puddles, dripped off rooftops and pooled in abandoned half-dug-out holes in the road. Our wandering light passed over dead curling posters offering beer, six cans for £4, wine, £3.99 a bottle, advertising wholesalers of wigs, makers of bead jewellery, packagers of Chinese rice crackers, purveyors of Turkish olive oil by the gallon, launderettes and chippies, hairdressers showing the same photo of the same bright-eyed man with the same charismatic-yet-domestic haircut beaming out of the window; and local stores where you can top up your mobile phone, your Oyster card, pay your gas bill, call New Zealand and get a special offer on fabric conditioner too.

I took out my A–Z guide to London and turned to Sidcup.

The page, which had been blank, was now full, drawn in black dribbling ink, as if the map itself was turning to liquid.

"It's fine," I announced. "Burnt-out remains of a tower block, one of three, near a motorway. Dead easy to find."

We kept on walking.

After a while Dees said, "Where are the people?"

I shrugged.

We walked a little further.

Then Theydon added, "We're being watched."

No one broke stride.

The road was tending downhill; by my pink travelling light I found a large reflective board declaring that this was the way to Rochester,

Dover, Folkestone and the Channel Tunnel, please drive carefully. As we passed the shuttered door of a pub, Dees made a little sound, and we stopped.

There was a figure curled up in the doorway, a sodden sleeping bag drawn up around its shoulders. A thin pale face, lined with thinner blue veins, was visible underneath a stained woolly hat. The eyes were closed, but the woman was still breathing.

"Wake her?" asked Dees.

"If you can," I replied.

She knelt by the woman, brushed her shoulder, shook her gently. No reaction. She touched the woman's cheek, leant in, whispered, "Excuse me?" Raised her voice. "Miss? Miss?"

Nothing.

Theydon said, "Let me try."

Doubtfully, Dees stood back. The man in the red coat knelt down by the woman's side, considered her face, then leant down and kissed her lightly on the cheek.

Nothing.

"It won't work, you know."

Bakker was standing next to her in the doorway, nonchalant as anything, not a hair out of place. He reached into his pocket, pulled out a small orange bottle, thumbed the lid off, and tipped a couple of triangular white pills into his palm. Theydon straightened up, a look of confusion passing over his face at his failure to wake the woman. Bakker downed the pills with the ease of habit.

"You can't wake them up. This is Blackout's territory now," explained Bakker. "Endless night. This is what you find on the other side of the wall, this is what the city will be, when the sun doesn't come up. Sleeping until the rain washes away the streets, the city, and them."

"It should have . . ." mumbled Theydon.

"The rules are different here" was the nearest to comfort that Dees could manage.

"You're all going to drown, Matthew," explained Bakker as we turned away from the still-sleeping woman. "That's how it ends, for this city, you know. The lights will go out, the river will rise and wash away the last trace of sleepy mankind, and you'll all drown."

"Bakker's back," I growled out of the corner of my mouth as we walked on.

"Who?" demanded Theydon.

"He left?" added Dees.

"Is there someone else . . . ?" Theydon tried again.

"Never mind."

"And when you – if you – find this chosen one?" asked Bakker, falling into step beside me. "You know," he went on, when I didn't reply, "the whole silent treatment is going to get you nowhere. I understand that you're not in a hurry for our esteemed colleague" – a nod to Theydon – "to appreciate just how mentally unstable you are right now, or indeed, how unstable in every possible way, but this is hardly a profitable attitude to our relationship." His footsteps did nothing to disturb the surface of the puddles; he was the driest thing in South London.

We kept on walking.

"Murderer," said Bakker, not unkindly.

Walking.

"Hypocrite," he added.

Still walking here.

"Inhuman in human skin."

My fists clenched.

"Human with inhuman thoughts."

We looked at him then, straight in the eye, and he was grinning, knowing how we'd react, watching it, waiting for us; we could feel the electricity trying to get out of our skin, burn and rage.

"Not coping very well with mortality, are you? And, heaven help you, all the things that come with it! All these feelings, all that pain, skin, flesh – *saliva*. How does a creature as glorious as the blue electric angels deal with the fact that its body is constantly secreting substances: sweat, saliva, piss, tears, snot, puke; it's utterly repulsive, when you consider it. Which I imagine you don't. Not if you can help it."

We dragged our gaze away, focused on each step in front of us.

"Farting is a particularly gross physical reaction," added Bakker. "I don't know why people find it funny. Every decent society since time began has been rightly ashamed of the urge to fart. So many bodily reactions we can't control! I mean look at the pair of us. You and I, Matthew, could, if we chose, in our lifetimes have set the sky on fire. We can stop the hearts of our enemies, fill the streets with electric flame, summon barbed wire and boiling water from the pipes below us, clad our skins in concrete and still breathe, inhale exhaust off the back of the buses and with it brew a potion of sizzling oil that could power a plane from here to Shanghai and back again. And can we stop a simple little fart? Can we nothing."

The sole of my left foot itched, an insufferable, impossible itch. In the window of a Chinese takeaway, the outline of a cat's paw bobbed up and down in a perpetual Nazi salute, promising good luck, or many riches, or a decent dish of sweet and sour, or maybe none of the above. In the back seat of a Fiat parked on the side of the road, a mother lay asleep, child bundled in her arms, uncomfortable posture promising the pins and needles of a lifetime when she woke, if she woke. An opening up of the darkness ahead revealed a sad patch of grass. Wet litter blew through thick mud dotted with thin tufts of green. We could smell an old dead smell on the air, black and dry, cutting through even the wash of the rain. I threw my light up higher, bigger, until it cast a circus-sized tent of light across the ground around us. The shadows didn't cave away. They scuttled, catching hints of giddy shapes at the edge of the light that bore no relation to nature. The rain stung my eyes.

There was a fence. It was covered with sagging posters for bands, comics, faiths and politics, the inks dissolving one into the other.

If you don't vote

. . . for DJ Sax And His Sexy Babes . . .

. . . what is the meaning of . . .

twice winner of . . .

. . . entry £6 before midnight, £10 after . . .

There was a hole in the fence, cracked wood. I crawled through. Concrete on the other side, broken by the odd feeble tuft of grass, drowning in oil-slick thick rain. My light hit an obstacle, and spread upwards.

The obstacle was grey, stained black, its walls embedded with grit plastered over, as if the architect had decided that here was a building destined for cracks and unevenness, so why not embrace the idea at an early stage and make it an effect of art, not time? The ground-floor windows were covered over with thick, lightless metal grilles. The door had at some point been covered with plywood, which had then been ripped off in recent times and thrown to one side. A chain had been smashed off by repeated blows and left to hang from the metal door handles of the main entrance. Nothing to steal, go ahead and try. I looked up. Somehow, the tower, square and squat, had seemed a lot taller when I was jumping off it. From the fourth floor up, the windows were burnt black, like ash lips around a surprised square.

Theydon said, "Minjae San died here."

I thought of the sound the glass blade had made as it entered Minjae's back.

"She wouldn't have been able to kill him without you, you know," offered Bakker, casually leaning up against the wall by the door.

"Sure," I muttered. "The Court and the Tribe, both summoned to this place by a phone call about the 'chosen one'; and like monkeys you both come and whaddayouknow, some idiot's brought petrol."

"The Tribe attacked *us*."

"Sure. They said to themselves, 'Hey, that looks like a harmless bunch of sword-carrying wankers, let's go banzai on their asses.'"

"Arses," corrected Bakker. "We are not Americans, Matthew, regardless of the TV we watch."

"You prefer the Tribe's ugliness? Their destruction, loathing, self-contempt?"

"Gentlemen," interjected Dees, "considering that we are, at this exact moment in time, trapped in an endless night outside the laws of geography, could we save this diplomatic discussion for another time?"

"Pragmatism pragmatism pragmatism," I grumbled, marching up to the door and kicking it open. Broken glass swept back before it: glass from the door itself, glass from the lights that had popped, and tumbled from the ceiling beyond. The water had got in here too, dirty water full of wriggling dirt that twisted like worms with each drop from a torn pipe or cracked ceiling. The doors to a lift, coffin-sized, stood half-open, revealing a black fall with a short stop below, cables hanging limp and crooked. Thin brown mould had worked its way into every contour of every dirty tile on the dirty floor, but still there was the lingering smell of burnt metal and carbon, drying out the mouth even as the water drip drip dripped onto the floor. I tried the stairs cautiously, and felt only solid concrete beneath my feet. There was a slow hiss behind me. Theydon had drawn his short stabbing swords, one of green glass, one of brown. The air had the common sense to run away from the edge of their blades. In the gloom, his eyes clearly reflected with a lilac tint. The claws were back on Dees' fingers too, no doubting it now, nails turned to thick black bone, sharpened to a point, skin on the top of her hand half mortal, half metal, eyes flecked with mad dragon red, thin black smoke turning on the air every time she exhaled, like she'd not just smoked the cigarette but swallowed it too. She was between me and Theydon. I wondered if even a daimyo's glass blade could penetrate the metal back of an Alderman.

We climbed.

On the second floor, in the middle of the landing, was a dark eaten-out patch of concrete, seared deep and black. The smell of petrol was still strong here, and something else, a lingering trace of something just on the edge of sense, a taste of magic. I glanced at Theydon. "Your lot regularly use petrol to start fires?" I asked.

"The Tribe do," he replied.

I grunted in reply, kept on climbing. The metal handrails of the stair had been twisted by the heat, warped out of shape. A plastic bag had caught itself on a broken shard of glass in the window. Water ran down the inside walls.

A sound, one floor above; probably no louder than a cup falling on carpet, and to us, in that place, the sound of thunder. Our heart started running for the exit, leaving us behind; I heard Dees' breath, Theydon's coat move as every muscle tightened.

"Rat?" asked Dees when no more noise came.

"No," I answered softly. "They're sleeping too."

A sound.

This one, unlike the other, had meaning.

It went

Clop. Clop clop. Clop.

We stood. We listened.

It seemed to listen back.

Then it moved again.

Hard and sharp on concrete. Black dust trickled from a crack in the ceiling above us.

Footsteps.

Walking overhead.

Theydon said, "The chosen one?"

"You wish," I growled.

"Then who?"

"If you see a woman with a hole in her heart, try not to look her in the eyes, OK?"

"You talk in riddles," he snapped.

"See this serious face?" I asked. He looked. He saw. Something crawled away behind his eyes. "Don't look," we repeated. "You'll die if you do."

Footsteps.

Not overhead.

They'd moved without seeming to move. Beneath us now. A door banged back and forth on its shattered hinges.

Stopped.

Then again, just one set of feet, somewhere in the distance, now, far off, but not getting any further away.

I found that our hand was itching with electric energy. I squatted down and ran my hand over the black dirt of the stairs, rubbing it between my fingers, scratching under my nails with the dry sound of thick chalk on an old board. I licked my fingertips and for a moment tasted

heat

back blister heat flesh crinkle and curl

fire

too bright

smoke

Help me?

black dropping ash tongue to ash skin to ash

carbon in the lungs too tight to breathe every breath hurts

Kill me?

feet running in the dark help me?

grey eyes

eyes turned to blood

grey eyes

paint on the wall, letters running in the blaze

JG WOZ ERE

I straightened, wiped my fingers on my trousers. "Your Minjae San – he got a tip-off sending him here?"

"Yes."

"And the Tribe were already here?"

"Yes."

"And that didn't strike you as odd?" I sighed.

"Mr Mayor," interjected Dees before Theydon could get into a proper fume. "Your meaning?"

"JG woz ere," I repeated. "I saw it on the walls. The girl was here. Oda said 'Where's the girl?', but none of the bodies brought out of the fire were hers. She was alive when the tower burnt, she was alive when it finished burning. I think I can find her."

Footsteps. Scuttling, running overhead, picking up speed and stopping as quickly as they'd begun.

"Do we need to be here for you to do that?" murmured Dees.

"This building is the only connection I have to your damned chosen one," I replied. "It's the only link I can use. Ignore the footsteps. Oda seems to be on a slow-killing bent these days."

I started to climb, but Theydon's arm reached up and caught mine, a grip that went straight down to the bone. "Wait. This . . . Oda . . . is the creature Blackout?"

"Yeah."

"And what do you mean, she asked you 'Where's the girl?'"

My eyes flickered to Dees, for just a moment, and she half shook her head. We looked back at Theydon, straight in the eye, and his grip slackened. "Your life will be easier and simpler," we answered, "if you just stick with the war." We pulled our arm free, and I started to climb before he could object at our empty half-words delivered in the dark.

No footsteps.

Another floor up.

Nothing but falling rain tapping in through broken windows across burnt-out floors.

On the next stairway up, Bakker stood, leaning out of the shattered, scorched remains of a window, one hand turned up to the sky, trying to catch the rain. He blocked the stair. We walked straight through him.

"Rude," he remarked as we passed by.

Next floor.

I stopped, hesitated.

"It all looks so different when not actually in flame, doesn't it?" remarked Bakker, coming up beside me. Everything that had once been wood, door or frame, was now a black tooth, sliced to scraggly spikes. Everything that had once been metal, handle or wire, was withered out of shape. Everything that had once been clean, or cleanish, was now black, eating up the thin light my bubble of illumination cast. I started walking down the corridor, past doors to flats long since cleaned out, shattered remnants of gone lives, TV glass smashed out, sofa of burnt springs, glass melted from an empty picture frame.

Footsteps ran beneath us.

I thought I heard a woman laugh, or maybe cry, or maybe neither.

I pushed back what remained of a door. It creaked like the granite eyelids of a mountain opening after a long sleep. Dust and flakes of powdered wood trickled between my fingers.

The fire had burnt away the last trace of Oda's blood, but we knew this was the room.

Beneath us, a door slammed.

Dees said, "Something's coming."

I knelt on the burnt floor, scorched down to tortured concrete. It shifted beneath my weight, a stiff stone mattress feeling its age. I ran my hand over it.

"How do we kill it?" asked Theydon. "The thing outside?"

I looked around for Bakker. He wasn't there.

"Sorcerer!" A note of frightened urgency in his voice. "How do we kill it?"

"Her," I replied softly. "How do we kill *her*."

Our fingers running along the floor brushed a place rougher than the rest. There was power, thick, hot power, a sauna without the moisture, burning without light. It made it hard to breathe. My hand hurt. Right hand, where the scars were. I pulled off my glove. The thin scars, twin crosses of the Midnight Mayor, were filling with tiny lines of blood.

Outside, there was the sound of something whispering. Not a voice. Not dust falling. But something somewhere in between. I glanced over my shoulder. Theydon stood by the door, shoulders hunched like an animal. Dees' skin had a silver sheen to it, her features distorted, bones too sharp, nails too black, eyes too red. Aldermen, when trying to scare, took on some of the aspects of the city's dragon, that old symbol meant to guard the gates. It hadn't occurred to us that Aldermen would do the same when they were afraid.

I ran my hand along the floor, feeling in a wide arc around me.

The sound of whispering was now something more, not feathered wings, not wind full of snow, not quite human, but alive, and coming closer.

My fingers brushed something sticky. I pulled them closer to my face, examining the substance by the thin light. It looked almost black, was tough, barely liquid at all, and stuck to itself like dried glue. I looked closer. Flecks of red shimmered, caught the light, seemed to wriggle, writhe, try to burst out of each other like a living thing and flicker a dull electric blue. I looked down at the ground. Something was moving beneath me, trying to crawl off the floor, surfacing and falling like the back of a maggoty whale. I pressed my hand into it and it responded, a sudden flare of brightness, brilliant red, writhing crimson, spread out beneath my fingers and traced across the blackness, the raggedy outline of twin crosses, drawn in blood.

A foot moved next to me. A pair of suit trousers, knee bent, as Bakker squatted down on the other side of the cross. We saw how he pulled his trousers smartly up around his ankles, keeping everything neat and creased. "Fascinating," he murmured, as the blood of the twin crosses wriggled and wormed to life beneath my fingers. "You know, it occurs to me, Matthew, that the power of the Midnight Mayor is one whose potential you've never fully grasped."

I could taste dust on my lips, feel a wind, hotter and faster than the one that came with the rain, coming our way, and now the sound was a whooshing, a rush of something fast and dense moving on the wind, trying to push and pull all at once. The blood on the floor was moving too, spilling out of its ridged shape, flowing like water downhill, but there was no down to encourage it, sending out little tendrils of liquid like a nervous lake that wishes it had managed to do the river thing. Dees hissed, "Matthew!"

"Nearly there," I replied.

"Matthew!"

I heard her moving, felt the heat now, like the touch of moonlight, only the moon had got envious of its bigger brother and was doing the thermal thing with a vengeance.

A tendril of rolling red blood reached a crack in the concrete, slim and black, a fault line, paused, pooled, reached critical mass, and went, *drip*. I bent down until my nose almost touched the floor, peering into that crack.

Drip.

Another little red bead fell away. I could feel Bakker beside me, watching, and as I closed one eye tight and scrunched down right below, I saw that drop of blood fall, and keep on falling, down and down and down into a blackness further and darker and deeper than the tower block itself, before the distance travelled blotted out its light.

I breathed, "Damn."

Then Dees' hand was on my shoulder, yanking me up and there was a roaring in the corridor outside and heat that made my skin try to shrink in on itself and Theydon was yelling, or had perhaps been yelling all along and there was smoke pouring in through the door and a shaking underfoot and above and dust falling all around and Dees screamed, "There's something . . ."

Then it was in the doorway, moving so fast and so hot it blasted the hinges off the door frame, smoke and dust and dirt and ash that bloomed hot red before folding in on itself. I curled up tight, and our hands were in front of our face, throwing up a wall of thick colder air against the blast. It was like trying to stop a lorry with tissue paper. I rocked back as the blast hit, filling my world with smoke, above and on all sides, blotting out the rest of the world, pushing in at the little bubble I'd thrown up and the fire in the blood on the floor was blotted out and our hand hurt, it hurt so much and we could hardly breathe, not enough air in our bubble, a few lungfuls at best, and we were breathing too fast, unable to stop ourselves.

The moisture in our bubble turned to steam and curled around our face, stung our eyes, burnt our skin. I could see the cracks in the floor spreading, breaking out and expanding beneath my feet and a few more seconds of this and we'd have to breathe again, and when we did the magic at our fingers would fail and we'd breathe fire and smoke and die burnt from the inside out. I couldn't see Theydon or Dees, couldn't see anything beyond my own hands, curled in around my face, not an inch of air left between them and the fire. We shuddered and tried to force our bubble of air wider, give ourself more space to move, but the air was already burning out and we felt a rush like petrol sucked from the engine as the breath was sucked from our lungs with the effort. We screamed our rage, pushed harder, saw the ash buckle and burst around us, pushed again, saw it retreat a few precious inches, raised our head and roared sapphire fury, and without so much as a sigh it split, burst and rolled around us, spat out of the shattered windows and tumbled away into the night, leaving nothing more than sickly brown curling hot vapours rolling over the floor.

We slumped forward, the sweat that had been too hot to prickle before bursting out on our skin. The floor was too hot for skin to touch; it stung through our trousers, made the soles of our shoes sticky. We staggered, coughing and gasping in the sickly-tasting air, looking for the others. Something moved in a corner. A thing half woman, half something else entirely, the clothes on its back barely clinging black rags, its silver skin covered in ash and dirt, its hair stiff metal, its eyes mad red, its fingers adorned with black claws. The bones of its spine stood up like shark teeth, and its knees were bent back the wrong way. It watched us, and there was animal madness in its eye, every part of it quivering with power and rage.

I breathed, "Dees?" and took an uneasy step forward.

A lizard tongue, blood red, licked the air. A voice, human only in that it used the language, hissed, "Only just." Her head moved, sharp and fast, like an animal hearing a thing beyond human sense. One finger, a joint too many set in the bones, unrolled towards a shape in the corner. I crawled towards it, a smell on our senses that we did not choose to name. A red coat, burnt almost to nothing. Knees tucked up to chin, arms wrapped around face like a child afraid of the dark. Still breathing. Just. I knelt down by it, reached out uneasily, rolled one arm back. It resisted. I hissed, "Theydon! Theydon look at me!"

If anything, the limbs locked tighter.

"Look at us!" we snarled.

An arm moved aside. The head turned. There was a hole in his face. It started just below his left eye, where his cheekbone was clearly visible, whiteness protruding between pink tendon and red blood, and ran, criss-crossed only by a few shreds of muscle, to the bottom of his teeth, revealing gum and bone beneath. His left eye was closed, twice the size it should have been, the eyebrow seared away from above it, and his ears seemed to have tried to melt into the flesh around them. I could see the whiteness of three ribs in his chest, and one arm hung crooked, that of a puppet badly strung. He pushed me back, then hunched over himself, hands pressed again to his face. A sound, a moan, came from him. It was the sound of a hurt animal, that rose and rose, until the room was just that wordless mewl. He rocked back and forth, magic blooming and flickering out around him, like a match guttering in the wind. Still the sound kept on, until breathless sobbing changed one sound of pain into stop-start gasps. I crawled back towards him, saw the magic bloom again at his fingers, saw him try to wash his face in it, sweep power over his features, trying to work the glamour. It ran over his skin, settled into the cracks, seemed to linger, and then washed off again like water on oil. I tried to touch him and he swatted my hand away.

"Theydon?"

"Can't look can't look can't look can't look . . ." The chant came, low, tumbling out between each ragged gasp.

"Theydon?"

"Can't look can't look can't look can't see can't see can't see . . ."

"Let me help you."

"See look see look see look see look . . ."

"You need a doctor."

"So bright so bright so bright so bright so bright . . ."

"You'll die here. Come on . . ."

Again I tried to pull him up, again he shook off my hand.

Then Dees was beside me. "Leave him," she said, her voice the inhuman rattle of the silver-skinned dragon. "He knew the dangers."

"He'll die . . ."

"Yes," she replied flatly. "It was always likely to be the case."

We hesitated. Somewhere nearby, we thought we heard a woman laugh. Or maybe cry. Hard to tell. We looked towards the door. I looked back. "Arseholes to that," I breathed. "I've got enough bad karma without adding this."

She grabbed my arm as I reached forward, and this time her fingers didn't release me, and her grip was metal, ticking hot metal still adjusting to the changing temperatures around and within it, and her claws bit down into our skin. "Leave him!" she snarled. "Or we will both die here too."

I looked down at Theydon, still rocking, still sweeping his hands over his face. For a moment, a hint of skin where there was none, a suggestion of wholeness. Then it slipped away, and he was smaller than I had thought him, a little hunched man on the edge of becoming old, rocking, still whispering,

"See look look look look see do you see look look look at me see see see see can't you see look look!"

We looked away.

We turned our back.

Dees relaxed.

We took a step towards the doorway.

There was a woman standing in it. Her hair was burnt, her skin was cracked, and there was a bloodstain in the middle of her T-shirt, right above her heart. She stammered, "M-Matthew?"

I heard the little hiss of breath as Dees' back arched to strike. I stepped between them, turning my eyes down to the floor. "Oda?" I breathed, shuffling another step closer, shoulder first.

"Mr Mayor!" snapped Dees, edging after me.

I waved her back. Oda didn't move, just stood there, bewildered in the sodium light, face turned away from it as if it hurt. Her eyes, we had almost forgotten the black churned-up ruin that was her eyes. One look and we could feel our own begin to burn, so we looked away. Bakker stood by her now, peering intently at her face.

"Oda? Oda, do you know what's happening?"

"Careful," breathed Bakker. "Very careful."

Our hands were nearly touching hers. "Oda? Do you understand? Do you see what's happening?"

She glanced up, and again our eyes met, and again our eyes burnt, and we flinched away.

"Matthew?" she whimpered. "Can you hear it? Can you hear?"

"Hear what?" I asked.

"Hear it! Can you hear?" She pressed her hands to the sides of her head like she was trying to keep her brain from bursting out. "Listen! All the things that happened in the dark, all the dirty little things, can't you hear here, hear, here, there hear, listen!"

"Oda, I . . ."

She grabbed our hands suddenly, pulled us close to her. We couldn't feel her breath, her skin was clammy cold, we had to close our eyes and look away. I heard Dees start behind me, ready to attack, tasted her smoky breath on the air, laced with deep-down city magic. "Listen! All the things humans do when the lights go out. Can't you hear them? The dirty, disgusting things, the shameful things, because when the lights go out no one will see you do it, do you see? Sweat and lies and . . . and . . . I can't make it stop, Matthew, I can't make it stop, hear, do you hear, hear it?"

I shook my head. "I can't. I'm sorry, Oda, I can't. Oda, there's a thing . . ."

"Why can't you hear it?" she pleaded, her nails biting into skin as her hands tightened around mine. "Why can't you hear?"

"Oda, there's something happening here. There's a creature, a . . . a thing called Blackout, it possesses people, takes over their thoughts, their bodies, it's . . ."

"Why don't you ever listen?!" she screamed, and suddenly let go of our hands and slammed her own, palms first, into our chest. I felt the floor go out from beneath my feet, the breath expelled from my lungs, as a force, more than just muscle, slammed into our middle and threw us backwards, landing us with a crunch on the black cracked floor in the middle of the room. I saw something bright and fast move by me and Dees leapt, fingers stretched for Oda, the sound of a thousand burglar alarms at bat-slaughtering frequencies coming from her throat. Oda fell back beneath the weight of her, and for a moment all I could see was fists and claws struggling at each other's face, a flash of blood and I couldn't tell whose, spilling out across the floor. I crawled to my feet in time for something dark and hot to bloom between the two women, pick Dees up by the scruff of the neck, throw her against the ceiling, then down onto the floor, then throw her up again like a yo-yo. I shouted, "Oda! Stop it!" and as she staggered back to her feet we gathered electricity to our fingertips, crackling walls of it, and hurled it at her.

It would have set an ordinary human on fire. It slammed into the middle of Oda's chest and she staggered backwards, blinking and shaking her head, clearing it of sparks. Dees dropped to the floor, smoke pouring out of every metal joint. Oda looked down at Dees, head on one side, curious, then bent down and with one easy fist picked Dees up by the throat and held her, toes barely scraping the ground. "Alderman," she said, and her voice wasn't her own. "We remember the Aldermen. They lit lamps to drive us away, thought that was all it would take, just a twist in the angles of the shadows in the dark. Little scuttling mortals who can't understand that they made us stronger when they grew afraid."

Dees wheezed, claws scrabbling at Oda's arms. I saw Oda's blood seeping from her, but she didn't flinch, didn't move. I gathered more electricity about myself, letting the scent of gas fill my nose and the feeling of flame ignite in my belly.

"Oda," I whispered, "put her down. Put her down now!"

Oda looked past Dees at me, and smiled. Her fingers opened and Dees flopped to the floor, gasping for breath. I realised that my eyes were on hers, felt blood burn in the corners of my eyes, looked away, watching her feet, power dancing off my skin. "Oda," I breathed. "You know that there's something inside of you. You know it's magic, you know it's bad. There's still time."

"Time?" she asked, stepping over the fallen form of Dees and moving towards me. "Time for what? Time to change, time to grow, time to burn, time to brighten, time for day, time for night, time for darkness, time for this, time for there, time for here, time for now, time for us, time for you, time for them . . ."

"Stop it."

"Big time little time passing time time standing still time racing time rushing and we never change! All that time! We've been waiting for so much time. Do you know what we are?"

She was right in front of us now. The room flickered crazy blue-white with the power running over our skin, ready to strike.

"You're Blackout," I breathed. "You're the thing at the end of the alley."

"But what does it mean?" she asked.

"The thing that comes with the night." To my surprise, it wasn't Oda, or me who had spoken. Bakker stood just behind her, his eyes holding mine, keeping mine away from hers. "Blackout isn't just the fear of the dark. No one fears the dark. You fear the things that happen in it."

I felt Oda's – or the thing that was not Oda's – fingers run down my arm, exploring it, every dent and line.

"You tell me," I gasped between breath.

A little sound, almost a croon, a whine, passed between her lips. "I didn't mean to," she moaned. "Didn't mean to it seemed all right at the time, so sorry, so sorry, won't tell, it wasn't my fault, wasn't my fault, no one need ever know what happened here just you and me just you and me and it's not like anyone cares not here not now we can do anything because no one will ever know anything at all what can you imagine anything at all it doesn't matter no one will see no one will judge us now the sun's gone down it wasn't me wasn't mine didn't see isn't yours hasn't come didn't mean couldn't stop didn't care mustn't tell hasn't heard didn't didn't didn't didn't didn't . . ." She stopped. Her voice was an animal whine. "Do you understand yet? Can you look us in the eye?"

"Yes," I whispered. "I know what you are."

Her fingers jerked shut around my wrists, shaking now.

"Matthew?" she whimpered. "Do you know how to kill me?"

Sparks snapped from my skin to hers. I could see the clothes on her arm singe and burn where they struck, see little yellow blisters bursting out on the palms of her hands where she touched the fire wrapped round me, and she didn't seem to care.

Bakker stood behind her, saying nothing.

I looked at him. "Help me?" I asked.

He didn't move. Didn't frown, didn't smile, just stood there.

I looked at Oda. Blood was running down in little tears from the corners of her eyes. I tasted salt on my lips, and realised the same was happening to me. "Can't," I whispered. "Can't. Sorry."

Her face darkened, drawing tight. Her fingers bit so hard and deep into my skin that I gasped. "Then what use are you?" she snarled, and I couldn't look away, I tried but I couldn't, tried to turn my head but there was just mad blood-red blackness and burning and no way out, nothing to hold on to, a great big drop into a great big nothing and we tried to burn and tried to scream and perhaps these things happened, somewhere a long way off, but she didn't let go, and we kept falling and there was blood on our face and on our lips and then

then a thing with a hole in its face, screaming rage, caught Oda, or the thing that had been Oda, by the throat with one hand and with the other rammed a short glass stabbing blade up to the hilt into her belly.

Her eyes went to it.

I staggered away, covering my face with my hands, wiping blood clear from my burning eyes, ears ringing, the sensation of glass bottles exploding above the bridge of my nose. I heard Oda make a little "uh" sound and glanced back. Theydon was there, her blood soaking his hands, the only thing holding her upright, blade buried so far in you could see the end poking out the other side. She stared at it, then, slowly, looked up and met his eyes. He stared back, face twisted into a grin of tooth and gum, even as his eyes started to bleed. She reached up slowly, put both hands around his face, like a mother holding a child. The grin on his face faded. He began to shake, quiver like paper in a gale, then he closed his eyes – much too late – and screamed, and there was blood running down from his eyes, his nose, his ears, and he screamed and screamed and then just stopped, head on one side, every contorted muscle locked, as if the body didn't even have the strength to relax, and flopped in her grasp. She let him go and he hit the floor with the final thump of a creature fated not to rise again. Then Oda looked down at the sword rammed through her middle. Carefully, she closed both hands around the hilt and, without a word, drew the blade out. Blood stretched and slid along it. There was the sound of things parting. It came free. She held it up, examining it, running her finger along the edge, testing it. It cut the end of her finger, a thin little slice, and she examined that too.

Bakker said, "Run."

I didn't move, couldn't move.

She sliced it a few times through the air, more curious than anything else, testing its weight.

"Matthew, run!"

She inclined her neck to examine the stab wound in herself, probing it as someone might see how bad a moth hole is in a bit of reasonably regarded clothing.

Bakker was right by me, trying to shake me and making no touch. "Matthew, I am trying to help you; if you want to live, run!"

She pulled her jacket tight around the wound, and looked up.

At us.

At me.

We ran.

Dees was in the corridor outside, half staggering, half crawling, fingers still around her throat. I grabbed her by the armpit and pulled her up; she wheezed as she came, hissed, "Matthew?"

"So much shit as you would not believe!" I sung out, hauling her towards the stairs. "Bloody hell you're heavy when you're doing the dragon thing."

"Blackout . . ." she stuttered.

"Yeah, about that. She's got a stab wound to the heart and another to the stomach now and is still doing fine. We've got to go *now*."

I reached the stairs, started dragging her up.

"Where are we going?"

"Roof."

"Why?"

"I know where the chosen one is."

"Lovely."

Behind us I heard footsteps in the corridor, the buzzing of flies, the sound of steam, the whisper of voices, the . . .

"Come on, come on!" I snarled, as Dees clung to the twisted handrail and hauled herself upwards.

"She's coming for us," she replied.

I glanced back over my shoulder, and there was for a moment in the shadows a woman moving, a child running, a trolley rattling, a door slamming, a TV crackling, a . . .

"Ignore them, Matthew!" snapped Bakker; he was above us, looking down from the next landing. "They're just the things you fear; just fear, nothing more!"

Next flight of stairs and here the sound of a woman, an old, old woman, slippers shuffling, someone crying in the night, a child's voice raised, something falling on the floor above, the sound of a radio out of tune . . .

"What's happening?" I demanded.

"You asking me?" replied Dees.

"Things that happen in the night." Bakker right by me now, head half turned back down the stairwell from where we'd come. "All the things that happen in the night, the things we don't talk about, this is where they happen, this place, Blackout's place, all the shameful, guilty, despised things that people do, this is their place that you've walked into. You have to keep going upwards."

A door ahead.

A familiar door, burst open, twisted to one side, rainwater pouring in under it, forming a flood that flowed around and over our feet as we climbed, and outside, a wide unlit darkness of twisted scorched TV aerials and pools of water. I half fell through the door, Dees slipping from my grasp onto the ground, gasping for breath. The water sloshed around my wrists, cold and black, and now I could hear them, crawling out of the walls, feel sweat on my back and excitement in my belly and fear in my heart and hear

did not

go on

just this once

who knows

never need know

won't tell

you a coward

try it

go on

go on

go on

no one will ever find out what you did

My fingers in the dark pool of water brushed something. It was small and hard and gleaming. I pulled it out. A small length of golden chain, the ends shattered and twisted out of shape. I thought of Minjae San, the chains he had worn, and the look on his face when he'd died. Then a hand fell on my shoulder and Dees was by me, gasping for breath, eyes somewhere halfway between human and animal.

"She's coming," she breathed. "What now?"

I staggered to my feet, every muscle objecting, every nerve sulky to respond. I dragged myself to the centre of the roof, keeping my little bundle of light down low, searching through the pools of water; and there it was. A crack, wide and deep enough that the water flowed into it, tumbling down, almost fat enough to squeeze a child's finger into. I knelt by it, sweeping the water with my hands. Dees flopped down beside me.

"I know where the chosen one is," I stammered.

"Well?"

"You heard of people falling between the cracks?"

"Yes . . ."

"This place, this building, all cracks, all broken, all old. Very easy to fall through the cracks. I saw it happen to the blood, my blood, Oda's blood, whatever, the blood that drew the symbol of the Midnight Mayor; it fell between the cracks, and not just . . . not just physically, I mean . . ."

"Mystically?" growled Dees. "I know what it means."

"That's where she is. JG, the chosen one. She's fallen between the cracks."

A sound on the stairs, more human, louder, than the constant whispering of the dark. Dees' head snapped towards it, then she looked away. "Fine," she said. "Three questions – can you get us in there?"

I nodded dumbly.

"Can Blackout follow us?"

I looked to Bakker, who shrugged.

"Don't know."

Dees' scowl deepened. "Can you get us out, if we go in?"

I dug at the crack, felt dust mingling with water beneath my fingers. "I think so," I said. "Yes," we added.

I felt Dees' hand close around my own. "Fine," she breathed. "Do it."

There was a footstep on the top of the stair. I glanced up. A woman in the doorway, darker than the darkness, a bloody sword in one hand; and all around, other things moved, and I tasted sweat and blood and salt and smoke and ash and . . .

"Do it now!" roared Dees.

I looked down at the crack in the roof, dug my fingers deeper, forced it further apart, until it was now a hole, a torn fissure, a slice through the earth, a fault line, no bottom, no depth, no walls, just an endless fall beneath us growing wider and wider and wider and as Oda screamed with a sound that wasn't human any more and ran towards us, blood running off her skin, I felt Dees' hand in mine and threw us both, head first, into the darkness.

Part 4: Between the Cracks

In which it all begins to make a horrible sort of sense; a war begins; an army is destroyed; and a conspiracy unravels.

Dust.

It was thin and beige, lit up by the yellow tungsten glow of a single flickering 15W bulb. It stuck to my fingers with the quiet tenacity of that possessive girlfriend unable to understand the meaning of 'it's over'. It was on one side of my face too – presumably the side that had been resting on the uneven lino floor. It was on the cracked tables and the tatty crooked chairs. It was on the piles of paper that had spilt across the floor, obscuring all writing. It was on the dirty brass handle on the door, and inside the shattered remnant of the TV screen, trying to smother the still-snapping sparks of life that leapt within the broken interior.

It was on my clothes, in my hair.

I tried to get up.

Something hard and sharp knocked into the middle of my spine, sending me the short distance back down to earth, and stayed there. A voice, that tumbled in on itself like it couldn't say the words fast enough, gabbled, "Who the hell are you where did you come from why are you here?"

I tried pushing myself off the floor and the weight on my back responded by pushing a little bit harder. A thing that might have been a toe prodded my side for added emphasis.

It took several attempts to get enough moisture in my mouth to answer.

"Hi," I wheezed. "Name's Swift. Sorry to drop in like this, I don't want to cause trouble."

The weight on my back shifted uneasily. "But I mean really who are you why are you here you don't have coffee do you lots and lots of big black coffee or maybe you're from the tax man you're not from him are you because I told the council I told them leave leave me alone and they kept saying they couldn't but if I didn't ask them for anything why should they trouble me do you see?"

"Um . . . yes. I think I do. Can I get up now?"

"You're not from the council are you only I told them they mind me I'll mind them you understand what I'm saying do you?"

"I'm not from the council, no."

"Oh."

The weight on my back eased. A hand, skin like the frozen back of a frozen ocean, reached down. I took it, let it pull me to my feet, turned slowly, ready for pretty much whatever I had to see.

What I saw was a man. His nose was round, his beard neat and grey, his hair showing signs of receding on the top, his posture hunched. He wore a torn green waxy coat, a pair of ragged corduroy trousers, a pair of trainers through whose holes I could see equally holey grey socks, and was carrying a crooked piece of pipe. The dust had settled on his back like fine snow, and was settling even now, a continual gentle shower tumbling from the spider's web of cracks sliced through the ceiling. The only disturbance in the dust was on the floor: a set of footprints, his, from a crooked rocking chair to the scuffed marks of where I'd fallen. No others, not in, not out of the little windowless room.

I held out my hand uneasily. He looked at it for a while, then put the pipe down, and shook it. "Hello," he stammered. "Sorry about that but I don't usually have people just fall through my ceiling like that and you did give me a start and I like my privacy but don't think I'm rude will you?"

"Not at all," I mumbled. "Um . . . and in an equal spirit of openness, where am I?"

"Here, here." He gestured grandly round the room. "Where else would you be?"

"And where is 'here'?"

"It's where I live isn't it!"

"And that is . . . ?"

"Here! I live here!"

"I see. And . . . how long have you lived here?"

His eyes narrowed. "Why are you asking so many questions?"

"I'm just . . . confused and bewildered, you know."

"You sure you're not from the council I don't want anything to do with . . ."

"No, I'm not from the council. Honest." I looked round the little room, but I saw nothing, food, sink, bed, that suggested this was a place a man could live. "Um, you haven't seen a woman disguised as a dragon walking about here, have you?"

"Disguised as a dragon?" he echoed. "No sorry not that."

"But . . . you have seen a woman?" I hazarded.

"Oh yes a while back I think."

"How long ago?"

He shrugged. "About sort of around I think maybe well it was certainly after but . . ." His voice trailed off. He smiled a desperate grin of gaps and inclines.

"Thanks for your help," I mumbled, and headed for the door. He didn't try to stop me. It opened in clouds of dust. It felt like it hadn't been opened for a very long time, and left an arc scoured in more dust outside. The corridor outside was dark, barely lit by dull fluorescent light streaming in the small window at one end. He didn't move. I stepped out, then hesitated and looked back.

"What's your name?" I asked.

"My name?" he echoed. "Um well it's uh it's . . ." He started riffling through the great pile of paper stacked up against one wall, wading in knee-deep. "It's somewhere here it's um . . . hold on I'm sure I've got it somewhere . . ."

"Never mind."

He looked back up, unease behind his wide grey eyes. "Close the door on your way out will you?" he asked.

I smiled, and pulled it shut behind me.

The corridor was covered in the same dust. Debris was strewn about, creating dense islands and archipelagos for the traveller to sidestep. There the torn-off arm of a plastic doll. Here, an envelope, open, a letter, half-written, inside, the stamp never attached; a pen, its plastic case cracked, the ink spilt out in a solid dry stain; a folder, its paper torn and curling; a ticket to the theatre, never used. A pram still in its plastic wrapping. A pair of false teeth tumbled out of their glass, liquid long since evaporated, grinning for ever at nothing. And always, falling around it all, the thin beige dust. There was nothing in this place that wasn't shattered and broken, and no sign that it had ever been disturbed.

I walked towards the small square window at the end of the corridor. It was frosted: all I could see beyond were thick patches of flickering light, and its lock didn't give. Upstairs, I heard a human sigh and headed towards it, past books with half their pages torn out, broken fridges with doors standing open and the shattered silver pieces of broken CDs. My footsteps left uneven splodges in the dust.

A single door stood open on this floor, a dull yellow light spilling from it. I walked towards it, knocked. No answer. I peered round.

A man stood in the middle of the room, arms stretched out at his sides, head turned upwards. His flesh was nine parts blue vein to one part white skin, his hair tatty and frayed, his eyes wide and darting, fixed on nothing. He wore a pair of blue underpants and a knee-high pair of black socks that had rolled down in thick bands to his ankles. I said, "Excuse me?"

He didn't move.

"Excuse me, mister?"

Didn't budge.

I walked up to him, touched him on the shoulder. Nothing. I shook him harder. Nothing.

"Mate! Hey, you!"

We shook him again, his head snapping back and forwards like a toy puppy in a car, but his eyes never once fixed on us. I let him go, and slowly he seemed to reset to where he'd been, head fixed upwards, unmoving, silent.

A voice behind me said, "He won't answer."

I jumped, hands flying up ready to fight.

How he'd got there, this man in the door, without my seeing, I didn't know. He was pushing a shopping trolley, one wheel stuck on with gaffer tape, the basket laden with old coat-hangers, bent teaspoons and bits of rusted metal. He had a broad dark beard, salt and pepper hair, raggedy padded coat, and a body odour that should have made him stand out like a samurai in the Senate. His face was familiar, the taste of his magic more so. He looked at us a good long while, and seemed mildly dissatisfied with what he'd seen, then, with a shake of his head, and a rattle of his trolley, he walked on. I followed a few paces behind, and when this didn't annoy him, I came closer. He stopped suddenly, bent down, and from beneath the dust picked up a silver watch, the face shattered. He shook it, listening for a beat, then with a sigh threw it onto the trolley and kept on rattling.

I said, "I'm looking for someone."

"Yeah?"

"Will you help me?"

He chuckled. "And why'd I help you, squire?"

"Fond sentiment?" I suggested meekly.

He ground to a slow halt, then turned, leaning back on the handlebar of the trolley, and examined us again. One hand reached up behind his ear and removed a knuckle's length of cigarette. He stuck it in his mouth, patted his pockets, didn't find what he was looking for.

"Got a light?" he asked.

We cupped our hands together, huffed a shimmer of fire in between our fingertips. The magic was slow here, sluggish, and we had not realised how tired we were. Our hands shook as we pressed the fire to the end of the stub of cigarette. The man took a deep breath, held, and puffed out a blue-grey cloud. He took the cigarette between two fingers and waggled it at me.

"So," he said. "You made Midnight Mayor, huh?"

"Got made," I replied. "In the passive sense."

"You don't seem very passive now."

"Midnight Mayor is sorta like having a sign saying 'kick me' on your back. You may not have stuck it there, but someone's going to take up the offer sooner or later." I stuck my hands in my pockets to hide the shaking. "What about you? I didn't know the Beggar King hung out in places like this."

He grinned, yellow teeth flecked with black. "In between the cracks, the place in the city where all the forgotten things go? Where else would you expect to find the Beggar King?"

"I heard a rumour you'd got yourself a pad underneath the Westway bypass."

He shrugged, smile fading. "Gotta move with the times. My kingdom's got big these days – too big. Too many people just slipping between the cracks, and damn all use it is trying to get them back." He raised one great curling eyebrow. "You got a way out?"

"Sure."

"Yeah. Can't see a guy like you coming to a place like this without a way out."

"Will you help me?" I repeated. "I don't know if the Midnight Mayor is supposed to go around begging . . ."

"He's not," said the Beggar King, flicking ash away with the ends of his fingers.

"I will."

Now both eyebrows did their thing. "You sure you're the right man for the job, Mr Swift? The Midnight Mayor isn't without his power, or his pride. An institution, is the Midnight Mayor, that's always got to think of the big picture, not of little people lost somewhere in the dust."

"An institution," I replied, "that's been run by arseholes."

"And you're running things differently, now?" he asked with a knowing grin.

"Muddling by."

"Going well?"

I looked down.

He patted me companionably on the back. His nails were ragged yellow stumps of bark. "Try the fifth floor, room right at the end."

"Thank you," I breathed, touching my hands together in a mimicry of grateful prayer. "Thank you."

He shrugged, turning his back. "You mind your business, I'll mind mine . . ."

The trolley rattled off down the hall.

I climbed the stairs upwards.

Fifth floor, much like all the others. A mug, handle knocked off, half proclaiming *I LOVE* . . . before time had erased the secret of its heart. A broken umbrella, the joints bent backwards, a pair of child's pyjamas stained with some fading sauce, shoes with the sole coming away, a handbag, its contents of half-used lipstick and dirty tissues spilling out across the way. Dust.

A door open at the end of the corridor. I could hear dull voices coming out from inside.

One said, "Then who's the father?"

Another said, "Oh babe, oh babe I wanted to tell you so much . . ."

The first one said, "But if Tom's not the father then . . ."

The second one said, "Babe, don't be mad at me!"

I knocked on the door, and when there was no answer, eased it open.

The room was empty of furniture, just a television on the floor, its aerial sticking up like a pair of comical ears. In the screen the grainy image of a man and a woman bickered in front of an electric fire. The dust was thicker here than anywhere, the floor almost felt. On the walls it formed a thin brown layer. Someone had written in the dust with the end of their finger, over and over and over again, a thousand times, criss-crossing across its own words,

Help me
Let me out
Help me
Let me out
HELP ME
HELP ME
HELP ME!

There was a girl sat in front of the TV, utterly focused. Her legs were crossed, back bent, chin stuck towards the screen as if pulled by invisible string. Her fingers were loose, open. Her hair was black, and had been shining before the dust settled on it, artificially straight and done in a ponytail round to one side of her head, sticking out behind her right ear. She wore gold hoop earrings wider than a wrestler's wrist, baby-pink shining lipstick and thick green eyeliner. Her skin was the colour of milky espresso, but her eyes were the same dark brown that Oda's had been, when Oda had eyes. Spittle hung in the corner of her lips, and her eyes, as she stared at the screen, did not flicker, twitch nor blink.

I sat down next to her, watched her; watched the TV.

On screen another man was shouting, "How could you lie to me, you slut, how could you make me think the baby was mine, I loved him, how could you do this to me? To us?"

I said, "Excuse me, miss?"

Her eyes didn't leave the TV, but the fingers of her right hand seemed to twitch, curl in a little on themselves.

I looked back at the TV screen.

"Oh, don't you take the high ground with me, Jimmy," screamed the woman. "I know what you got up to with Debs last week, I heard all about your sordid little affair . . ."

"I don't watch much telly," I said as we sat there, dust slowly settling across our shoulders. "I'd like to say it's because I get out lots, you know, go to the pics and the theatre and stuff. But I don't. Bit behind the times, really."

Nothing.

"You like this programme?" I asked.

Nothing.

On screen, man two had hit woman one. She was now sitting sobbing uncontrollably while man one comforted her. Man two was saying, "You know I only do it 'cause I love you, babe, I love you so much . . ."

"There's a lot of rubbish made," I confided, nudging the girl next to me conspiratorially. "I mean, everyone says how quality's declined – you know, Shakespeare to Dickens to *X Factor* and all that, but I don't think so. I just think that there's so much stuff made these days that of course ninety-nine per cent of it's going to be shite, and you've just gotta weed out that one per cent that takes your breath away. That's what I think. It's just a theory, though."

Nothing.

I could hear footsteps walking overhead.

A pair of fingers dipped in liquid nitrogen walked the walk down the back of my spine.

"You wouldn't know a girl by the name of JG, would you?" I asked.

A twitch, just in her fingers, no more, but it was there, real, a response.

"Only thing is," I went on quickly, "I'm looking for her. Not in a bad way or anything, but I think she might be in a bit of trouble and I was kinda hoping I could lend her a hand, you know?"

Nothing.

The footsteps upstairs had stopped, hard and sharp.

"My name's Matthew," I added, holding out my hand to her. "What's yours?"

Nothing.

I heard the footsteps move again, heading away, towards the stairs.

On the TV screen, the story had now cut to the interior of a grubby pub, where two completely different women were discussing the infidelities of their husbands and the demands of being both old and loyal at the same time.

One said, "Yeah, I know, it's like terrible."

The other replied, "You don't say, and I have such a hard time with him. He's only ever interested in the footie these days."

I stood up, walked round and stood directly in front of the girl. She couldn't have been out of her teenage years, seventeen at a guess. She craned round me, mouth still hanging open, to see the TV.

"Look," I said, every bit the enforcer, "I'm really sorry about this and I understand that it might be a difficult thing but time is a factor here . . ."

She kept craning. I turned round, knelt down in front of the TV, fumbled down its side and, with a sharp electric snap, turned it off.

Behind me the girl screamed. Before I had a chance to turn she was on me, beating at my back with her fists, kicking, scratching, long nails dressed in red paint trying to tear at my ears, my neck, my face. I rolled over, and she came with me, flopping onto the floor in a mess of ear-ring and rage, and went straight back onto the attack. I managed to get a grip on her wrists and still she kept on screaming, teeth bared and white, trying to get in close enough to bite. I pushed her back and in the moment that she was off me threw up my hands and caught her in a fist of thick shimmering air. It picked her off her feet and pinned her back against the wall, destroying the scramble of words underneath.

"Enough!" we snarled and the dust trembled and trickled at our voice. Her struggles grew less, but her eyes were wide and frightened, looking everywhere all at once. She licked her lips, tried to speak, then licked them again and managed a shriek of

"You fucking arsehole I'll fucking kill you I'll fucking kill you who the fuck do you think you are who do you think you fucking are I'll fucking kill you!"

She drew in more air ready for round two, and I let my spell go, dropping her onto the floor on her hands and knees, pushing the air out of her. Before she could speak again I caught her by the wrists, dragged her upright and hissed, "Where do you think you are? Tell me that! Where do you think you are?"

Her eyes danced around the room, and some of the strength began to leave her. "I . . . I . . ." she began.

"Look around!" I hissed. "Tell me where you are!"

"I don't . . . you don't fucking touch me, you hear, if you fucking touch me don't fucking touch me!"

She pulled free, staggered back a few steps, seemed to curl in on herself, hugging herself, quivering with too many things to name any one distinctly. We watched her, a creature not much more than a child, too frightened to be anything more than what it was. I said softly, "My name's Matthew. I'm here to help."

"Piss off."

"Look around. My name's Matthew. What's your name?"

"You think . . . you think you can just . . . just fucking come in here and be like 'I'm Matthew' or whatever and that's like I'm fucking going to trust you?" she snarled. "You come one step closer and I swear I'll rip your eyes out."

I backed away a pace, raising my hands in a gesture of surrender. "Fine, fine. Look. I'm not coming any closer. Just tell me your name."

She wiped the end of her nose with her sleeve, straightened up, forced her shaking hands onto her hips in an expression of defiance. "I'm JG," she snapped, and then faltered, too much to say, unable to say any of it.

I pinched the bridge of my nose. Something harsh and static was buzzing at the end of the corridor outside. I couldn't hear the Beggar King's trolley, or any footsteps any more. "JG, hi," I said. "Nice to meet you. We've got to go."

"I'm not going anywhere with you!"

"Look around. You want to stay here?"

She looked, and for the first time seemed to see. She curled in tighter on herself and in a little voice asked, "Where is this?"

"Bad place. I think it's starting to make some sort of sense but it's a bad place, and there are bad things happening here tonight, and I've really, really got to get you out of here."

Her eyes flickered back to me and for the first time she seemed to see me too. "You've got blood on your face," she said, backing away. "My God what kind of freak are you? You're a fucking freak keep away from me!"

"There was a fire, wasn't there?" Her eyes were burning, but they were at least looking at me. "A tower block in Sidcup, a place scheduled to be demolished, everyone else had cleared out, but not you. You liked it there, you wrote on the walls and hung around there with your mates and then there was a fire. It spread too fast, and it was below you, and there were people. You ran and ran until you didn't know where you were running to and you felt like there was this hole opening up beneath you and then you were here. Wherever here is. In all the dust. And you couldn't find a way out. Am I right?"

"You're one of them," she whispered.

"One of who?"

"One of them that's been watching me. I told the priest but he said I was imagining it. They laughed at me, cops said I was trying to get attention and I shouldn't waste their time, come back when there's an actual crime to report. You're one of them."

"No."

"You are! How d'you know all this unless you're one of them!"

"I . . . I know this woman . . ." I stammered. "Look, now is not the best time . . ."

"What woman?"

"This woman, a . . . a friend of mine, I . . ."

"What's her name?"

"It doesn't matter."

JG suddenly sat down, legs tucked into her chest, arms folded around her knees, glaring at me. "Fine! If it doesn't matter then it doesn't matter what I fucking do does it so I'm going to sit here and it won't fucking matter and you can just fuck off!"

"You're not making my life any easier . . ."

"Her name!"

I flinched as she shouted the words, waited for the dust to billow and resettle around us. Looked down at her. Knelt down in front of her, closer now. "My friend's name was Oda," I said. "Do you know her?"

JG licked her lips. Then she said, "What d'you want?"

"To get out of here."

"No way out of here," she replied. "I looked. No way out."

"I can get us out of here, but we have to find my friend."

"What friend?"

"Her name is Dees, she came here with me looking for you."

"Why'd you look for me?"

"Because . . . because Oda said 'find the girl'. She asked me to do it."

Her eyes narrowed. "You're lying," she said. "You're lying, you're going to try and use me or something, you're like all the rest."

"Please! I've risked a lot to come here! Please! Trust me? For now?"

I held out my hand, smeared in dust and soot and blood. She looked at it with contempt. Then, ignoring me utterly, she levered herself to her feet, and looked at the darkness of the door. "What's out there?" she asked.

"Dust," I answered with a shrug. "And stuff." I stepped into the corridor, looked back. She was still standing there.

"You don't want to be lied to, huh?"

"I know if people lie," she replied.

"Good. That'll make this easier." I ran my finger through the dust. "There's something out here you've got to be scared of. And I am really, really trying to keep you alive."

For a moment, we thought she wouldn't come.

Then she did.

We walked together to the end of the corridor, to the foot of the stair. I fumbled in my pocket until my slippery fingers closed around the cold weight of my phone. I thumbed it on. "Dees!"

Our voice echoed and bounced away.

The stair seemed to have no top, no bottom.

"Dees!"

"Why you fucking shouting?" hissed the girl. "You dense, you'll bring . . ." Her voice trailed off.

My phone came on. No signal.

I thought I heard feet run, further away, somewhere a long way off.

"Up," I said. "We keep going up."

"I'm not doing anything you say!"

"Sure. I'll let you make up your own mind on this one," I sighed. "But I'm going up no matter what happens, since up is where out is."

I started to climb. She waited nearly two flights before following me, tutting and shaking her head like I was a reckless child, demanding my whims were indulged. Still no phone signal. Below us, something went *pop*. Then something else joined it, then another.

I leant out over the stairwell and looked down.

Beneath us, one at a time, heading from the bottom up, the lights were going out.

I almost found myself wishing for Bakker.

Then a voice overhead said, "Nearly there!" I looked up. Bakker was leaning out over the railing, staring down. "But will you make it in time?" he called, voice echoing away.

I grabbed JG by the sleeve, dragged her upstairs. She came, struggling to pull her arm free but still running, bright enough for that at least. The darkness kept on rising, pop, pop, pop the little snapping sound of the little white bulbs in the tight dark stairwell going out. The dust was slippery beneath our feet, puffing up in little beige clouds as we climbed.

"Dees!" I shouted again. "Dees, get your arse here now!"

The darkness was five floors below; three. Then it hit us and I ducked as the lamp overhead burst and went out in a shower of glass. I caught a sliver of light between my fingers as it went out, tossed it over my head and everything here was so slow, the power so distant. We kept climbing upwards, even now as the darkness overtook us, rose up over our heads, snuffing out light after light until all that seemed to remain was the pinprick of a distant star, and then even those stars started to go out. I rounded another stair, turned another corner and she was right there, my little bubble of light was too dim to see her clearly but she was right there, Oda standing on the stair above me and she kicked out, knocking me backwards straight into JG, sending me tumbling back into the corner of the landing. Her shoulders were shaking, her fist closed tight around Theydon's bloody glass sword, her face set in mute rage. I heard JG gasp and shy back, covering her face instinctively with her hands, heard the air part and threw up my hands, unleashing a blast of electricity that crackled its way through the air slow and sluggish, slamming into Oda's chest and throwing her backwards. JG screamed, the high-pitched scream of someone who's watched too much TV and knows that's what you do under these circumstances, and I drew my fists back and dragged out what little heat was left in my soul and threw another blast at Oda even as she staggered upright, then another, knocking her to her knees. The clothes on her back were smoking. We crawled onto our feet and, as she tried to rise, forced out another blast. The effort nearly knocked us flat again, the dust filling our eyes as the air parted around us, but it hit Oda in the heart and she clasped her fists to her chest and seemed to rock back, head snapping up to the ceiling. I drew my hands back for another, last shot, and Bakker's voice was beside me, around me, in me, shouting "Matthew, no!" and then there were arms around my neck, across my shoulder, and JG was screaming, "Don't touch her! Don't you fucking touch her!" and her weight propelled me backwards, knocking me off my feet and sending me sprawling back down to where I'd begun. I landed badly, barely aware of JG's fists against my side, one leg caught under the other. I tried to crawl up and my arms were putty, my feet scrambling in the slippy dust. Oda was already back on her feet, heaving herself up, supported by Theydon's stabbing sword.

Bakker was by me, hands gesturing uselessly in the air, unable to help me up, hissing, "You can't kill her do you hear, you can't kill her, you can't win this you have to get out of here now!"

Oda was coming down the stairs, and there was nothing human, nothing merciful, in those not-eyes.

I felt for the phone in my pocket, wiped dust off the screen with the corner of my thumb, started to dial. Our fingers were shaking, exhausted from the effort of trying to throw Oda-Blackout back, and then she was there, pulling JG away from me by the scruff of her neck. I felt sharp cold glass in the hollow of my throat, and closed my eyes shut before the blood could begin to run out of them.

Then JG whispered, "Oda?"

And death failed to come.

I half opened my eyes. Oda was staring at JG, and JG was staring at Oda, and JG's eyes were not bleeding. The two looking straight at each other and there wasn't anger in Oda's face, there wasn't hate or fear but something I'd never quite seen before. JG reached out uneasily towards the other woman, hand shaking. "Oda?"

The blade drew back.

Oda seemed almost to smile.

Then JG saw her eyes, and screamed again, this time for real, an animal sound of distress and terror, and screamed and screamed and Oda drew away, covering her face with her arm, and the sword went back and

Something silver, burning, fast, rose up behind her and dug its silver teeth into Oda's neck. Oda shrieked with pain, clawed at the thing wrapping itself around her, even as flame danced between them, and I saw a pair of mad red eyes.

"Dees!"

I tried to crawl to my feet, but Oda had got a grip somewhere on Dees' metal skin and thrown her back, and was diving after her with blade in hand. "Dees!"

I saw claw break skin like skin was silk, and Oda didn't even stop, didn't slow, didn't flinch, but drove Theydon's glass blade into the middle of the silver-skinned Alderman with the sound of metal cracking and glass shattering. Fire flared in Dees' eyes, and began to go out. The silver covering of her skin began to fade, her hair became charred human blonde, her fingers curled in pain, breath, human breath, shivered across her lips. Oda drew her hand back, and all she held was a glass hilt, the blade shattered into a thousand parts. I saw Dees stagger back, trip on the top stair, fall, press her hands to her belly in surprise, pick free from the bloody mess of it a shard of broken green glass, hold it up to the dim light. Her mouth opened in an "o" of horror, tears, half salt, half blood, welling up in her eyes. She whimpered, "But I . . . never said . . ."

The glass fell from her fingers.

"I . . . didn't have . . . time to . . ."

She fell back on her elbows. Then on her back. Her feet dangled over the edge of the stairs, her head locked, staring bloody-eyed at the ceiling. Oda walked up beside her, stared down into her face. No more blood came from Dees' eyes.

We stood up.

Our hand burnt.

We could feel the blood rolling out of the scars in our hand.

Bakker hissed, "Matthew . . ."

Oda turned, stared straight at us, and we stared back. We held up our hand towards her, and saw Oda flinch. *"Domine dirige nos,"* I whispered, tongue of leather, lips of sand. *"Domine dirige nos."*

Fire flared, on our skin, in our blood, behind our eyes. It bloomed around us like ripples in a pond, the red mad dragon fire; it stretched out from the crosses in our palm and tumbled up, and out, and around, spilt over the corridor, slammed into Oda and sent her staggering back, shielding her not-eyes from it. It wasn't hot, it wasn't bright, but it was the dancing madness in the pit of the dragon's eye, the dancing, unmentionable thing that had grown from a city built on the ruins of a city built on the ruins of the city, a thing fuelled by the embers of the fires that had never quite gone out, fed by the bones of the bodies buried beneath the bodies buried beneath the bodies buried beneath the stones on which one day more bodies would be lain. I advanced up the stairs, legs moving without being asked, and Oda cowered back. I could see blood trickling from a thousand burns on her, see her lips cracking before the fire, I was level with Dees now, standing over the body of the Alderman, and we screamed, our voice, my voice, and another voice too, the one that had a lizard tongue and guarded the gates, *"Domine dirige nos!"*

And Oda shrieked, threw her arms back even as the fire tore away at her and shrieked, howled like a hurt dog, shrieked and shrieked and shrieked and then was, without any warning, laughing, hyena laugh, and the gesture I had taken for pain and terror was the open-armed joy of acceptance. And briefly I saw, beneath the wound in her chest, through the hole in her heart, a thing move underneath it, a liquid, living thing, not human, not bound to flesh, crawling its way free of hers.

Bakker roared, "You can't kill it with fire!"

We faltered.

The fire flickered and began to die around us.

Our legs had no more strength to hold us.

Oda's laughter died with the flames.

I flopped down to the floor next to Dees. Her blood was slow, thick in the dust. Bakker tried to grab me by the arms, hissing, whispering, "Get up you have to get up you have to go Matthew! You have to go now!"

Oda sank down against the wall opposite me, still shaking from laughter and pain. A body like that was dead, so much broken and torn and bloody, she was dead, a dead body and a thing beneath it and . . .

"Matthew!" Bakker was pawing at the phone still clutched in my left hand. "The more you destroy her, the more powerful it becomes! Matthew! You have to go now!"

I turned the phone, peered at the screen. A single grey bar of signal sat, wobbling and weak, in the top left-hand corner.

I found I still had a thumb. It dialled, one number at a time, each little digit a triumph of concentration. Oda tensed as she saw the thing in my hand, tried to get up, slipped, tried again, crawled on hands and knees towards me, reaching out for it. I found the last number, rolled with a grunt of pain onto my side and slipped feet first down the stairs. Oda's hand snapped at the air where I'd been, I heard her hiss of rage. JG was huddled in a corner, hands wrapped around her head, shaking, sobbing, frozen in place. I saw Oda stagger to her feet, reaching out towards us. "No," she gasped. "No, give me the girl, Matthew! Give me the girl you have to give me . . ."

My finger found the dial button, my hand pressed the phone to a far-off object that might have been my ear. Oda launched herself, screaming, "Give me the . . .!"

A voice on the other end of the line said, "Matthew?"

"Get us the hell out of . . ."

The universe went bye-bye.

I smelt soy sauce.

It cut through all other smells, sharp and rich and bright.

So far so good. I risked opening one eye.

The light outside was too bright, so I closed it again for a while to reconsider my position.

My position was horizontal, belly down, on a hard floor.

It seemed as good a place as any, so I stayed there a while.

Bakker said, somewhere not far off enough, "Time is wasting, Matthew."

I groaned.

This seemed to attract more attention. I heard footsteps, felt air move. Then Penny's voice was by me and she was blurting, "Bloody hell are you all right I mean obviously you're not all right you look like a fucking bulldozer has been using you for practice and getting it wrong but I guess what I'm asking is, are you bleeding internally?"

I risked opening my eyes again. Somewhere in front of the brightness, a hair-shrouded blob that might have been Penny's face shifted in and out of focus. I coughed dust and ash that scratched all the way up. I crawled onto my elbows, and mumbled, "Hi Penny."

"Bleeding internally?" she repeated.

"Is there some easy way of checking?" I asked.

"I just kinda assumed you'd know."

I risked looking a little further.

I was sprawled on a plain concrete floor in a room full of boxes. The boxes said in several languages, 'Finest Fortune Cookies; Export Only'. Someone had cleared a space in the middle of this floor and laid out, in a clear and careful magical circle, hundreds and hundreds of first-class postage stamps. Some of them were still smoking now. I prodded one with the end of my finger. It crumbled into dust at the touch. I said, "Jesus, how much postage and packing did you use?"

"You said you needed rescuing!"

I managed to make it into an upright sitting position, and lingered there. "It's a recorded delivery," I explained. "You're supposed to use an equal postage relative to the mass of the object being delivered. You've got enough stamps in this damn summoning circle to summon the ghost of Orson Welles and a five-course meal."

"I did work out the masses!" she replied. "It's not my fault you're a weird skinny freak!"

"The Post Office even issues a chart! Number of stamps relative to mass times distance of object being teleported . . ."

"But I did it, didn't I?" she triumphed. "I mean, all by myself, your kick-ass apprentice, I like totally did it, a spell that most people can't and I did it and I got it right and you're here and safe and that's what matters, see?"

Sweat glimmered out on her forehead, ran down her neck. Her hands were shaking, her grin wide and uncontrollable, eyes darting all over my face as if scanning for one muscle out of place.

"Yes . . ." I began.

"I mean it's like I just did it and there was so much power but I controlled it and you are here I saved your life, I mean, I saved it, I did it right and . . ."

And some of the sweat below her eyes was tears, not sweat, and some of the shaking in her hands was terror, not tiredness. I caught her fingers as she gestured feebly at the magic circle, held them tight. It didn't seem enough. Not knowing why we did, or what we did, we leant over and caught her in our arms, pulled her tight. We did not know if we did it for her, or for us. We held her and she held us and she was shaking, tears rolling freely down her face. When to hold her any longer was to never let go, we pulled ourself free, looked her in the eyes, bright, brilliant, human eyes, and smiled.

"Yes," I said. "You did it. You saved the day. Again, may I add. I am dead on proud of you."

She wiped the tears away with the corner of her sleeve, sniffed noisily, straightened up. "I wasn't . . . don't think I was crying because of you!"

"I know you weren't."

"I . . . I was worried but it wasn't you."

"I know."

"I thought that the power . . . there was so much power and when I did it, when I made the spell work, I knew I could . . . that if I didn't . . . I can do so much, Matthew."

"I know you can."

"I can do too much, Matthew."

"Me too. But right here, right now, you did exactly what was needed."

She bit her bottom lip, even as her mouth parted in a nervous smile to mask her tears. There was a slow clapping, one heavy slap at a time. I looked round. Bakker was sat, pristine as ever, half on, half off a case of fortune cookies.

"Well done," he said. "You have trained an apprentice who, in her wilder days, nearly destroyed all of London by mistake, and you gave her even more power than she already had, and the confidence to try and use it. Very well done."

An absence slowly impressed itself on the corner of my mind. I looked a little further, then quickly back to Penny, who was straightening out her top self-consciously, like an applicant before an interview. "Penny?" I asked, struggling to keep my voice calm.

"Yeah?"

"Where's the girl?"

"The . . ."

"The girl. The girl I snatched from the jaws of death to bring here, that girl."

"Oh yeah, her. She arrived screaming like a banshee, punching and kicking and talking crazy shit. Aldermen took her upstairs to give her a wash, a drink and, with luck, a tranquilliser." She hesitated, then added, "Matthew . . . where's the Alderman? The psycho-nut Court guy? Where's Dees?"

I looked down, hands burnt and stained with blood.

I heard Penny take in a sharp breath, let it out deliberate and slow. "They . . ." Then she stopped.

We were silent.

Even Bakker was silent.

Then Penny said, "There's a toilet in this place. You'll want to get cleaned up. And there's food. The chef is . . . sleeping. So's the staff. But I think there's prawn crackers and stuff."

She held out one hand, palm soft and clean and pink. I took it. I could feel things screech and scratch inside as I stood up, and nearly lost my footing, clinging to her shoulders for support. "I'm fine," I wheezed. "I'm fine. I'm tired, that's all. I'm just . . . very, very tired."

"Toilet? Food? Drink?"

"Water," I said. "Water would be good."

"I'll get you some. It's going to be OK, Matthew. You know that, right? You'll do the whizzo Midnight Mayor shit and some of that blue electric angel shite and it'll all be cleared up by . . . by sunrise. It's going to be OK."

"Yeah," I lied. "I know."

The toilet was a chipped thing of broken red tiles and suspicious odours.

I sat for a long time, head pressed into the wall.

When I felt like the wall and I had shared every secret we had to tell, I crawled to my feet and stood for a long time, fists curled round the edge of the sink. There was a face in the cracked mirror above it. Blood and ash and dust had made it a monster in the dark, eyes too white and blue, the only thing about it left with any brightness.

When I grew sick of that face, I ran the cold tap and washed it.

Not even the icy water could take the tiredness away now.

I stayed friends with the wall all the way out of the toilet, up the stairs, past the kitchen. It was a dirty off-white thing, mates with many more species than just human, in which sacks of rice and bags of noodles waited to be cooked on the now sleeping stoves. Hushed voices beyond it kept me climbing, through a processed wooden door and into another room. This one had pink wallpaper adorned with thin white cranes, images of wild horses and flowing water. It had round tables covered with plastic tablecloths, a fish tank containing one lonely fat carp, and a trolley containing cold half-eaten plates of food. A chubby Asian woman in a white frilly shirt and black skirt lay, head in her hands, across the table next to it. At the table behind her was a group of Aldermen. Skin pale, eyes red, what little low conversation they'd had stopped as I entered. There was a jug of water on the table between them, empty, and several packets of pills, popped. Penny leant, arms folded, against the wall beside them. Her eyes were puffy and pink.

All the Aldermen stood as I approached. All sat when I took the one spare chair. There was silence. Then one, the oldest, blurted, "Dees . . ."

"Blackout killed her."

Silence.

I said, "Where's the girl? JG? Where is she?"

"Upstairs," said another. "She was hysterical."

"Guarded?" I added.

They nodded.

"What's happening?" I asked. "Why's there no one here? Where are the rest of you? What's going on with the Court, the Tribe?"

They shifted uneasily. Then the one who'd spoken first said, "People are falling asleep. Technically, we've all been awake for days. Some people napped at first, but now when they nap, they don't wake up. And more places have . . . vanished."

He pushed an A–Z across the table to me. I flicked through the pages. Kentish Town, Hammersmith, Bethnal Green, Elephant and Castle – all gone. Just blank pages. There was more whiteness now on this map, than there were streets. I closed it and pushed it back to the Alderman.

"The Neon Court's man?" asked one.

"Dead," I replied.

"He . . ."

"Blackout killed him too. Oda. She was there, in the darkness."

"But you got the girl out. The . . . chosen one? This girl upstairs . . . is the chosen one?"

I nodded dully. "Yeah. That's her. Right pain, isn't she?"

"What does this mean? Can we fix it?"

I didn't answer. Looking past the Aldermen, I could see through the restaurant window the cheery lights of Chinatown, red lanterns and windows full of ducks, bright calendars made of bamboo strips, nests of thin translucent noodle and little custard cakes. But no people. The signs on all the doors said closed; no one walked the streets, not even the dustman with his barrel and brush. The Aldermen waited. Not like them.

"Any food in this place?" I asked.

"Just left-overs and a microwave," offered Penny.

"That'll do. The girl – JG – is she still hysterical?"

"Should be calmer," answered an Alderman.

"Good. I'm going to have a chat with her."

I managed to drag myself to my feet. We felt old, horrifying, crippled old, a concept which once upon a time we would have had no means to understand.

A small staircase, grey, walls painted dull pale green, led upwards. A single Alderman sat by the door, her eyes flickering on the verge of sleep. I walked past, knocked on the door she guarded. No answer.

"JG? It's Matthew? I've got some food coming, some drink. You OK in there?"

No answer.

Slowly I turned the handle, eased the door open.

A single unsheltered bulb burnt from a wire in the ceiling. JG sat on an abused, sheetless bed, knees tucked into her chin, staring at the one picture on the wall. It showed a Chinese pavilion, a lady in flowing robes meeting a man with a mighty beard beside the still waters of a lake. I sat down on the bed beside her, resisting with every ounce the desire to lie down, just for a moment, just a little moment.

She didn't acknowledge my presence, but there was a concentration in her face that hadn't been there before, in that dust-filled room with the TV.

"Are you all right?"

She didn't bother to reply.

"I need to ask some questions. I'm sorry. But I have to know."

"Why?" she asked.

"Lives at stake."

"Whose?"

"Everyone's."

"I hate you. Go away."

She went back to her studies.

Penny came in, a grubby silver tray in her hands. "Right!" she said. "I've got reheated rice, reheated sour and sweet pork, reheated chicken with mushroom, reheated chow mein with ginger and, as a special treat, reheated duck with plum sauce and pancakes."

She laid it out on the bed. JG didn't bother to look at it. "Don't want it."

Penny's smile didn't falter. "I am not," she said, "a fucking waitress."

"You look like a fucking waitress," replied JG.

"And you look like someone who didn't get enough thick ears as a kid . . . oh, no, wait, you still are a fucking kid! Eat up or you'll go to bed and never wake up!"

JG grabbed a plate at random and made to throw it at Penny. I caught her wrist before she could, prised the plate free from her, put it back down. Penny's face was bright with anger, her fingers twitching at her side. "JG," I sighed, "I don't care what you think right now, and I'm too tired to try and puzzle it out. But you should probably know that the nice lady you just tried to cover in plum sauce saved your life out of the goodness of her shiny little heart, so try and be nice."

"Fuck off fuck off fuck off!" screamed JG. "Why won't you people leave me alone?!"

"Is it too late to send her back?" asked Penny.

JG was on her feet, glaring straight at my apprentice. "Do it!" she hissed. "Go on, do it, fucking do it, send me back there, I want to go back, do it now! You can't keep me a prisoner here!"

"You're not a prisoner," I sighed, trying to rub some of the fluff out of my eyes.

"Yeah, then why's there a guard on my fucking door?"

"Because all sorts of nasty people are probably out to get you right now, including, I gotta tell you, the woman you and I know as Oda."

She spat. A round blob of spit rested on the thin carpet and began to sink in. We watched the dark dampness of it spread in busy silence. Penny's face was a twisted pattern of disgust. JG slumped back down on the end of her bed, face puffed and furious, and said nothing.

Penny said, "You going to let that pass?"

I shrugged.

"You are one bloody crap childminder."

"Not a child!" snarled JG.

"You're acting like one."

"Am not!"

"Oh yeah, that's so mature."

"Get out get out get out get out!" shrieked JG, and as she screamed, she beat her fists against the air and the bulb in the middle of the room hummed and dimmed, and it seemed, for a moment, that there was something wild and bright behind her eyes, and a taste of smoke on the air.

Penny's eyes met mine. I said, "That wasn't . . ."

"Not me," she replied, raising her hands in defence. "You know me, boss, I am cool-cat-Ngwenya these days, super sorceress extraordinaire. If I want the lights to schiz out, I do it properly."

I looked back at JG. The girl was still shaking with rage, fists clenched, eyes tight. Rage, and a bit more besides.

"Great," I sighed. "Because all the situation needed was a little more complexity." I shuffled round, closer to JG and, in her pride, she didn't move. Bakker was in the doorway, watching now, back again for the fireworks.

"JG?" I breathed. "JG, please listen to me. No one here wants to hurt you, no one here is your enemy. I think you know that. I think you understand that. But I need to know things, otherwise it's all going to get much, much worse. I need to know how you know Oda."

"Go away."

"I know you knew her. I said her name and you trusted me; she told me to find you, she seemed . . . she looked at you and you didn't go blind. JG? You must know something's wrong with her. I was . . . I am Oda's friend. I want to help her."

Her head snapped up, she glared at us. "You attacked her. I saw you do it! You nearly killed her!"

"She attacked us," I replied. "You know that's true. You saw it. She . . . she killed my friend. You saw that happen too. You saw it, JG, you saw her kill my friend, a woman with a husband, a child, Oda killed her and didn't have a moment's regret. You saw Oda's eyes. You saw what happened to her in the fire. You must know, you must, you must understand that whatever your relationship with her is, that relationship is as good as dead."

A flicker of doubt? Then, "You're lying! You lie about everything!"

"Think about it, JG. I haven't lied about one thing. I've told you the absolute truth. Oda asked me to find you. 'Where's the girl?' she said. She was in that tower block when it began to burn, she called me to try and help her."

"Then what are you?"

"Matthew Swift. I'm a sorcerer. This is Penny, my apprentice."

JG's eyes flickered from me to Penny then back again. Her fingers tugged unconsciously at the neck of her hoodie. "If you hurt me," she whispered, "my sister will hunt you down and kill you."

We had not thought the human body could reel from words spoken, as if words were weapons. Yet we reeled, our eyes flying to Penny's and seeing in them equal shock as suggestion danced the dance with realisation. Even Bakker detached himself from the door where he'd been leaning, craning in closer to hear.

I licked my dry lips, tasted broken skin. "JG," I murmured, "is Oda your sister?"

Silence.

"Oda's sister is dead," breathed Penny. "Sinclair told us; Oda's sister died, she was . . . killed by her brother, by Kayle, Oda's sister was . . ."

Bakker's nose almost brushed JG's as he leant in closer. "There is a resemblance. Although suggestion does prompt imagination."

I grabbed JG by the shoulders and she flinched away, face crinkling in dislike. "Get off me!"

"JG, this is absolutely the most important thing you can tell us. I need to know right now – is Oda your sister?"

"Why do you care, you hate her, you hate her and you want to kill her!" Tears were building in JG's eyes, but she kept on staring as if daring anyone to point it out. We realised we were still clinging on to her shoulders and let go, drawing back.

"You are . . . you are Jabuile Ajaja," I breathed. "Your older brother, Kayle, tried to . . . he tried to use you to fuel his own magics and . . . and Oda found you and killed him . . . how are you still alive, Jabuile?"

"That's not my name any more."

"Why not?"

"It's not my name it's not my fucking name!"

"Listen to me!" Blue fired flashed in front of our eyes and for a moment, JG was afraid, afraid of us. I closed my eyes, drew in a shuddering breath. "Listen to me," I said again, softer. "Please . . . just listen." I eased myself off the bed, knelt in front of her, holding her clammy hands in mine. "All you need to do is listen. Oda . . . your sister . . . has been hurt. And when she was hurt something moved inside her, tried to possess her. It took her eyes, it took her blood, and it's taken a lot of lives too. When any of us – me, Penny, anyone – looks in your sister's eyes, we go blind, and then we die. But when you looked into her eyes, you didn't. I think even now she's trying to protect you, keep you safe. I think . . . whatever part of her is still Oda, not the thing wearing Oda's flesh, you are our very best chance of talking to it. How did you survive?"

"I . . . why are you telling me this? What kind of freak are you, telling me this?"

"Name any way of proving it that I haven't already done, and I'll do it. You saw, JG, Jabuile, you saw Oda. Is she still your sister?"

"I . . . I don't . . . I didn't . . ." Her fists were unclenching. Even Penny's face was breaking out into something nearing pity.

"Tell me – please, just tell me. What happened to you? With Kayle, with Oda, with everything? What happened?"

"I . . . he hurt me. He was . . . was like you" – her lip curled with contempt as she spat the words – "sorcerer, he said, a sorcerer, and you're a sorcerer . . ."

"Yeah, and if Matthew is running on blood magics, then it's really bad PR for the business," added Penny helpfully, but for all we scowled, it seemed to be enough to push JG on.

"They took me to the hospital," JG went on, voice wandering through some distant place as she spoke. "When Kayle . . . he didn't . . . he couldn't do it, couldn't . . . do everything he had to do, he hurt me so bad and then . . . then he stopped and they came and took me to the hospital and the priest was there and he . . ."

"Priest?" My voice was hard, sharp, she shrank away from it. "What priest?"

"The priest at the hospital. He told me when I woke up that my brother was dead, and my sister killed him. He said the police were after me, that I was in big big trouble and . . . I was so scared, he said that nowhere was safe for me and I had to go into protection. He said he'd look after me, keep me safe, but that I mustn't tell anybody. He got me a new home, looked after me . . . sort of. I don't think he liked me. Not ever. All those years and he just said 'I'll keep you safe' and he got me clothes and shit and gave me cash and didn't care what I did with my friends – I mean, parents are supposed to care, right, they're supposed to get all mad and he was like a priest, he could have got mad with like bells on – but he didn't and I guess that was cool but he never . . . liked me. Saved me and all, but never . . . They said I couldn't see her again. Oda. That there were people looking for her, people who . . ." Her voice trailed off, eyes darting to mine, then to Penny's. "Who are you? I mean like more than fucking Matthew and fucking Penny, I mean . . . what's your beef? What's in it for you? Are you like the police?"

"No, not really. Hell, it's not like we're even big on the goodness and light business, are we Penny? But we're the guys left awake when everyone else has fallen asleep, so I guess that means we're the good guys by default."

"You talk a lot of shit, man."

Despite ourself, we grinned. "That's what people tell us. Go on, please. Who was this priest?"

"He said he was a friend of Oda's. He knew about me and the tower, and stuff, he knew that I like, liked to hang out there. He seemed cool with it. Then one day Oda turned up there, I mean . . . she just turned up and she was so much older, I mean like, old inside too, but she was still my sister and she said she was going to look after me, look after me for ever and ever and never leave me and she cried, my big sister cried and . . . and then there was the fire . . . and men came looking . . . and I remember running and there was this . . . this crack in the floor and I was so scared, so scared and then it just . . . what happened to her?"

"She was hurt," I replied. "In the fire; she got hurt. JG? This priest . . . the man who took you from the hospital, took you away . . . what was his name?"

JG gave a little shrug, small and dismissive. "Father Anton. Why?"

I felt my fingers uncurl, my breath unravel. I stood up slowly, forced myself to take a breath, then another. "Father . . . Anton Chaigneau?" I suggested. "White hair, dark skin, big voice?"

JG nodded.

"He took you from the hospital?"

Nodded.

"Knew you'd be in that tower block?"

Hesitation; nod.

We felt like we ought to laugh. It seemed like too much effort.

I fumbled for the door. "Be back in two ticks," I muttered, opening it and staggering onto the stairwell outside. I made it downstairs by touch and instinct, Penny following a few seconds behind, reached the dining room, the Aldermen all rising as I entered, found a table to prop myself against and sat down with my head in my hands. "Get me," I growled between the slits in my fingers, "caffeine, aspirin and the psychotic head of a magician-hating institution called the Order." The Aldermen hesitated. I looked up through my parted fingers. "Guys. I really, really do mean it."

Penny was at the foot of the stairs. "Anton Chaigneau?" she demanded. "The weird religious-nut guy who told us in a pub by Euston that Oda was doing the dark-power business? He's . . . involved?"

"Oh, hell, yes," I groaned. "I think it's all starting to make sense. The Order, the Tribe, the Court, the chosen one, Oda . . . yeah. I think I'm close to cracking this one."

"Matthew?"

It wasn't Penny who'd spoken. Bakker was there, standing by the trolley of leftovers, face drawn in tight concern. "What?" I snapped, and then flinched as all eyes turned to me in curiosity. "Caffeine," I repeated. "Aspirin. Psychotic nut-job. Any time, please."

"Matthew," repeated Bakker, voice darker, deeper. "We have to leave this place."

"All right, wow me!" I scowled. "Why do we have to leave this perfectly civilised place, right, right now?"

"Uh, boss?" mumbled Penny. "You're kinda talking to yourself now."

I flapped her into silence. She fumed.

"We're being observed," replied Bakker. "At this exact moment, everything that happens here is being watched."

"I don't feel it," I said. "No scrying, nothing."

Wordlessly, Bakker raised his hand, and pointed at a pile of magazines on the bar. Something inside my chest tried to head for my knees. I got up, walked to the bar, picked up the first magazine on the top of the pile.

Its front-cover headline read:

Eternal Youth – 10 Top Tips!

More cover lines added:

Men – how to keep them hot!!!

5 great romantic get-away ideas, for the budget traveller!

Exclusive interview with the Queen of the Night!!

There was a picture of a woman beneath this title. Her face was lightly obscured with a thin white veil, but that didn't prevent you seeing beneath it the pale, silk skin, the laughing mouth, the twinkling lilac eyes. I looked at Lady Neon on the front cover of the magazine, and she, indefinably and inescapably, looked back.

I threw it down, marched over to Penny, grabbed her by the sleeve, hissed, "Get JG, we're going, right *now*."

"But we . . ."

"Right now!"

She took the stairs two at a time, slamming the door to JG's room behind her. I grabbed the nearest Alderman, an Indian-looking woman on a mobile phone, said, "The Neon Court's coming. We have to go."

She had the good sense to look afraid, and nodded. "I'll call the car."

"Don't say I can't be useful, Matthew," said Bakker easily as I pressed my nose up to the steamy glass of the window.

"Yeah, so far you've been a right pleasure," I growled. "Thanks for the ride."

Penny reappeared with JG and her token Alderman protector in tow. JG looked mute now, a bundled-up child that had given up trying to pretend to be an adult. Another Alderman opened the restaurant door, ushering us out. We scrambled outside. Rain. The same thick relentless rain that had been falling in Sidcup, that seemed to have been falling for ever. It fell on crumpled cardboard boxes, on stray rotting cabbage leaves and bones that even the rats were too tired now to gnaw on. It dripped off the red arches that closed off either end of Gerrard Street, the hub of Chinatown; ran off the lintels of Georgian houses converted into restaurants, herbalists', acupuncturists' and flats for dozens. The Aldermen wore big black hats and carried umbrellas, shielding JG from the rain like guards around a visiting minister. There was a car, black, engine running, windows tinted, waiting by the fire station, whose banner declared in Cantonese and English the importance of smoke detectors. One Alderman asked another, hushed but not enough, "How does he know that . . ."

"Magazine," I snapped, marching towards the waiting car. "Lady Neon was on it, in it. The Neon Court can watch you from any picture bearing their features. You know the phrase 'its eyes followed me round the room'. That thing."

We reached the car, yanked the door open. The driver was a professional chauffeur, from his peaked hat down to the tips of his white soft gloves. His eyes were open, his mouth hanging down, drool pooling in one corner. He stared at nothing, fingers gripping the wheel, and did not move. We smelt magic on him, not the thick smothering stuff of Blackout, but something lighter, brighter, and infinitely more persuasive. The bright lights of Shaftesbury Avenue shone down on empty sleeping streets, from the roofs above theatre doors and the windows of the cinemas. They shone on double-decker buses that had lost the will to move, on diners in restaurants whose heads had tipped forward into their soup, on overflowing dustbins and the frozen silent faces of Bollywood movie stars pinned to the darkened windows of the video store. The falling lights scampered across the shutters drawn shut over a bureau de change. On the shutters someone had written, in bright green paint:

TOXIK WOZ ERE

The paint was still dribbling downhill, fresh and wet, mingling and thinning in the rain.

They shone on a group of stretch limos, five, hogging the middle of the road and reaching almost round the corner. Most were black. One in the middle was white. The one at the very front was pink. As I watched, the door opened. A girl got out. She had blond hair done in pigtails, and wore not much more than two straps of blue fabric, across those parts the police considered it polite to cover. She looked straight at us and giggled, her left hand held to her mouth, like she was locked in a perpetual battle to not chew her nails. She said, "Mr Mayor? My lady isn't very happy with you."

I shuffled back to Penny and JG. More doors opened. Limos, it turned out, could hold surprisingly large numbers of people. They were armed. None of them looked pleased. "You two?" I murmured.

"Yeah?"

"When you run, and yes, we're going to have to run, don't go into Soho, don't go into Leicester Square. They'll gobble you up like biscuits to a puppy if you do."

"Who are they?" asked JG.

"Neon Court," I replied. "They think you're a chosen one."

"Uh – what the fuck? Chosen for what?"

"Oh, ending a war, starting a war, being a war, Christ knows. You're not, if it's any comfort. Although," we grinned, a sickly tired grin washed in the stench of humanity, "in an ironic way, you are. Dig that philosophy."

The white door to the white limo opened.

A white shoe stepped out, half hidden by a white silk hem. Then the rest of the white body. Lady Neon's veil twisted in the breeze. There were dozens of them, thralls and even a number of daimyos, necks bound in silver, watching us. I eased in front of JG, took a step towards the crowd, smiling my most charming dentist's smile.

To our surprise, Lady Neon walked towards us, alone. We moved towards her, until just the two of us stood on the tarmac between Aldermen and Court. I felt the water in the pipes below, smelt electricity in the cables overhead, the taste of glass and heat of gas ready to ignite.

We stopped just short of arm's length apart.

Nothing happened.

Not a pigeon, not a rat.

I licked my lips. "Theydon's dead."

Her head inclined a little to one side, like someone trying to recall the name Theydon. If she made the connection, she didn't care.

"You're being used," I added. "This whole chosen one business – you're being used. There is no chosen one. There never was. It was made up to lead you into a war with the Tribe. You've been manipulated. And you've walked right into the trap. Hurrah. But I imagine you don't really care about that, do you?"

She was silent. Then she reached up, and lifted the veil.

The spell hit us hard enough to hurt, got its fingers into our belly and twisted like it was squeezing juice from a lemon. It made our eyes water, filled our ears with the sound of blood, made the veins ache in our head. It said, *beautiful, beautiful, beautiful* . . .

and much more than that, so much beauty that it could do no ill, that nothing other than perfection could come from this face, beauty that bypassed all senses and went straight down to that unknown spark in the soul that talked without using words. It slipped its hooks into our skin, tangled itself in our hair, dripped one nectar drop at a time onto the tip of our tongue. I spoke, and it took every breath I had, every inch of air in my lungs, one word at a time. "Don't . . . play silly . . . buggers," I wheezed.

She smiled, and the sheer force of the expression, the sheer innocent, joyful playfulness of it, the invitation and the offer, nearly knocked us flat. "Don't!" we snarled. "We are not . . . we are not just flesh . . . not just flesh not just . . ." Her smile widened. Laughing. Sapphire rage flickered in front of our eyes. "Try and spin one more spell," we hissed, "try and work one more magic into our skin, and we will teach your blood to burn like oil."

Her smile twinkled, lilac eyes full of more than life, of stories that couldn't be spoken out loud, feelings that language hadn't yet got the tools to express. But not laughing. Not now. She gave a little half-bow, and as her head dipped, she swept the veil back across her face. We remembered what it had been like to breathe. She straightened up slowly, hands folded neatly in front of her, like a priest about to bless.

"Do you know," she asked, her voice light on the empty air, "what it means to be a chosen one?"

"Buggered about," I replied.

A thing that wore the look of genuine humour, if anything about this creature could be said to even hook little fingers with the hand of truth, flickered across her shaded features. "*You* are a chosen one. You were chosen by the blue electric angels, a mortal shell for their mind. You were chosen by the Midnight Mayor. You were chosen by me. We did not ask your opinion, we did not seek your counsel, whether you wished these things was of no relevance. It was what we wished, and you could neither run nor resist. Now, this chosen one, this girl hiding behind you, she may have been chosen by a higher power. There may be a god looking down on us, proclaiming that this is the end of days. But I do not think so. And even if I were to believe that she were *not* chosen, the Tribe will believe that she was, and thus, she is. They have chosen to make, of her, a war. And as she is the cause, and the heart, and the mystery inside this conflict, regardless of herself, or you, or me, so I shall have her. If only to destroy her and end for all this mystery. Perhaps that was always her purpose – chosen to die for no greater reason than she was there. Yet she must die."

"And what gives you the power to decide?" I asked.

She laughed, the sound of falling glass, and flexed her fingers, encompassing almost without moving the men and women around her. "Will and means, my beautiful blue-eyed fire. Will and means are all that power ever is."

I half nodded, turning my face up to catch the rain. Something moved along the gutter line of the buildings above us, old former houses, once dignified, now mingled with newer brick slabs and steel concoctions, as time, commerce and disaster mingled together. The air still rumbled with the half-faded sound of distant traffic, of voices raised in drunken merriment, and carried the smell of boiled rice. Not even the perpetual falling rain of Blackout could wipe away the stamp of magic trod like chewing gum into dirt on the paving stones of Shaftesbury Avenue. The green-painted words on the shuttered shop behind Lady Neon were almost entirely gone, washed out with the rain.

TOXIK WO

I said, "How'd it start? Your lot and the Tribe? I mean, how'd it really, really start?"

Lady Neon seemed to think. Then, "I don't think it's important any more."

Something misshapen up in the chimney pots. "Blimey," I mumbled, eyes fixed on the dark, rain-washed roofline. "That trivial, huh?"

For a moment, doubt. It was just a glimmer like the dimming of a bulb when moved around the wire, but it was there, just for a second. Lady Neon's gaze flickered to the roofs; it was obvious that she saw what we had already seen and, for just a moment, there it was, something small, and real, and mortal. Bakker said, "Kill her now."

We felt fire on our fingers.

"Do it, Matthew, this is your one chance, do it now and end it!"

Her head turned back towards us, slowly. Fear. No one else would ever sense it, but it was there, sticky fear clinging to her perfect skin. Then her look drifted to our fingers, saw the flame. She tensed in an expression of surprise, and I heard her whisper, "Treachery?"

Bakker was right beside her, head turned to the roof. I half shook my head, clenched my fist until the blood was driven down deep, taking the fire with it.

"More people will die by your inaction than will be saved," sighed Bakker.

Then a voice spoke from the corner.

It belonged to a man standing before a nearby cinema. His face was half shrouded in darkness, his back crooked, his stance uneven. His words came with a flare of sudden match-light, which quickly dimmed in the rain to the orange puff of a cigarette. The voice said, "If u giv her da chosen 1, we wil kil u."

My eyes wandered back to the roof, and yes, there they were, dozens of them, maybe more than dozens, creeping out of the shadows, humans, or once-humans, or humans that had cut away every outward sign of humanity, skin and flesh, in the hope that when they no longer looked human, they'd no longer have to obey human rules. And for some of them, it had worked, for there were men crawling along the brick walls of the houses like they were exploratory ants, and women hunched like bats on the ledges of the darkened windows, ready to dive and strike, and they stank of deep-down airless places and iron, of blood and all the magics that came with it. The Tribe, turning out in force, ready, as promised, to claim their prize.

Toxik, the shaman of them all, stood alone by the cinema entrance, and puffed. I called, "You hear all that stuff I said about how you're being used?"

He drew the cigarette slowly back from his slashed lips with a pair of fingers more bone than flesh, let out the blue-grey smoke in a slow rolling wave. "Yeh," he said. "i herd. but if der is a chosen 1, n we didnt do da chosin, den wat kinda sukers does dat mak us?"

I could feel Penny dragging in power around her, taste the sharp sparking of her magics moving in the street. The Aldermen were tight and silent around the motionless car, the shadows turning at their feet, and I could hear . . .

rumble of bus rumbling for ever

chatter this tongue that tongue chatter chatter look!

get out of the way where'd he learn to drive?

I said two for one two for one

which way for Piccadilly Circus please?

You know, it occurs to me, Matthew, that the power of the Midnight Mayor is one whose potential you've never fully grasped.

And if I half closed my eyes I could hear . . .

five quid mate yours a bargain

go again next time?

Taxi! Taxi!

The fucking Midnight Mayor, mystic fucking protector of the city!

I opened my eyes. They were all watching. Tribe, Court, Aldermen. I became aware of a nasty smell. I looked down. At my feet, the black tar used to patch the uneven roads was hissing, smoking, melting. I looked at my hands. Our nails were black, clawlike, stretching out beyond their natural growth. I looked at Lady Neon. She took a step back. I looked at Toxik. He took a shaky puff of smoke. I half turned my head and looked at Penny. Her eyes were bright, and of all of them, in all that place, she was the only one who didn't seem afraid. I grinned, turned back to Lady Neon, turned back to Toxik, turned my head to the Court and the Tribe and gave an expansive shrug.

"You know what?" I said, and our voice wasn't our voice, our voice was dripping with city dragon, forking off the end of our tongue. "You guys are absolutely right. Fuck it. I've got way more to worry about tonight than what you guys do to one stupid kid from Sidcup. I mean Jesus Christ, there's five million people who are going to die tonight all because I got my sense of perspective from a discount destiny store off Dalston Lane. Here!" I marched up to JG, grabbed her by the shoulders, pulled her into the middle of the road. "Go on! Here's your chosen one! Now you lot have a lovely bloodbath over her while I go and make the sun come up. Come on!"

They hesitated, not one knowing exactly what to make of this.

"Although," I added quickly, before the moment could snap or JG could bite my hand off, "I would add, just so that you don't think I'm not a professional when it comes to these sorts of things, mind where you walk."

They looked down.

And perhaps for just a moment, everyone in that street, from mutilated kid who thought the key to being perfect was to cut away the bad things, to wanky lady who thought that being herself wasn't nearly as good as being someone else, perhaps for just a moment they heard it, the sound of . . .

footsteps footsteps footsteps a thousand footsteps walking on stone on tarmac on cobble on mud on dirt on dust on sand on leather on iron on steel on plastic on rubber on

lost i'm lost sorry can you help me?

late dear for the show

north to cambridge circus south to piccadilly

and the tarmac began to crack

camera flash!

just want to go home

you wait all day for one and then five turn up at once

did you see

looking for the way to

walking fast slow up down back forward late here now then coming going coming going coming going in between coming going and

the tarmac began to split and tear apart, black chasms opening up inside it and we could hear

fire engine siren wailing

another bloody hole already

was it coffee or tea?

I said left idiot!

excuse me which way to . . . ?

And there were fingers, each a shadow-blade, whisper-thin, crawling out of the cracks, and behind the fingers stick-arms, and each stick-arm attached to a body no wider than the tears in the earth itself, stretched long and thin as time and memory, crawling out of the street and they were coming alive, shadows and whispers and memories, pulling themselves free of the bricks, slipping out of the windows, flopping from the gutters and dragging themselves one joint at a time from between the paving stones. There were hundreds; then thousands; a blink of an eye and there were thousands on thousands, and still they kept coming, their touch the shiver of a cold wind blown off the river, and they were speaking without mouths, empty black spaces mumbling at the air but their voices were deafening, all around, everywhere, unstoppable, ringing so big and loud together that all we could hear were

Brake of engine
Rain falling
Foot snap on stone
Umbrella swish open
Phone ringing
Hello?
Which way for . . .
Did you see . . .?
I lost my . . .
Is it far to . . . ?

The memories of the street came crawling up in the dark and talked, pawed at every daimyo and shaman, every thrall and crawling warrior of the Tribe, begged and wheedled and whispered in their ears, an eardrum-shattering whisper that went straight to the brain without bothering to stir the air, and as the street filled and the shadows became too thick to see through I grabbed JG by the hand and turned and ran.

Chaos was too clean a word.

Too much, too much information across the senses, we couldn't see for too much seeing, hear for too much hearing, we bent double and charged head first through a thousand thousand shadows still crawling up from a street ripping apart so wide and deep we could see the pipes cracking, the cables rupturing, concrete and rubble and mud and cobbles and deep down the bones upon bones laid on the streets below. They pawed at us with fingers of steam and dust, tried to put their words in our head, tried to crawl inside us through our ears and lips, they were everywhere, hugging the feet of the scrambling thralls, pulling at the clothes of the Tribe's warriors, and everywhere magic bloomed, random, giddy, out-of-control ignorant magic that tried to blast the shadows away and found itself impacting on nothing more tangible than a little too much time. I saw the Aldermen, or not the Aldermen, things that could have been Aldermen when the lights still burnt, mad red eyes and at their backs, wings, made of black folded nothing, too big and deep to ever end, stretching up almost as high as the rooftops, teeth turned to fangs, fingers to claws, and I saw Penny, and the air around her was brilliant with wildfire. We wondered what she saw when she looked at us, and then ducked as the glass shattered in the windows overhead, popping like bubbles under pressure from the inside out all along the length of the street, and I could half see the shaman Toxik running along the pavement, hands over his ears, eyes half shut as the glass snapped and popped around him, cutting at clothes and skin, not that he cared. I shouted, "Penny!"

She turned, and there was barbed wire spinning up like ivy from the ground around her, and her hair stood on end with static and her fingers were tangled in blue-yellow burning gas. "Not this time!" she shouted back. "Not tonight!"

I tried to shout something more and a figure dropped from right above me, from the black metal pipe of a black dirty wall, spun and dropped onto all fours like a leopard, and the skin of his face was stabbed through with little metal pipes and so was the skin of his hands and he made an animal noise that had nothing to do with any human feeling and leapt, fists first for JG. She covered her head with her hands and we lashed out, tackling him mid-leap and knocking him to the ground. I got a kick in somewhere in his midriff and briefly all I could see was wild eyes laced with blood and broken teeth raging back at me, then we drew our hand back and slammed it palm first into the point between his eyes, static flaring off them and dancing white fire earthing itself through his flesh as we struck. He went limp, steam rising off the pavement beneath him, and I grabbed JG again and pulled her down the street. Behind me I felt fire bloom, fuel pulled from the mains beneath our feet, and I knocked JG against the nearest wall as the road split and gas flames burst upwards, stabbing into the air like the questing tongue of a frog, gnawing at feet and the wheels of the cars behind. A fistful of flame caught the inside of an engine, made it tick, then groan, then twisted it up into the air and out, blooming with a blast wave that sent all to the ground around it. I pressed myself flat against JG as metal and glass sliced into the wall. Half a wing mirror embedded itself there, a sliver away from my ear, and wobbled, shedding shards of plastic and glass. A pair of pink bouncy dice, one side burning and black, rolled along the pavement and came to a stop by my feet. I waited for the worst to pass, caught JG by the arm and ran again, the shadows spinning as we passed. I could see the lights of Cambridge Circus ahead, taste the older, deeper magics of Covent Garden off to the south, darker spells for smaller streets than the pounding dazzling magics of Soho. JG staggered and tripped; I looked behind, saw a woman dressed in not nearly enough for the weather, her hair stood up in great blue spikes, sprawled in the gutter, clinging to JG's ankle. Her nails were painted with the image of a writhing green snake that crawled and became worms, living little worms that were crawling from her hand up JG's leg, wrapping themselves round it.

Bakker whispered right in our ear, "Cut her hand off!"

We grabbed the woman by her blue spiky hair, pulled her up until we thought her back could bend no more, while JG kicked and scrambled and wriggled her way loose, and then slammed the woman's head down as hard as we dared into the grey tarmac of the street. She went limp, the snakes snapping back in retreat to her nails. JG's leg was grazed from the writhing of the things that had tried to hold her; she limped and said nothing as I pulled her along. Cambridge Circus: the theatre, great walls of bare yellow bulbs that hissed and sizzled in the falling rain, narrow buildings on the triangular corners of winding streets peeking out onto the not-quite-roundabout, bars and pubs, banks, a long red-brick arcade holding sleepy shops selling furry hats, novelty souvenirs and porcelain miniatures of Big Ben, second-hand bookshops offering books in English, Latin, French, Swahili, Sanskrit, German, Dutch, Hindi and ancient Greek, music shops, windows gleaming with brass instruments and polished guitars; life here, so much life if you just knew what to do with it.

Behind me, I heard another whoomph followed by a sound which seemed to flatten all the world around it; I risked glancing back and for a moment, in between the moving everything, the heaving, hauling sea of darkness and light, I glimpsed Penny, her skin clad in thick grey concrete, swing a fist etched with steel knuckle into the glass blade of a daimyo. Then we were round a corner, a narrow little street, the sounds of fighting muffled by the walls of the houses tight around us, wheelie-bins and shops offering beads, wool and organic food for silly prices, our feet shattering the surface of the growing puddles, the light buzzing and humming around us. We got fifty yards before JG, staggering, her injured leg bleeding, slipped and fell on her hands and knees. I tried to pull her up, but she was a dead weight, hot and prickly to the touch. She put her hands to her head and whimpered, "Can't stop them can't stop them can hear can hear . . ."

Something moved at the end of the road behind us, too fast to see, a shimmer in the dark. I grabbed her hands, pulled them back from her head and hissed, "Look at me!" She looked, and the whites of her eyes were foggy with swirling smoke. I shook her gently. "Jabuile Ajaja," I hissed, "sister of a sorcerer, you are going to get up right now, and you are going to live, and you are going to be so much more, do you understand?"

She nodded dully, allowed herself to be pulled back to her feet. With one arm slung across my back, she half walked, was half carried to the end of the narrow little road. Another theatre, tucked away, pictures on the walls of men in suits and women in floral dresses looking respectively shocked and awed; a shop ahead, wide windows lit against a dark background offering action-figure dolls carrying wands, guns, rifles and the occasional sonic screwdriver against a backdrop of aliens, demons, screaming women scantily clad and non-specific tentacled monstrosities. Bars with blacked-out windows and posters inviting playful and perky young ladies to be hostesses at the best-paying social club in all of London; restaurants offering menus of snails in garlic butter or leaves of lettuce at £8.50 a throw.

I couldn't hear the sounds of battle now, but the voices were still there, thousands of them, fingers trying to break out of the walls, faces trying to pull themselves free from the shadows. I saw a light up ahead shining on blue and gold, pulled myself onwards, slipped on the edge of a deep puddle pooling in a blocked-up drain and nearly dropped JG onto the steps of a tall once-white pillar in the middle of a child's-sized roundabout. On the top of the pillar were seven different faces, painted gold and blue, each adorned with an elegant and utterly non-functional sundial. I looked around, counted seven streets leading off in seven directions, pressed my head against the cold stone steps of the pillar and for just a moment, breathed.

Bakker said, "Where are you going to run?"

I raised my head slowly, taking it one vertebra at a time. He was sat quite casually next to me, watching the street we'd come up, a white napkin tucked into his shirt. In one hand he held a small white biscuit, adorned with a dollop of white cream and pink salmon. He ate it with one mouthful, his other hand shielding his legs from any fallout from the same. He sighed, eyes half closing with every sign of pleasure, and licked his lips with the sharp end of his tongue.

JG was lying beside him, gasping for breath, sodden and shaking. I crawled over to her, murmured, "You OK?"

She looked up and I could taste the magic on her now, see it flicker and flare in the air around her like a lighter trying to start in the wind. "Something's coming," she breathed.

"No shit."

"Oh look," sighed Bakker. "Oda's little sister picked up some of her big brother's less sanctified traits – what a family!"

"We've got to keep moving," I murmured.

"Where?"

I opened my mouth and found I had no answer.

"Oh look!" added Bakker with sickly sweetness. "The lights are going out!"

He unfolded one long pale finger, stabbing at the street up which we'd just come. I followed it. Above the shop selling DIY Jedi kits, the pink sodium street light flickered, buzzed, thinned to a point, and went out. Then the next one. And then the one after that.

I didn't move. Didn't run. "JG?" I murmured.

"Yeah?" she breathed.

"You are what saves us. You are the only thing left that Oda knows and loves. You are the only thing left that makes her human, the only thing that can bring her back. Do you understand?"

"No," she whimpered. "I don't understand any of it."

I found her hands in mine, her eyes fixed on mine, every part of her shaking, cold, fear, name it. "Jabuile Ajaja," I breathed. "You're probably the most human thing left in this part of town."

She almost smiled, though she didn't seem to know why. I rubbed water out of my eyes and tried to stand up. Someone had replaced the bones in my legs with rubber. I leant against the cold wet stone of Seven Dials and forced myself to breathe, watching the approaching darkness.

"Well!" I said brightly. "Isn't this a right old . . ."

Something brushed the side of my neck.

Something warm.

Something living.

I tried to turn my head to see what it was and couldn't. I tried to spread my fingers, move my feet, tried to speak, and couldn't.

I felt breath brush the inside of my ear. Heard a little sigh. Heard silk move. Bakker rose to his feet, arms folded, face stern.

Lady Neon stepped round in front of me.

She was smiling. (Beware her violet kiss.)

Her veil was up, and her lipstick was smudged. I wondered if I'd see some of that colour on the side of my neck, if I ever got to look again. She looked at me, then, no longer interested, down at JG. JG tried to crawl away, scrambling backwards from Lady Neon, kicking away like a stranded starfish.

Lady Neon said, "There's nothing for you to worry about. You are the chosen one. We will protect you."

She held out one hand. I saw JG hesitate. I tried to scream. We raged and kicked and tore and tried to reach out, tried to grab her, shake her, tell her to run, to get away. Couldn't.

"You can fight it, Matthew," breathed Bakker in our ear. "The kiss of Lady Neon binds all to her will but it can't hold you for ever, it is as false and shallow a magic as everything else about her!"

JG's fingers slipped into Lady Neon's. She rose to her feet, eyes locked on the lilac smile of the white-clad woman. Her hands rested in the palms of Lady Neon's, like a child about to be led on its first dance. We shook, managed to taste saliva on our lips, force out a gasp of air, a little sound, barely a syllable and even that effort nearly knocked us flat, opened up a pit of hot darkness at our feet. The lights were nearly out in the street in front of us, and going out around too, snapping out in the streets on either side, closing down in a tighter and tighter circle on the little point of light left at Seven Dials.

Lady Neon began to lead JG away, and the girl didn't resist.

"Come on!" roared Bakker. "Come on, you are the Midnight Mayor! You are the blue electric angels, you are gods on this earth, power made flesh, you are rage and light! Come on!"

I felt my left hand move, half an inch, a twitch, I tried to push power into it, felt my fingers part like my skin was dry clay, sensed the smell of ozone and the hiss of power in the air. From the pit of our throat we managed to make a sound, a bare whisper, a croak, "JG . . ."

She didn't look back.

Then something hard and fast flew out of the darkness and caught Lady Neon on the shoulder. She staggered, her touch on JG breaking for just a moment, and looked at the thing which had hit her. It was half a brick. Slowly, disbelievingly, she craned her head round to examine the silk on her shoulder where it had struck. A tiny tear in the perfect fabric, which was slowly turning crimson with blood. She turned, looked back at the thing that had thrown the brick. Another went flying past; she ducked, avoiding it easily, and JG, blinking as the spell began to snap, pulled herself free and staggered away, turning all around to see that the darkness was at the edge of the Dial, was lingering on the edge and all sounds had gone out except the fall of the rain, not even the whispering now. Then her eyes fell on me and she ran towards me, grabbed my hand and at that touch the spell snapped and we staggered forward, gasping for breath, clinging on to her for support as our limbs finally decided to report themselves in for duty. I half turned my head to see who'd thrown the brick, and there he was, Toxik, every crooked part of him, leaning on a dustbinman's broom, dirt on his face and in his hair, hatred in his eyes as he stared straight at Lady Neon.

I hissed, "Wait . . ." Toxik raised one hand in command and nausea gripped me, sent me slipping further down in JG's arms. "Blackout!" I tried to gesture at the darkness all around, at the places where street lights should have been, but he and Lady Neon neither looked nor cared.

"Ugly man," said Lady Neon finally, "I don't suppose you're here to surrender?"

Toxik grinned, shook his head. "U dont lok lik u is givin up 2."

Lady Neon nodded, drew her hands together in front of her. The white silk sleeves closed around her fingers, hiding them from view. I heard hard surfaces move. Toxik raised his broom, and I saw that the wood was black, embedded with dirt and time and a little bit more besides. Lady Neon drew her hands apart again, and from inside the white folds of each sleeve came a curving blade, of perfect crystal glass.

"I don't think we need bother with apologies," she murmured as the two faced off.

"No," agreed Toxik. "dat is mayb da 1 rite thin u av said."

They charged.

I supposed their fight might have held some points of technical interest. I supposed that if I wasn't trying not to throw up on my own shoes, I might have keenly observed their battle, staff on swords. As it was, I was, so I didn't. JG whimpered, "My sister's coming."

I nodded, tasting bile.

"Can we go?"

I looked around. Black streets all about, no light burning in any of them, just the sound of rain and weapon on weapon. Neither Toxik nor Lady Neon was obeying the laws of nature in their battle; their leaps were too high, their moves too fast, and when their blades met, the air stank of solder.

Bakker said, "Oda will kill both Lady Neon and Toxik. Problem solved."

"Yeah, because the Tribe and the Court will sure believe that story. 'Wasn't me, guv, was this walking sun-stopping darkness.'"

JG hissed, "You talking to me?"

"No."

"Oda will kill you too."

I fumbled at JG's arm until I had a good enough grip. "Help me up," I groaned.

She did.

Lady Neon and Toxik seemed happily preoccupied. "These two plonkers," I said, "are fighting over you."

JG stared as Lady Neon nearly – and not nearly enough – took Toxik's head off with a swipe of glass sword. "Seriously?"

"Yeah. Seriously."

"Why? What's so special about me?"

"Absolutely nothing," I replied, coughing up dry air and the last lingering sickly taste of other people's spells that had lodged in my belly. "No magic scars, no epic destinies, no mysterious meteor-showered birth; I gotta tell you, you are pig shit ordinary." Toxik managed a swoosh of his broom at knee height. Lady Neon backflipped over it like some squirrel had been written into her DNA and didn't even crease a sleeve doing it. "Great thing about not being a chosen one, is you get to do your own choosing. And now . . ."

"Yeah?"

In the windows around Seven Dials, the lights were going out, first on the top floor, then the floors below.

"Now I need you to stop these guys fighting."

"Me?"

"Yeah."

"How d'you think I'm supposed to do that?"

"Dunno. You're the girl that everyone wants to get to know better. Think of something."

She looked uneasily at the two fighters. "Hey, you!" she shouted. "Oi! You! I'm fucking talking to you!"

If they heard, they didn't care. JG let go of me; I slipped back down onto the steps of the pillar, clinging to it for comfort and strength. She marched out onto the street between them and nearly got a broom to the head for her pains. "You fuckers!" she screamed. "I am your fucking chosen one and you will listen to me are you dense yeah?"

Nothing.

"Stop it!" she shrieked, and the girl had a mighty pair of lungs on her when she wanted to. "Fucking stop it!"

Lady Neon, as casual and calm as anything, without breaking stride or movement, turned beneath a swipe of Toxik's staff and as she did, kicked out deftly behind her with one white shoe, caught JG squarely in the middle of her body and sent her flying. I started up, felt electricity snap, weak now, so weak, to my fingertips.

Then JG moved. She staggered upwards, one hand curled around her belly, back bent with pain, eyes narrow. She raised her head, opened her lips, and screamed.

I covered my ears, though that barely dented the pain: the volume and pitch of it sliced straight through the stomach, made glass crack, mortar dust sprinkle down, sent ripples racing across the surface of the puddles, twisted the shape of the falling rain into a cocoon around the girl, and still she kept screaming, Toxik and Lady Neon bending back and away from the sound, covering their ears, the glass of Lady Neon's sword shattering, Toxik's staff bending and twisting out of shape with the force of it and it went on and on and on until

it stopped. JG doubled over, gasping for air. Lady Neon lay on the ground, staring wide-eyed at the breathless girl; Toxik leant against a wall heaving down lungfuls of air, blood running from the hollows of his ears. Slowly, painfully, JG half straightened up and wheezed, "So like, yeah, this guy wants to have a word."

Their eyes moved slowly to me. I crawled up one joint at a time, made it to my feet and stood there, wobbling in the dull breeze. I clenched my fingers into a fist, and opened it out. The little bubble of sodium light was faint now, so very faint, but I cast it up overhead anyway to spread a dull pool on the soaking earth and said, "So guys, the last light will go out . . . now."

In the doors of the bright white theatre on Seven Dials, the last light went out.

We waited.

Nothing but the sound of falling rain.

We waited a little longer.

Footsteps.

Footsteps on stone.

We put our head on one side and now everyone was watching us, Lady Neon, Toxik, even JG, and everyone had the sense to be afraid. "Hear that?" I asked. "That's the sound of Blackout."

The footsteps stopped. Then started again, somewhere else, just one pair, too loud in the quiet patter of the falling rain. Getting closer.

"She does that," I explained. "Darkness and footsteps. It's all part of what Blackout is: the thing at the end of the alley. It's all about fear and shame. All the things that you can get away with when the lights go out, that's what Blackout is. The thing at the end of the alley is no more and no less than fear. Pure and absolute fear of a thing unknown. Regrettably, this unknown thing has a sister. And regrettably this sister's name is Jabuile Ajaja."

I watched Toxik and Lady Neon. Their eyes were now locked on JG.

"She's coming," I murmured. "Blackout. She's coming right here, right now. London is closing in on itself, shutting down. We're probably part of a very small bubble that remains. I can't imagine she's going to be impressed with the pastoral care on offer. Does any of this strike you as odd? That the Court and the Tribe are both told, at the same time, to go to the same place, to find the same chosen one, and this chosen one happens to be the sister of the woman who's now going to come through the darkness and kill us all?"

Footsteps running, then stopping.

Silence.

We all craned to hear, but there was nothing.

Then again the sound: three short steps, pause, then three more, like feet finding their way.

"You've been used," I said. "None of it was real. And look what unintended consequences we now have to deal with."

Feet on stone.

A sound that might have been a woman laughing, might have been her crying, fading to distant nothing.

Then Toxik said, "Prov it."

Lady Neon said, "It's not just about the chosen one . . ."

"I can prove it. You two have bigger problems than each other."

The edges of the shadows were growing ragged, things in them that didn't obey the same rules as light.

"They are . . . they are . . ." Lady Neon stabbed a quivering finger towards Toxik. "They are so *ugly*!"

Toxik's lips curled in an animal snarl.

"Look at it!" she shrieked. "How can anything good come from that?"

"We r beautiful!" roared Toxik. "We r beautiful we r beautiful we r . . ."

JG took a nervous step forward. Something moved in the darkness of a window, a hint of blackness out of shape caught in the light of my little spell. I began, "Wait, JG, wa . . ."

There was a flash of star-shaped light. A sound like a mosquito having a heart attack. I saw JG stagger and fall, slipping face first onto the tarmac. I ran forward and grabbed her, hauled her up, looking to the windows for that flash again. Lady Neon started, hiding her face with her hands, I heard the breath rush from Toxik's lips. I felt something hot beneath my fingers. I was too familiar with the feeling of blood to mistake it for anything else. JG's eyes were wide, her lips moving, she was trying to feel round at her back, trying to find the source of the pain. A single bullet, straight to a lung, fired from behind. She coughed, and there was blood on her breath.

Bakker said, "Matthew, get out of the firing line."

I held her closer and whispered, "JG? Jabuile?"

"Matthew, get out!"

"Is she . . ." whispered Lady Neon.

"Jabuile?"

Her eyes began to close. I shook her gently. Then we shook her harder. "JG? Jabuile!"

Toxik raised his head, fixed his eyes on Lady Neon. "U did dis," he breathed.

She shook her head. "You did."

I watched the air steam around JG's lips as the breath went out. I kept on watching, shaking her, pressing my fingers into her back, trying to force the blood back in. She didn't move. The air didn't steam. "Jabuile?"

It wasn't me that had spoken.

I looked up.

Oda stood on the very edge of the light, eating it, the darkest thing in the night. Her hands were shaking, and from her mashed-up eyes, thin lines of blood were beginning to trickle down her face. She took a step forward, staggered, as if she was about to fall, then picked herself up and managed another, pulling her tatty clothes tighter around herself like a shroud. I eased JG to the ground, scrambled away from her, the blood washing like smoke into the puddles beneath my fingers. Oda knelt down slowly by the still body, leant right over it, covered it entirely, cradling it to herself and her to it. Her back shook, a constant tiny vibration, no more and no less, just shaking, her fingers tangling in JG's hair. She didn't speak, didn't whine, didn't moan, didn't scream, just knelt there and shook.

Bakker said, "Too late now."

I heard a little hard clink. I looked round. Lady Neon's hand closed round one of the shattered glass pieces of her blade. I shook my head mutely. Toxik, seeing what Lady Neon was doing, flexed his fingers and reached out for his staff. Lady Neon rose silently, advanced towards Oda, shard glinting in my little sodium light. I shook my head desperately and she ignored me.

"No, it won't . . ." I blurted.

Lady Neon caught Oda by the back of the head, yanked her up by her hair and slashed the glass smartly across the line of her throat. Blood spilt across the stones – not enough – and with peacock pride

Lady Neon let go of Oda's head and the other woman flopped back forward, bowed over her sister.

The rain fell.

The world waited.

I saw Oda's fingers tighten at her side. Then, without raising her head, she lifted herself up, and turned, as slow as a tidal wave, and looked Lady Neon straight in the eye. I saw blood bloom behind Lady Neon's perfect lilac gaze, saw the glass shard fall from her fingertips.

Bakker said, "There is nothing left here for you!"

I crawled to my feet.

Toxik tried to ram his staff into the side of Oda's head. She didn't even look at him and the staff shattered into burning ash in his hands long before it was even close. He staggered back, clutching at his eyes, scrabbling at his eyes. I heard the beginning of a scream from Lady Neon, felt the darkness tumble in thick and hard, pushing down on my little bubble of light, snapping it out, and, as Toxik's voice joined the wail, we turned our back, on them, on Oda, on Jabuile and, feeling through the dark with our toes and fingers, ran away.

I didn't summon fresh light until the sounds of pain were lost far, far behind.

I crawled on hands and knees, feeling my way between parked cars, fingers needling round the edges of the pavement and into the cracks of the stones, recalling a path by nameless instinct and guesswork. I crawled until my knees bled, then I wriggled up onto my feet and staggered like a drunk man, hands out in front of me, banging into bins and slipping on litter spilt across the street until at last I staggered face-first into a hedge someone had inconsiderately left in the way, and slipped down to the ground beneath it. The darkness was universal. Not one light flickered, not one creature stirred, man or rat. I could hear no traffic. Just the sound of rain. I could see nothing and dared not call a light, in case I stood out like a lighthouse and called something a little bit more.

I remembered my mobile phone and, thumbing it on, found I had no signal. It gave off a feeble little light, and by that I saw I had staggered into an alley of small elegant houses with white walls, and potted plants beside their low doors. The light went out on my phone. I thumbed at the buttons until it came back on and, by its grey-blue glow, staggered to the end of the alley and out onto a wider shopping street. The rainwater was already two feet deep in the muddy hole dug for perpetual building works down the side of the road. In the shop windows stood mannequins sporting clothes for him, clothes for her, their perfect, unrealistic bodies all curves and flat paint. I looked closer. There was something wrong with the mannequins' eyes. They were bleeding.

A voice echoed off the building, loud and rich and confident.

"We're coming for you next, sorcerer! We're coming for you!"

It bounced between glass and brick, steel and concrete, and faded away.

I ran again, fumbling with one hand pressed into the changing shape of the walls until I reached the shuttered shape of Covent Garden Tube. The light was out in the Underground sign, the screens on the ticket machines read:

OUT OF ORDER

A single guard in a blue hat slept behind the counter. The doors stood halfway open to the lifts, the lights off inside.

I fumbled my way round the corner, down a street that usually hummed with tourists, shoppers, jugglers and children, and which was now empty, save for the odd piece of litter that tangled in the hair of a sleeping beggar lodged under a dripping bench. Even the smell of greasy pies had been washed away. At the end of the street Covent Garden Market was a dark squatting rectangle with nothing to recommend itself to the traveller except, perhaps, shelter from the rain. I staggered under its arches, down aisles where during the day they sold jewellery, hats, scarves, ornamental bits of wood with no apparent purpose, and all those pretty things that made a perfect home, a perfect home with a bit of wood in it.

There was a light shining.

Just one.

It burnt beneath a great set of neo-Greek pillars across the street, a single bright spot of yellow illumination supported by a huge antique iron cage. It fell on slippery stone slabs beneath the pillared portico.

We thought for less than a second about this, then ran through the rain towards that glow. It was a church, a grand thing in front of a space where in summer pigeons fluttered and businesspeople ate their sandwiches on benches dedicated to fond memories of the dead. Beside this one light a gate stood unchained to the churchyard and at the west end of the building a pair of doors, set in red brick, opened easily enough into the cool dry interior. Over this entrance, another light burned.

As churches went, it was neither decadent nor overly restrained; it made it clear in its ornamentation that it could do stuff if it wanted to, but didn't like to boast. Long pews of polished wood. The walls were adorned with names of patrons and devotees, and in two tight banks candles were burning, the wicks crooked with their own heat. A small mahogany cabinet smelling of rosemary opened up to reveal various silver dishes, an empty glass beaker, and several immaculately folded white altar cloths. I hauled a bundle of these off their shelf. Pulling off my sodden coat and shoes, I sat down by the larger bank of candles, dragged the altar cloths around myself like a blanket, and shivered.

The rain pattered on the windows.

I listened for footsteps, voices, any sign of life, heard none.

Then the creak of a leather shoe.

I looked up to see Bakker sit down on the pew beside me, hands folded between his knees, head bowed. I watched him for a while and then blurted, "You are *not* praying."

He sighed, raised his head and said, "You know, if I had been, that would have been very rude."

"I think we're past good manners."

His eyebrows contracted in mild disapproval. Then he said, "You're getting blood on the altar cloth."

I shivered, followed his gaze. My hands had left dirty black-red stains in the starched material.

"It's all right," he added. "It's her blood, not yours."

We felt something hot sting our eyes, the need to swallow, found it hard to breathe. I tried to speak and found the words sticking at the back of my throat.

"Crying at this time would be self-indulgent," went on Bakker. "I have no doubt that in your own way you feel you ought to cry, out of a mixture of guilt and grief – mostly guilt, I may add – but if you could put off the event until after we have dealt with the current situation, that would be far more practical all round."

"Dealt with what?" I managed to blurt out the words between shuddering breaths. "Dealt how? She's . . . JG is dead. She's dead and . . . Dees is dead and Lady Neon is dead and Toxik is dead and Penny is . . ."

"An unknown factor," replied Bakker. "Good God but it is tedious having to share your consciousness, Matthew. So much 'could be' and 'might be' and 'what if' and 'if I could' and 'but I should' and all these empty empty sounds that make you believe yourself to be doing the right thing even as sheer necessity and the demands of the time force you to do what is in fact the needful thing. The only thing that there is to be done. I sometimes think that the only difference, to you, between what you classed as my wickedness and your goodness was that you wasted time lamenting those you'd forced to die of necessity, while I accepted that necessity has no time for grief and got on with it."

I pulled the sheets up over my head, wrapped my arms round my knees and stuck my chin in my chest.

Bakker was silent a while. Then with a puff of frustration he exclaimed, "Hark at the ostrich! Shall I find you some sand to bury your head in?"

"Go away."

"Yes, wallowing is so much more dignified in private, isn't it? In public it's called self-pity, misery and vanity. In private it's called respect for the dead and contemplation. I do hope you're not planning on wailing, Matthew, I can't abide wailing."

"Go away!"

"Can't. You inhaled me. It wasn't even like you argued much! Dees said 'this seems like a good idea' and you did it. Not because you respected Dees – and let's face it, in the grand scheme of things, you didn't respect her, not one inch, which was generally shallow of you – but because, I think, there was some part of your soul that wanted it. That wanted me here. I may suggest it was a masochistic part, but it's there. The same little corner of you that wants to feel grief for Dees despite the fact that you hardly knew the woman, to grieve for the girl JG despite the fact she was a rather obnoxious pawn. I imagine you're even managing a few shivers of guilt for the death of that tedious man Theydon. Or did you forget him? One has to prioritise when it comes to big feelings. One can only feel big feelings for so many people, otherwise one has to feel lots and lots of little feelings for lots of little people, and then frankly you'd stop being the hero."

"Go away go away go away!"

"There'll be speeches, if you live – *if* of course being a frail argument at this time. You'll go to memorial services and stand above Dees' empty coffin – I assume it will be empty – and you'll talk about how she was a soldier who fought and died and that's what a true hero is and there'll be tears punctuating the quiet solemnity. I mean, Christ." Bakker slapped his hands together in contempt. "You may even go to JG's service and throw flowers on the coffin – this one will have a few bits in it – and, while I think you'll have the good sense not to cry, I am sure you'll like playing the part of the quiet black-clad mourner who understands a tragic truth that cannot be shared."

"Get out!" we screamed, the candle flames twisting around us. "Get out get out!"

Bakker waited until we had no more breath, then rested his chin in the palm of his hand, bending closer to us. "You know," he murmured, "you have so much more life now you're not entirely human. Look at you. Matthew Swift, sorcerer who was born, went to school, travelled a bit, and died. Barely three lines in the obituary. Just lay in his own blood too surprised and hurt and scared to do all the wonderful things I taught you to do. Crawled to a telephone box and called for help, didn't fight, didn't rage, didn't blaze, just called for help and died. I mean what is the point of that? And now look at you!" His eyes sparkled, his pale skin flushed. "Look at everything you are now that you're not quite . . . not really . . . hardly at all . . . Matthew Swift. Look how hard you fight, how well you live. You came back from the dead and if you'd just been human you would have run away and curled up into a ball and got religion. But you're not. You went about setting things right. Vengeance and retribution. When you killed me it was the most spectacular thing I had ever seen, the most power and passion and beauty that had ever been struck from a spark; you were blazing! And then the business with the Midnight Mayor, and the Midnight Mayor is notorious for sitting on his arse and letting things take their natural effect, but oh no, not you. Because the blue electric angels don't care for the laws of men, or the practicalities of this world, or what should or should not be. They have the morality of six-year-olds, stripped down of all complexity and, like children, you will scratch and claw and kick and bite even when the thing you're clawing at is the rope that will pull you to safety. Such a pity there's still a little human left. With those left-over human things, pain for example, that really a sensible deity would have burnt away. After all, it's only the human part of you that can ever truly die."

I peered up into Bakker's eyes. There was an unhealthy sheen on him now, a hint of yellow in his skin, a blackness in his nails. I said, "Dunno if the dead have feelings, but if you were alive, I bet I could tell what you're feeling now."

He drew his lips in thin, curling in towards his teeth to wet them inside his mouth.

"I bet," I went on, "you're feeling hungry."

His fingers tightened, flexed. The candlelight cast a flickering dark shadow along the wall behind him, dancing from side to side, and at each dance, it was never quite the same shadow that moved. I shifted onto my knees, staring right up into his face.

"Go on," I breathed. "It's just you and me now. The lights are out everywhere else, what does it matter what's done in the dark? No one need ever know. Go on!"

His eyes glittered, his lips were parted, his chest rising and falling with steady breath.

"Go on! All you're going to get from this experience is destruction and grief; you might as well make the most of it. It's the end of everything, nobody cares what's said and if you're a bastard, nobody is left to care or be impressed, so go on!"

His shadow twisted on the wall behind him: it was too thin, too angular, too many joins and joints, too many claws. Then the candlelight twitched again in its own hot air, and there was just Robert Bakker, old man dying from too much time, sat on the pews of an empty church, staring at nothing.

I shuffled back down into my nest of sheets.

"You know," I mumbled, running my hands through the hot air around the little candles, "it's a lot easier to identify absolute evil when you're a kid. Evil, you see, wears black, has glowing red eyes, puts prepositions at the end of sentences and cackles. When you get a bit older you begin to understand that most of these things may just be a lifestyle choice. But you, Mr Bakker – I would have thought even you were smart enough to realise that your shadow, your living shadow, the moment it started eating people and drinking blood and stuff, was probably not going to win you any moral philosophy prizes."

Silence.

Then, "Matthew?"

"Yeah?"

"When you came to kill me, did you know why?"

I rubbed my fingers together, trying to work some life back into them. "I thought I did. At the start. I mean, I told myself some really smart things. How you were a threat to everyone, how you had to be stopped, the good of the city and so on and so forth. That it wasn't about killing you, it was about stopping your shadow, you know. That stuff. Then by the time I found you, there were so many people dead on the way, just . . . on the side, you know? People who'd died in the name of saving the lives you'd take and if I hadn't . . . but by then I was so far down the line, and I had nothing, just . . . We hated you. We hate you. You made us mortal, made us see things . . . *feel* things . . . we have found names for things we could not have conceived of. Colour. Smell. Taste. Desire. We had no conception of such things. Nor did we conceive of pain. Horror. Fear. Disgust. And you made us feel all of that. You thought you would control us, make yourself better, through us. Diminish us. For that arrogance alone we would have . . . but humans complicate everything. Things that should be clear become . . . bewildering. We had never killed before."

"But you still went through with it." He didn't sound angry, or sad, or accusing. Just old, tired.

"Dana Mikeda."

A little sigh passed his lips at the name; a slight nodding of the head.

"You are right about that, at least," we conceded. "The death of Dana, it was . . . it made complex things simple."

He nodded. For a while neither of us moved. Then with a great grunt of effort he stretched, from his toes to his fingertips, turning his head this way and that, like a man working out an old ache. "You can't kill Blackout," he said flatly.

"I know."

He raised his eyebrows. "Do you? Do you indeed? Well, I suppose your education wasn't completely wasted. Do you know why?"

"Yes. Blackout is the things that are done in the night. Eyes bleed because we cannot look. The lights go out because we do not want to see. And yet these things will still happen. Can't kill that. That much I sussed way back."

"You can't kill Oda," he added, stern.

"Because she's already dead," I interrupted. "Yeah, I worked that bit out too. I even worked out why JG was really important, and who stands to gain if the Tribe and the Court go to war. Dig that IQ."

To our surprise, Bakker smiled. "You were a very average sorcerer, Matthew."

"Gee, boss, thanks."

"But, I think," he went on, "a slightly above-average person."

"I'm coming over teary-eyed."

"If a little flippant."

"It's a defence mechanism."

"You know," sighed Bakker, standing up and patting invisible dust off his trousers, "if I hadn't trained you from childhood, nurtured you down the paths of magic, killed you, been killed by you, and finally concluded my already concluded time by sharing the rather self-indulgent place that is your consciousness, I might never have guessed."

We found ourself smiling. I said, "I know how to stop Blackout."

"Wouldn't want to be in your shoes," he answered with a little shrug.

I pulled myself up one limb at a time. Everything seemed distant and heavy, even thought was shuffling about looking for the slippers. "You know, it occurs to me that things would have been a lot simpler if you had just agreed to tell me, straight up, Mr Bakker, how you beat Woods in the first place."

He feigned outrage. "And give away my great secret? My reputation was built on that battle."

"You're an arse."

"Petty petty."

"A murdering arse."

"I have killed no one."

"No," I growled. "The charge would be manslaughter, not murder, wouldn't it? Death by association, never by action." I marched to the church doors, pressed my fingers against the cold walls. Outside, the rain fell on darkness.

"Afraid?" asked Bakker.

"Petrified."

"Sensible man."

"You wonder why this light" – I gestured back at the flickering warmth of the church – "stayed lit when everything else went out?"

"I imagine the Christians would say it has something to do with Jesus."

"And you know that's bollocks?"

"Of course," he replied. "I mean, the symbolism is curious but entirely predictable. The light burns because Oda wants it to burn. Some tiny part of her left alive, some tiny flicker of her that won't let all the lights go out. Not all of them. Not quite yet."

"Yeah," I sighed. "I never thought the day would come when we cheered for Oda's immortal soul."

"She could have killed you," he chided quickly. "On many, many occasions, and with sufficient motivation at each. And yet, quaintly, she didn't. Don't get too relaxed – I personally wouldn't lay any money on you surviving past . . ." He glanced at his watch, then tutted and looked away, up at the darkened sky. "What does it matter anyway?"

I followed his gaze, and saw nothing but darkness stretching upwards.

"I cocked this one up something shitty, didn't I?" I heard myself say. "All those things I was supposed to stop, all those dead, all that blood, and they died anyway. I didn't make anything any better. May have made some of it worse."

"Maybe," sighed Bakker. "Not for want of trying, though. I suppose that just leaves want of ability."

"I don't suppose it'd be too much to ask for a little moral support at this time?"

"Speaking as the only one of us who is currently deceased and incorporeally being projected via your subconscious into a semi-hallucinatory form, I really feel you're asking me to act beyond my remit."

"So . . . no. Thanks."

I reached out beyond the doorway, watched the rainwater splatter and run down my hand, pool in my palm. Didn't move.

"Matthew." A note of warning in Bakker's voice. "Sooner or later she'll come find you."

"Yeah. I know."

"There's no glamour in being the last thing left alive."

"Yeah."

Didn't move.

"If it was Dana's death that convinced you to kill me," he said, "then surely there has been enough blood, more than enough, for you to do what has to be done tonight."

"Oh yeah," I replied with a little laugh. "Don't get me wrong, this isn't lack of motivation. I know what I've gotta do and that's fine; it'll get done because frankly, there's nothing else to do. This is . . ." We plucked at the words. ". . . watching our life pass before our eyes. We concluded that it was better to stand here, out of the rain, and contemplate all the sights that we have seen now, rather than later, when we might be preoccupied."

"And?" prompted Bakker.

"And . . . all things considered . . . it's been interesting." We thought a little longer. "If perhaps rather brief."

I stepped out into the rain, dragging down the last glow of yellow tungsten from the light above the church doors, spreading it around myself in a little umbrella of illumination. I started walking, down the wet flagstone path towards the iron gate to the darkened street outside. A chill made me look back. Bakker was still standing in the doorway of the church. I said, "Come on, then, if you're coming."

"If you could stop it," he called back, "if you could not die, make it so you didn't have to fear dying, would you do it? If you could?"

I laughed, the sound running off the high walls of the buildings all around and melting into the churned-up muddy grass of the churchyard. "Mr Bakker," I chided, "now what is the use of sharing my head if you have to ask a question like that?"

I kept on walking. After a while, he fell into step beside me.

The city slept.

Even the rats and cats and dogs and pigeons, even the thieves and midnight-delivery men, even the sweepers and the underground engineers, the maintainers of wire and painters of roads, slept.

We walked down the middle of streets where, in the day, traffic roared and bicycles skidded, in a little blossom of yellow light, alone, except for a well-dressed ghost.

I stopped at a supermarket on the corner. Its lights were out, its shutters drawn. I smashed one of its high windows and crunched my way through the crumbled glass. The alarm didn't even bother to wail. The shelves were almost entirely empty, just a few sad not-wants sprawled on clean metal racks. I found a squishy pack of tomatoes and a ham and pickle sandwich. I ate the sandwich while wandering down the drinks aisle. A bottle of sugary tooth-eating not-really-water washed down a second course of coffee beans coated in chocolate and pick-me-up pills. I bundled bandages and plasters into my pockets from the medicine shelf.

"Assuming," pointed out Bakker, "you've still got enough fingers to use them."

I considered leaving money on the till. The idea was rejected without much in the way of qualms. A small rack carried umbrellas by the door. I picked one at random. Opened up, it carried the face of Minnie Mouse, complete with a pair of round stick-up ears.

"Tasteful," sighed Bakker.

Out on the street, I stood in a crooked crossroad. Old newspaper blew down the street, caught itself in the wheels of the parked cars. I looked left, right, up and down, then glanced at Bakker. "High road or low road?"

"All roads will lead to Oda."

"For such a patron of the arts, you're a right charmless bastard, aren't you?"

I walked left, not knowing why, not caring much either. Sushi bars and bookshops, sandwich cafés and dealers in rural watercolours.

"If we're discussing art, there are at least three cultural institutions that are now going to run short on donations, courtesy of you killing me," pointed out Bakker as we walked together down the middle of the street, which bubbled and bounced with rainwater.

"What three?"

"A theatre, an opera house, and a small pottery workshop in Suffolk."

"Does a pottery workshop count as a cultural institution?"

"The fact that you ask suggests you don't have the capacity to appreciate the answer," he replied.

"Didn't you bequeath them something in your will?"

"I never actually wrote a will," he sighed.

"You are joking me."

"It seemed like an expression of giving in to do so."

"My God, even in death you manage to screw over the little guy."

"I do admit that my sponsorship of the pottery workshop was something of a whim," he conceded. "But I suppose we might ask – what price art?"

"No!" I blurted as we crossed over St Martin's Lane, the balconies of the theatres dripping and the lights out. "No! We don't ask 'what price art?', because your currency started with the blood of the innocent and didn't account for inflation!"

"Here speaks a child of the banking crisis."

I scowled, marched a little bit faster down a wide alley of darkened restaurants and purveyors of leather coats. This was Theatreland, where the lights were meant to never go out, and the air was thick with the buzz of illusion. Posters lined the walls, showing various productions with well-known faces caught doing dramatic things. Bakker suddenly exclaimed, "Good God, is *he* playing Hamlet too?"

"Not now," I growled.

"Matthew, if you just looked beyond your preoccupations, you might find yourself on the verge of having fun."

"You know, if it had been anyone else who knew anything about Blackout," I grumbled, turning past a greasy pizza shop and down towards the smell of the river, "I might have enjoyed this experience. I really might. A chance to chat with a peer, to get to know the life and times of an interesting practitioner of the art, share knowledge and experience. But oh no, it had to be you; you just couldn't leave well alone, could you?"

"So now you're blaming me for being dead?" suggested Bakker.

"Maybe there is a God. And if he's up there . . ." I turned my head up to the sky, shook my Minnie Mouse umbrella and shouted, ". . . enough already! Give a guy a break will you? I mean how much more testing are you looking for?"

The words died away.

And I heard it.

The sound, just there, just beyond the rain, of footsteps.

Bakker coughed politely. "Now, Matthew . . ." he began. I gestured him to bewildered silence, listened.

Footsteps muffled by the rain, now splashing through a puddle, now pausing, now back on hard paving stones. Walking, slow and steady. Coming closer. I started to walk faster, turned past a spaghetti house and down towards Trafalgar Square. Our hand ached, we could smell the river, more than just a washing coolness to the wind, a power, rich and vivid and flowing, that would always be the last thing in London to stop.

"Scarf!" exclaimed Bakker as I passed a shop window. I paused long enough to look into a newsagent which ran a sideline in hats, scarves and thin black gloves. The lock on the door parted without bothering to argue at our touch, I grabbed a scarf off the shelf, price tag still dangling, and marched on.

The footsteps were louder now, all around, not from any one direction. Just one set of footsteps, but they bounced off the walls, spun down the side streets and echoed off glass, everywhere all around, behind and in front, growing, getting louder. And with them came a voice.

"Sorcerer!"

It rolled rich and bright and merry through the darkness.

"Sorcerer! You next!"

I crossed the zebra crossing outside the National Portrait Gallery out of habit, not reason, headed down towards the long slope of Trafalgar Square. Memory dictated what was there, not sight, sight was up to little more than grey shapes on the edge of my bubble of illumination. Memory of Nelson's Column at the heart of the square, a giant off-white spike holding a very little man adorned with admiral's hat and a good deal of bird droppings. Great black lions, four of them, guarding wide shallow pools of greenish-blue water in which, so it should have been, fountains played. There should have been children running, beggars begging, teenagers ignoring the "do not climb" signs and scrambling over every statue and monument. There should have been protestors campaigning against racism and for the environment, tourists turning their maps this way and that as they tried to work out which was the exit for Parliament, which for Buckingham Palace; music, Caribbean steel drums and Scottish bagpipes, policemen and snipers hidden on the roofs of the embassies.

None of that tonight.

Just footsteps.

I scuttled down the steps into the bowl of Trafalgar Square, and they were everywhere, snapping feet on stone, the sound of Oda's – of not-Oda's – laughter. Bakker hissed, "Hurry!"

I dropped my umbrella and fumbled at the scarf I'd stolen, wrapped it unevenly round my eyes, looping it twice round and tying it off at the back of my head. I let the bubble of yellow light go out and all was darkness.

True, eyelid-sealing darkness.

The memory of Trafalgar Square suddenly didn't matter. No amount of reason, of knowing the layout, compensated. I staggered forward and bumped into my own fallen umbrella. I fumbled, bending at the knees, until I found its handle, picked it back up, shaking out the rain, folded it up and pushed it out in front of me like a blind man's walking stick. I thought I could hear laughter behind me, a change in the rhythm of the footsteps, as of feet on stairs. Then they stopped. I kept walking forward, one shuffling step at a time, swaying unevenly. My fingers found rough curving stone. I traced its shape down until they hit water, then deeper; I plunged my arm in to the elbow until I could feel pipe, and tile, and the little copper coins thrown by travellers into the pool.

Then, "Sorcerer?"

It was right behind me. I turned, splashing water and nearly slipping on the stones, clinging on the edge of the stone fountain at my back like it was the wall of Jericho.

Footsteps. They moved around me, from left to right, then right to left, describing a small arc. I stammered, "Hi, Oda."

The footsteps stopped.

"Not Oda," she replied. "Much more."

"Sorry. My fault. Hi, Blackout. How's the woman you're wearing?"

Something brushed the top of my head. We flinched back, fighting with every breath not to let the fire flood to our fingers, turning our face away and bending over the line of the fountain.

"What is this?" asked not-Oda, brushing the scarf around my eyes.

"Um . . . a scarf?"

"And why are you wearing it" – fingers pressed along the line of my eyes – ". . . on your head?"

"You know . . . protection against blindness, bleeding eyes, runny nose, brain damage and death," I mumbled. "The usual." Her hands moved towards the knot at the back of my head. We caught her wrists. We could feel cuts, sticky drying blood on her skin. She didn't seem to feel the pain. "Uh-uh," I said. "My sensory deprivation."

Slowly, she drew her hands back, freed her wrists.

Not touching her was worse, much worse, than feeling where she was.

Footsteps.

They swept left, they swept right. They stopped. They paced again. Then, "Look at us."

"Can't, sorry."

"Look at us!"

Sparks crackled from our skin, we couldn't help ourself, couldn't push it away.

"Not today, no."

"Look at us!"

She screamed it, the words hitting us like a bag of bricks; we buckled and bent double and, as we unfolded again, the static built up around us snapped, sliced through the air around us and went outwards. We heard a crack as it hit Oda and a thump, further off, as she hit the ground. We smelt ozone and felt the moisture of the water on the surface of the fountain turning to steam. I slid onto the ground, fumbling my way along it, shaking with fatigue, my fingers passing over the handle of the umbrella, and stone.

I heard Oda get up, and froze, on hands and knees.

"Lady Neon begged," she said softly.

I leant back onto my knees, resting my hands on my legs and hauling down ragged breaths.

"The other one, the Tribe man, he fought a bit. And begged at the end. It'll go faster if you beg first."

"Oda . . ." I began.

Something hard and fast and hot burst across my back, knocking me to the ground. I hadn't heard the move, and Oda's voice, when it came again, seemed as calm and stationary as before.

"We heard that the blue electric angels are too proud to be human. That they think they're gods, somehow better, above the rest. What a fall for the mighty."

"I'm not a god," I groaned, hauling myself back up.

"But they are!"

Something hot burst across our belly, we doubled over, crying empty animal sounds at the pain. I could feel blood between my fingers.

"Are you better now?" asked Oda. "Are you bigger, faster, stronger, brighter, wiser, better? Are you more than everyone else?"

"We . . . we are . . . *more* than you," we hissed. "We are . . . we are the sum of everything you are, we are the creatures you made, all that everything you poured into the telephone lines, all that knowledge, all that feeling, all those secrets, all that everything you are, digitised and sent into the wire, we are all of that. Yes. We are faster, brighter, better. We are glorious. You are tiny. But we are me."

"And what are you?"

"It is only because we are me that we are alive."

I heard her move right in front of me, felt her breath on my cheek. "Yes," she encouraged. "But what *are* you?"

"Just me," I said. "That's all."

The palm of her hand slammed into the side of our face, knocking us down. We tried to crawl up. She hit again. We stayed down. I could hear the rush of her breath. "*Sorcerer*," she hissed. "What pleasure you must have, walking among mortal men, knowing what you are."

"I have it on good authority," I mumbled through the taste of blood, "that I am at best, a very average sorcerer."

Her fingers crawled round the back of my neck, grabbed a clump of hair, dragged me back onto my knees, tilting my head to stare at the place where her bloodied face ought to be. "Which one are you now?" she asked.

"Uh . . ."

"Which one? Human or angel, human or angel, which one?!"

"Doesn't work like that."

"Human angel human angel human angel human angel?!"

She shook us. We were not made of stone. We shook.

Through rattling teeth I stammered, "Both!"

The shaking stopped. The pressure at the back of my head relaxed. I flopped onto my hands and knees again, too dizzy to deal with the pain. I felt something move near me and blurted, "Which one are you?"

Stopped. It stopped, and there was rain. Then she said, "I . . ." and stopped again, the word sticking. Then, "I . . ."

"Oda?" I breathed.

"I . . . I did not . . ."

"Come on, did not what?"

"I . . . we did . . . I did . . . we . . ."

"Oda Ajaja-Brown, raised in God help us of all places, Reading. Psycho-bitch, remember me? I ran out of fingers for the number of times you could've killed me. I've been chatting with Satan lately, we've been doing the crossword together. I said 'seven letters', he said 'got any?', I said 'third letter "p", I think it's an anagram', he said 'in your dreams' and waltzed off with a swish of his tail to order another round of martinis. Remember that hysterically entertaining time some nutter shot me? And you helped me back up? Or that nasty little incident with the dead guy walking underneath Holborn, and you dragged me out of the dust. Remember Balham, remember growing electric wings, remember flying? I thought that was particularly Satanic, that incident. I could practically hear the hoofs over the sound of the Underground."

Something soft and warm wrapped itself around my windpipe and became a lot less of both fast. I fumbled, felt wrist, sleeve, scrambled at her fingers, couldn't pull them away. I could hear the blood in my ears, every breath was like trying to push cricket balls through a sieve.

"I hate you," she breathed.

I made the sound of sandpaper running over blackboard, the only sound I could make.

"I *hate* you. I hate you, Matthew, I hate you."

The wasp orchestra was back in my brain now, playing its final tango.

"Why didn't you . . . why didn't you . . . why didn't you do it? Why didn't you when I told you to? Why didn't you kill me?"

"Sorry," I wheezed.

"You never listen!"

"Sorry."

It didn't seem a good enough answer: Oda shook us. "Why do you never listen?!"

"Sorry!"

"Why didn't you save her?!" She screamed the words, even as static rose up in front of our eyes, and with a final shake pushed us backwards, letting go and sending us to the ground. I curled up instinctively, hands over my head, knees up to my chin, waiting for it to get worse. It didn't. I heard . . .

. . . what might almost have been a woman crying . . .

I whispered, "Sorry, Oda. I tried."

"Not good enough!" The voice that shrieked the words wasn't Oda, not entirely, and the sound of it went straight through our ears and out the other side, turned our stomach to water, filled our nostrils with hot blood, tingled on our tongue with the taste of iron, burnt across the surface of our skin.

"Oda!" A voice, somewhere, that might have been mine. "Stop it! Oda! Stop! Look at yourself!"

It stopped.

For a while, all we could do was breathe, and that by an act of will that would have crippled Hercules.

Silence.

I didn't even know if she was still there.

"Oda?" I asked between my hands. "Oda?"

Then, "We want . . . I need . . ."

I tried getting onto my feet, and gave up.

"I can't . . . please I can't . . ."

"Get up, Matthew." Bakker's voice, inside my head.

"I can't." Oda's voice, somewhere just outside.

"Get up!"

"I can't go . . ."

"The blue electric angels do not die like this!"

We tried again. No heroic task could demand more care than we took in trying to move. We could feel blood, sticky, ugly human blood, hot and wet, between our fingers, taste its sickly taste on our lips, feel it rolling down the inside of our nose, pooling in our ear. The sense nearly knocked us down again, nearly crippled us before we had time to conquer it. We thought of Robert Bakker, arrogance and vanity. Of Penny, the air around her catching fire. The way Theydon had clawed at his own face; the way Toxik had blown smoke into the air; the touch of Lady Neon's lips, the way Leslie Dees had looked when she died, the way JG's head had bounced when it hit the earth.

We said, "It's all right. You'll be all right."

And couldn't quite believe it was us who was speaking.

"Sorcerer?"

"You're all right, Oda. You'll be OK."

"You made me go to hell."

"Didn't mean to. Didn't want to."

"I'm going to burn. For ever and ever. I'm going to burn."

"No."

"Up in flames."

"No."

"I . . . I am . . . we . . . I am . . . please I . . ."

We reached out crookedly across the ground, found the tip of her shoe, rested our fingers on its edge. "We're sorry. Oda? Forgive us."

"Can you . . . can you stop us?"

"No."

"Why not? Why can't you stop us?"

We crawled a little nearer, shaking with the effort. "We know what hell is, Oda."

A sound that might almost have been a laugh started from her. "Of course you do."

"It's the pit. The big, black, endless falling pit. The one that sends sane men mad. The one that's so wide and dark and deep that you don't even bother to try to climb. It's the one with no hope at the bottom but just enough light at the top that you can remember the things you've lost, even though you can never get them back. And just enough light gets through that you can glimpse countless horrors, but you have no way to tell anyone else what they are, and not enough light to see that they are anything more than shadows. You are going to hell, Oda."

A laugh that might have been a sob.

"You've seen it, haven't you? That big black pit, lined with human arms that try to grab you as you go by. You'd have to have seen it, otherwise Blackout wouldn't have been able to get in. You see, that's what

Blackout is. An endless falling into black. Doesn't just join with anyone, doesn't just eat the eyes of anyone. Only those who've seen too much."

"Perhaps we should eat you," she whispered. "Everyone sees what we are, at the end. No matter how rich or beautiful or powerful or bright, everyone sees. It's why they tear their eyes out."

"But only a select few *become* what you are. You wiggle in under their skin, get into the blood, this big black endless pit sitting in the middle of them, and you keep them walking and you keep them talking and anyone who so much as looks at you, they get a glimpse, just a glimpse, of what you are and that's more than enough, more than much much more than enough. I can see why you decided to use Oda."

"We are the same."

"Her body, her life."

"We are . . . I am . . . we are not using. We are the same."

"Which one are you now?" I asked.

"I . . . we . . ."

"Monster, human? Monster, human, monster, human, monster, human, which one?"

"Matthew? I didn't mean it . . . the ones who died were . . ." Her fingers found mine. "Kill me?"

"Can't."

"Kill me?"

"Can't. Sorry. Can't."

"We are . . . we are so strong and we are . . . we are for ever and so . . . we have seen so far. Please make it stop?"

"Can't. You're dead, Oda. You've been dead a while. Blackout got into the blood. Keeping you alive. That's why I can't kill you. Even if I destroyed your body, Blackout would live on, a shadow in your bones, a darkness in your dust. I'm sorry."

"Then what use are you?" she snarled. "You couldn't even save her!"

"I'm sorry. We're sorry."

"We were . . . we had . . . it is the fear that keeps us alive, you can't stop that, not ever, you can't make us go away, you can't stop it, there'll always be a footstep in the dark, a thing at the end of the alley . . ."

"I know."

"You can't ever kill us!"

"I know. You going to kill me? Oda?"

Hesitation. Her grip was driving the blood from our hand. Then, "You are damned, sorcerer."

"You and me both."

"I didn't . . . I don't want to . . ."

"By your theology, Oda, you're going to hell. And me too. And so many other people. JG. Dees. Toxik and Lady Neon, Penny and Sinclair. The liars, the gamblers, the cheats, the men who lust, the women who succumb, the desperate who pulled one last desperate act, the rich, the greedy, the overweight, the vain, the glorious, the proud. We're all going to burn. This being the case, are you really ready to drag us all down that little bit faster?"

She said, "How do I make it stop?" And in the same breath, "We won't!" cut off sharp.

I crawled onto my knees, head turned in what I hoped was vaguely her direction. "Blackout needs you."

"We don't we don't we are for ever we don't stop we don't we don't!"

"You're the only girl in the city can stop it."

"We won't go we won't we won't we won't!"

"I can't help you."

"Useless useless useless we won't!"

I tangled my fingers tighter in hers. She heaved down a ragged breath, hissed, "Sorcerer!"

"Still here."

"This could be you, huh?"

We felt something tighten in our – my – stomach. "No," we breathed.

"Just you wait until you're like us me us me I . . ." She gasped in air again, shaking with the strain. "How do I make it stop?!"

"Two of you in one body," I replied. "Two of you, tied up together. Can't kill one without killing the other, no Blackout without Oda, no Oda without Blackout. Do you see?"

"No!"

"You look at Blackout and you go blind, your eyes run with blood, Blackout is so powerful now, he's so much of you, Oda, he's got so deep inside. Do you see?"

"No, I don't I don't we won't we won't . . ."

"You got to push him out."

"I . . . I . . . we . . ."

"Do you know how Robert Bakker beat Blackout last time?" I asked.

"No no no no no we weren't we weren't never beaten never . . ."

"He was there when Blackout moseyed on into Woods, turned his eyes to putty. He was there when everyone else was dead and do you know what, the great secret of how he beat Woods, the great, towering mystery at the heart of it all? Woods was an orphan. So was Bakker. They were children together. Woods killed everyone who came near him, but couldn't quite bring himself to kill his one and only friend. Oda-Blackout. Not one without the other."

I could hear ragged breath, an asthma attack happening in wheezing gulps beside me, words trying to form between lips shaking too hard from the effort of speech, and then, blurted like vomit trying to come, "Look at us!"

"No."

"Look at us!"

"No."

"We are we are we are the pit we are we are the things in the night the things the we are the things you made made us fear fear shit disgrace shame fear the thing in the night thing at the end of the alley nothing there nothing there just shadows but fear so much fear we are we are we are . . ."

"Oda."

"We are we are *we are We Are . . .*"

"Oda Ajaja."

"*WE ARE . . .!*" She shrieked out the words and then caught them, seemed to fold in on the sound and force it back down before it could find its way.

Silence.

The rain drummed busily on the square.

Water rolled between the paving stones.

"Look at me," she said. "Matthew? Look at me."

I reached up to the scarf around our face. Hooked my fingers under the fabric. We shrank back inside. I pulled it away, eyes still shut underneath, opened them a crack, saw darkness, opened them a little further, light coming unbidden to our fingertips. Blinked away dryness and blurry fatigue. Oda was right in front of me, a few inches at most, eyes like pudding, face scratched, dirty and bloodied. Nail marks in the skin around her eyes, shallow and hesitant, stop-starting. She stared at us with broken bloody eyes and it took every ounce of my will to stop us closing our eyes.

She looked.

I looked back.

I mumbled, "Hi."

"Which one are you?" she asked, her fingers tracing round the hollows of our blue eyes. "Human, angel?"

"Right now?" I sighed. "Neither." I reached up, my fingers leaving thin bloody paint lines where they brushed beneath the empty mess of her eyes, and rested on her skin. "You?"

"We . . . I . . . I am . . . I . . ."

"Oda Ajaja," I repeated gently. "Sister of Kayle, who went mad and did evil. Sister of Jabuile, who was none of the above." I put my head on one side, and added, "Oda, also known as psycho-bitch. Hi there. Nice to see you."

She smiled.

"Hi," she replied. "Nice to see you too." Then, "Bye, Matthew."

"Goodbye."

And she closed her eyes.

She let out a sigh.

And the breath kept on coming.

The air around her lips shimmered like a heat haze. It twisted and writhed like something living in it, trying to break free. Smoke curled from her nostrils, hung in the tiny cracks of her lips, condensed, thickened, spread upwards. It rose up from her and stretched out, turning in on itself like a storm in a bottle, snapped and flickered little black tongues at the air, drifted upwards and out further, and still it kept coming. It seemed as if an elephant's breath had been held inside her tattered lungs, as if the smoke had been pumped into her and through her, and as it went out her body twitched and jerked like a stiff puppet on a string, or the spasms that precede vomiting, her head turned back, her fingers clenching and unclenching at her sides, and for a moment in the smoke that spun and spiralled around her, I thought I saw fingers, clawing, trying to get out, before being sucked back down into the fumes. Blood began to roll down her face. It began to spread from the hole in her heart, beating out with a faint pulse, began to trickle down her middle and along her arms, spill from a dozen injuries she hadn't even noticed that she had.

Her shoulders bent forward, her chest seemed to curl in on itself. Her arms bent back and then forward, covering her head as she doubled down and the flow of black smoke from her mouth faltered, began to trickle to a nothing while overhead this cloud spun and writhed and tried to break free of itself. I staggered to my feet, staring into it, and thought I could hear . . .

No no no no no no
Please don't
He's coming for
Never find out
Won't tell
Nothing to fear
Nothing to see
Footsteps in the dark
We're waiting for you

Then I smelt it. The cold breeze, it smelt of the river, even through the rain, it tangled itself into the belly of that spinning cloud and split it in two, then spun and split it again, gentle and silent. I saw Bakker, standing to one side, watching the smoke tear and part and begin to clear. I felt blood in the twin crosses on my right hand. I thought I could hear . . .

Water running out to sea
No no no no no no!
Waiting . . . for . . .
Rain falling on a metal roof
No no no no NO NO NO NO *WE ARE*
The beating of mighty wings
we are we are we are we
Footsteps walking away

Something sizzled.

We looked slowly.

A single lamp, on the edge of the square, a fake-Victorian thing of black iron. I saw the filament heat up orange-red inside the fat round bulb. It flickered out for a second, then tried again, made its way to hot white and, with a splutter, burst into light.

Then another.

There was almost no smoke left now, melting in the rain.

Another lamp.

Inside the waters of the fountain, floodlights warmed up, casting illumination up the misformed backs of things that might have been dancing fish, or dolphins, or some entirely other unlikely marine species.

The lights went on outside St Martin-in-the-Fields, striking proud white columns and dirty white steps. They went on in the National Gallery behind great barred windows and polite shopfronts selling books and art and impressionist tea towels, in the windows of the embassies and the fronts of the shuttered cafés. They snapped on one at a time down the length of the Mall and behind the leafless trees that ran towards Hungerford Bridge. They went on inside the sleeping taxis parked outside Charing Cross, in the station and the subway stairs, in the theatres of St Martin's Lane and above the little ATMs nestled behind Leicester Square. They went on in the CCTV cameras and the patient spinning yellow domes of the waiting repair trucks. They went on in the distant shapes of the London Eye, the BT Tower, and Centre Point, where once, not so long ago, a sorcerer called Robert Bakker had fallen to his death at the hand of one very angry apprentice, only to have his last breath bottled and filed for further reference.

From Hampstead to Hammersmith, Maida Vale to Morden, Hackney to Hounslow, Seven Sisters to Streatham, the lights came back.

Something fell to the ground.

I looked at it. I knelt down and turned its face up to the rain, to wash away some of the blood. Its eyes were closed, and I had no desire to open them again. It didn't speak, didn't breathe.

Oda Ajaja was dead.

Epilogue: A Temporary Truce

In which those loose ends that can be are tied, and those that can't be are studiously ignored by all.

The sun was down over Surbiton.

A man got off the train from Waterloo, as he did nearly every day of every week at this hour, and went to the bank. In the bank he paid in a couple of cheques, picked up a leaflet entitled "Pensions: What You Need to Know", walked into the launderette next door, paid £5 for his freshly starched and pressed shirts, and, his goods safely stowed on his lap, rode a small single-decker red bus, into the heart of nowhere in particular.

At the end of a street of semi-detached half-timbered houses identical to all the other streets of semi-detached half-timbered houses, save for the addition of a Chinese takeaway on the corner, he got off the bus. He walked for some ten minutes past gardens of neatly mown grass, parkways lined with diligently cleaned Vauxhalls and Volkswagens, turned left past the local Conservative Party office, and cut down a small alley between a bank of houses and a line of children-friendly gardens, complete with the occasional trampoline.

Halfway down this cut-through, which was one he used every day, he hesitated.

Did he hear anything behind him?

Did his heart miss a beat at the thought that there might be something watching?

Probably not.

Probably just his imagination.

At the end of the alley he came out onto a wider street of detached houses, their front gardens a mixture of smooth lawn and raked gravel, and walked along until he came to a red-bricked, sloping-roofed number much like all the others. A light came on automatically at his approach. He reached into the pocket of his coat, pulled out a set of three keys, and unlocked the front door. The house was warmer, drier, than the outside world, the central heating rumbling somewhere in the distance. He closed the door, wiped his feet and in a sort of glass antechamber between the outside world and the inner, took off his coat, and his shoes, and swapped them for a pair of slippers.

He turned on a few lights as he went inside.

They illuminated some fairly banal pictures – a painting of a medieval peasant scene in France at harvest time, a black and white picture of a happy family, presumably the man's, grinning cheesily at the unknown photographer. A series of pictures of old rotor aeroplanes, each one annotated at the bottom with details of make and model. There were a few bills on the floor which he put in a neat pile on the table, and a letter from his local MP inviting him to Do Right by Your Community.

He went through into the pink-floored terracotta kitchen and – as he always did – put on the kettle, made himself a small plate of cold ham, bread and cheese, and when the kettle had boiled, poured himself a cup of herbal, foul-smelling tea.

He didn't bother to turn on the lights to the study as he went into it. The books were on their places on the shelves, ranging from treatises on theology to detective novels to guides to the political conflicts of the last fifty years, the newspapers folded up and ready to be recycled, the desk neat and tidy. The curtains were drawn across the window, and as he sat down, he might, perhaps, have noted that the seat of the leather chair he sat in felt warm.

As luck would have it, he didn't.

He turned on the lamp on the desk, an old-fashioned thing cast in the shape of a giant vase and wearing a hat that was mostly tassel. The light fell across neat folders stacked up one above the other, a medical manual bookmarked at the entry on diabetes, and a Bible.

It also, not entirely by chance, fell on my feet, where I'd had them resting up on the other side of the desk.

I'm not as neat around the house as I should be.

The man considered my feet for a while, showing no sign of surprise. Then he said, "Have you had any tea, Mr Mayor?"

"I had a nose around," I replied. "But all I could find was that herbal stuff."

"It's very good for a queasy stomach."

"Just no good with custard creams."

He leant back in his chair, folding his hands behind his head, and contemplated us for a while. Then, "How may I help you today, Mr Mayor?"

I detached my feet from the desk, put my elbows in their place and rested my chin on the palms of my hands. "A free and frank discussion, Mr Chaigneau. Sound good?"

Anton Chaigneau considered, then gave a little nod. "If you will be free and frank with me, of course. I don't want us to engage in an unequal relationship."

"Fair enough," I said. "Where'd you like to begin? I know – Oda's dead."

"I was aware of that."

"You didn't turn up for the funeral, did you?"

"And you did?" he asked, eyebrows raised in challenge.

"Oh yeah," I replied. "It was a ball. There was me, and Penny, and this big man called Dudley, who I think turned up to see if anyone would cry. And a wereman called Charlie, who kinda goes where Dudley does. It was in Abney Park – you ever been there? She's buried by the image of an angel, half tangled in ivy. I didn't pray, because I figured it'd be kinda hypocritical, but Penny did. She's good that way. She considers that God would be looking for what is right, not what is written. Drizzled a bit. But we brought umbrellas."

"I am glad Oda received a decent ceremony, of a kind," he replied.

"You should have been there."

"Alas, duty called."

"Alas. Oh, and I'm sending you the bill, by the by, for her headstone."

"That seems fair."

"I'm sending you the bill for her sister's, too."

He raised his eyebrows. "Her . . ."

"Her sister," I replied. "Jabuile Ajaja. She's buried in the plot next to Oda's. We got a special offer you see, two for the price of one. There were tears at that one. Penny, again. She gets all het up over these sorta occasions. Penny's fine, by the by. Just in case you're wondering. I mean, you know, it's not every day that you get plunged into an epic battle between the Court and the Tribe and I gotta tell you, apart from a little sloppy hexing in the final furlong, she excelled herself. She's going to be difficult for your lot to kill, is my Penny Ngwenya."

"And I see you're recovering too," he added breezily. "I heard rumours that you were in a bit of a state."

I shrugged. "I know this amazing little woman in a crypt. She gets NHS funding and all. You wouldn't approve. Taxpayers' cash going towards the restoration of shell-shocked sorcerers. You might almost think we were people."

"In your very specific case, Mr Mayor, I fear you're not quite that – but please, do go on."

His hands had drifted down from his head and were now resting in his lap, his back straight and neck stiff.

"Had a look through your files, by the by," I went on, crumbling a piece of cheese off his plate and rolling it between my fingers. "I had no idea the Order was so petty. Going after minor witches and druids, when all this time, there's angels and demons and sorcerers and Midnight Mayors and all sorts of stuff you could be dealing with, but oh no. Little sinners are so much easier to dispose of than big ones. Very disappointed."

"Yes – I am curious, Mr Mayor, how you actually found this address."

"Oh, a man called Dudley. Big guy. Lots of connections. Fingers in pies. I said 'Dudley, I think Anton Chaigneau is the man responsible for nearly bringing about the destruction of the city'. He said 'no', I said 'yeah!', he said 'seriously?', I said 'look at my face' and he said 'oh well, then you'd better go forth and do something about it, here's his home address . . .'" Chaigneau moved. He had the drawer open and the gun out before I had a chance to get to the next syllable. It was a nasty little thing, but a little thing over a little distance would still do the job. I pushed the cheese back onto the plate, sat back in my chair. "You know," I went on, "I think the problem was in the overengineering. You had a lovely plan. A really good plan that exploited one of the greatest weaknesses of the magical community – our willingness to believe pretty much anything on the basis that almost anything can be possible. You paid O'Rourke for a false prophecy. Or blackmailed him or threatened him or something."

"His daughter," replied Chaigneau calmly. "We threatened his daughter."

"How economically efficient of you," I said, watching the gun in his hand. "Anyway, you got O'Rourke to make a false prophecy and frankly, the Tribe and the Court were ready to go for each other anyway, you just needed to give them a shove. 'There's a chosen one,' you said, 'who's going to destroy one or the other of them' and then you spread the word. O'Rourke told Minjae San at the Neon Court, and you leaked the information to the Tribe. It only took one of them to even consider exploring the possibility for the other side to go 'oh my God, our enemies believe it, so we must' and fairly quickly you've got Lady Neon shuffling in and warriors in Sidcup and it's all going swimmingly. You keep them dangling for a while and then you think, 'Hey, I know what – I need a body count! Let's send them to the same place at the same time chasing a ghost and see who kills who!' So you send them off to Sidcup, ready to go and claim the chosen one. And here's the bit where, personally, I think you got tricksy. You decided to give them an actual chosen one. I mean, shit."

Chaigneau's thumb ran up and down the side of the pistol, thinking about firing. We looked at him, waiting. He said, "Go on. This is fascinating."

"You thought, 'Genius! Let's get rid of all the rotten eggs in one go!' and what do you know, there was Jabuile Ajaja, Oda's should-have-been-dead sister. Should have been killed by Kayle but oh no. You saved her life, plucked her away from her family, told Oda that she'd died and in the process made this potentially fluffy woman the psycho-bitch vessel of vengeance that we all knew and loved. For all those years Oda thought her sister was murdered by a sorcerer, and for all those years you kept JG under your wing until you began to suspect that the traits manifested by her older brother were also, possibly, beginning to kick off inside Jabuile. Oh whoops. But killing her – way too easy. You got clever, decided to screw with Oda one last time and see which way she dived. Stop me if I get any of this wrong."

He smiled, tight and thin. "So far, Mr Mayor, so good."

"You knew JG hung out in that old tower in Sidcup. You sent Oda in there. Would she kill a sorceress in the making? Even if that sorceress was her own sister? And of course, the answer was no. Oda took one look at Jabuile and any inclination she'd had to go around doing the decapitating thing vanished in an instant, all she was at that second was JG's big sister. Not a servant of God at all."

"It's your fault, you know," he said suddenly. "It's your fault that Oda fell." I raised my eyebrows, waited. "Even from your first association we detected . . . imperfections . . . in Oda's attitude. It's true that we ordered her to keep you alive during that business of Robert Bakker, since we considered you the most likely means to destroy a greater evil. When you became Midnight Mayor we further considered your destruction, but again the business of the death of cities had broken out and, again, your utility exceeded your potential threat. But even from an early stage it was clear that Oda was . . . expressing a willingness to kill you that perhaps she did not genuinely feel. We felt that her requests to end your life were increasingly coming from a desperation, an act, almost, of spiritual self-defence as if she was concerned not that you might live and cause harm, but that time might strengthen the bond between you, to the point where she would be unable to do her duty. By the end, the consensus among the Order was almost universal. She considered you . . . practically human. She had lost her perspective. Then there was that night in Moorgate . . ."

"I think I know the one."

"You were being attacked by spectres. The pair of you. And you, Matthew Swift, armed a spell in a beer bottle, and gave it to Oda, and she, whether intentional or not, performed an act of magic. She confessed it to me, almost two months after the event. I should have killed her then, but she begged and wept and seemed repentant. So we sent her to Sidcup. One final test. One last chance to prove her loyalty, to repeat the act that had won her place in the Order. Kill her sorceress sister. And she failed."

I drummed my fingers on the edge of the desk, looked at Chaigneau and saw only iron and fire.

"I'm curious," I said at last. "Did you drive a blade into her heart yourself, or did you get someone else to do it for you?"

He hesitated. "There is no place for me in heaven," he said at last. "I know that. I know where my soul is heading. But, for the sacrifice of my soul, generations may walk with the angels, that would otherwise have burnt with me."

"Sounds sweet. Except! Unintended consequences! So you've killed

Oda for betraying you, left her for dead in the tower block in Sidcup. The Court and the Tribe are coming, they're going to run straight into each other while chasing a very fast, very frightened rabbit. JG runs, and, having, as you said, some of the tendencies of her big brother, manages to fall through the cracks, and is thus saved, where she should have burnt along with everything else in that tower. Court and Tribe are furious, blame each other, fighting breaks out and you, just to make absolutely certain that there are going to be bodies on both sides and this thing has nowhere left to go but full-blown war, start the fire in the lower floors, trapping the fighters, including Minjae San, daimyo of the Neon Court no less, and condemning all within to death. Court, Tribe, Oda, JG, and one bearded beggar man who, I'm sure, you considered an acceptable loss. Fantastic. Bodies all round, JG gone, Oda dead, Tribe and Court at war. The Order's work is done. The magical community will tear itself to shreds, hurrah.

"And then the snag.

"Oda isn't just a woman with a hole in her heart. She's a woman who's been betrayed. Killed by her mentor. Her dead sister, not dead. Her faith shattered, her body hurt, the things she believed in, as you yourself pointed out, dented. What a perfect vessel for nasty old Blackout to slip inside, what a wonderful opportunity. In it goes, kicks her into something resembling life. Flames are flickering at the wall, she's panicked, scared, confused, bleeding. She needs help and, not really understanding or knowing what she's doing, the Oda–Blackout fusion calls for help the only way it knows how, and summons us. Summons me. And now you've got the Midnight Mayor involved, and the sun isn't rising, and Oda is walking, and JG's body wasn't among the ashes, and the city is shutting down and sure, the Court and the Tribe are still going to war: but what unintended, what terrible unintended consequences. It took you a while, I think, to realise what a total balls-up you'd made of the situation. That's why you contacted me at Euston station – sheer panic about what you'd done. That was a mistake. If you hadn't come forward then it might have taken me a good few hours more to work out that, basically, it was you, Mr Chaigneau. You did it. You did it all."

His finger closed around the trigger.

The gun clicked.

Nothing happened.

"My mate Dudley," I went on, "did I mention him? He knows a lot of different people. He knows where they live. He knows what they do, their habits, their hours of work and days of rest. He even knows, Mr Chaigneau, where they keep their guns."

Chaigneau fired again.

Nothing.

His smile grew wider, he half nodded and, slowly, put the gun down on the table between us. "Very good, Mr Mayor. I didn't think the blue electric angels planned much in advance."

"It's the new me," I explained, waving my hands jazz-style in greeting. "Matthew Swift, Midnight fucking Mayor – I've got multicoloured highlighters and everything."

He sighed, putting his hands up behind his head and leaning back to study the ceiling. "And what now?" he asked. "Kill me? You have great roads of corpses behind you, Mr Mayor, but very rarely do you have the courage to push the knife in yourself."

"I thought about it," I admitted. "I mean, I don't think anyone would really care, in the grand scheme of things. And when you shot JG . . . we could have killed you then. We wouldn't have thought twice about it, and there wouldn't have been a body left to bury when we were done. That was, I think, your most despicable act. You shot a girl, a kid, in the back at Seven Dials not because she was a threat to you, or because it was going to change anything, but because your carefully laid plans were unravelling and you didn't know what to do. You had no better idea. My God. The righteousness of the terrified. Yeah. We would have killed you, if we could.

"But then I realised, I've still got this whole messy Tribe–Court thing to deal with! I mean, Lady Neon and Toxik, they're both dead, and I've got a gathering of very angry daimyos and very angry shamans who I've got to convince that actually, ripping up Shaftesbury Avenue in their attempt to obliterate each other is not the best course of action. So, in case you're wondering, the reason it's taken me all this time to get round to you is because I have been locked at a negotiating table in a kebab shop in Willesden trying to get these two sides to understand that there never was a chosen one, and that this war is just a thing invented by a greater enemy, a worse enemy. Two weeks it took to convince them. And oh boy, the Court and the Tribe aren't very happy with you. Amazing, really, the power of hate. They hate you so much that they're practically buddies on the subject."

He didn't speak, didn't move.

I stood up, pulling my coat off the back of the chair and slinging it over my shoulder. "You know, it was futile," I said. "There will be another Lady Neon. A woman so beautiful it hurts to look at her, a vision of things you never can be, a world you can never have. And there will always be a Tribe too, the ones who can't have so badly that they decide to have nothing at all because that'll show them. Your war . . . was nothing new. There'll be others again, and other truces. The fact that Lady Neon and Toxik are dead merely sped up the peace. All that blood, all that talking about bigger pictures, all that scheming, and for what? The temporary gratification of an ageing man worried about his blood sugar levels and the final destination of his immortal soul."

"I don't fear death, you know," he replied softly. "Not that."

I walked to the door, pushing it open and letting the light spill in from the corridor outside. "You heard of the night bus?" I asked. "You heard about how it gets its driver? Chained to the wheel, they say, every night, never sleeping, just driving for ever and ever through the streets of the city. They say it's a curse, bestowed upon the bitterest enemies of Lady Neon. Nothing can break those chains, once they're forged. If death is the best your imagination can run to, then I'd say you're in for a bit of a shock. Good night, Mr Chaigneau. I'll show myself out."

I closed the door behind me, leaving him alone in the gloom.

There was one more funeral to attend.

I stood at the back with Penny. A handful of Aldermen had turned out, but not enough. There was a contingent of financial advisers, muffled in black hats and coats. A gaggle of smartly dressed women from the local tennis club. A group of governors from the school. An uncle and aunt. A husband and a daughter. Neither of them cried: he didn't cry, for her sake, and she didn't cry, for his. As services went, the priest kept it short, accurate, and as true as manners would allow. Mr Dees, a man barely taller than his departed wife, asked who we were. Business associates, we said. He invited us to the local tennis club, where drink would be drunk, memories shared and Leslie Dees, who was after all twice women's lawn champion, would be honoured in a brighter spirit than that celebrated in those endless neat rows of neat gravestones in the cemetery.

We smiled, said it was kind, said no more, didn't go.

When all the others had left, Penny and I stood by the grave of Leslie Dees.

Finally Penny said, "I didn't really know her, you know?"

"Me neither."

"Yeah but you . . . you know . . . you knew her more, right?"

"I don't know. I didn't know . . . stuff. Friends, family, background. No idea where she went to school, college, how she became an Alderman, what she did for fun, where she went on holiday, favourite food . . . you know. Stuff. The stuff you're supposed to know. I guess I figured we'd work it out as we went along."

We stood a while longer.

Then Penny said, "I didn't know her, right, but I figured . . . she seemed like the kinda lady who wouldn't do nothing she didn't mean to."

"Yeah. You may just be right about that."

Time stretched by.

"I am a disgrace to the office of Midnight Mayor."

I hadn't been aware that I'd spoken. But looking round, I didn't see any other likely candidates.

Penny said nothing, stared at me, waiting for the rest.

So, since she seemed to be expecting something, I went on. "All those dead. Dees, Oda, JG, Theydon, Lady Neon, Toxik, all those dead, all that blood in the city streets. What is the point of me if I don't stop it? What's the point of this" – I waved my scarred hand, crosses aching – "of this" – we tapped our forehead, just above our bright blue eyes – "of this" – I stretched out my fingers through the air and let the sparks flicker and flash between the gaps, "of us, what is the point of all that we are, if we could not stop this?"

Silence.

Then Penny said, "You know, yeah, it seems to me like there are two kinds of chosen one. There's the kind who gets chosen for a thing without any say, like someone who gets picked – kings and queens and shit. Then there's the other kind of chosen one; the guy who stands up when everyone else is afraid, when no one else can decide. Guy who chooses to fight, or do the thing that no one else will, 'cause it has to be done, yeah? I mean, most times, that guy's a total shit. And sometimes he's the hero. Seems to me that you're a bit of both."

My shoulders shook, which I guessed meant I was trying to laugh. "That's me," I sighed. "Bit-of-both Matthew. Bit of both, bit of everything, bit of nothing really whole."

Silence again. Then, "Right!" she blurted. "Come on you!" She grabbed me by the arm and began to march me down the gravel path.

"Where we going?"

"You're buying me supper."

"I am?"

"Yeah."

"Why?"

"Because you're my mate and that's what you do."

"But I . . ."

"Nope! No arguments!"

"But we should . . ."

"Nope! Only thing is . . ." She stopped so sharply I nearly walked into her, her index finger flailing with righteous certainty. "Thing is," she repeated carefully, like one testing out an idea for size, "you're not a very good Midnight Mayor, yeah, and you're not exactly great at being human, yeah, and you're like, way off with being an electric angel, yeah, so all that's really left, all that you've really got, is buying someone like me a curry."

"That's what I've got," I echoed numbly. "Buying you curry."

"Yep."

"I've got to tell you, Penny, as life-changing bits of philosophy go, it's not exactly a winner."

"Matthew," she said firmly, "there are men who would eat their left foot to buy a girl as totally kick-ass awesome as me a poppadom, let alone a whole fucking curry, you see what I'm saying?"

I thought about it.

We began to see what she was saying.

"Oh," we said, finally, seeing as she seemed to want us to say something at all. Then, as we thought about it a little more, "OK," we added. "When you put it like that."

She beamed. "You know," she began, as we turned towards the exit of the cemetery, "I was thinking, this being Midnight Mayor shit . . . does it come with expenses?"

We walked away, between the neat lines of grey stone.

We had supper.

When it was done, we walked, and talked, about nothing much, to nowhere in particular.

A little before midnight, Penny blurted something about catching the last train to Lewisham.

We walked her to the station. Because it seemed like the right thing.

The last train was a dull yellow-white worm on a background of upside-down tungsten stars spread across the earth, as far as the eyes could see. We watched it from the bridge above the line, listened to it with our toes, tasted the flash of blue-white electricity from its metal wheels.

Then we started to walk.

We walked north, without map or clear direction, but almost never veering from our course. We walked through the streets of the sleepy and the sleeping, down roads humming with trucks and cars, past windows in which voices could be heard arguing or laughing or in low earnest talk, restaurants smelling of garlic and cumin, kebab shops dripping grease, amusement arcades clattering with the sound of artificial gunfire. We walked down slumbering residential streets of houses, windows flickering with the blue-grey glow of late-night TV, past great grey schools, windows full of posters about Tudor history, the nitrogen cycle and tectonic plate movement, past the noticeboards of churches offering lessons in truth, God, judo and advanced yoga, round the back door of the late-night cinema where zombies and ninjas were tonight's midnight offering. We ran our fingers over the rough wooden tops of the pub benches, chained to the streets, the cold metal of the lampposts and pedestrian railings, scratchy red brick and cut grey stone. We wove our way down great fat shopping streets and little suburban paths, between concrete estates and detached mansions. We thought we could hear behind us . . .

. . . but it was just our imagination.

For a while, a lone urban fox, wondering what we were, walked beside us, nose turned up, curious at our passage. As we crossed Clapham, a family of rats tracked us in the sewers below our feet, scuttling with every footstep we made. The pigeons bustled as we passed, the shadows turned to watch. After a while, even they left us alone.

We walked until the shallow spread of South London gave way to the taller buildings that clustered the river, until we could see the chimney of Tate Modern, the floodlit glow of St Paul's, the ever-burning lights of Guy's Hospital, the pinnacled tower of Southwark Cathedral. The traffic was a thin nothing as we crossed onto London Bridge, the waters of the river flowing out to sea, a great busy churning beneath us. We could just make out the dark round shape of Greenwich Hill to the east and, upriver, the red letters of the Oxo Tower. We leant on the cold balustrade of London Bridge and looked towards the sea.

"All right," I said. "Don't get me wrong, it's been a ball. But you – out."

Bakker sighed, reclining back against the edge of the bridge, face turned up to the sky. "It's probably about time," he admitted.

"About time?" I echoed. "When I agreed to this, I thought the words 'temporary experience' meant a few hours, a day at most. Do you know how disconcerting it is to wake up to find you in bed next to me?"

"Judging by the fact that you fell out of the bed on the first occasion, I would hazard that it is very?"

"I'm not ungrateful, mind. Strip out the psychopathic stuff, and you've come in handy at the odd moment."

He half bowed in acknowledgment.

"But," I added, "time to move on. Both of us."

He sighed, stared into space. "I find at times like these that the inspiring words I've been mentally preparing for such an eventuality utterly fail me. It is rather compromising for a man of my stature to be reduced to empty banalities."

"You'll live with it."

"No," he replied, almost sad. "No, I won't." Then he straightened up, slapped his hands together. "Bye, then, Matthew. Be good and all that. Try not to murder anyone unnecessarily, keep a sense of perspective, if you have one; don't get consumed in your own electrical glory and so on."

"Bye, Mr Bakker."

"Be seeing you."

"Until then."

He turned and looked out towards the river, spread his arms wide and closed his eyes. I took in a deep breath, turned my eyes towards the sky and let it go. The breath ran out from the tips of my toes, shivered up my legs, curled the inside of my stomach, ached out of my chest, crawled from my fingertips and out from behind my eyes. It was warm and tasted faintly of dust and earth. It spread out from me, filling the air with its quiet busy shimmer.

Then the breeze off the river caught even that, and whisked it away.

And Bakker, too, was gone.

We stayed a while longer, watching the river.

After a while, pale and discreet, as if embarrassed to be caught stirring at this delicate time, the sun began to rise.

We watched for a while, until the sun was too high and bright to look at.

Then we watched a little bit more.

extras

orbit

www.orbitbooks.net

about the author

Kate Griffin is the name under which Carnegie Medal-nominated author, Catherine Webb, writes fantasy novels for adults. An acclaimed author of young adult books under her own name, Catherine's amazing debut, *Mirror Dreams*, was written when she was only 14 years old, and garnered comparisons with Terry Pratchett and Philip Pullman. She read History at the London School of Economics, and studied at RADA.

Find out more about Kate Griffin and other Orbit authors by registering for the free monthly newsletter at www.orbitbooks.net

if you enjoyed
THE NEON COURT
look out for
THE DROWNING CITY
by
Amanda Downum

1229 Sal Emperaturi

CHAPTER 1

Symir. The Drowning City.

An exile, perhaps, but at least it was an interesting one.

Isyllt's gloved hands tightened on the railing as the *Black Mariah* cleared the last of the Dragon Stones and turned toward the docks, dark estuarine water slopping against her hull. Fishing boats dotted Ka Liang Bay, glass buoys flashing in the sun. Cormorants dove around them, scattering ripples as they snatched fish from hooks and nets.

The west wind died, broken on the Dragons' sharp peaks, and the jungle's hot breath wafted from the shore. Rank with brine and bilge, sewers draining into the sea, but under the port-reek the air smelled of spices and the green tang of Sivahra's forests rising beyond the marshy delta of the Mir. Mountains flanked the capital city Symir, uneven green sentinels on either side of the river. So unlike the harsh and rocky shores of Selafai they had left behind two and a half decads ago.

Only twenty-five days at sea—a short voyage, though it didn't feel that way to Isyllt. The ship had made good time, laden only with olive oil and wheat flour from the north.

And northern spies. But those weren't recorded on the cargo manifest.

Isyllt shook her head, collected herself. This might be an exile, but it was a working one. She had a revolution to foment, a country to throw into chaos, and an emperor to undermine with it. Sivahra's jungles and mines—and Symir's bustling port—provided great wealth to the Assari Empire. Enough to fund a war of conquest, and the eyes of the expansionist Emperor roved slowly north. Isyllt and her master meant to prevent that.

If their intelligence was good, Sivahra was crawling with insurgent groups, natives desperate to overthrow their Imperial conquerors. Selafai's backing might help them succeed. Or at least distract the Empire. Trade one war for another. After that, maybe she could have a real vacation.

The *Mariah* dropped anchor before they docked and the crew bustled to prepare for the port authority's inspection; already a skiff rowed to meet them. The clang of harbor bells carried across the water.

Adam, her coconspirator and ostensible bodyguard, leaned against the rail beside her while his partner finished checking over their bags. Isyllt's bags, mostly; the mercenaries traveled light, but she had a pretense of pampered nobility to maintain. Maybe not such a pretense—she might have murdered for a hot bath and proper bed. Sweat stuck her shirt to her arms and back, itched behind her knees. She envied the sailors their vests and short trousers, but her skin was too pale to offer to the summer sun.

“Do we go straight to the Kurun Tam tonight?” Adam asked. The westering sun flashed on gold and silver earrings, mercenary gaud. He wore his sword again for the first time since they’d boarded the *Mariah*. He’d taken to sailor fashions—his vest hung open over his scarred chest, revealing charm bags around his neck and the pistol tucked into his belt. His skin was three shades darker than it had been when they sailed, bronze now instead of olive.

Isyllt’s mouth twisted. “No,” she said after a moment. “Let’s find an extravagantly expensive hotel tonight. I feel like spending the Crown’s money. We can work tomorrow.” One night of vacation, at least, she could give herself.

He grinned and looked to his partner. “Do you know someplace decadent?”

Xinai’s lips curled as she turned away from the luggage. “The Silver Phoenix. It’s Selafaïn—it’ll be decadent enough for you.” Her head barely cleared her partner’s shoulder, though the black plumage-crest of her hair added the illusion of more height. She wore her wealth too—rings in her ears, a gold cuff on one wiry wrist, a silver hoop in her nostril. The blades at her hips and the scars on her wiry arms said she knew how to keep it.

Isyllt turned back to the city, scanning the ships at dock. She was surprised not to see more Imperial colors flying. After rumors of rebellion and worries of war, she’d expected Imperial warships, but there was no sign of the Emperor’s army—although that didn’t mean it wasn’t there.

Something was happening, though; a crowd gathered on the docks, and Isyllt caught flashes of red and green uniforms amid the blur of bodies. Shouts and angry voices carried over the water, but she couldn’t make out the words.

The customs skiff drew alongside the *Mariah*, lion crest gleaming on the red-and-green-striped banners—the flag of an

Imperial territory, granted limited home-rule. The sailors threw down a rope ladder and three harbor officials climbed aboard, nimble against the rocking hull. The senior inspector was a short, neat woman, wearing a red sash over her sleek-lined coat. Isyllt fought the urge to fidget with her own travel-grimed clothes. Her hair was a salt-stiff tangle, barely contained by pins, and while she'd cleaned her face with oil before landfall, it was no substitute for a proper bath.

Isyllt waited, Adam and Xinai flanking her, while the inspector spoke to the captain. Whatever the customs woman told the captain, he didn't like. He spat over the rail and made an angry gesture toward the shore. The *Mariah* wasn't the only ship waiting to dock; Isyllt wondered if the gathering on the pier had something to do with the delay.

Finally the ship's mate led two of the inspectors below, and the woman in the red sash turned to Isyllt, a wax tablet and stylus in her hand. A Sivahri, darker skinned than Xinai but with the same creaseless black eyes; elaborate henna designs covered her hands. Isyllt was relieved to be greeted in Assari—Xinai had tutored her in the native language during the voyage, but she was still far from fluent.

"Roshani." The woman inclined her head politely.

"You're the only passengers?" She raised her stylus as Isyllt nodded. "Your names?"

"Isyllt Iskaldur, of Erisín." She offered the oiled leather tube that held her travel papers. "This is Adam and Xinai, sayifarim hired in Erisín."

The woman glanced curiously at Xinai; the mercenary gave no more response than a statue. The official opened the tube and unrolled the parchment, recorded something on her tablet. "And your business in Symir?"

Isyllt tugged off her left glove and held out her hand. "I'm here to visit the Kurun Tam." The breeze chilled her sweaty palm. Since it was impossible to pass herself off as anything but a foreign mage, the local thaumaturgical facility was the best cover.

The woman's eyes widened as she stared at the cabochon black diamond on Isyllt's finger, but she didn't ward herself or step out of reach. Ghostlight gleamed iridescent in the stone's depths and a cold draft suffused the air. She nodded again, deeper this time. "Yes, meliket. Do you know where you'll be staying?"

"Tonight we take rooms at the Silver Phoenix."

"Very good." She recorded the information, then glanced up. "I'm sorry, meliket, but we're behind schedule. It will be a while yet before you can dock."

"What's going on?" Isyllt gestured toward the wharf. More soldiers had appeared around the crowd.

The woman's expression grew pained. "A protest. They've been there an hour and we're going to lose a day's work."

Isyllt raised her eyebrows. "What are they protesting?"

"New tariffs." Her tone became one of rote response. "The Empire considers it expedient to raise revenues and has imposed taxes on foreign goods. Some of the local merchants"—she waved a hennaed hand at the quay—"are unhappy with the situation. But don't worry, it's nothing to bother the Kurun Tam."

Of course not—Imperial mages would hardly be burdened with problems like taxes. It was much the same in the Arcanost in Erisín.

"Are these tariffs only in Sivahra?" she asked.

"Oh, no. All Imperial territories and colonies are subject."

Not just sanctions against a rebellious population, then, but real money-raising. That left an unpleasant taste in the back of her mouth. Twenty-five days with no news was chancy where politics were concerned.

The other officials emerged from the cargo hold a few moments later and the captain grudgingly paid their fees. The woman turned back to Isyllt, her expression brightening. "If you like, meliket, I can take you to the Silver Phoenix myself. It will be a much shorter route than getting there from the docks."

Isyllt smiled. "That would be lovely. Shakera."

Adam cocked an eyebrow as he hoisted bags. Isyllt's lips curled. "It never pays to annoy foreign guests," she murmured in Selafaïn. "Especially ones who can steal your soul."

She tried to watch the commotion on the docks, but the skiff moved swiftly and they were soon out of sight. A cloud of midges trailed behind the craft; the drone of wings carried unpleasant memories of the plague, but the natives seemed unconcerned. Isyllt waved the biting insects away, though she was immune to whatever exotic diseases they might carry. As they rowed beneath a raised water gate, a sharp, minty smell filled the air and the midges thinned.

The inspector—who introduced herself as Anhai Xian-Mar—talked as they went, her voice counterpoint to the rhythmic splash of oars as she explained the myriad delta islands on which the city was built, the web of canals that took the place of stone streets. Xinai's mask slipped for an instant and Isyllt saw the cold disdain in her eyes. The mercenary had little love for countrymen who served their Assari conquerors.

Sunlight spilled like honey over their shoulders, gilding the water and gleaming on domes and tilting spires. Buildings crowded together, walls of cream and ocher stone, pale blues and dusty pinks, balconies nearly touching over narrow alleys and waterways. Bronze chimes flashed from eaves and lintels. Vines trailed from rooftop gardens, dripping leaves and orange blossoms onto the water. Birds perched in potted trees and on steep green- and gray-tiled roofs.

Invaders the Assari might be, but they had built a beautiful city. Isyllt tried to imagine the sky dark with smoke, the water running red. The city would be less lovely if her mission succeeded.

She'd heard stories from other agents of how the job crept into everything, reduced buildings and cities to exits and escape routes, defenses and weaknesses to be exploited. Till you couldn't look at anything—or anyone—without imagining how to infiltrate or corrupt or overthrow. She wondered how long it would take to happen to her. If she would even notice when it did.

Anhai followed Isyllt's gaze to the water level—slime crusted the stone several feet above the surface of the canal. "The rains will come soon and the river will rise. You're in time for the Dance of Masks."

The skiff drew up against a set of stairs and the oarsmen secured the boat and helped Adam and Xinai unload the luggage. A tall building rose above them, decorated with Selafaïn pillars. A carven phoenix spread its wings over the doors and polished horn panes gleamed ruddy in the dying light.

Anhai bowed farewell. "If you need anything at all, meliket, you can find me at the port authority office."

"Shakera." Isyllt offered her hand, and the silver griffin she held. She never saw where Anhai tucked the coin.

The she stepped from the skiff to the slime-slick stairs and set foot in the Drowning City.

The Phoenix was as decadent as Xinai had promised. Isyllt floated in the wide tub, her hair drifting around her in a black cloud. Oils shimmered on the water, filled the room with poppy and myrrh. Lamplight gleamed on blue and green tiles and rippled over the cool marble arch of the ceiling. She was nearly dozing when someone knocked lightly on the chamber door.

"Don't drown," Adam said, his voice muffled by wood.

"Not yet. What is it?"

"Dinner."

Her stomach growled in response and she shivered in water grown uncomfortably cold. She stood, hair clinging to her arms and back like sea wrack, and reached for a towel and robe.

The bedroom smelled of wine and curry and her stomach rumbled louder. The *Mariah*'s mess had been good enough, as sea rations went, but she was happy to reacquaint herself with real food.

Adam lit one of the scented-oil lamps and sneezed as the smell of eucalyptus filled the room. The city stank of it at night—like mint, but harsher, rawer. Linen mesh curtained the windows and tented the bed. The furniture and colorful rugs were Assari, but black silk covered the mirror, true Selafaïn fashion.

Adam sat, keeping the windows and doors in sight as he helped himself to food from the platter on the table. He'd traded his ship's clothes for sleek black, and the shadows in the corner swallowed him.

"Where's Xinai?" Isyllt asked, glancing at the door that led to the adjoining room.

"Scouting. Seeing how things have changed. The curry's good."

She tightened the towel around her hair and sat across from him. The bowls smelled of garlic and ginger and other spices she couldn't name. Curries and yogurt, served with rice instead of flat bread, and a bowl of sliced fruit.

"We should find our captain tonight." She stirred rice into a green sauce. "The Kurun Tam may take all day tomorrow."

The *Black Mariah*'s legitimate business would keep her in port at least half a decad, but Isyllt wanted to make sure their alternate transportation was resolved before anything unexpected arose. She scooped up a mouthful of curry and nearly gasped at the sweet green fire. A pepper burst between her teeth, igniting her nose and throat.

The sounds of the city drifted through the window, lapping water and distant harbor bells. Night birds sang and cats called to one another from nearby roofs. Footsteps and voices, but no hooves or rattling carriage wheels—the city's narrow streets left no room for horses or oxen.

"You don't want to be here, do you?" Adam asked after a moment. Shadows hid his face, but she felt the weight of his regard, those eerie green eyes.

She sipped iced-and-honeyed lassi. "It isn't that, exactly."

"You're angry with the old man."

She kept her face still. She hadn't cried since the first night at sea, but emotions still threatened to surface when she wasn't careful. "I know the job. My problems with Kiril won't interfere." Her voice didn't catch on his name, to her great relief.

"I hope not. He'll skin me if I don't keep you safe."

Isyllt paused, cup half raised. "He said that?"

Adam chuckled. "He left little room for doubt."

Wood clacked as she set the drink down. "If he's so bloody concerned, he could have sent someone else." She bit her tongue, cursed the petulant tone that crept into the words. The side door opened with a squeak, saving her from embarrassing herself further.

Xinai slipped in, feet silent on marble. "I found Teoma. He frequents a tavern on the wharf called the Storm God's Bride." Izachar Teoma had made most of his wealth and notoriety smuggling along Imperial shores, but sailed north often enough to have encountered Kiril's web of agents before. A ship quick and clever enough to escape harbor patrols would be useful if they had to flee the city.

Xinai tossed a stack of cheap pulp paper onto the table. "News-scrawls, from the past decad or so. The criers will have stopped spreading those stories by now."

"Thanks." Isyllt flipped through the stack—wrinkled and water-spotted, and the ink left gray smears on her fingers, but the looping Assari script was legible. The latest was three days old. She took a moment to adjust to the Assari calendar; today was Sekhmet seventh, not the twelfth of Janus; 1229 Sal Emperaturi, not 497 Ab Urbe Condita.

She often found the pride of nations silly. Trade and treaties between Assar and Selafai had to be twice dated, because the founders of Selafai had abandoned all things Imperial when they fled north across the sea five hundred years ago. But if not for the pride of nations, she'd be out of a job.

She sipped her drink again, watery now as the ice melted. Moisture slicked the curve of the cup. "Did you hear anything about the protest we saw?"

"Not much. The guards ran them off not long after we arrived, it sounds like. There were arrests, but no real violence." From Xinai's tone, Isyllt couldn't tell if she was disappointed in that or not.

Adam rose, taking a slice of mango with him. "Finish your dinner, Lady Iskaldur." The title dripped mockingly off his tongue. "We'll leave when you're ready."

Night draped the city like damp silk. Heat leaked from the stones, trapped between close walls; sweat prickled the back of Isyllt's neck. The end of the dry season in Symir, but the Drowning City would never be truly dry. Insects droned overhead, avoiding the pungent lamp-smoke, and rats and roaches scuttled in the shadows. Charms hummed around them, soft shivers from doors and windows. *Safe*, some murmured, *home*. Others pulsed warnings—*stay back, move on, look away.*

Shadows pooled between buildings, leaked from narrow alleys; the glow of streetlamps drowned the stars. Voices drifted from taverns, floated up from the canals as skiffs passed. Water lup-lup-lupped against stone and wind sighed over high bridges, rattling the chimes that hung on nearly all the buildings. Hollow tubes and octagonal bronze mirrors flashed and clattered—in Erisín, Selafai's capital, no one left mirrors uncovered and even still puddles were avoided, but here it seemed they were lucky.

The crowds had thinned after dusk, stores closed and shuttered, the last clerks and shopkeepers hurrying home. More than once they passed guard patrols, green uniforms edged with Imperial red—a whispered word kept the soldiers' eyes off them.

A cool draft wafted past Isyllt, and a whisper light and hollow as reeds. Her bare arms prickled and the diamond chilled on her finger. She smiled—the touch of death was comforting, made the city feel less foreign.

She studied Adam's easy stride, the roll of Xinai's hips as she kept pace with him, the dangerous grace with which they moved. At home she worked alone more often than not—probably more often than she ought—but Kiril had insisted she bring backup this time. She could have brought someone familiar, but it was better this way. Too many people in Erisín knew her bitter history with Kiril, offered her sympathy and sad glances. She preferred the quiet solace of strangers. And, she admitted to herself, in this strange place she was glad of their presence.

They crossed a wide canal into the dock district—Merrowgate, the map named it. The Phoenix lay in Salt-lace, the tourist and market quarter. The night grew louder as they neared the docks, bare and sandaled feet slapping the stones, laughter and music echoing from taverns, bells tolling to guide ships in the dark. The cloying spice-sweetness of opium drifted out of an alley mouth.

As they passed a narrow walkway along the water Isyllt heard a soft cry, like a child's muffled sob. She paused, searching for the source. It sounded like it came from the water.

Xinai laid a hand on her arm as she leaned toward the black offal-reek of the canal. "Don't. It's a nakh."

"A what?"

"A water spirit. Like your sirens in the north. They mimic children to lure people close to the water, then pull them in."

Isyllt frowned down at the black water. "Then what?"

Xinai shrugged. "Eat you. Drown you. I don't know. I doubt you'd care once you were at the bottom of the bay. The inner canals are warded, but they slip in around the edges of the city sometimes." She leaned over the railing and called out in Sivahran; the word shivered with a weight of magic. Something below them croaked, then splashed and was still. Xinai turned away and Adam and Isyllt fell in behind her.

The Storm God's Bride lay on the far side of the district, nestled between storehouses, with cheap rented rooms stacked above it like a child's precarious block tower. The sound of flutes and drums drifted through the door and firelight fell from the windows in oily-gold streaks.

Isyllt was glad to find the Bride little different from the disreputable dock taverns at home. Smoke and sweat and spilled beer thickened the air, and the tiles were cracked and sticky. Dried plants hung from warped rafters, wards or decoration or something else entirely.

Xinai twisted through the crowd in search of the captain; Isyllt stayed close to Adam, careful not to foul his sword-arm. She ran a surreptitious hand over the hilt of her own knife, though the mood in the room seemed pleasant enough.

Musicians played on a low wooden platform against the far wall, mostly ignored by the custom. Sailors and dockworkers, Isyllt guessed, watching the people slouched on low benches or gathered loudly around the gaming tables. Wiry men and women, scarred and wind-scoured and plainly dressed, bronze skin and ocher, shades of black and brown. Ninayans and Sivahri and Assari alike laughed and gambled and drank bowls of beer, and none seemed less welcome than the others. She even saw a few fairer heads, from Hallach or lands farther north.

Xinai reappeared soon and led them across the room, toward a door beside the stage. As they moved down a narrow corridor, Isyllt heard the rattle of dice. They entered a cluttered storeroom and found a man sitting alone, rolling bones across a scarred table.

She'd known Teoma was a dwarf, but the leather cuff that capped his missing left forearm was a surprise. Dark eyes gleamed under heavy black brows as he glanced up at them.

"Good evening. Here for a game of chance?"

Adam's lips curled. "Since when is there chance in your games, Izzy?"

The dwarf's grin rearranged his creased face; lamp-light winked off two gold teeth. "It's dangerous to accuse a man of cheating." He nodded toward his maimed arm. "Look what happened to me."

He turned his eyes to Isyllt. "But if you haven't come for the bones, what can I do for you?"

Isyllt twisted a red-gold ring off her finger and held it out. "Among blind men—" She gave the first half of the code in Selafaïn.

"The one-eyed reigns," he finished. He reached out to clasp her hand and palm the ring in one smooth gesture.

As his calloused fingers touched hers, a shiver ran up her arm. Isyllt barely managed to keep her face still; no one had mentioned the man was a sorcerer. The sensation vanished so quickly she almost doubted her instinct, but his eyes narrowed as he studied her.

"Well met, I hope. I'm Izachar Teoma."

"Isyllt Iskaldur."

His eyes flicked briefly toward her left hand. "What is it you wish of me, Lady?"

"I want to hire your ship."

"The *Rain Dog* can take you anywhere you need to go."

"Actually, I want you to stay in port. We'll be in Symir for perhaps a month—hopefully it will be a peaceful visit and we'll leave quietly. But it may come to pass that we'll need to leave the city very quickly, and we'll need a fast ship we can trust."

"Ah." Izachar ran a hand over his curling beard. His chair creaked as he leaned back. "I understand. But a month . . . My crew have families to feed, and I'll lose business." A gold tooth gleamed with his smile. "And with the new import taxes, my business is booming."

"We're prepared to compensate you."

Adam slid a purse across the table. Izachar hefted it, listened to the clatter of metal and stones. He loosened the ties and pulled out a coin. Silver gleamed smooth, unstamped.

"I'll keep the *Dog* in port for a decad," he said at last. "My first mate's daughter is sick, anyway, and she'd like to spend some time with the child. After ten days, find me again and we'll negotiate further."

Isyllt nodded. She'd expected no better. "A pleasure doing business with you, Captain."

"The pleasure's mine, Lady." The money vanished off the table.

The door swung open and a dark, scar-faced man leaned in. "Time to go," he said. His hand moved against his thigh, a sign Isyllt didn't recognize. Then he was gone.

Izachar cursed softly. "A raid's coming. Business is booming a little too well." He pushed off his chair and crossed the room, quick enough for his short legs. "We'll use the back door," he said, motioning them on. "It'll be clear for a few more minutes—Desh pays his bribes on time."

Isyllt and Adam exchanged a quick glance and followed the dwarf down the hall. From the main room she heard a door slam, then a flurry of curses and shouting and the clatter of an overturned table. They stepped outside into a dark alley, as empty as Izachar had promised; the last light caught his grin before the door shut behind them.

"Welcome to Symir," he called after them as they escaped into the sticky night.

Xinai moved through her exercises by the light of one guttering lamp. The flame gleamed on her knives, shattered on their razored edges. Her breath hissed through clenched teeth as she thrust and spun and stretched. Normally she flowed like water from one stance to the next, but tonight tension trembled her limbs, made her movements too quick and jerky.

The smell of the canals breathed across the casement: water and waste, eucalyptus and brine and citrus-sweet champa flowers. Beneath it her own sour salt sweat clogged her nose.

She'd thought she could do it. She'd thought she could come home after twelve years gone. On the voyage she'd told herself that the city would have changed, that time would have made her memories bearable.

She'd almost believed it.

The exercise wasn't calming her. She stopped, stretched, and put her blades away. Adam watched her from the shadows of the bed as she stripped off her vest and trousers. He'd asked if she could take the job, one of the rare times he acknowledged all the things she'd never told him about her past. In Erisín, spending the wizard's money on food and wine, she'd said yes. Even the necromancer hadn't deterred her, for all the woman's magic made her skin crawl.

She could do this. She didn't have a choice.

She threw herself down beside Adam and buried her face in a cushion. His familiar scent was a comfort—oil and leather, musk and iron. Nothing that reminded her of home.

He propped himself up on one elbow. "Is it so bad?"

"It's—" Pillows muffled her sigh. "It's the same. Things have changed, but it's still the same."

He knelt over her, running his hands over her shoulders. She grunted softly as he pressed against knotted muscles.

"They think they're lions," she muttered, thinking of the customs inspector with her expensive coat and hennaed hands, her perfect Assari. The Sivahri soldiers in their red-trimmed uniforms. "Only dogs licking their masters' boots." She gasped as Adam dug his thumbs into her back.

He worked down, calloused hands strong and steady. She forced herself not to stiffen as he brushed the scars on her back. It had been a long time, even after they were lovers, before she let him touch them. Not until the nightmares faded and she didn't wake up gasping, expecting to find her skin slick with blood.

Years of partnership had left his touch as familiar as her own. By the time he reached the small of her back she could breathe easily again, the angry stiffness gone from her limbs.

"It's only a job." He leaned down to kiss her shoulder. "When it's over we'll go somewhere else. Anywhere you like." He caressed the unmarked skin on her sides and she shivered. "You want to be a pirate?"

She chuckled and rolled over, stretching out the last of her tension. "You might be able to talk me into it." But she pulled him down and kissed him before he could try.

CHAPTER 2

Isyllt and Adam crossed onto the mainland north of the Mir early the next morning and rented horses to carry them up the foothills to the Kurun Tam. Mount Haroun loomed above them, its shadow casting a false twilight over the western hills.

The sun burned away the dawn mist, embroidered the mountain's green skirts in gold and amber. Summer heat left leaves curled and drooping, baked the roads cracked and dusty and withered the ferns that grew in the shade.

Ward-posts lined the road, simple charms to keep predators away and something else, a spell to hold the stones steady if the earth shook. Isyllt wasn't sure she understood the intricacies of it, but the implication was unsettling. Far above the canopy, white smoke leaked from Haroun's summit. Liquid fire still bubbled in the mountain, but it hadn't erupted in the hundred and fifty years of Assari occupation. The mages of the Kurun Tam expressed nothing but confidence in their ability to keep the mountain quiet—since they'd be the first to burn if Haroun stirred, Isyllt tried to take comfort in their assurances.

The trail turned sharply and she saw the sluggish waters of the

Mir below them, and the broader, gentler slope of Mount Ashaya on the far side of the river. The South Bank was home to politicians and merchant moguls, mansions and plantations. Whatever native families had lived there were long gone, driven out or bought off and their lands divided up for gifts to those who pleased the Emperor. The North Bank was poorer, home to Sivahri who couldn't afford to live in the city proper. From the ferry she'd seen clay and brick buildings, thatched roofs and packed-earth roads.

And between the two banks and the bay, Symir shone in the morning light, all colorful roofs and gardens and glittering webs of water.

Isyllt swallowed bitter dust and the smell of horse. This assignment was one others would have vied for, exotic and expensive. And important.

They'd lost three agents in Assar—clever, well-trained spies. Two had simply vanished from their posts, and the body of the third was found dumped near the Selafaïn embassy in Ta'ashlan. And in Erisín, Kiril had caught two Assari agents already—one trying to seduce a Selafaïn inventor whose clever designs would make wonderful instruments of war, and the other worming his way into the palace bureaucracy. The latter had fallen on a blade before Kiril could question him, but his presence was story enough—the Emperor was growing bolder.

In the five hundred years since refugees fleeing the al Sund dynasty's armies had crossed the sea and founded Selafai, several Assari emperors had tried to take the younger kingdom. Assar had never established a solid presence on the northern continent, and every other generation some general-prince with dreams of fortune and glory thought to be the first to do so. And now Rahal al Seth sat the Lion Throne, young and greedy and itching to match his grandfather's conquests—and backed by generals canny and greedy enough to give him a chance.

She pressed the tip of her tongue between her teeth and tried not to scowl. What Kiril said was true—she was his best student, his most trusted agent. And what he didn't say was true as well, that given a job as important as this she'd die before she disappointed him. He needed her here. But he'd sent her away, and it gnawed.

She tried to relax, but the jolt of hooves stiffened her back and shoulders. Adam rode more easily beside her, his eyes on the trees. The jungle clamored around them, screeching and chirping and rustling. Jewel-bright lizards and long-tailed monkeys watched them from tree branches, calmer than the birds that took fl ight whenever the clatter of hooves grew close. The trees hid all manner of exotic beasts.

And bands of desperate men as well. She just had to find them. Trade gold and weapons for warriors to wield them. To die for them. Thousands of Sivahri lives in exchange for Selafaïn ones.

She looked up and caught Adam watching her, pale eyes narrowed. She schooled her face and smiled at him. Then she shivered as they passed through a tingling web of wards. The trees fell away and they rode into the courtyard of the Kurun Tam.

The Corundum Hall. A long building of crimson granite, pillared and domed in Assari style. Faces watched them from the wall, bound spirits staring through stone eyes. Neat green lawns stretched within the walls, shaded by slender trees and pruned topiaries—all the jungle's wildness tamed.

A young stablehand appeared to take charge of their horses, and Isyllt dismounted with a wince and brushed at the dust on her clothes. The gray-green linen hid the worst of it, at least. She breathed deep, tasted magic like spiced lightning in the back of her throat. It tingled down her limbs and prickled the nape of her neck.

They climbed broad red steps and entered a columned courtyard. Isyllt sighed as cool air washed over them—a subtle witchery and a welcome one. A fountain played in the center of the yard and she worked her dry tongue against the roof of her mouth. The air smelled of fl owers and incense and clean water.

Isyllt washed her face and hands in the basin beside the door, and she and Adam added their boots and socks to the neat row of sandals and slippers. She didn't hear the footsteps approach over the splash of the fountain until Adam spun around. She turned as a shadow fell across the stones at her feet.

"Roshani," the man said, bowing low. Light gleamed on the curve of his shaven head, set mahogany skin aglow. He wore robes of embroidered saffron silk, the hem brushing the tops of his bare feet. "Or should I say good morning?" he asked in Selafaïn. "You must be Lady Iskaldur."

"Yes." She lifted her ring in warning as he offered a hand. "I'm *hadath*." Unclean. Had she been born in Assar, she would go gloved and veiled and touch no one but the dead.

"Ah. It's not often we see necromancers here." He took her hand and raised it to his lips; his skin was warm, his magic warmer still as it whispered against her. His smile was wry and charming. "I'm not devout. My name is Asheris. Vasilios mentioned that he was expecting you. I'll take you to him."

"Wait for me," she said to Adam, and followed Asheris down a shadowed arcade.